P9-EJT-939

INTO THE DEEP

ALSO BY KEN GRIMWOOD

Replay

The Voice Outside

Elise

Breakthrough

INTO THE DEEP

KEN GRIMWOOD

To Connie —
Sorry you weren't able to make
it here -- hope you're doing great!
All the Best,
K

WILLIAM MORROW AND COMPANY, INC.

NEW YORK

FOR COURTNEY

Copyright © 1995 by Ken Grimwood

All rights reserved. No part of this book may be reproduced or utilized in any form or by any means, electronic or mechanical, including photocopying, recording, or by any information storage or retrieval system, without permission in writing from the Publisher. Inquiries should be addressed to Permissions Department, William Morrow and Company, Inc., 1350 Avenue of the Americas, New York, N.Y. 10019.

It is the policy of William Morrow and Company, Inc., and its imprints and affiliates, recognizing the importance of preserving what has been written, to print the books we publish on acid-free paper, and we exert our best efforts to that end.

LIBRARY OF CONGRESS CATALOGING-IN-PUBLICATION DATA

Grimwood, Ken.
Into the deep / Ken Grimwood.
p.   cm.
ISBN 0-688-08799-X
1. Dolphins—Fiction.   I. Title.
PS3557.R497D45   1994
813'.54—dc20   94-1283 CIP

Printed in the United States of America

First Edition

1 2 3 4 5 6 7 8 9 10

BOOK DESIGN BY JESSICA SHATAN

When her tasks are done, she swims for pleasure: now a burst of liquid speed just beneath the surface, now a dive to gain still more momentum, now an exhilarating leap straight up into the light— wind rushing warm along the smoothness of her body as she rises free of the ocean in a graceful arc, the water droplets fanning out behind her in a rainbowed mist.

At the top of her arc comes the paradox she so enjoys: the weightless moment, floating free as if at rest in her familiar sea, yet suspended merely in the insubstantial air above the waves.

Now down again, flexing her sleek form into a sensual curve that brings her headfirst back into the water, slicing the surface so cleanly there is barely a splash as her supple body makes its reentry into that deeper blue beneath the pale blue through which she has, for an instant, flown.

The filtered light from on high begins to dim as she descends, the blue becomes a formless gray, then black . . . and still she dives, thrilling at the sudden, unaccustomed blindness. The dark envelops her, and she allows it, relishing with gleeful trepidation its power to turn this everyday world of hers into a place of unseen, scary wonder.

The game becomes a bit too eerie, and she scans, turning in place to inspect her surroundings on all sides. Detailed shapes emerge from the blackness, as distinct as if a powerful searchlight has been lowered into the depths: hard-shelled, many-legged things crawling upon the sandy bottom; fish undulating everywhere, some darting about to devour still smaller fish; a wary squid scooting past, propelling itself with jets of expelled seawater.

Ch*Tril chitters a high-pitched sound of self-amusement; the awesome darkness she had forced upon herself for fun is, after all, no more and no less than her own familiar home.

Growing short of breath, she rises again to the light, lifts her head from the water and opens her blowhole to gulp the sweet clean air. The others are not far away, leaping and playing and loving in their own after-task diversions. Ch*Tril wriggles her flukes, twists her dorsal fin in that direction, and swims to join them.

BEFORE

1948

The boy was shamed by the sound of his father's voice; shamed not merely by the words he spoke, but by the language in which they were said, the musical, slightly nasal Portuguese with its trilled *R*'s and its sliding *Zh*'s that branded the man forever an immigrant, a worker in a land of managers and administrators . . . a fisherman, with the smell of the sea embedded in his clothes, his hair, his rough brown skin.

"O que disparatado rapaz!" his father said, laughing. Silly boy, foolish child.

"It's a lie, what you say," the boy broke in. "Try to make me look dumb, what for?"

"Fala português em casa," his mother admonished; "Your *pai,* he work too hard to study English like you." She glanced at her husband, then back at the boy. "An' you never call your father liar no more, hear me?"

The boy looked down at the linoleum floor of the kitchen, warped with age but spotless. *"Sim, mãe;* but what he says, it makes people laugh at me, they—"

"Português!"

He reluctantly switched to his parents' tongue, oblivious to its beauty, conscious only of how different, how wrong, the words felt in his mouth after two years of speaking English everywhere but in his own home.

"I didn't talk to no fish."

His father's laughter filled the cramped little room. "No, but the fish they talk to you, right, Toninho?" He shook his head, grinning, and poured himself another glass of the sweet red *oporto*. "What they say, they tell you all about little mermaid girls, huh?"

"*Bastante,* Paulo," the boy's mother said. "You embarrass him."

"He said it, not me. *Verdadeiro,* Toninho? Tell the truth."

The boy shrugged, his eyes still fixed on the scuffed linoleum. *"Eu não recordome."* And it was true, he could not remember, or at most could recall only the faintest outlines of the incident, like a cloud-shape dissipating in the wind even as he watched.

He remembered being in the dinghy this afternoon, out past sight of land, his father teaching him things he didn't want to know, preparing him for a life he hoped he could avoid, his father's life: how to steer the little boat into the waves, how to spot the signs that told of tuna schools below, how to alert the men on the larger fishing boat nearby so they could cast their long, heavy lines into the sea at just the right point.

He could remember, too, their return to the docks as the sun fell, the laughter of the wiry brown men from the other boats— family friends, relatives, *compatriotas*—as his father mockingly recounted what had happened out there on the alien waters just beyond the sheltered familiarity of San Diego Bay.

"O rapaz que fala com peixes," they had called him, "the boy who talks to fish." Ruffling his hair as they said it, touching his face and talking around him, not to him, with their airs of adult superiority and privilege.

But the time in between, the time his father kept so ruthlessly teasing him about ... what *had* happened out there among the languid, rolling swells of the Pacific? The part of him that seemed to know, to remember, felt distant and muffled; and every time he struggled to recall some minor detail of the day's incident it only slipped farther and deeper into that peculiar well of unawareness. It was as if one part of his mind was keeping a secret, an enormously important secret, from the rest of him.

Maybe if he just pretended it had never happened, whatever it was, and stopped trying so hard to remember ... maybe then his father would forget, too, and the other men who had laughed at him.

Or maybe it would come back to him one day, and then it could be his own secret to keep.

1959

The hills that surrounded the schoolyard on every side were ablaze with Carolina autumn at its peak, but Daniel saw only the tangled green jungles of East Africa, the dense growth of vines and leaves so thickly intertwined they blotted out the harsh sun above and darkened their own emerald hue to a green so shadowed it was almost black.

That was what he'd call it, he realized at once, and flipped the nearly full notebook back to the first page. "THE BLACK JUNGLE, BY DANIEL COLTER," he penciled in large block capitals, and then he went back to fill in each letter carefully with ink.

"Whatcha doin', Danny?"

The boy slapped the notebook shut and slid it, upside down, beneath a geography text. "Nothin'."

"Hey, c'mon, lemme see." The other boy, shorter and huskier than Daniel, reached to grab the notebook, but its young owner jerked it from his grasp.

"I'm not done with it. Maybe you can look at it later."

"Bet it's a love letter, that's what it is. Love letter, love letter ... to Mary Beth!"

Daniel's face flared hot. Mary Beth Jessup was the scrawniest, dirtiest girl in the fourth grade. Her parents were some kind of Holy Rollers, and they made her wear long-sleeved plain cotton dresses all the time, even in the summer.

"You're stupid, Bobby. You don't know crap."

The stocky boy put his hands on his hips and jutted his chin forward. "I know I ain't queer, like some people I could name."

Daniel smiled, despite his anger. "Can't even make up your mind. What am I, queer or in love with Mary Beth?"

"You're *weird* queer, that's what. Always actin' like you know somethin' special, somethin' nobody else does. Well, you're the one don't know crap, turd-face."

Bobby Rastow turned away and strutted arrogantly across the playground, confident that he had made the final, telling point; but Daniel didn't give a damn what that ignorant little bully thought of him, he didn't care what any of them thought. He *did* know things they didn't, though sometimes he wasn't sure exactly what it was he knew.

It was that time last summer, on his uncle's sailboat off Cape Hatteras, that had him most confused. Usually he remembered most everything that happened to him, particularly the fun or exciting things, could play back his experiences in his mind like a movie, even months and months after they'd happened.

That day was different, though. There was a kind of fog in his head when he tried to think back on it, and the harder he tried the fuzzier it got. All he could remember was being alone back in the stern of the boat while his dad and his uncle were drinking cocktails up on the front deck and his mom and his aunt were fixing lunch down in the galley. He'd been trailing his hand in the boat's cool, white wake, watching the retreating shoreline of Roanoke Island and thinking of the Wright brothers launching their flimsy cloth-and-wood airplane among those isolated sand dunes, when—

Something. Something . . . gray? Dark, anyway, darker than the frothing bubbles of the wake, and big, and . . .

The rest of the image wouldn't come. His memory had simply faded out after that moment, and the next thing he could recall was sitting at the little table in the galley, eating a peanut butter and banana sandwich and staring out the thick round windows at the ocean with a wholly new sense of frustrated wonder. Certain that his life had undergone an immense, irrevocable change, but having not the slightest notion of what had caused it or of what the change entailed.

It hurt his head too much, trying to remember. He opened the notebook again, went back gratefully to the story he was writing. That, at least, he could control, could picture and shape and modify in his mind and on the blue-lined paper with complete assurance. It was almost finished, forty neatly printed pages of menace and adventure and stolen native idols that had nothing whatsoever to do with that disturbingly missing afternoon out on the ocean. Miss Hess had already said he could use the mimeograph machine to make a hundred copies of his story, and he planned to sell them in the cafeteria for a quarter apiece.

Bobby Rastow wanted to see what the big secret was? Fine, Daniel thought with vengeful satisfaction; let him pay for it.

1969

An uncommon quiet had descended on the throng as the sun began to burn the morning haze from the thick, still air. There were people everywhere, hundreds of thousands of them, most having spent the night in their cars or camped on the narrow beach; but as the moments ticked forward—or was it backward?—the earlier festive atmosphere had given way to one of awe and uneasy anticipation.

The horizon spread, flat and empty, in every direction: to the north and south stretched the thin strip of sand, packed smooth but now unseen beneath the multitude of human feet; looking west

there were the marshy shores of the Banana River, and eastward
lay the shallow, smooth expanse of the Atlantic. Only two features
broke the circle of apparent infinity: one was a square, gray building
without windows, said to be the largest enclosed space ever con-
structed—so massive that it would sometimes rain inside the structure when outside the skies were cloudless.

On any other day, this hugely impressive successor to the Pyra-
mids of Egypt would be the focal point of considerable interest
and speculation; but this morning, all eyes were centered on the
second object that rose from the endlessly level terrain. In truth,
it was a pair of objects: one a gangly, rust-orange assemblage of
girders and platforms . . . the other, a pristine white needle pointed
straight upward, as high as a thirty-six-story building but anchored
to no foundation, no piece of earth. All night the needle had shone,
diamondlike and icy, in the glare of a hundred spotlights; now
it stood poised in the brilliant Florida sun, visibly eager to be
away.

Sarah Roberts grasped her husband Leland's arm and spoke in
a near-whisper, mindful of the reverential hush that had fallen over
the crowd. "Honey, it's really happening, isn't it? I mean, right
now, right *here*."

He put his hand over hers and nodded slowly. "I never thought
I'd live to see this. But here we are."

"Sheila, can you see O.K.? Can you see the rocket?" Sarah pulled
her daughter closer to her with her free hand.

"There's too many people, Mommy," Sheila complained, squirming away.

The public address speakers that had been set up amid the scrub
came to life again. "This is Apollo-Saturn launch control; we've
passed the six-minute mark in our countdown for *Apollo 11;* now
five minutes, fifty-two seconds, and counting . . . we're on time at
the present time for our planned liftoff of thirty-two minutes past
the hour."

"You want to sit up on my shoulders?" the little girl's father
asked.

"I want to go in the water."

Sarah and Leland exchanged a glance; he was frowning, impatient.

"Honey, she can probably see it better from the water," Sarah said. "There's not so many people over there."

"Damn it, this is no time to have to be watching over her like—"

"It's shallow way, way out, and you know she can swim like a fish. She'll be all right for a few minutes."

"I don't know whether—"

"Launch operations manager Paul Donnelly reports go for launch . . . launch director Rocco Petrone now gives a go, we're five minutes, twenty seconds, and counting."

"Come on," Sarah said, "let's go." The three of them wound their way through the crowd, and as they reached the edge of the placid green water Sarah let go her daughter's hand and gave her a look as full of love as it was of caution. "Don't go out to where it's any deeper than your waist, now, all right?"

The girl nodded gravely, her nine-year-old's eyes restless with the urge for freedom. Sarah smiled, nodded, and watched the child dash away into the shallow water.

"We've passed the fifty-second mark, power transfer is complete; we're on internal power with the launch vehicle at this time. Forty seconds away from the *Apollo 11* liftoff."

Sarah glanced again at the inviting expanse of warm, smooth water; Sheila, free of the thick forest of adult legs, seemed to have a clear view of the rocket now as she splashed about in the shallows.

"All the second-stage tanks now pressurized, thirty-five seconds and counting, we are still go with *Apollo 11;* thirty seconds and counting."

"I love you," Sarah whispered to her husband, squeezing his fingers tight in her own. This was a moment, she knew, that he had waited for since he was Sheila's age or younger.

"T minus fifteen seconds, guidance is internal . . ."

In the midsummer heat, Sarah felt a rush of chill bumps across her bare arms and back. Billows of condensing fog had begun to rise from the base of the towering white needle in the distance, as the cold from the river of liquid oxygen inside it hit the warm, humid surrounding air.

"Twelve ... eleven ... ten ... nine ... ignition sequence start ..."

A low murmur, a spontaneous, wordless prayer, began to rise from the assembled watchers. Between the beach and the launching pad, a trio of seagulls soared lazily, their wings tilting in unison as if performing a choreographed salute.

"... four ... three ... two ... one ... zero ... all engines running ..."

Dense clouds of flame burst from beneath the rocket, in perfect, momentary silence. Then the shock wave, not mere sound but a tangible wall of sheer force, hit Sarah, hit her husband, hit all the many thousand others who watched the scene in anxious awe. The huge cone-tipped cylinder in the distance shuddered, shaking itself awake; slowly, almost imperceptibly at first, it began to lift itself up from the place where it had stood, monumentlike, seemingly so permanent and immovable an edifice.

"Liftoff! We have a liftoff; thirty-two minutes past the hour, liftoff on *Apollo 11*!"

Sarah had somehow expected it to streak swiftly across the sky, like a low-flying jet, but the great ship maintained a majestic, labored dignity all its own as it rose toward the heavens. The massive, physical wave of sound that emanated from its monstrous engines grew in intensity, battering the spectators on the ground and drowning out their screams of encouragement.

Sarah looked at her husband's face, saw his tears, and huddled close against him. His hope and enthusiasm for this very event had, over the years, become her own, and she knew full well what this moment meant: They were watching mankind leave the cradle for the first time, to take his first baby steps on a world not his own.

On a column of flame ten times longer than the rocket itself the ship ascended, ever higher, the stunning sight and sound and even feel of it gradually diminishing as the craft thrust onward toward its incomparable destiny.

Sarah tore her eyes from the magnificent vision, and looked out at the water to see if Sheila had been as transfixed as all the others, if she had—

Her daughter was thirty yards from the beach, in water up to her neck, staring at a sharp gray fin that was knifing its way through the water at shocking speed, straight toward her.

"Leland! My God, Sheila!"

Her husband jerked his gaze away from the shrinking flame of the rocket, saw first the terror in Sarah's face, and then the cause of it. He dashed for the water, his Leica still strapped, unnoticed, around his neck. The water slowed his running pace, but for the first several yards it was too shallow for him to swim.

Sarah stood frozen at the water's edge. "Help! Shark!" she screamed, and a hundred faces took their attention away from the receding dot of fire in the crisp blue sky.

The creature had reached its target, and stopped, and reared its head from the water only a few feet away from the immobile girl.

All around Sarah, people were yelling and running: some toward the highway to escape the frightful scene, others toward a nearby lifeguard station to get help, others into the ocean after Leland to do whatever they could do. Everything seemed to be happening more slowly than it should, just as the rocket had seemed to take forever in its long ascent from the shackles of earth.

The bullet-headed creature remained suspended in the water, stock-still, its snout no more than three feet from Sheila's face, its rows of teeth white in the harsh sunlight.

"Sheila! Don't move!" Leland shouted, swimming now with all his strength. There were a dozen men just behind him in the water, splashing and screaming to frighten the beast away.

Suddenly it spun and seemed to regard the oncoming swimmers for a moment, then looked back at the little girl, shook its head, and raced away toward the depths from which it had come. As he reached his daughter, Leland could see dozens of other fins, no more than a hundred yards away, circling in the bluer water.

"I've got you, honey, I've got you. Just hold tight to me; now, let's get back to the beach."

When the water was knee-deep he stood, exhausted, the girl still clutched tightly in his arms as he gulped the salty air.

"Hey, mister," one of the men who had followed him into the water called, "it's O.K. Them ain't sharks, they're porpoises."

Leland didn't give a damn what they were; one of them had almost killed his daughter. "Are you all right, angel?" he asked her between heaving breaths.

"I'm fine," the girl said calmly. "Did you see . . ."

"I saw it, yes. Are you sure you're O.K.?"

She looked puzzled. "Of course I am." She looked around at all the faces watching them, and her own cheeks colored with embarrassment. "Put me down now, Daddy."

"I know it must have been scary, that . . . thing coming up so close, but—"

Sheila struggled impatiently against his protective grasp. "Daddy, *please*. People'll think I'm some kind of baby."

He set her down in the gently lapping water. "Anyway, it's gone now, honey. It can't hurt you."

She frowned up at him, curious. "What?"

"That big fish. It won't come back, not now."

"I don't remember . . ." The girl shook her head, dark hair wet and glistening. "I watched the rocket go up, and then I was swimming, and . . . I don't know. It's hard to think."

She must be in shock, Leland realized. The only way a child her age could deal with the level of danger she'd just faced was to block it out entirely, banish the memory as unacceptable, intolerable.

"It's not important," he said, feigning unconcern. Let her forget what had happened; he never would. "How'd you like the launch? Pretty impressive, huh?"

She brightened, glad to be steered away from more difficult, more confusing thoughts. "I couldn't believe how *loud* it was! And they're really going all the way to the moon?"

He knelt in the shallow water, hugged her thin, precious shoulders. He had gone from exhilaration to terror to relief in a matter of seconds, and he was only now beginning to realize how close he had come to a loss that would have been beyond his capacity to absorb.

"Yes, angel," he murmured against his daughter's tiny, sun-pink ear. "All the way to the moon."

NOW

1

The earth ripped, groaning and trembling as it did so, the great Pacific plate shifting another inch or so northward on its stately, endless voyage across the face of the planet. Such ponderous pacing, such unthinkable scales of breadth and interval: ocean traveling upon ocean, the vast blue Pacific itself a passenger atop an enormous raft of oceanic crust, drifting through the eons on the surface of a great global sea of semiliquid rock. Time as measured by the tides of granite.

With that laborious and violent rending of the earth, a fracture opened beneath the shifting ocean floor, a cavity within the solid crust. The opening was a mere bubble in comparison to the immense plate itself, but by other standards the cavern would be judged respectably large, containing as it did a volume approximately equal to that of the Great Pyramid at Giza.

The shaking earth quieted, the drifting oceanic plate settled into place for another year, or ten, or fifty. Teardrops of superheated, molten rock from beneath the earth's brittle and plastic mantles seeped upward through a thousand snaking fissures, and filled the newly opened chamber.

Equilibrium—however temporary, however illusory and fragile—was established once again.

* * *

Daniel hadn't really thought about what to expect from the offices of the Ocean Coalition, but now that he saw them he realized the physical premises of the environmentalist group fit his unconscious preconceptions to a T. Five plywood-partitioned cubicles filled the interior of what had previously been a Vietnamese restaurant in a Santa Monica mini-mall; the two street-front windows were boarded over, casualties of the recent earthquake. Daniel noticed that the unframed Bob Talbot whale and dolphin posters covering the window areas were new; the numerous similar ones that decorated almost every other wall were beginning to curl at their Scotch-taped corners.

"Can I help you?" The young woman's ash-blond hair was pulled back into a long ponytail, and Daniel wished she'd turn her head to the side so he could see just how far down her back it went.

"Daniel Colter. I'm supposed to meet Mitch Creighton here at two, for an interview."

"Anybody seen Mitch around?" the girl shouted, swiveling her chair about to address the dozen or so people visible in the open cubicles. The ponytail didn't quite reach the denim-encased cleft of her ass, but almost.

"He was in for a few minutes this morning," one man said with a vague shrug, and then went back to disassembling the dingy-gray hulk of a copying machine whose warranty had probably expired around the time of the Tet offensive. The whole place felt like the other end of a time-warp, littered with pamphlets and cheaply printed newsletters: STOP THE SLAUGHTER one was headlined; another, in large crimson type, read FOREIGN TUNA = DEATH!! Change the slogans to FREE HUEY! or BOYCOTT DOW CHEMICAL, Daniel thought, and it would be as if the decades had never passed.

"I don't know," the ponytailed girl said, wrinkling her eyes in what was apparently intended to be a thoughtful manner but had more the effect of making her look as if she'd just emerged from sleep into a brightly sunlit room. "Usually he comes in about every afternoon. You said you had an appointment with him?"

"At two," Daniel said, glancing pointedly at his watch. Years of constant deadlines had made him impatient with those less punctual than he, even though now, as a free-lancer, his deadlines were largely self-imposed.

"Well, he'll probably be here anytime now." She waved a brace-leted arm at a pair of metal folding chairs against one wall. "You're welcome to wait if you want to."

"Maybe I should reschedule—"

"No, no, really, I'm sure he'll show up soon. Here, why don't you take some of this stuff to read while you wait." She leaned across the battered desk, scooping up a random handful of the pamphlets and newsletters. The loose neck of her baggy sweater fell away with the movement; Daniel could see the freckled roundness of her small breasts, the pink nub of one nipple. A couple of years ago—hell, two or three months ago . . .

He looked up to see her staring at him with a fixed, polite smile. Daniel took the sheaf of booklets from her, nodded his thanks, and retired to one of the folding chairs. Yeah, a few months ago he would've chatted the girl up a bit, pretended to agree with whatever convoluted political beliefs she'd temporarily settled on, and with any luck would have passed a pleasurable night—maybe even two—burrowing into the softness of that long hair, those apple-perfect little tits. Fending off, for a matter of hours at least, the wildly conflicting emotions that had plagued him since Ruth died.

But suddenly there were no more emotions left to fight. For weeks now, months, a curious emptiness had occupied his soul, as if all the anger, the grief and betrayal, the never-to-be-resolved mysteries of his wife's death had finally just canceled each other out. What had once been a firestorm of opposing feelings was now mere residue, the damp, cold ashes of remembered rage and sorrow that had buried all trace of joy as well.

He shifted his butt left and right in the plain metal chair, trying without success to find a position approaching relative comfort, and looked at one of the pamphlets the young woman had given him. It was headlined STOP THE KILLING!, and beneath that was a photograph of a dolphin, presumably dead, hanging from some sort of winch mechanism above the deck of a boat. The picture was indistinct and poorly lit; the dolphin looked pretty much like any large fish, strung up in a proud display of a day's catch.

It wasn't a fish, of course, Daniel knew that: Dolphins were mammals; they were friendly; they were as intelligent as dogs or chimps or humans, depending on who you listened to . . . and so on, and so on, and so on. Still, it was hard for him to understand the emotional attachment so many people claimed to feel for the creatures. Damn it, they just looked too much like *fish* to him.

"You the newspaper guy?"

Daniel looked up to see a sturdily built, bearded man in his late twenties or early thirties. He was wearing Levi's and a checkered flannel shirt that had to be much too warm for Santa Monica at this time of year. His face was red with new sunburn, and his eyes were among the most intense that Daniel had ever seen.

"Mitch Creighton?" Daniel asked, freeing himself from the discomfort of the chair.

"Yeah."

"Daniel Colter. And I'm free-lance, I'm no longer associated with any specific paper."

The man waved his hand dismissively. "Whatever. You're a reporter, right? A writer?"

"I've had pieces in *Rolling Stone, The New York Times Magazine* . . ."

"Fine. You want coffee?"

Daniel hesitated, annoyed at having had his summary of recent credits so brusquely interrupted. Who the hell was this guy, this neo-hippie eco-freak, to treat such hard-won achievements so lightly? What had he done that was so fucking great, save a tree?

"I might have a cup," Daniel said tightly.

"Back here," Creighton told him, leading the way toward a small table behind the Arrowhead dispenser. There was a coffeemaker and a row of personalized mugs; no Styrofoam cups, but Creighton pointed out a cracked and stained yellow mug with the word GUEST painted on it in red fingernail polish. Daniel poured himself a cup of black coffee from a full pot labeled CAF; the other pot said simply DE, and it was almost empty.

"So, what's your angle on this, Dan? You on our side or theirs?"

"The name's Daniel." He hated it when someone took the liberty of using one of the diminutives of his name without so much as asking. His mother had called him Danny whenever she'd wanted to belittle some statement or action of his as juvenile; and Ruth had called him Dan in an exaggeratedly sexy tone of voice when she was trying to be persuasive, or to deflect his attention from something she was trying to conceal. "And I'm not on anybody's 'side,'" he added. "You ever hear of journalistic objectivity?"

The man grunted with distaste. "Yeah, that's what they always call it. You any good, then? Your stuff, I mean."

One more remark like that, Daniel decided, and this "interview" was over; two more, and Mitch Creighton would have bought himself a fat lip.

"I'm damn good. So why don't you just tell me what makes you worth writing about?"

"Hey, you called me, remember?"

"I'm doing an article on the conservation movement, a general overview; you're one of about a hundred people I'll be talking to."

Creighton nodded, and pointed toward the pamphlets Daniel still held in his free hand. "You read those?"

"I've looked at them. Aren't they a bit out of date?"

"O.K., so you haven't read them."

"What's the point? I mean, this whole 'boycott tuna' deal was over back in '90, right, when Starkist caved in."

"No, it's not over," Creighton said, and the permanent fire in his eyes flared hotter. "Not by a long shot. You know the background on this?"

Daniel shrugged, took a sip of the weak coffee. He reached

automatically toward his shirt pocket, then stopped himself as he noticed there were no ashtrays in sight. That figured. "Tuna boats used to catch dolphins, too," he said, dredging the old controversy from his memory. "Environmentalists raised a big stink about it for years: newspaper ads, boycotts, letter-writing campaigns ... so they finally quit catching dolphins."

Creighton gave a small, bitter smile. "I guess that pretty well sums up what most people think. But you're wrong on several counts.

"First of all, the tuna fishermen don't purposely 'catch' dolphins; they set their nets, huge nets, around schools of dolphins because some species of tuna, like yellowfin, tend to follow along under dolphin schools."

"Why?"

"Nobody knows for sure. Maybe they eat the same kind of fish, or something."

"Why didn't they just let the dolphins go, then, or throw them back?"

"Some do get away," Creighton said. "But most get stuck in the net and can't get loose; they're crushed to death, or they drown. Dolphins breathe air, you know. And the ones they throw back usually die from the fall. Those boats have high decks."

"You keep talking about this in the present tense, like it's still going on."

"That's because it is. Foreign boats mostly, but American ones, too; they sell the tuna for export, and for other uses. The only companies that ever agreed to stop buying tuna from dolphin-killers were the U.S. canneries that put out the stuff with the cute little mermaids and bees on the labels."

"So where does the rest of it go?"

"Fertilizer. Cat food. Third-rate canneries that can't afford to be picky about their sources."

Daniel frowned. "How come we never hear anything about all this?"

"Americans like happy endings. Marines come home from Somalia, people'd rather celebrate than think about the millions of children still starving in all the other Third World countries. Starkist and Bumblebee say they've suddenly decided they love Flipper, and nobody wants to hear about the dolphins—thousands of them, every year—that are still dying in tuna nets."

"So you want me to write about that."

Creighton drained his coffee and started brewing a fresh pot of decaf. "Yes and no. Mainly, I want you to document what I'm going to do about it."

"You gonna call for another boycott?" Daniel asked. "'Cause I'll tell you, that'd have all the news value of a PTA meeting. Like César Chavez; he did that so many times, who the hell cared anymore whether or not they were supposed to eat grapes?"

Creighton's sun-red face was set with grave determination. "No boycotts. That's not even what really did it the last time. Remember Sam La Budde?"

Daniel had to think for a moment, then the name struck a familiar chord. "The guy who took a video camera on board a tuna boat a few years back, right?"

Creighton nodded. "It was mainly the publicity from that footage that convinced Starkist to stop buying tuna from boats that set on dolphin schools. But after all the hoopla had died down ... like I said, everybody figured the problem was solved. Only it wasn't."

"And you ..."

"I'm going to show the world how little everything has changed."

"With a camera? On a tuna boat?"

"That's the plan."

Daniel mentally awarded the guy one point for bravery, and deducted two for foolhardiness. "I doubt that'll be easy."

"I expect not," Creighton agreed. "La Budde did it on a Panamanian boat, with the camera right out in the open; he just pretended he was making souvenir pictures. I'm going to have to sneak one on board, and I want it to be an American boat. Drive the message closer home."

"And if you get caught ..."

35

"They'll destroy the camera and the tape, I know that."

"Jesus," Daniel said, exasperated by the man's messianic obtuseness, "they'll probably do a lot worse than that. Those fishermen are tough motherfuckers; you'll be lucky if they don't throw you in the goddamned ocean. Nobody'll ever see that tape; they won't even know what you were trying to accomplish."

Creighton turned those burning eyes full on Daniel's own. "That's why I want you to come with me," he said.

Antonio Batera was in a bad mood. Here it was Friday, and he should've left on his second trip of the season by Wednesday at the latest. On top of that, Maria was in one of *her* moods; all day long she'd been in the bedroom playing those goddamned fado records they'd bought last year in Lisbon, and the constant mournful wailing was doing nothing to brighten Batera's disposition.

He figured she must be doing it on purpose, trying to drive him out of the house. The thirty-five years he'd spent on the boats had accustomed them both to the seasonal routine, and any unexpected break in the cycle was hard for either of them to deal with. They'd miss each other during his weeks at sea, they'd be mutually relieved and delighted every time he returned ... but when the time came for him to go out again, he was damned well supposed to go, and a delay like this made them both so cranky they could hardly carry on a conversation.

She probably even liked the periodic bouts of solitude by now, particularly since the boys were grown and out on their own. She could listen to her fados, she could watch the Portuguese soap opera videos she rented every other day, she could chatter on the phone with the other wives about whatever it was they discussed when the men were out on the boats.

Batera couldn't take the high-pitched, melancholy music anymore. He tossed aside the magazine he'd been trying to concentrate on and put away his hated reading glasses. He'd always been proud of having perfect eyesight, could spot a school of porpoise ten miles off; now he didn't even like to look at his charts or his codebook when anybody else was on the bridge, because of those damned glasses.

"Maria!" he shouted over the whining song as he took his car keys from the hook by the door. "I'm going out for a while, be back around six, six-thirty."

She turned the record down and leaned out from the bedroom door. *"Obtesses algum peixe ou frango para jantar,"* she called down the hallway.

"I wasn't planning on stopping by the market." She always lapsed back into Portuguese when she was moody, and that annoyed him, too, brought back the childhood years of shame over his father's obstinate old-country speech. Portuguese was O.K. for boat-talk, because some of the younger guys were straight over from Oporto or Setubal, but in his own home Batera had always insisted on English. Mainly for the boys' sake, and it had helped them get out of fishing and into good schools and jobs—Jorge had even changed his name to George, and he was a computer programmer in Phoenix, about as far away from the old life as he could get—but Batera was certain his own good English had been important in his career, too. He'd never have made first mate at twenty-seven, and skipper by thirty-six, if all he could do was *falar português.* Now, when Maria talked like that, she reminded him of some deckhand's girlfriend, his *namorada;* which of course was exactly what she'd been, back in the fifties when Batera had started out on the boats, forced by economic reality to fulfill his father's wishes instead of his own.

"Bom," she said with a bored shrug. *"Comes comida congelada."*

Antonio shut the door behind him, and by the time he was halfway to his car he could hear the melodramatic lamentations of the fado again. He cringed; if the neighbors didn't know better, they'd think the Bateras were uneducated immigrants.

He started the big Chrysler New Yorker, turned the air conditioner up all the way and put in a Tony Bennett tape. Music, now *that* was music. Humming along to "This Is All I Ask," he pulled out of the driveway and drove up to Chatsworth Boulevard, past Point Loma High where Jorge and Gilberto had gone to school. Batera's house was close to the top of the hill; he'd bought it just a couple of years after he made skipper. It was a good neighborhood, nice homes and a strong sense of community. Mostly Portuguese, and about half the families were or had been connected to the tuna business. Funny thing, Batera thought; you could tell which ones were in the industry by whether they had a boat in the driveway. The ones that did, they didn't have to spend six weeks at a time at work out on the ocean.

He stopped at the corner of Rosecrans, took a left and got onto Sports Arena Boulevard, past the Marine Depot and the back of the airport. He didn't feel like going to Nunu's today; too dark, no damn windows in the place, and they had that soft-rock crap on the radio. He got off at Washington, headed over to Mission Hills, and parked the Chrysler across the street from some yuppie takeout joint called Pasta La Vista. He shook his head and smiled as he locked the car, then jaywalked and pushed open the familiar big wooden door of the Lamplighter.

Only one of the booths against the walls was occupied, and the tables in the other room off to the right were all empty. Back on the other side of the U-shaped bar, a couple of younger guys were playing pool, and two men closer to Batera's age sat on stools at opposite ends of the bar.

"Hey, Chico!" he called to the bartender as he swung his still-wiry frame onto one of the many empty stools.

"Hey, Toninho! Bud?"

"Yah, I guess. João been by?"

"Not today. Could be over to Nunu's, maybe he'll drop by later." The bartender handed him his bottle of beer, no glass. "Tough luck you had, man."

Batera took a swig of the beer. "It happens."

"Found anybody to sign on yet?"

"Nah, not yet." He glanced over his shoulder, indicated the pool players with a jerk of his thumb. "What about those fellas, they in the business?"

Chico shrugged. "Didn't say. Prob'ly."

"Never hurt to ask," Batera said, getting up off the barstool. He stood by the pool table for a few moments, waiting as one of the muscular young men made a corner-pocket shot.

"Falais português?" he asked them.

"Italiano," said the shooter. "But English, too, me and him."

"You on the boats?"

They both nodded.

"My name's Batera, skipper on the *Sea Master*. We had a bad thing last trip, winch cable snapped; one guy lost his hand, the other one got hit in the head real bad."

"Yeah, we heard tell about that around the docks."

"So anyway, I'm still laid up in port, two men short. You guys lookin' for work?"

The taller of the two shook his head. "We got places on the *Pacifica,* goin' out tomorrow morning."

"O.K., you hear anybody needs a spot on a boat, you send 'em down to me. *Sea Master,* G Street Mole."

"Yessir. Hey, we was sorry to hear what happen."

Batera smiled glumly. "Thanks. And you guys ... good luck to you, O.K.?"

"Yeah, O.K. You too, sir."

Antonio left them to their game and settled back on his stool. The grizzled stranger at the end of the bar had put a quarter in the jukebox: Louis Prima's frenetic version of "That Old Black Magic."

"Any takers?" the bartender asked, setting him up a fresh beer without being asked.

"Fuck, no. You know how many days I'm losin'?"

"Too many, right?"

"You got it, Chico. Too goddamn many." He sucked the head

off his beer and watched the door. Hell, *somebody* in this town had to need work, and however soon he could find them wouldn't be soon enough.

Sheila Roberts sat at her computer keyboard, adjusting the parameters of her latest algorithm. She made some slight alterations in a few lines of code, and after a moment's thought added another line to the program. Then she reset the digital audio tape loop, checked the hydrophone connections, and jumped into the pool.

The water was warm, as always; she kept this end of the system heated to a comfortable temperature year-round. Even without the heating system, though, the Santa Barbara winters were nothing like the ones she'd grown up with in the high desert chill of Santa Fe.

Nor was the setting anything like New Mexico, she thought, swimming to the far end of the pool where a pair of sliding underwater doors connected the pool with an artificial lagoon next to her house and office, and from there to the open sea. So much water, it was hard to believe that the area suffered from almost constant drought; but this was desert, too, despite the proximity to the sea.

At least the water to refill the pool had been free, aside from what it cost to pump it in. The earthquake had jostled the pool like a too-full soup bowl on a bumpy airplane flight, emptying it by two thirds and flooding the adjacent house. Sheila and her grad-student assistants had spent the last ten days mopping out her house and office, and pumping a fresh supply of seawater from the lagoon to the pool.

Sheila reached the doors and rested her hands on top of them, bobbing buoyantly in the salt water. Her petite body felt so light that it might almost rise free of the water itself at any moment, and go gliding effortlessly above the beach below the house.

She called out once, and almost instantly a sharp gray fin appeared in the lagoon, speeding toward her from the ocean. When it neared the doors it dipped beneath the surface, and after a moment the doors began to slide apart, opening the pool to the lagoon.

Ringo swam in and immediately touched his snout to the button in the pool wall that closed the doors again. He liked it warm, too, and was always diligent about keeping as much of the heated water from escaping as he possibly could. His smooth, sleek head raised up from the water, nodding excitedly as Sheila stroked him. Then he dove abruptly and swam beneath her, brushing her legs like a friendly kitten.

"Good morning," Sheila said, smiling, when he surfaced again. "You ready for some TV?"

Ringo gave one of his Bronx-cheer squawks, and splashed her lightly with a shake of his flippers. She reached into the zippered pouch at her waist, took out his rubber penguin toy, and gave it a squeeze to fill it with water. Ringo spotted it right away, and opened his long-beaked mouth expectantly. Sheila raised the toy just above the surface and carefully directed a thin stream of water toward the dolphin's head, letting it play over his rounded snout and his rows of sharp little teeth. He squeaked contentedly, moving his head slowly from side to side as the warm water tickled him.

"Had your breakfast yet?" she asked. He made a noncommittal click-sound, and waggled his still-open mouth for another refreshing stream of water from the rubber toy. Sheila complied, then swam back to the edge of the pool and took a fresh mackerel from the bucket she'd left there.

"Go for it, fella! Midair catch!" She tossed the fish toward the east side of the pool, and Ringo put on an instantaneous burst of speed in that direction. He leaped straight from the water just as the fish began its downward arc, caught it easily in his mouth, and with a quick flick of his head tossed it twice as far toward the west, over the underwater doors and into the lagoon.

Sheila laughed; either he'd already had his fill out in the ocean, or he was conveying a strong disdain for the taste of mackerel on this particular morning. Or, even more likely, he'd thrown the fish away just for the sheer mischievousness of it, to get a rise out of Sheila. Dolphins were swiftly bored by routine, and were always looking for some way to perform the unexpected.

"O.K., Ringo," she said, lifting herself out of the water. "Enough warm-up, it's TV time."

He rolled on his side and swam cooperatively to the near corner of the pool. Embedded in one wall, two feet under water behind a thick plate of glass, was a twenty-seven-inch Panasonic color monitor. It was flanked by a set of customized sound-wave generators and a pair of sensitive underwater microphones, called hydrophones.

Ringo submerged himself slightly and floated in place, staring impatiently at the blank screen. Sheila sat at the poolside control console, toweling dry her close-cropped dark hair. She flipped a switch, and a brief segment from a nature documentary appeared on the underwater monitor: two dolphins making love. Ringo's interest in these sessions, Sheila thought wryly, always seemed to be heightened by starting off with a little porn.

He watched the screen intently, surfacing only once for a quick breath, as the dolphin pair on the tape enjoyed a vigorous copulation. When the segment was finished, Sheila immediately triggered another control, one that did several things at once: It changed the monitor's function from VCR output to computer link, turned on the delicately tuned hydrophones in the pool, and started one of the digital audio recorders rolling.

Ringo stayed where he was for a few moments, still and apparently silent; but the oscilloscope on Sheila's console showed her he'd responded to the blinking prompt on his screen with several rapid emissions of extremely high-frequency sound, in the range of 125,000 cycles per second; far beyond the hearing capability not only of humans, but of dogs or cats or any other land-dwelling creature.

This was the famous dolphin "sonar," or echolocation beam; using it, a dolphin could construct a precisely detailed auditory image of its surroundings, from a millimeter-thin wafer nearby to a fish or another dolphin four or five miles away, even in the murkiest of waters. The image was at least as distinct as that afforded by human sight—the acoustic perception centers of the dolphin's brain were as large, and as complexly developed, as the human visual cortex. Using an echolocation scan, a dolphin could clearly "see" an entire three-dimensional landscape beneath the water; and since flesh, being largely water itself, was also permeable to the dolphins' sonar beams, they could observe an X-raylike image of the internal organs and skeletal structure of the creatures around them, dolphin or fish or human.

But Ringo wasn't scanning anything; he had no reason to. He was intimately familiar with this and every other corner of the pool, had scanned them all exhaustively when he'd first been introduced here over a year ago. There was nothing novel in the environment that would call for a scan, and his ordinary vision was sufficient to give him a good look at the audio-video equipment in front of him.

Sheila was convinced that right now he was doing something entirely different with his sophisticated echolocation powers; and this conviction was the basis of all her research for the past four years.

It was a simple enough equation, on the face of it: If a dolphin can send out a beam of concentrated high-frequency sound, and then translate the returning reflection of that beam into a well-defined, holographic image of its environment ... then why could it not, using those same highly evolved stereophonation organs, transmit an original wave of sound purposefully modulated so as to already contain the same type of shape-and-distance information as one of the reflections?

In other words, *send a picture.*

All previous experiments in human-dolphin communication had been hampered, perhaps fatally flawed, by one fact: Dolphins in the wild almost never used those audible squeals and squawks so familiar to generations of television viewers and aquarium visitors. They usually produced those sounds only in the company of human beings, and dozens of well-intentioned researchers had stumbled along for decades either trying to decipher the possible meanings of those noises or attempting to teach the dolphins to modify them into English or Russian or Norwegian.

Sheila, by contrast, was working from the premise that the sounds the dolphins made with their heads above water might well be devoid of logical content—cetacean nonsense syllables produced solely for the amusement of human observers. Either that, or some rough equivalent of grunts or groans or laughter. It was entirely possible that the dolphins had no concept of linear, symbol-structured, grammar-oriented language in the human sense; they might find the very notion so alien as to be forever incomprehensible.

But, Sheila thought, thrilling even now at the notion she'd conceived six years ago ... if they could send each other *pictures*!

A chime sounded from the direction of the house, and she switched the monitor on her console to display the front-door camera view. It was the mailman, probably with an express delivery of the new image-enhancement software she'd been promised from a friend at MIT.

"Back in a minute, Ringo," she called to the dolphin, who squawked disapproval at her departure. She padded barefoot through the kitchen and living room, not bothering to grab a cover-up on the way; her working uniform was a swimsuit, and she felt as thoroughly dressed as if she were wearing pumps and stockings and a navy wool "power" outfit.

"Morning, Miz Roberts. Certified letter—could you sign here, please?"

Sheila scrawled her name on the slip, disappointed that it hadn't been the new software; she was looking forward to trying that out, seeing if it could bring out enough detail in the tapes to finally discern a recognizable image.

She thanked the mailman, closed the door, and only then did she take note of the return address on the envelope: the Hellerman Foundation, Philadelphia. Sheila frowned; her grant check wasn't due for another six weeks.

She tore it open; no check, just a one-page letter. "We regret to inform you ..." she read, and "... insufficient results from your research ..." and "... all funds to be terminated ..."

God, no, they couldn't. They damn well couldn't, not now!

But of course they could. And had.

Sheila sank into the nearest chair with a sense of utter devastation.

She was about to lose not merely her life's work, but also her most cherished friends. With no further money to support the research, Ringo and the two other dolphins with whom she had lived and worked so closely would, at best, be sold to an aquarium; at worst, they would be turned out to fend for themselves in the open sea, with no protective school to return to.

She had six weeks in which to convince the foundation to reverse its decision; six weeks in which to produce the definitive results that had eluded her for the past four years.

2

The *Sea Master* was docked at the foot of a stubby little pier just off Harbor Drive, behind the U.S. Navy Supply Center. Daniel was surprised to discover that it was only a few blocks from the center of downtown San Diego; he and Mitch had walked there straight from the train station in less than ten minutes.

The boat itself was a couple of hundred feet long and fairly modern-looking, though the black paint of its hull was worn through in spots from salt and battering waves. Behind the two window-lined decks at the front of the boat, one atop the other, was a large expanse of flat, open deck. In the middle of that space stood a fifty-foot mast with an enclosed crow's nest at the top. The mast also served as a support for a large metal boom as long as the mast was high. Below the boom was a gigantic black pile of net, what looked like tons of it, all carefully folded and stacked along with an array of buoys, rings, and chain.

There was no one to be seen on board the boat; the only person around was a shirtless young man on a skateboard, doing jumps and spins on the adjacent pier. He looked to be in his late teens, maybe early twenties.

Daniel readjusted the straps on his backpack, and Mitch rolled his faded blue duffel bag off his shoulder and lowered it to the pavement.

"Whatcha think?" Mitch asked, frowning. "We ask the kid?"

"Let's hold off a minute or two," Daniel said. "He doesn't look like he belongs to the boat, somehow."

Mitch shrugged, nodded. Daniel shook a cigarette out of the pack in his jacket pocket, and stared out across the narrow channel of the bay toward the plush homes of the peninsula that everyone mistakenly called Coronado Island. Away to the south, the graceful white curve of the bridge connecting Coronado to the mainland arced high above the choppy water. He and Ruth had spent a long weekend over there once, at the splendid old Hotel del Coronado, when Daniel came back from his first China assignment. She'd cut her foot on a shell one day when they were walking on the beach, and she bled, she bled . . .

He ground his half-smoked cigarette out on the dirty concrete pier, and looked up to see someone walking purposefully across the open deck of the *Sea Master,* toward the netpile at the stern.

"Hey!" Mitch shouted. "Any work to be had on board?"

The darkly tanned man stopped and looked at them. *"Falais português?"* he called back.

"Yo hablo un poquito de español," Daniel answered.

The man stared back in silence. *"'Spera um momento,"* he said at last, and disappeared back into the interior of the boat. As they waited for him to return, the kid on the skateboard took a tumble. He got right back up and started practicing his tricks again, ignoring the nasty red scrape on his elbow.

Somebody else, a shorter and lighter-skinned man about thirty, stuck his head out the door of the boat's lower front deck. A dirty-brown dog, half-retriever by the looks of it, peered out beside him. "Can I help you guys?" the man asked.

"Hope so," Mitch told him. "Got any crew slots open?"

"You ever work seiners?"

"Sure," Mitch lied. "Out of Costa Rica."

"Skipper's in town right now, but he oughta be back soon. Come aboard, take a load off while you wait."

" 'Preciate it," Mitch said, lifting his duffel bag and stepping onto the gangway.

"Name's Carlos," the man said, extending his hand. "Chief engineer. But I guess you could tell," he added with a grin.

Daniel wasn't sure what he meant; sure, there was grease caked under the guy's fingernails, but a glance around the open deck showed there was grease on half the exposed working surfaces. Couldn't be anything about the way he was dressed, either; he was just wearing jeans and sneakers and a blue T-shirt.

Carlos saw their lack of comprehension and shrugged. "Engineroom tan," he explained, rubbing his smooth, almost pale cheek. "What boat you guys say you worked down south?"

"Couple different ones," Mitch said hurriedly. "Not so nice as this here. You suppose we could get some coffee while we wait for the skipper?"

"Sure," Carlos said. " 'Less you rather have a brew?"

"Yeah, I could go for a beer," Daniel said, his mouth dry with nervousness.

"Coffee's O.K. with me," Mitch said.

They followed the engineer into the galley. Four restaurant-style booths were set along the walls, and two other tables were bolted to the floor in the center. A framed reproduction of *The Last Supper* hung over one of the booths, and on the opposite wall was a chart of the southeastern Pacific, from California to Peru. At one of the tables sat a dark-haired girl of fifteen or sixteen. She was sipping a Diet Dr Pepper and leafing sullenly through a copy of *Spin*.

Ignoring the girl, Carlos raised a partition and walked through a long wooden serving counter that separated the cook's working space from the dining area. "Bud O.K.?" he asked, opening a big metal refrigerator.

"Yeah, fine," Daniel said, though he would have preferred a Beck's or a Dos Equis.

The engineer tossed him a can of beer, then poured a mug of thick, black coffee for Creighton. The dog stayed by his side, watching the newcomers; it neither barked nor wagged its tail, reserving judgment.

Carlos opened a beer for himself and indicated one of the two corner booths. The three of them sat down, Daniel next to a window overlooking the dock. The kid on the skateboard was still at it.

"So, what you think, any slots open?" Mitch asked.

"I hate to say one way or the other," Carlos said apologetically. "That's for the skipper to do."

"He a good man to work for?" Daniel asked.

"Better'n some," Carlos said after a moment's reflection. "He's a fair man, and he's got a nose for where the fish are."

A large, swarthy man suddenly filled the door that opened onto the outside deck. *"Olá, Carlos,"* he boomed, *"êsse central tanque?"*

"Pressure's back up now," the engineer said. "Had a leak in one of the ammonia pipes, *e reparado agora.*"

"Bom," the big man said. "Who these fellas?"

"Lookin' for work," Carlos said. "I told 'em Antonio be back anytime now, they waitin' to see him."

"Name's Mitch," Creighton put in. "And this is Daniel, here."

The beefy man grunted, his face dour.

"This is Manoel," Carlos said. "He's the mate."

Manoel grunted again, and didn't bother to offer his hand. Daniel glanced away from the man's stern gaze, and saw a big blue Chrysler pull up on the pier outside and stop next to the boat. "That the skipper?" he asked.

Carlos leaned forward to look out the window. "Yeah, that's him. Hang on, I'll tell him you're here." He chugged the rest of his beer and tossed the can in the trash, and went out to greet the captain. Manoel moved aside to let him pass, then lingered in the doorway, alternating his silent frown between the teenaged girl and Mitch and Daniel.

The skipper was a well-groomed, graying man in his fifties, still lean and ropy. He looked curiously at the young girl with the magazine when he came into the galley, but said nothing to her; then he turned his attention to Daniel and Mitch. "Antonio Batera," he said, shaking hands as the two men introduced themselves. "Come on back to my cabin; we'll get you a real drink, O.K.? And, hey, Manoel, you come on by for a minute, too, I need to talk to you."

They followed him down a hallway past the crew's quarters, then up a steep flight of steps to the top deck. Batera's cabin was just behind the bridge, and surprisingly well-appointed: There was a large writing desk, a wet bar, and a teakwood cabinet containing a TV, VCR, and stereo. On one of the walls next to the full-sized bed was an open gun rack stocked with a couple of rifles, a shotgun, and a .45 pistol. Daniel and Mitch sat down on a sofa across from the bar; Manoel remained standing.

"Vodka? Scotch? Bourbon?" Batera asked, taking three glasses from a cabinet above the bar.

"Bourbon and water, thanks," Daniel said.

Mitch hesitated. "Ah . . . vodka, I guess."

"Straight up, water back?"

"Rocks and tonic."

The skipper took an ice bucket from the mini-fridge, and put a few cubes in each glass. He spoke to Manoel over his shoulder as he mixed the drinks.

"So, who's that kid in the galley? And the one outside, on the skateboard?"

"A garôta, I think she's a runaway," the big man told him. "She was hanging around the park. Gilberto get to talking to her; he say she could use his bunk last night. Since he was home, you know?"

Batera stirred the drinks. "And the boy? The skateboarder?"

"He just show up today. See the girl out on the deck, come over and try to talk to her, show off for her."

The skipper handed the drinks to Daniel and Mitch, then sat in an overstuffed reclining chair across from them. "I don't like it," he told Manoel. "You know the troubles we could have with strangers on the boat, and kids besides. Nothin' but bad news."

Manoel nodded. "Bad news," he repeated.

"The times the way they are," Batera said in oblique explanation. "And the insurance."

"I go tell her *deixar o barco,* and not come back no more."

·"Good. Good. And have a word with Gilberto about it, too, O.K.?"

"You got it," Manoel said, and moved his heavy frame back down the hallway toward the galley.

The skipper took a sip of his Johnnie Walker and gave Mitch and Daniel the once-over. "So, you boys looking for work. You drive a speedboat?"

"Some," Creighton said. "Not really good enough for herding porpoise, though, tell you the truth."

"Mmh. Well, I guess I still got enough drivers; what you want, general deckhand work?"

"Yeah, that's basically it," Daniel said.

"You know brailing? You know how to stack the netpile?"

Mitch jumped in before Daniel could answer. "We might be a little rusty," he said, "but we can pick it right up again, no problem."

The skipper frowned. "You boys ever work a tuna boat before, or not?"

"Oh, hell yeah," Mitch said. "Down south, out of Puntarenas, you know?"

"Yah, I know Puntarenas." Batera's long-fingered hands idly stroked the frosty glass. "Where you guys usually stay down there between trips?" he asked. "The Colonial? The Portobello?"

Daniel barked a quick, loud laugh to drown out whatever Mitch had been about to say. "You kidding, sir? On Costa Rican deck-hand's pay? Most of the time, we'd double up at a place called *Cabinas Orlando,* at San Isidro. They've got those little kitchenettes, you know, so it works out even cheaper if you do most of your own cooking."

"You ever eat in those Chinese places downtown?"

Daniel made a disgusted face. "Not if I can help it. I don't think

I ever found a decent Chinese place in Puntarenas yet. And, shit, that's damn near all they got!"

Batera laughed, nodding. "If I'm going out to eat down there, I like *Fonda Brisas del Pacífico.*"

"Right near the wharf, right?"

"Yeah, you got it."

"Now *that's* where you can get a real plate of *casado,*" Daniel said, grateful now for all those weekend R & R trips when he'd been writing about El Salvador for *Mother Jones.*

"Well," Batera said, getting up to replenish the drinks. "You boys be ready to head out tomorrow morning?"

"It must have come as a terrible shock," Richard Tarnoff said, straightening the creases of his gray wool slacks as he sat down on the living-room sofa. So like Richard always to wear wool, Sheila thought, even in Southern California; he belonged in New England somewhere, maybe at a small private college or one of the almost-Ivy-League universities. UCSB had never really suited him, despite his professional success here.

"Of course it did," Sheila said distractedly, glancing out the window toward the nighttime blackness of the ocean. Ringo and Georgia and Paulette were out there right now, unseen but all-seeing; they had twenty-four-hour access to the sea, and used the privilege frequently.

The wine-dark sea . . . what must it be like, she wondered, to explore those ominous night depths with such utter ease and assurance? With their sonar, the dolphins could scan each hillock and plain and improbable creature on the ocean's bottom with as clear a view in total darkness as in the brightest sunlight.

". . . your 'babies,' after all," Richard was saying, with that little clucking sound he used to express both sympathy and disapproval.

"I don't need that, not now," Sheila snapped. He'd started calling the dolphins that when he and she were lovers, and always with a tone of ill-concealed condescension. It had been the factor that had finally driven them apart, his jealousy of the time she spent with Ringo and the others. His own field was ichthyology; he preferred his undersea creatures with gills and minuscule brains, and, ideally, fossilized.

"I was only trying to—"

"I know, Richard. I appreciate your coming by, really I do." She was embarrassed by her outburst. What did it matter whether he still thought her obsessed with her work? The work was finished, or would be soon, all her efforts and devotion wasted; and he was married now, to a very pretty and very pregnant lady named Leslie, whose interests apparently ran the gamut from gardening to horse-back riding to taking care of Richard.

"Well, I knew you'd be upset," he said. "You can't really blame the foundation, though; they did give you four years to try."

"It wasn't enough."

"Then how long would have been enough? Five years? Ten? I mean, for God's sake, Sheila." He gestured at the workstation across the room, where she had been reviewing one of the dolphin tapes when he'd arrived. The tape was still running, filling the screen of the monitor with an ever-changing array of apparently random patterns: sometimes swirling, sometimes jagged, always amorphous and indistinct.

"There's nothing meaningful in all that jumble," Richard said. "There's nothing there to decipher. Isn't it time you put your talents to better use?"

"Like what?" She felt her fists clench, the flush rise to her face. "Playing academic politics?" It was a low blow, but she no longer cared. Tarnoff hadn't produced any original work in years, and they both knew his position as chairman of the Department of Marine Biology was the result of his constant involvement in fund-raising affairs, alumni dinners and the like.

"Anything would be better than this . . . this bullshit," he retorted, stung.

Sheila fought to control her anger. "You have no right to say that," she finally managed to get out, in a tone at least approximating some degree of calm. "You know damned well how much I believe in this project, how much it means to me."

"Wishful thinking doesn't make good science," Richard said. "It may be a very appealing notion in some circles, this idea of yours that dolphins can communicate by sending each other imaginary pictures, but where are your results? Where's your proof?"

"I told you, I need more—"

"More time, right. And more money. Well, the foundation board decided you'd had enough of both, didn't they? I mean, face it, Sheila, this whole theory of yours is straight out of science fiction. It's just too damned . . . alien."

"Jesus, what would you expect? The cetaceans *are* alien; they've been on a separate evolutionary path from the land mammals for tens of millions of years. They're almost like extraterrestrial beings, and all that excess brain mass they have didn't develop for no reason; it's there for thinking, for communicating."

Tarnoff gave her a maddeningly smug half smile. "Then why have all the attempts to communicate with them failed? Don't you think some bright dolphin involved in one of those experiments would have realized what was going on and would have met the researcher halfway? Just once?"

"Damn it, Richard!" How much of this was still personal with him? Sheila wondered. He had his wife, their baby on the way; would he not be satisfied until he'd finally proved Sheila wrong about the project that had driven him away from her? "You know that's my whole point," she said, exasperated. "They may be using something radically different from what we think of as language. For all the jabbering we've done at them over the past twenty years, the dolphins may still think we're their equivalent of deaf-mutes."

Richard shook his head. "That's still too bizarre for me to accept," he told her. "I think you were always grasping at straws, and it's just as well it's over."

An unexpected and sickeningly awful thought abruptly struck

her. "You haven't ... Richard, you didn't talk to the foundation, did you?"

He looked away, suddenly uneasy. "Well, of course I'm regularly in touch with all sorts of—"

"Did you?"

"They asked me for my opinion, that's all. I couldn't very well be less than honest with them."

"You bastard! It was you!"

He held up his hands, placating, defensive. "Like I said, I only—"

Sheila had never quite believed that one could literally shake with rage; now she found herself trembling uncontrollably, desperate to lash out. "Goddamnit, *why?* Whatever you may have thought of my theories, that grant was a plum for the university, too, and—"

"It was becoming an embarrassment to the university, Sheila. The department doesn't need that kind of reputation; it could've endangered future grants for more ... respectable work."

She couldn't look at him anymore, was afraid she might do something childish and violent and regrettable. "Get out of my house," she told him in a measured voice.

"You've got to understand that my responsibilities as—"

"I said get out. Now."

He was already halfway to the door. "I'll expect to see you at the department meeting on Thursday," Tarnoff said over his shoulder. "This phaseout needs to be handled properly. Rationally."

Sheila said nothing in reply, just waited until she heard the door click shut behind him and then let the tears come.

He'd never agreed with her ideas, that had always been made abundantly clear; but to sabotage her like this, to willfully destroy four years of dedicated work ...

She wiped her eyes and looked across the room at the computer workstation. On the screen, the wavering, enigmatic patterns continued to unfold without a hint of any recognizable shapes or symbols. They were there, though, of that she was convinced; she might have to rework her translation algorithm yet again, she might even have to start from scratch with a whole new approach to the problem ... but one way or another, she was determined to prove Richard Tarnoff wrong.

In the next six weeks.

They'd been on the ocean for almost a week now, doing essentially nothing: coiling and recoiling lengths of rope, swabbing out the big refrigerated holds, plugging oil leaks in the miles of pipe that snaked their way to and from the engine room.

Daniel had begun to wonder if this was going to be a wasted trip, after all the planning and the careful subterfuge. He'd spotted a gray whale or two, a school of flying fish, even a few isolated pods of dolphins as the boat moved south past Mexico; but nothing had come of any of the sightings, and the Portuguese crewmen seemed as bored and restless as he.

They were in the placid tropical waters off Costa Rica when the call to action came, a spirited cry from whoever was taking his turn that day in the crow's nest: *"Toninhas, uma hora!"*

"What'd he say? *Qué dice?*" Daniel asked the crewman next to him, with whom he'd been futilely polishing the rusty cleats on the gunwales.

"Marsopas," the man said, grinning and dropping his dirty rag and brush to hurry toward the netpile at the stern. "Porpoise, one o'clock."

Daniel stood up and peered across the flat blue water; it looked empty to him, but a sudden air of robust festivity had seized the men on deck: There was laughter all about, and jubilant shouts in Portuguese and English; three men in bathing suits jumped into the red speedboats as if getting set for an impromptu race, a game for a sunny day on the open Pacific. Someone brought a boom box out onto the deck, and turned it up loud: Gal Costa belting forth a joyous, spirited samba, the music ripe with gaiety and life.

The chief engineer's dog was as caught up in the excitement as any of the men, dashing back and forth between the piled nets and the speedboats, tail wagging, his bark an arrhythmic punctuation to the blaring, pulsing Brazilian music.

The boat veered slightly to starboard, picking up speed, and in a moment Daniel saw them: half a mile away, hundreds of dolphins were leaping and playing in the gently rolling swells. He stood immobile at the portside rail, watching the dolphins, as the first of the speedboats to his right was lowered into the water fifty feet below.

"This is it," he heard Mitch Creighton mutter at his side. "Go get the camera."

"You're the one who was supposed to—"

"Manoel wants me on the net winch. You start—then when the set's made we'll try to switch off."

"I don't have any place to hide the damn thing."

"Put on your jacket, hold it under your arm."

Daniel was perturbed at the sudden change in plans. Accompanying Creighton on this trip was one thing, but actually operating the camera was more than he'd intended or agreed to do. "It's ninety degrees, for God's sake; it's gonna look weird if I put on a jacket now."

Mitch scowled and looked around the deck. He and Daniel were the only men not furiously laboring with either the nets or the speedboat cables.

"Just do it! One of us has to get to work, and Manoel's already pissed off at me. I can't go back to the cabin now."

A speedboat engine's steady whine cut through the vibrant music from the cassette player. Daniel could see the battered, dull-red craft wheeling in tight circles on the ocean below, waiting for the other two boats to join it. The dolphins, closer now, heedlessly continued their uninhibited romp, spinning like dancers as they jumped clear of the water's surface.

Creighton turned away and headed toward the massive stack of folded netting at the boat's stern. Manoel, the heavyset mate, glared at him through droopy lids as he went.

Shit, Daniel thought, it was do it Creighton's way or blow the whole story. He made his way back along the railing, then down a companionway to the crew's quarters below the bridge. There were five cabins: two single ones for the mate and chief engineer, and three four-bunk cabins like the one Daniel shared with Creighton and two other men. All were empty now as the pace of the work outside increased to a fever pitch.

Daniel shut the door of the cluttered cabin, wishing he could lock it. He pulled Creighton's duffel bag from beneath his bunk and rummaged through the dirty laundry at the bottom of the bag until he found the Sony camcorder, no bigger than a coffee mug. He put in a fresh battery and checked to make sure the camera was set to autofocus.

The heavy engines beneath Daniel's feet roared once as the big boat heeled about, then idled. He pulled a light windbreaker over his T-shirt and wedged the camcorder under his right arm, its lens almost hidden by the half-zipped jacket.

Stepping back out on deck, he saw the three speedboats rush away in a looping curve to the right of the dolphin school. At the stern, Creighton and several other crewmen were playing out the huge black folds of the net, easing it into the water through the oily power winch fifty feet above the deck.

Daniel steadied himself against the portside railing and angled his body in the direction of the swerving speedboats. He glanced down at the partially open windbreaker, where he could see the camcorder's upward-swiveled electronic viewfinder; there was nothing on the tiny black-and-white screen but blank sky. He leaned forward a bit, readjusting the slight weight against his forearm. Now the little screen showed a perfect miniature image of the racing speedboats.

The *Sea Master* had begun to move again too, in a slow leftward semicircle that was a mirror image of the speedboats' arc. Behind the larger vessel, a smooth curve of evenly spaced cork floaters marked the area where the thick net trailed deep below the surface.

Daniel watched the speedboats break their close formation as they rushed the dolphins and moved into a pattern of tight circles, one on each side of the school and another behind it. The sleek silver creatures were now boxed into an ever-shrinking space of water—one that moved, as it diminished, toward the impassable net the boat had laid.

Over the sound of the samba music that still bellowed from the deck, Daniel could hear the whoops and shouts of the speedboat drivers as they herded the obviously agitated dolphins in the direction the men wanted them to go. He risked another glance at the viewfinder: still on target, but when the hell was Creighton going to take over? This was his goddamn mission; Daniel was just here to report on it, not carry it out.

The nearest few of the dolphins had encountered the net, and strained without success to swim back through the hemmed-in mob of their fellows. Daniel could hear the first high-pitched squeals of panic: babies separated from their mothers, other dolphins thrashing and squirming as their sensitive fins or flippers were caught in the thick strands of the net, still others struggling for a breath of air as they were forced beneath the water by the inexorable crush.

The *Sea Master* moved to complete the deadly circle, enclosing the dolphins on all sides. Daniel noticed with surprise that his breath was coming in short, strained bursts, as if he, too, were caught in that claustrophobic net below. Where the *fuck* was Creighton?

The engines of the big boat shifted into reverse and began to pull the net through the water. Daniel gripped the railing to maintain his footing, and when he looked back down he saw that a few of the dolphins had managed to escape through a small opening in the back of the net. Within moments, a panicked mass of dolphins formed around the intended escape route, like people jamming a single exit from a burning theater. Most of them were drowning.

The *Sea Master*'s engines went to idle again, and the net began slowly rising, lifted by the massive steel pulleys of the hydraulic winch high above the deck. As it was hoisted clear of the water, the net closed tight like a gigantic drawstring bag. Daniel watched, transfixed, as the dolphins at the bottom of the net ceased their anguished writhing, crushed lifeless under the weight of their enmeshed brethren.

He looked around; no one was paying him the slightest attention, they were all too busy. He slid the camera partway out of its place of concealment, held it in both hands and tilted it upward as the cargo of dead and dying dolphins ascended toward the deck.

Four crewmen guided the heavily laden net to the flat open space in the center of the boat and let it drop to the deck with a rough thud, where a dozen grasping hands eagerly opened it. Of the hundred or more dolphins caught in the net, only a handful now showed any signs of life.

The chief engineer's dog had singled out one of the survivors, and ran back and forth near the helpless creature's head, yapping furiously as the agonized, intelligent eyes watched its movements. Every few seconds, the dog would dart in close to snap at the dolphin's flippers or its dorsal fin.

Another live dolphin lay behind the one the dog was tormenting; its abdomen heaved with labored breaths as its delicate skin dried quickly in the relentless sun. Its dorsal had been broken off by the thick strands of the net, and a gush of bright red blood spurted from the wound with each remaining heartbeat.

Daniel felt himself about to retch, then suddenly there was a hand on his shoulder. He started, made a reflex motion to cover the camera with his windbreaker.

"Give it to me," he heard, and turned to see Mitch Creighton behind him.

"They'll see it," Daniel protested.

"The jacket, too, then."

"Let me get the rest of it for now, and tomorrow—"

"Jesus, half an hour ago you didn't want to touch the damn thing—now you want to do it all?"

Two crewmen passed by, carrying a trembling dolphin about five feet long. At the railing, they pitched the terrified young creature overboard, a drop as high as a two-story building. It struck the water broadside, then sank slowly, unmoving. If the impact hadn't killed it outright, Daniel thought, it would undoubtedly drown, too weak from shock and internal injuries to return to the surface for air.

"Give it to me," Mitch insisted in a raspy whisper.

Daniel shrugged wearily and slipped the shiny blue jacket off, keeping it wrapped around the camcorder as he did so, and handed the package to Creighton.

Out of the corner of his eye he saw one of the crewmen watching the exchange. The man frowned, said something to the beefy mate, Manoel, and pointed in their direction.

"Hey, new-boy," Manoel shouted, coming toward them, "what you got there, huh? You got dope?"

Creighton tried to move toward the cabins, but Manoel's hamlike hand was already on his arm.

"Gimme that, boy. You got dope in there, you in a shitload of trouble."

He snatched the rolled-up jacket from Creighton's grasp, and impatiently unfurled it. The compact video unit looked even more minute in Manoel's burly hands. He stared at it in confusion, having expected to see a package of cocaine or marijuana; then his scowl of bemusement was swiftly transformed into one of rage.

"Greenpeace! You motherfuckers from Greenpeace!"

"No," Mitch said. "Not Greenpeace. The Ocean Coalition."

Manoel hit him in the mouth with the back of one of those massive hands. "Same fuckin' thing!"

Creighton managed to stay on his feet, spitting his own blood onto the already wetly crimsoned deck. Daniel stood his ground, silently; there was nothing to say, nowhere to flee.

Behind the mate, the crewmen went on with their work, indiscriminately heaving the bodies of dead or living dolphins into the sea. The prizes for which they labored were set aside in a separate stack: twenty or thirty large yellowfin tuna, destined for the canneries of Europe or Japan.

"Hey!" Manoel shouted over his shoulder. "*Éstes filhos de cadelas são de* Greenpeace! They takin' fuckin' pictures!"

The men stopped what they were doing; one of them dropped a live dolphin in a grimy pool of oil near one of the speedboat bays. He pulled a knife from the belt of his shorts, and led the others toward the spot where Mitch and Daniel were cornered.

"The fuck make you think you get away with a stunt like that, huh?" Manoel's dark face seemed even darker now, with anger. The crewmen hovered, waiting for the mate's lead.

"You were killing dolphins," Creighton mumbled, his voice thick through bruised and puffy lips.

"Ah, Cristo ... escuta éste idiota," Manoel said to the deckhand on his left. The man was holding a large wrench at the ready near Daniel's head, and the others had armed themselves with various tools or knives. "Put that fuckin' thing down, Chico," Manoel said, and handed the man the tiny video camera. "Take this up to the skipper, an' the rest of you get back to work."

Daniel slowly let out his breath as the men walked away toward the bow, across the blood-soaked deck. So goddamned much blood today ... the whole boat stank of blood and grease and fish.

"We want to talk to the skipper ourselves," Daniel said. "See what he has to say about all this."

"Sim? I thought maybe the way you like the fish so much, porpoises an' all, we'd maybe just put you down in the wells." Manuel grinned. "Not so hot down there. Nice an' cold, you know?"

Daniel pretended to ignore the threat; any response, he sensed, would only increase the likelihood of its being carried out.

"They're not porpoises," Mitch managed to say. "They're dolphins. Porpoises are a different breed."

"Whatever."

The crewmen had finished heaving most of the tuna into the wells; the set was over, and nothing remained of the dolphins except their blood, smeared everywhere across the grimy deck. Daniel heard the power block rumble to life, its taut steel cable straining against the weight of the skiff. The smaller boat lifted from the water, and the men fought to steady it as they eased it back on board.

"The skipper," Daniel demanded. "Now."

Manoel stared at him, indecision in his broad, brown face. Finally he shrugged and jerked his head toward the companionway that led up to the bridge. Daniel headed in that direction, with Mitch and Manoel marching along behind him. A jet of water shot across the slippery deck; one of the crewmen was hosing it down, washing the blood back into the sea.

They were near the railing at the side of the boat now, almost to the stairs. Whatever else he might be, Daniel thought, Batera was a businessman; he couldn't afford the luxury of violence. Daniel could see the man already, his shaded eyes looking down from the bridge at the three of them.

Daniel turned to Mitch, about to offer a word of optimism, and was stopped by a sudden cry of pain from Manoel. Creighton had kicked the big man in the kneecap with his heel, hard.

"Filho de cadela!" the mate shouted, clutching at his knee as Creighton flailed to keep his own footing; the impulsive kick had left him off balance, his left foot skidding wildly in the slick of oil and blood and water that covered the deck.

Daniel grabbed for him, touched the sleeve of his T-shirt but couldn't hold on. He watched in disbelief as Mitch fell against the waist-high railing and pitched over it headfirst, arms windmilling helplessly as he plunged into the water below.

"Help!" Daniel screamed, "Man overboard!" He clutched the steel railing with a rigid grip, scanning the waves below for a glimpse of Creighton's bobbing head.

"Idiota!" Manoel spat out through teeth clenched with pain. *"Paulo! Chico! Uma corda aqui, rápido!"*

Daniel stood transfixed at the rail, staring at the empty sea. He heard the crewmen behind him, running forward with the rope, but he still hadn't seen any sign of Creighton; and then he realized with sudden horror that the boat was turning, that its massive steel hull was already moving directly, unstoppably, over the very spot where Creighton had fallen.

3

It was the time of dark, but that was of no consequence to Ch*Tril and her companions. They swam in tight, precise circles around Ek*Tiq, brushing lightly against her now and then to offer a simple Touch or a little boost to the surface so that Ek*Tiq could conserve her strength for the ordeal ahead.

Ch*Tril was honored to have been chosen to attend her old friend, as Ek*Tiq had once attended her in her own bringing-forth. She was relieved that everything was going well; another of their pod-sisters had gone through a tragic bringing-forth not long ago, with the one-to-be coming out headfirst. It had drowned before the birthing was completed.

This would not be such a sad time, Ch*Tril was sure. She scanned Ek*Tiq again; the one-to-be, a male, was strong and well-formed, and its placement in the womb was as it should be.

Ch*Tril lifted her head above the surface for a breath. The sea was calm, and the moon above it a perfect thin crescent, its tips pointed straight upward. That was a good omen; it was said that such a crescent cool-light symbolized an arc of buoyancy, whose delicate form would keep those born beneath it always near the surface.

Ch*Tril bobbed her head and made a silly-silly sound to herself, then dove back down to rejoin the circle around her friend. She was an educated female, and knew better than to believe such nonsense as signs and omens, but the old myths still had their pull on her now and then.

She imaged the scene of the calm sea and the crescent cool-light to Ek*Tiq, and then directed the same image to the one-to-be, who was just beginning his arduous journey from the womb into the birthing passage. Perhaps his nascent mind would instinctually recognize the intended message of serenity and support.

Ch*Tril circled steadily about her friend, keeping pace with the two others. One of them, Tr*Qir, would be Ek*Tiq's nursing companion and protector as the young one grew, and Ch*Tril envied her that. Ch*Tril had been Ek*Tiq's first choice for the role, but her first duty was to the School, and it had been decided there was urgent work for Ch*Tril to perform.

The trip she'd soon begin would be a long one, as the nearest Sources were far to the north at this season. Dj\Tal would not be coming with her; he was needed here with the School, so she must choose others to accompany her on her travels. She wished that it were otherwise; Dj\Tal had seemed curiously preoccupied of late, and that concerned her. They had been exceedingly well-matched when first they'd mated, but now she sensed that there were certain images and thoughts, important ones, that he was holding back from her.

Ek*Tiq suddenly imaged a depiction of herself contorted with pain, and Ch*Tril sent back a scene of Ek*Tiq basking at the surface in a cool, soft mist, her healthy new young one beside her. Similar reassuring images came from the others in the circle, and Ch*Tril soon scanned a slight relaxation of Ek*Tiq's anxiously constricted muscles.

Waiting for the birthing to proceed, Ch*Tril let her mind roam back with pleasure to the occasion of that first mating with Dj\Tal. It had happened on a journey much like the one she was about to begin. The Sources had been to the south then, in a lagoon of the warm seas; it had been their own time of bringing-forth.

Dj\Tal had been one of three companions Ch*Tril had chosen for the mission, though she'd scarcely known him before then; oh, there'd been the occasional polite Touch in passing, but their separate tasks and friendships had kept them relative strangers. Tr*Qir had suggested she invite him on the journey south; Tr*Qir had mated with Dj\Tal a few times, and the erotic scenes she'd imaged had been recommendation enough.

Ch*Tril's tasks for that trip had been brief and uncomplicated, and when the work was done she and her companions had lingered in the warm lagoon, marveling at the birthing ritual of the great, gray Sources, at the mighty chorus of their deep bellowing songs that echoed through the darktime. Naturally, the experience had inspired Ch*Tril and the others to engage in respectful and abundant sex, in honor of the life-force so much in evidence all around them.

The four of them had mated in all possible combinations there in that lagoon, but Ch*Tril had found herself drawn time and again to Dj\Tal in preference to the others. Not merely because of his mating-skill, or his strong and unmarred body: Above all, she treasured his imaging, mysterious and beautiful scenes with a power that more than compensated for their relative infrequency.

On the long swim back to the School, she and Dj\Tal had kept largely to themselves, imaging privately to each other and mating often in the warm, clear water. He would send her images that seemed to have sprung from some secret world of his own: views of the sea and hills from high above, as a flying-creature might see them; or strange scenes of the mysterious land, with no ocean in sight. They were breathtaking images, often frightening but ultimately compelling.

Ch*Tril, in turn, would send him re-creations of the ancient myths and tales she had uncovered in her work as a Historian, or depictions of bizarre beings that had once swum in the seas but were no longer found.

It had been the most satisfying of all her journeys, Ch*Tril reflected fondly; and when they had returned to the School, she and Dj\Tal had remained all but inseparable. Thirty cool-lights ago, she had brought forth a young one from their mating, and their son Dv\Kil was now almost as strong, and as unblemished, as Dj\Tal.

So many events and scans shared in the time since they had come to know one another in that lagoon of the Sources; what, then, was he holding back from her now?

Her ponderings were interrupted by an image from Ek*Tiq: contortion and pain again, more extreme than before. Ch*Tril sent her another pacifying scene, then scanned her friend's abdomen. The one-to-be was near the end of the birthing passage now, beginning to emerge: There, a tiny set of flukes was coming out, moving rapidly now, followed by the little dorsal, then the head . . .

Ek*Tiq immediately guided the young one to the surface for its first breath, and Tr*Qir hovered nearby, ready to help if needed. Ch*Tril imaged a happy scene of seaweed-play to her friend, then hung back a ways, scanning as Tr*Qir maneuvered the newborn male into the proper position for suckling.

There was nothing more for Ch*Tril to do here now; mother and son were safe, everything was under control. She imaged her friends matched scenes of leaving and returning, then swam back toward the main part of the School, scanning for Dj\Tal.

Their School was a large one, numbering almost three thousand. A major fish-herding procedure had just been completed, and the individuals were now sorting themselves out from that highly disciplined mass exercise to rejoin their own much smaller pods, or to wander off in pairs or groups for play and sex.

Tr*Til, another friend from her youth, came swimming alongside with a slow, gentle Touch. Ch*Tril imaged her a speeded-up sequence of the birthing, and ended with a long still depiction of Ek*Tiq floating at the surface, serenely nursing her newly brought-forth young one.

Tr*Til imaged back leaping-pleasure, and paused a moment before tentatively sending a scene of herself and Ch*Tril swimming together, with the School nowhere in evidence.

Ch*Tril was touched that she would want to come along on the trip; her friend had never left the School before, was known as one who seldom even strayed more than a few beak-to-flukes from her own pod unless assigned to do so for a herding maneuver. She imaged Tr*Til a long series of lights and darks, then a scene of a cold sea with unfamiliar currents and fish; it would be a long, arduous journey.

Tr*Til gave an accepting jerk of her head, and imaged back an intentionally monotonous cycle of identical scenes: pod and herding, pod and herding, pod and herding. She was bored with her safe and comfortable life here in the School.

Ch*Tril mused on this. It would be good to have an old friend along on a trip of such length, and even though Tr*Til was inexperienced, she had always seemed both quick and adaptable. Why not give her a chance?

She echoed her friend's image of the two of them far from the school, and brushed against her in an amiable Touch.

Tr*Til dove swiftly down, almost to the sea bottom, then ascended at full speed and broke the surface in an impressive, joyous leap. At the top of her arc she stretched her body straight, and fell flat-bellied back into the water with a tremendous splash, almost landing on a couple who were mating nearby.

Ch*Tril arched her head again in amusement, and imaged a comical sequence of what might have happened if Tr*Til had indeed landed on the distracted couple. They shared the humor of it for several moments, then Tr*Til did a sensual undulation with her hind quarter and imaged an interrogatory blankness, followed by a scene of the two of them accompanied by a male Ch*Tril recognized: Nk\Jin, Tr*Til's latest temporary mate.

This enforced separation from Dj\Tal was sad to contemplate, but Ch*Tril knew it would be impossible to tolerate such a trip without the pleasure and release of sex. She waggled her pectoral fins to show indifference to the selection of Nk\Jin as a journey-mate, but at the same time imaged her assent. Tr*Til did two enthusiastic full rolls, then darted off to give her lover the good news.

Ch*Tril moved on, still searching for her mate, Dj\Tal. For a time she thought he might be in yet another meeting of the Circle, the group entrusted with the making of important Choices for the whole School; but then she saw Qr*Jil, the Old One, in the company of no one but her protector/companions, and knew that no meeting had been called.

Still no sign of Dj\Tal, but at the far edge of the School she came upon their male offspring, Dv\Kil. He was resting in half-sleep, and she waited quietly, knowing her son was aware of her presence. He, like all the others of their kind, normally slept in brief, frequent snatches, with only half his brain asleep and the other always conscious and alert, so that the half-sleeper would not forget to regularly rise to the surface for air. Surfacing to breathe was a voluntary act, and any of their kind who were rendered unconscious by accident or illness would drown unless held above water by others.

He looked so vulnerable, so young, in half-sleep; funny how she still thought of him as their "young one," even though he was now almost as long and as broad as Dj\Tal.

After a few moments, Dv\Kil roused himself to full alertness and greeted Ch*Tril with an image of tranquil seas. She returned the wish, and then she noticed a young female swimming in impatient circles just a few beak-to-flukes away. Ch*Tril imaged a querying depiction of her to Dv\Kil, and he responded eagerly with a scene of himself and the young female sharing a series of spirited Touches.

So, Ch*Tril thought with pleased amusement: Her young one's interests had expanded beyond the delights of games and fish-herding. She called out her signature to the newcomer, who shyly sent back her own: Lr*Xin, she was called. Ch*Tril imaged her a scene of welcoming, and the lustrous young female hesitantly swam to Dv\Kil's side.

After the proper formal greetings, Lr*Xin seemed at a loss for images, and Ch*Tril could scan that she was still nervous.

]Seaweed-Tickle[, Ch*Tril imaged playfully, breaking the momentary awkwardness. She searched around for a floating strand of seaweed, then swam forward and began moving it gently back and forth within Lr*Xin's open mouth, trailing the tiny brown bulbs across the younger one's teeth. Ch*Tril herself had invented the game when she and her pod-sisters had been even younger than Lr*Xin, and it had enjoyed a brief popularity throughout the School. She still liked the soothing delicacy of the seaweed-tickle against her own sensitive gums and tongue, and it seemed a good way to show affection and acceptance to Dv\Kil's young female friend. Lr*Xin soon relaxed, and offered to return the tickle, while Dv\Kil watched their game with appreciative amusement, swimming round them in a tight circle.

There was so much that she had missed, Ch*Tril thought sadly. Her journeys and her tasks fulfilled her, certainly, and they had never been more valuable to the School than now; but so many of the joys of taking part in her son's growth had been denied her, and now here he was a robust young male apparently ready to take on a mate.

She stayed with the two of them a while longer, sharing hopeful images and offering Dv\Kil a truncated version of her upcoming journey. At last she gave them each a fond Touch, lingering just a little longer as she brushed against Lr*Xin to reassure the bashful young female of her welcome to the fellowship of Dv\Kil's pod. Then she whirled and left the couple to themselves.

Ch*Tril swam a while longer, then finally dove a beak-to-fluke down and rotated slowly in place, scanning the School in all directions. There was still no sign of Dj\Tal among the throng, and she was tired of searching for him; this would be their last time together for a long while, and it was foolish to waste any more of it. Surely this would count as an exception to the precepts, wouldn't it?

Despite her studied rationalization, Ch*Tril felt a twinge of guilt as she used the Link-Talent to call out to her mate. Only one in twenty of her kind possessed the gift, and by long tradition its use was restricted to matters of great urgency. She had known Dj\Tal for many cool-lights before she'd even learned that he, too, possessed the Talent.

His reply to her Link was swift in coming; it appeared directly in her mind, bypassing the normal sensory inputs of her eyes or lower jaw, and its form was unlike sight or scan or imaging:

>Here<

it seemed to say, but nestled within the simplicity of that momentary contact was a wealth of information and emotion surpassing even the lengthiest of imaged sequences: There was love, and longing, and desire; concern, curiosity, regret for absences past and future; assurance of personal well-being, a flash of private humor, and a clear indication of exactly where he could be found.

No wonder such strict limits on the use of the Link-Talent were imposed, Ch*Tril thought as she swam in the direction he had told her; if those few who had the gift were permitted to exercise it freely, they would soon retreat unto themselves, would communicate with no one but each other. Such a sundering of the Schools must never be allowed, she knew; her own young one, Dv\Kil, lacked the talent, and it was unthinkable that he and all the others should be left behind by Ch*Tril and Dj\Tal and their like.

Dj\Tal was precisely where he'd told her he would be: off to the far side of the School, meditating in the seclusion of a large bed of kelp. She moved toward him for a Touch, and as their smooth bellies slid against each other Dj\Tal twisted to gently bite one of her pectorals. She returned the bite, and abruptly darted away into the shadows of the kelp. Dj\Tal followed close behind, giving chase as she spun and dashed among the long, thick stalks, the dark forest that fell away into the invisible depths below.

Ch*Tril broke the surface for a breath, and as she did Dj\Tal playfully nipped her flukes. She swatted them at him, splashing the warm seawater across his beak, then dove again, doubling back so that she was now behind him. She twisted on her side to let their white bellies rub again as she swam past, and she could feel his firm, extended penis tracing its way along the softness of her proffered flesh.

He entered her, rolling her above him to the surface as he did. The tendrils of the drifting kelp caressed her back as he thrust into her, and her flukes slapped limply against the level sea in time with the frenzied motion of their bodies. As they arched hard together for the final thrust, Ch*Tril's mind filled with a single, flawless burst of oneness as Dj\Tal Linked to her:

>Here<

came the shared thought, in a euphoric flood of tenderness and ardor:

>Here<

"You crazy, fella? Are you fuckin' *crazy?*"

Batera's forehead shone with sweat, despite the chill of the air-conditioned galley. Daniel focused blankly on the beads of perspiration, unable to respond. He knew he wasn't crazy, but he was no longer certain that he wasn't simply dead, in every way that mattered save the physical.

Daniel had hoped that taking part in Mitch Creighton's project might rekindle some sort of emotional response within him, some residue of the passionate feelings that had once come so naturally but had, in recent years, been gradually anesthetized. Pride, fear, disgust—those were the emotions he had considered most likely to emerge. Instead, the senselessness of Mitch's death, and of the dolphin slaughter, left him more desensitized than ever. It truly seemed there was nothing left worth caring about, no outlet from the smothering void that had enveloped him since his wife's own brutal death.

Daniel turned his face away, toward one of the thick, salt-pitted windows; the passion of the captain's anger was like something foreign, and it exhausted him merely to see it. In the distance, a low rise of land was growing steadily nearer.

"A man is *dead*," Batera shouted at him, slapping his palm down hard on the scarred Formica surface of the table where they sat. "Only one time before in my life I have a man die on my boat, he had a heart attack. People get hurt, there's always accidents, but this . . ." He shook his head, his voice trailing off.

"I think he thought of it as a kind of war," Daniel said, his voice a monotone that felt thick and gauzy in his throat.

"The fuck does that mean, 'war'?" Batera spread his hands and frowned questioningly. "Who's fighting who? This look like a fuckin' battleship to you?"

No, Daniel thought, it looked more like a floating charnel house, an abattoir of the seas. "Your men are killing dolphins. That was important to him."

"Ah, shit, get serious; a few goddamn porpoise is worth a man's life?"

It always came back to mathematics in the end, didn't it? Equations of life and death, of worth, of reason; Ruth, the man who'd killed her, the now eternally unknowable potential future that had died with both of them . . .

"I imagine he thought so," Daniel said, forcing himself to break off that pointless train of thought, that open invitation to blank, blind despair.

"Then he wasn't just crazy, he was stupid!" Batera cast a sudden sidelong glance at the faded print of *The Last Supper* on the bulkhead, and crossed himself. "I mean, not to speak ill of the dead, but that just don't make sense."

The boat was making its way into a small harbor, Daniel saw; several fishing boats, including two or three other tuna seiners, were tied up at the aging wharfs. "I don't know," he said truthfully. "Maybe not."

"We do the backdown," Batera said, as if making a point in a court of law. "We save as many porpoise as we can."

Daniel shrugged, his tired shoulders aching with the movement.

"That was Mitch's thing. I just came along to report on what he was doing."

Batera went on as if he hadn't heard him. "These men work hard, goddamnit; they got families to support. Tuna fishing's all they know. Then you come along, you lie your way on board—"

"Where are we?" Daniel interrupted, watching out the window as the boat pulled alongside a ramshackle wooden dock.

"Panama," Batera said. "Port of Mensabe."

"What are we doing here?"

Batera's eyes were dark, unreadable. "This is where you get off my goddamn boat." He reached into his shirt pocket, took out Daniel's passport, and threw it on the table.

"You went through my cabin," Daniel said, aggrieved.

"The fuck you expect? You come on here with a goddamn camera, I start to wonder what else you maybe got. A gun? A pipe bomb?"

"Where's the rest of it? Where's my money?"

Batera paused a moment, then put down two twenty-dollar bills next to the passport.

"Jesus Christ," Daniel exclaimed, "I had close to a thousand dollars in—" Something outside on the dock caught his eye, a flashing light stabbing blue through the pale sunshine. He craned his head to look; there were two white Volvos marked POLICÍA and five men in khaki uniforms with automatic weapons slung across their shoulders.

"That was money I advanced you for this trip," Batera said, ignoring the scene on the dock. "You didn't do the job, you don't get paid."

The crewmen had finished tying up the boat, and the uniformed men were filing on board, their expressions grim. "What's going on here?" Daniel asked nervously.

Batera leaned his head back against the bulkhead, where a dark, oily spot had been worn from years of such use. "A man dies, you think nobody wants to know how it happened? Even in Panama?"

The doorway filled with the thud and clatter of boots, of heavy weapons. The men in khaki stood behind Manoel, peering around his bulk into the galley.

"*Ésse homem,*" Manoel said, pointing at Daniel. "That's him, right there."

The flight from Houston had been an hour late, and Jeb Sloane glanced again at his watch as the cab moved in fits and starts up La Cienega Boulevard. The driver, an Asian of indeterminate age and national origin, caught the movement in his rearview mirror. "Freeway's even slower," the driver said.

Sloane mumbled a grudging acquiescence and sat back in the seat, its clear vinyl covering sticky to his touch. He probably should have gone ahead and rented a car, even though he'd have no use for one after tomorrow; but at least the drive up the coast would have been pleasant, a chance to unwind a little and prepare himself for the job ahead.

There hadn't been much of an opportunity for him to relax back home in Houston; hell, he'd only been there three days when this assignment had come up, barely enough time to get the desert sand out of his hair before facing up to the prospect of sea spray and damp clothes again, the taste of crusted salt always on his lips.

He hadn't worked an offshore job in more than two years, not since that stint in the North Sea. This one promised to be somewhat different, though, for which he was grateful; that platform in the East Shetland Basin had always been either frigid with Arctic gales or hellishly hot beneath its trademark eternal flare, commemorating nothing but the waste of enough unrecoverable natural gas per second to heat an average home for years. Sometimes, out there on that hugely improbable structure in the wind-lashed seas between Scotland and Norway, he'd felt he might never again be truly comfortable, never again be dry.

This new job should be a literal breeze compared to that: balmy weather off the temperate shores of Southern California, and work-day duty in the clean, high-tech environs of one of the new laser-drilling exploratory rigs; a far cry from the stench and the constant danger of the big North Sea semisubmersibles with their monstrous diesel engines driving a million pounds of muddy pipe.

Lindy would have appreciated this assignment, he thought glumly. An airy little cottage by the sea, civilized shopping streets and restaurants galore, restaurants where you could get a nice cabernet or fumé blanc to go with your dinner ... movie theaters, for God's sake, and beaches where he and she could have actually gone *together* on a sunny weekend afternoon, could have splashed in the cool surf in bathing suits and laughed out loud, could have held hands or kissed each other without looking over their shoulders for the *mutawiyyin,* those hovering black crows of judgment ever alert to any breach of "decorum," ever prepared to wield their curses and their sticks against Saudis and foreigners alike.

Hell, Jeb Sloane mused, if he'd gotten this posting to Santa Barbara two years ago instead of the one to Dharan, his marriage just might have survived ... for a while at least. Until the next, inevitable, "exotic" assignment.

He looked out the window of the cab, which had finally picked up speed a bit. They were passing a small forest of oil wells, each one a twenty-foot-high working replica of those "perpetual motion" water-drinking-bird toys that had been so popular when he was a child. Right here in L.A., on the main boulevard between the airport and the upscale West Side, a goddamn oil field.

They could have lived here, Pacific Palisades maybe, or Santa Monica, where the offshore rigs were disguised as colorful apartment buildings or hotels on palm-strewn little islands. They could have stayed in Texas, even lived in Dallas where Lindy could have been close to her family.

There were a dozen places, a hundred, that would have provided them with all the comforts of home; stable environments, safe and simple ones in which to raise a family. That had been the gripe Lindy had hit him with most often: "This is no place to raise a child," she'd complain about wherever they might be, or if their latest country of residence *was* a genteel, civilized corner of the earth, as Scotland had been, it was "You're never home long enough to help me with a baby," or "This may be all right, but what kind of a hellhole will they send you to next?"

Yeah, Jeb thought, lots of places they could have lived and not fought about it, could have had the kids they both had said they wanted: Texas, California, even Alaska would have been O.K., for Christ's sake.

If.

If he'd settled on straight production drilling, had tied himself to one company, one location—supervising rig operations from an air-conditioned office in Dallas or Anchorage or L.A., showing up at nine o'clock in the morning with a jacket on his back and a tie around his neck. Spending his days on a radiotelephone, telling the exhausted, grime-covered, sweltering or freezing men in the field what they should or should not be doing, and then going home again at five P.M., his hands clean, his hair in place, relaxed and warm and dry and hating every fucking second of his fucking useless life.

Right, they could've done it that way.

Lindy'd known his heart was set on exploratory drilling since the first week they'd met, back at U.T. Austin where Jeb was getting his master's in petroleum engineering and Lindy was wavering between art history and English lit. That was how much they'd had in common, other than the mutual desire to fall in love and get laid, in one order or another.

She was from Dallas, her father a banker in that quasi-easternized city of banks, where the "awl bidness" was often looked upon with ill-disguised disdain even in its flush years, and with open contempt when the wells were too frequently coming up dry or the prices for home-drilled crude were plummeting.

Jeb Sloane's father had been the living embodiment of one of those Texas stereotypes that fed the high-toned Dallasite contempt for the dubious though sometimes wildly profitable enterprise of pumping thick black goo out of the ground and selling it. Arvin Sloane was a "roughneck" through and through, had been in the coarsest sense of the word even before he'd first found work in the grimy cacophony of the busy fields that had ringed Beaumont and Port Arthur.

Young Jeb, enthralled by his father's coarse vitality, had grown up loving oil, loving the idea, the romance, the smell and even the *taste* of the viscous stuff: Summer weekends, whenever Arvin Sloane was between drilling jobs, he'd take the family down to the beaches of South Padre Island, where the sands were sticky with lumps of black tar, the petroleum in that region so ubiquitous that it came oozing up out of the ground even when no one went digging for it.

Arvin would pluck up a wad of tar, rinse the sand off and chew it like a plug of Red Man tobacco, swearing all the while that it tasted better and wasn't near as habit-forming. As in so many other areas of life, big and small, the boy Jeb soon followed his father's lead in this odd quirk, eschewing his usual jawful of Juicy Fruit or Wrigley's Spearmint for a sun-warmed gob of pure, foul-tasting tar ... and before too long the taste was no longer foul but familiar, and then pleasant, and by now a deeply evocative and nostalgic sensory memory: Proust's madeleine reconstituted as a black clump of gummy, slowly solidifying petroleum.

To each, Jeb thought with a wry smile as the cab picked up speed and left the flock of bobbing oil wells behind, his own. Not that Lindy would've shared that sentiment, let alone attempted to understand Jeb's uncompromising love of oil, the mystery and lore of it, and above all, the tantalizing, heartbreaking or gloriously rewarding *search* for the stuff, however and wherever it might be found, be it in a balmy, paradisiacal resort or in a teeming, filthy, and dangerous hell on earth.

Unfortunately for their marriage, most of the drillable oil heretofore discovered tended to be hidden away beneath the latter sort of place.

The cab was moving up the boulevard at highway speed now, the driver weaving among the suddenly sparser traffic with practiced ease. They passed the Santa Monica Freeway, took a left on Wilshire, and Jeb's memories of prior brief trips to L.A. suddenly kicked in to inform him that the driver was taking the long way around, two sides of an almost equilateral triangle instead of one. Freeway congestion or no, Jeb realized, they could've taken Sepulveda straight up from the airport and encountered the same amount of traffic as there'd been on La Cienega—or even less.

He leaned forward, anger rising, and just as he was about to verbally accost the driver he caught sight of the gleaming white spires and gold statues of the Mormon Temple in among the high-rise condos and office buildings. Something about the vision struck him as funny; ludicrous, actually, as if he'd suddenly glimpsed a twisted, out-of-context image of Riyadh's Jami Mosque in some unexpected locale: the Reflecting Pool in Washington, say, or by the harbor in Vancouver. For an unsettling, head-swimming moment they all merged in Jeb's mind, and he sat back in the hot, sticky vinyl seat, his eyes closed.

Fuck it, he thought, and let the driver's little roundabout-route scam go unchallenged. It's all the Third World nowadays anyway, he thought; it's all a bunch of thieves and fanatics, wherever you go.

The PetroGlobe building was on Lindbrook, just north of Wilshire and east of Westwood Boulevard. Jeb paid the fare on the meter, an outrageous sum, and pointedly added a single quarter for the larcenous driver. The young man smiled smugly, impervious to insult, aware that Jeb had realized his scheme and that he'd gotten away with it.

"Next time take the Super Shuttle," the driver said, throwing the old Chevy station wagon into gear. "That's my tip for *you*."

Jeb shook his head in resignation; if he was thin-skinned enough to let a simple asshole like that piss him off, he'd never have made it in the places he'd wound up these last eight years; he'd've bailed, just like Lindy had.

Milton Harris had the penthouse office, of course, with a panoramic view of the multicolored layers of smog and the sclerotic arteries of city traffic stretching from East L.A. and downtown to the edges of the ocean at Venice. A man less enamored of oil in all its forms and stages than Jeb was might have seen it as somehow fitting that the CEO of PetroGlobe should be forced each day to look out on the increasingly noxious leavings of his primary product . . . but Harris himself never noticed, and neither did Jeb Sloane.

Harris was on the phone when Jeb entered, and the burly company head waved his visitor toward one of three leather chairs in front of the desk. The chairs were comfortable, even plush, but Jeb noted with amusement that one tended to sink into the folds of them, and that they were set about six inches lower than Harris's own high-backed swivel chair.

"... give a good goddamn *what* that bunch has to say, we start work on it this Wednesday, right on schedule. Matter of fact, I've got the project drilling engineer here in my office, even as we speak." Harris gave Jeb a nod and a wink. "That's right, he's *damned* confident, and rarin' to go, I might add."

Jeb smiled politely and tuned out the rest of Harris's conversation, focusing instead on the lingering pleasant aftertaste of the two Scotch and sodas he'd had on the plane. He wasn't much of a drinking man, but the absolute prohibition of any simple luxury tended to amplify one's desire for it. In truth, the pleasure of actually drinking the liquor had been equaled, if not outweighed, by the satisfaction of doing so in public, in full view of a planeload of strangers, with no fear of imprisonment or flogging for taking those delectably bracing sips of iced J&B.

"Good flight out?" Harris asked as he hung up the phone.

"Very smooth," Jeb said, thinking of the Scotch.

"Good, good. You staying in town tonight, or going straight on up?"

"I'm taking a four o'clock train."

"Just as well," Harris said, proffering a box of cigars, which Jeb declined. "City's gone to hell, no matter what the Chamber of Commerce would have you believe about rebuilding or reviving or whatever. The gangs, you know, and that element . . . they cater to them, is the problem."

Jeb nodded vaguely and gave a noncommittal grunt.

"You'll like Santa Barbara," Harris went on, lighting a cigar. "Patrice and I, we have a little getaway home in Montecito ourselves." He puffed on the thick, slightly squarish cigar, getting it going. "Of course," he added, "you won't be seeing much dry land the next few weeks or so, but your wife'll appreciate the shopping and the—"

"We're separated," Jeb said.

"Oh, sorry," Harris said uncomfortably, glancing at an open folder on his desk. Jeb wondered if the "sorry" meant sympathy for the failed marriage, or regret that Harris hadn't taken an extra minute to more closely peruse Jeb's personnel file before meeting with him. As if to make up for the lapse, the executive picked up the folder now and ran his finger down one of the pages, his head tilted back in deference to the necessities of both the rising cigar smoke and the half-frame reading glasses he had now put on.

"Looks like you'll have a friendly face on board the boat," Harris said, "or at least I hope that's the case. Old classmate of yours, Bryant Emerson?"

Jesus, Jeb thought, he hadn't talked to Bryant in five years or more, and he really didn't want to now. Not that there was bad blood between them; quite the contrary—they'd been close friends at U.T. Austin, Bryant had even introduced him to Lindy, for Christ's sake; they'd just fallen out of touch, the way people do whose jobs take them to some of the most remote corners of the earth. Now he'd have to tell him about Lindy, have to explain all that shit, relive it again. . . .

"Yeah, sure," Jeb said. "We're old friends. Be good to work with him."

Harris beamed, as if he'd personally planned the reunion of the two old college buddies. "Good, good. He'll be site supervisor, nominally speaking, but of course the drilling is all in your hands . . . though, God knows, with this new technology I'm not even sure if we should even call it 'drilling' anymore, heh? Maybe 'zapping,' or something."

The megapowered laser-drilling equipment that Jeb and his crew would be using in the Santa Barbara Channel had come into commercial use only four or five months before; Jeb himself had worked with it only once, on a site in Saudi Arabia's Rub' al-Khali, the so-called Empty Quarter where nine tenths of the country's oil wells were located. He had never used the laser apparatus at an offshore site; only a couple of exploratory drilling boats that he knew of had successfully used the technology, one for Gulf Oil off Louisiana and another for Dutch Petroleum in the North Sea.

"Crew in Saudi called it 'burning,'" Jeb said, "and they called the shaft the 'burnhole.'"

Harris shook his head admiringly. "Shit, I remember being amazed when the geologists started using computers. Now look what we can do. Are these things really as fast as they say, and as clean?"

"Faster, and cleaner. In Saudi we were burning down a thousand feet a day, with no mud to pump, no pipe to drive. Damn beam just liquefies what it touches, and it cauterizes the edges of the hole as it goes. Turns the rock itself into a smooth, solid pipe."

"Good, good. Got these goddamned environmental types on our backs again, you know."

"They object to the laser drilling?"

"Well ... we haven't exactly publicized the actual equipment you'll be using up there."

"You're keeping it secret, you mean."

Harris sucked wetly on the cigar. "Those goddamn Goreheads, they're all a bunch of Luddites; they think any new technology's a step backward instead of forward. Hell, they'd object to anything. Plus, we had us a good-sized quake out here couple weeks ago; they're scared of oil spills if there's an aftershock during the drilling. Santa Barbara, you know ... that's where they had the big spill way back when, '68 or '69; some people say that's what started the whole eco-nut movement, that and that book about DDT."

"And the moon shots," Jeb said.

Harris frowned at him, uncomprehending.

"The first photos of the earth from space," Jeb explained. "Nobody'd ever seen that before, this fragile-looking, blue-and-white Christmas tree ornament of a planet, floating all by itself in the middle of all that blackness."

Harris eyed Jeb strangely, one eyebrow slightly cocked. "Whatever," he said. "Is there gonna be a lot of steam to vent?"

"A fair amount," Jeb said, "and then of course there's a bit of molten rock overflow, like fresh igneous matter, at the entry spot. Steam pressure from the max-depth burn point forces it back up to the top, and the beam keeps it in a liquid or gaseous state until it emerges."

Harris puffed at his red-tipped cigar and frowned. "How the hell do you keep up with the accumulated flow? Doesn't it just build itself a goddamn little mountain right there at the site?"

"It would if we let it, but it oozes up at a pretty steady rate; slow enough to stay ahead of, and a lot just boils off as steam, like you said. Of course, it's gonna cool a lot faster on the sea floor than in the open desert ... a *hell* of a lot faster. That's where the robot secondary unit comes into play."

"You've worked with those before?"

"Yeah, but strictly for observation. Never used one as an actual tool before."

Harris grinned around the fat brown cigar. "Helluva 'tool,' " he said.

Jeb nodded, smiling back. The little remote-controlled sub he'd be using on this job would have a camera in its snout, just like the ones he'd worked with in the North Sea ... but mounted on its tubular hull would also be a laser as powerful as the one on the drilling device, with which Jeb and his crew could remelt the accumulated rock flow from the drill shaft as it billowed up and cooled. The little circling sub would thereby keep the area around the upper burn point relatively level; what would otherwise be a steadily growing undersea hillock, perhaps eventually even a small island if it rose as high as the surface, would instead be melted away like so much candle wax, and allowed to spread across the sea floor.

"Just think if we'd had a few of those little babies back during the Cold War," Harris went on, warming to his subject. The man was clearly entranced by the technology involved, by the sheer *expense* of it all and the fact that he could afford to pay for it. His eyes glowed like the cigar's hot tip as he flicked a length of ash away. "That sucker's not a tool, it's a goddamned *weapon!*"

Fort Myers was a town of proudly weatherbeaten old homes, their sprawling yards filled with a profusion of banana trees and bougainvillea and jacaranda. The avenue that Sheila had been told to take was flanked by what seemed to be an infinite procession of hundred-foot-high royal palms, and it paralleled a quiet blue river for ten miles or more.

What on earth was she doing here? she wondered again for the hundredth time. The trip had been a desperate act, a last-ditch effort to imbue her with the sudden inspiration she so sorely needed. She'd somehow known, almost from the moment she had first heard about the Fort Myers encounter, that she'd have to get to Florida immediately; now, here she was.

She was starting to worry that she might've missed a turnoff, when suddenly the road led into a causeway that stretched toward Sanibel Island, across the open water into which the river flowed.

Sheila had forgotten how much water there was here: not only the ocean and the Gulf, one or the other never more than a brief drive away, but a wealth of lakes, rivers, ponds, and springs everywhere you turned. It struck her as odd that she'd never come back here, as much as she loved being near the water; but her only other trip to Florida had been as a child, that time her father had taken the family to Cape Canaveral for the moon shot.

She pulled the rented Fort Escort to a stop at the causeway entrance.

"Mornin', miss," said the toll collector, a plump and darkly tanned woman in her forties. "Goin' shellin', are you?"

"No, not today. I'm here to see the dolphin I've heard so much about."

The woman beamed with pride, as if she'd personally invited the dolphin to visit. "Ain't he somethin'? Ain't he just somethin' else?"

"That's what I understand," Sheila said, returning the smile. "So, could you tell me where I might—"

"You just stay right on this road here, it'll turn into Gulf Drive once you're on the island, and you go to where the Pointe Santo resort is. If you come to the Shalimar, you went too far, you have to turn around. Take a right on Tarpon Bay Road—that's if you didn't have to turn around, else you have to take a left—and just go till you get to a little beach. That's where he comes."

Sheila thanked her and drove on across the causeway, rolling down her window and turning off the air conditioner so she could smell the salty air. As she came onto the island the tangy breeze turned sweeter, mingled with the aroma of the crimson and canary blossoms of a thousand twisted banyan trees. For a moment she almost forgot her omnipresent anger at Richard Tarnoff, and her dejection at the unlikelihood of persuading the foundation to reverse its decision; but then she felt a sudden stab of guilt, not the first, at having left Ringo and Georgia and Paulette alone at such a crucial time.

Of course they weren't really alone, she reminded herself; the graduate-student couple she had left in charge of the house and lab were almost as devoted to the dolphins as she was. More important, this trip might be her last remaining chance to obtain the results she needed—without which, she would soon be permanently separated from her cetacean friends and charges.

She saw the sign for the Pointe Santo de Sanibel, took a right and soon found herself at a widened cul-de-sac. About a dozen cars were parked there, most of them with out-of-state or rental plates. Sheila took one of her metal equipment cases from the backseat, double-checked to see that the car was securely locked, and set off down the path through the sea grass toward the beach.

She could see the water as soon as she'd crested the first gently sloped sand dune. There was no surf, no waves at all to speak of. The Gulf was on the opposite side of the island; this was Pine Island Sound, sheltered from the rougher, deeper waters to the south and west by the string of nearly contiguous islands that curved out from the mainland. The water here was as placid as a lake, and from its clear green hue Sheila could see that it was no more than three or four feet deep for at least twenty yards out.

She set the tightly sealed equipment case down in the sand and surveyed the scene from where she stood. There were thirty or forty people, ranging in age from toddlers to the elderly, gathered on the secluded little beach. All of them were staring intently at the calm and empty expanse of water, as if waiting for something to happen.

"There!" a woman suddenly shouted, her voice pitched high with excitement. "Right there—can't you see it?!"

The rest of the crowd looked where the woman was pointing, some with binoculars, others with hands cupped around their eyes to shut out the glare of the sun and sand.

"Daddy, Daddy!" a little boy burst forth. "I see him, here he comes!"

Sheila scanned the still water where it edged from green to blue. She couldn't see a thing except the flat, smooth surface. The woman and the child must have been mistaken, overeager; there was nothing out there, not a trace of—

And then she saw it, the sharp gray dorsal fin slicing cleanly toward the beach, its wake marking a clear path in the water through which the powerful creature had sped, was speeding yet.

A white-haired couple in matching sun hats were the next to spot it, then a pair of little girls, and soon the whole disparate group had located the fin. First one family, then another, waded and splashed into the shallow green water, cheering the alien visitor on as it came swiftly toward the shore.

The dolphin leaped, displaying its proud, sleek body for the appreciative assembly. When it reentered the water it slowed its speed considerably, careful not to bump or jolt any of the small, fumbling humans who immediately surrounded it. The children squealed with delight as the elegant being swam among them in an intricate, playful dance of its and their simultaneous devising: a touch, a spin, a brushing past, a slipping through ... and no fear, no hesitation about the spontaneous contact from either human or dolphin.

This sort of thing was not unheard of, Sheila knew; similar events had occasionally been reported for the past twenty or thirty years, from locations as far apart as England and New Zealand. This particular encounter had been going on for almost two weeks; she'd read about it in the *L.A. Times,* and a colleague had told her he'd seen a segment about it on *Nightline.*

She knelt in the sand and excitedly undid the straps on the metal container, then removed the digital audio recorder in its waterproof plastic casing. All her doubts about having given in to the wild impulse to come here had vanished the moment she saw the dolphin, saw the way it reacted to the people and the people to it.

This was an unprecedented opportunity for her, a chance to test her methods with a dolphin that hadn't been put through the rigors of anyone's research, hadn't suffered the trauma of capture and isolation. Above all, one that had sought out human contact on its own, and whose home was an ocean thousands of miles from the ones she'd been studying. A comparison of this dolphin's tapes with those she'd made of Ringo and the others might give her the breakthrough she needed, might offer the final key to deciphering the images she was convinced were somehow coded in the dolphins' ultrasonic signals.

Yes, she thought as she walked across the sand toward the water's edge, and the phrase that came into her mind surprised her, puzzled her: Yes, I was supposed to come here.

4

 "Su nombre es . . ." the khaki-uniformed Panamanian police inspector glanced down at a clipboard. "Daniel Cal-
der?"

"Colter. Daniel Colter."

"American, *sí*? I mean to say, not Latino, not Portuguese like
most the other fishermen?"

"Es verdad, yo no soy—"

"No, please, I enjoy the opportunity to practice English." The
policeman smiled disarmingly. "Since we get back the Canal, you
know, not so many Americans live here anymore. The most who
come here are tourists or are soldiers, and a man in my profession
has not so many reasons to talk to either."

The other four policemen, underlings apparently, stood guard
on either side of the galley door, their automatic weapons held at
a stiff, correct angle toward the ceiling. Not threatening, not yet;
but ready. What the hell had Manoel told them? Had he claimed
that Daniel pushed Creighton over the side?

"Do you mind, Captain . . . Batera, yes?"

The skipper shook his head. "English is fine. It's what I speak
at home."

"Good, good. Now, the man who died—"

"Mitch Creighton," Batera said. "A deckhand, his first trip out with me."

Daniel gave the skipper a quick sidelong glance, unreturned by Batera. Why hadn't he mentioned the camera?

"Also an Anglo, correct?"

Batera nodded. "Most of the time, we hire within the community, but ... tough times, you take who you get and hope they can do the work."

"I see. Mr. Colter, you have worked on tuna boats before?"

Daniel sat uncomfortably still, trying to appear at ease. If he told the same lies he'd told to Batera, the cop could check the Costa Rican records in an hour or so. But what was the point? Batera already knew he and Creighton had faked their backgrounds, there was nothing more to conceal from him.

"No, this was the first time. Mitch and I, we ... well, we thought it might be kind of an adventure."

The inspector frowned quizzically. "Adventure? I would think more hard work, no? Adventure is what one does on holiday."

Daniel risked another look at Batera, wondering when he was going to bring up what they'd really been doing on board. The skipper's weathered face was still expressionless. "I guess it depends on how you look at it," Daniel answered carefully. "We just figured, you know, tropical seas, chance to pick up some money at the same time ..."

"A very risky sort of adventure," the policeman said, with an edge of disapproval in his voice. "As your friend unfortunately discovered."

"I run a safe boat," Batera put in. "Always the chance of an accident, sure, like anywhere, but our procedures—"

"Tell me what, exactly, did take place?"

Maybe it was time to come clean, Daniel decided. After all, he hadn't committed any crime, and if Batera and Manoel were looking to blame him for Mitch's death, this was no time to lie. "Look, what really happened was, Manoel—that's the mate—had caught us—"

"Goofing off," Batera interrupted. "That's what they call it in America. They were lazy, *preguiçoso*."

The policeman laughed. "*Ah, sí,* in Spanish *perezoso.*" He turned back to Daniel, an amused gleam in his eye. "So, too much real work on your adventure, yes? Not what you expected."

Daniel shrugged and said nothing, curious to see where the captain was going with this.

"Too many dreamers today, not enough good workers," Batera said.

"*Lo mismo en nuestra policía,*" the man in uniform agreed, lapsing into his native tongue.

Batera was looking straight at Daniel now, waiting to see whether he'd contradict these misleading semi-truths. "These men never been on the boats before, they don't know how messy it gets. Deck gets slippery after a set, you got to watch how you step."

The policeman nodded and turned back to Daniel. "So your friend, he ... lose his footing?"

The galley was silent, close and silent, as everyone waited for Daniel's reply. The truth would gain him nothing, he realized, and might cost him everything: If he didn't go along with their version, there was still time for Manoel to jump in and claim he'd seen the two men fighting, even that Daniel had pushed Mitch over the railing.

"Yeah," he said at last, "There was blood and oil all over the place. I almost fell myself." True as far as it went; whatever happened later, no one could say he'd told the police any outright lies. And the death had been an accident; there was no question of that. Still, it rankled him to conceal the fact that he and Mitch had essentially been in custody when it had happened.

"Did you see this yourself, Captain Batera?"

The skipper shook his head. "Better ask my mate here, Manoel Ricosta. He was close by when the man fell."

"Señor Ricosta?"

The burly mate still stood in the doorway, flanked by the other policemen. "Like they say, he slip on the wet deck. No time to do nothing about it."

The inspector scribbled in his notebook. "You performed a search?"

"For an hour or more," Batera said. "There was no sign of him."

"Could the man not swim, do you know?"

"It's a long drop from the deck," Batera noted. "If he hit wrong ... and, too, the boat was coming about to starboard when he fell; he was most likely crushed beneath it before anyone had warning."

The policeman continued to write. *"Sí, sí ..."* he muttered. "So everyone agrees that this was an accident, and there were no suspicious circumstances involved?"

Daniel held his breath, and his tongue.

"That seems to be the case, Inspector," Batera said. "So, if there are forms to be signed ... you understand, we have much work yet to do."

So that was it, Daniel thought; Batera didn't want to be held up in port any longer than necessary. Silence for silence, that was the trade.

Batera was still dealing with the bureaucratic paperwork of death when Manoel marched Daniel unceremoniously off the boat. Cooperation or no, they still hadn't given him back any of his belongings; apparently they'd figured that being stuck in this rathole with forty dollars in cash and the clothes on his back was a fitting punishment for his part in the original deception.

As soon as he was away from the harbor area and into the center of town, Daniel sat down on a filthy curb and took off his left sneaker; the Visa card was still there, where he'd kept it hidden since he and Mitch had first arrived in San Diego.

He caught a bus from Mensabe to Chitre, but discovered on arrival that he'd missed the once-a-day connection to Panama City. He couldn't find anyplace in the dusty village that took credit cards, so he spent two dollars at a street stand for a single plate of shredded beef, mashed yucca and fried plantains, and spent the night in a cramped and stinking room in a *pension* on the Calle Manuel Correa. The mosquitos woke him early, and he passed the morning sitting in the hot shade on the steps of a little museum in the center of town.

The bus for the capital left at 2:00 P.M. Daniel was the only foreigner on board, and the bare metal floorboards beneath his feet were caked white with partially dried chicken dung.

They rode through brown, arid plains filled with anemic-looking cattle for the first two hours; then, a short way past a village called La Ermita, the land turned to green savannas dotted with clumps of palms and mango trees, followed by long stretches of carefully tended orange groves.

As the bus crossed the long bridge spanning the Canal, Daniel stared out at the massive sets of locks visible to his left. He could see the stacked containers of a great freighter rising as if by magic high above the level of the water beneath the bridge, while beside it the upper decks of a gleaming white westward-bound cruise ship sank into apparent oblivion behind the immense gates of the lock.

Just after six o'clock, the bus coughed its way through Balboa, in what had once been the U.S.-owned Canal Zone. The town stood out in bizarre contrast to all the others they had passed through that day: immaculate suburban streets, American-style ranch houses, street signs reading ROOSEVELT and QUARRY HEIGHTS and ALBROOK ... he might have been in Encino, or New Rochelle, circa 1957.

Leaving Balboa, the bus rounded a hill and finally entered the city. Daniel hadn't been here since the Noriega days, and he kept an eye out for familiar landmarks as the smoky old vehicle trundled through town. Yes, that park there, across from the breakwater; there'd been a bitch of a firefight there, he recalled. And over there, past the Holiday Inn, there was the Marriott, where he and the rest of the press corps had been trapped during much of the initial action. Hell, he wouldn't mind being trapped someplace like a Marriott tonight, he thought; mortar fire outside the window would be just fine, as long as there were clean sheets and unlimited hot water.

The bus station was a nondescript, unmarked building behind a grimy block of apartments near the harbor. Daniel shouldered his way through the crowd in the terminal, feeling grungy and exposed in the dirty shorts and T-shirt he'd been wearing on the boat. He took a *chiva* to the Hotel Continental, and shivered at the blast of cold air that hit him when he entered the lobby under the disapproving scowl of the doorman.

"You have no luggage at all, señor?" the desk clerk asked skeptically, his practiced eyes taking in Daniel's unshaven face and filthy, abbreviated clothing.

"I've been robbed," Daniel told him.

"And how will you be paying for the room, may I ask?"

Daniel handed over his credit card and waited while the man went off to call in the number. When he finally came back to the desk, the clerk's attitude had changed from one of suspicion to an almost equally grating obsequiousness.

"A view of the harbor, señor," he said, tapping at his computer keyboard. "Would that be satisfactory?"

"Fine, fine. I'll also be wanting some fresh clothes," Daniel informed him. "I'll call down with the sizes once I'm settled in."

"No problema, señor," the man said, smiling the smile of service people everywhere who know for certain that the plastic they've been given is valid.

Daniel took the elevator up, ignoring the curious stares of the immaculately groomed Latin businessmen and their undoubtedly expensive female companions. Once he was in the blessedly anonymous room, Daniel turned off the air conditioning, tossed his stinking shorts and T-shirt into the wastebasket, and started the shower running at the maximum *Calor* setting to build up a good cloud of steam. He carefully used the complimentary razor to shave his sunburned face, and when the bathroom was filled with a soothing, humid fog he finally stepped under the powerful spray. He washed his hair twice with the blue Euro-gel from the dispenser, then shampooed a third time just for the luxury of staying in the shower that much longer.

When he was done he put on one of the thick terry-cloth robes the hotel had provided, and headed straight for the refrigerated mini-bar. He poured himself a double brandy and soda and picked up the phone.

United had a flight to Miami the next afternoon, connecting with a red-eye to Los Angeles. Daniel booked an aisle seat, then called down to room service for some *seviche* and a bowl of *sancocho,* the stew made with chicken, cut-up corn on the cob, potatoes, and onions that he'd acquired a taste for when he was down here doing the "Cocaine Presidents" series for *Rolling Stone.*

He gazed out the window overlooking the harbor twenty floors below as he recited his shirt and slack sizes for the hotel men's shop; there were tuna boats as far as he could see. From his research and his conversations with Mitch he knew that the majority of them had originally been based in San Diego, but had moved down here to escape the U.S. quotas on dolphin kills. A good percentage of the tuna went straight back up to the States anyway, to the pet-food companies and the smaller, independent canneries.

There was just one more call he had to make, and he wasn't looking forward to it.

The hotel operator patched him through to L.A. information, and he got the number for the Ocean Coalition in Santa Monica. A melodious female voice answered, soft and lilting, a wonderfully feminine, *American* sound after all he'd been through. Probably the girl with the apple breasts and the ass-length ponytail, but he'd never learned her name.

"This is Daniel Colter, I—"

"Oh! Sure, you're the guy that went with Mitch, right? What happened, didn't you guys get onto the boat?"

Daniel turned his chair around so it was no longer facing the harbor. He closed his eyes and pinched the bridge of his nose between his thumb and forefinger, rubbing ineffectively at the ache that had been there for two days. "Mitch is dead," he told her.

There was no sound from the other end of the line, not even an intake of breath. Daniel waited.

"He— Oh my God, what happened?"

"It was an accident. They caught us, and he slipped on the deck and went overboard."

"Oh God, oh God, oh God . . . I told him it was too dangerous, I said he'd . . ." the girl's lovely voice cracked and dissolved into wailing, keening sobs. Daniel suddenly realized that she and Mitch must have been much more than merely co-workers.

"It happened very fast," he said. "I doubt there was much pain."

"When . . . ?"

"Two days ago. They just put me off the boat, in Panama."

The young woman managed to regain some temporary control. "Will they . . . are you going to be sending . . ."

"His body was never recovered. I'm sorry; listen, if there's anything I can—"

"When you write your story," she said, "tell them he died for something. That it counted."

When he'd hung up the phone, Daniel mixed himself another drink and turned the television on to CNN while he waited for the food and the new clothes to arrive. He stared at the screen, Bernard Shaw saying something about the budget deficit, but all he could see was Mitch Creighton falling, careening headlong with a dying scream into the already bloody sea. And the girl, the fervent and well-meaning young woman whose name he still didn't know, her pretty round face contorted with grief, with confusion and anger and impotent frustration. He didn't have to see her to know how she looked right now, her red-rimmed eyes alternately flashing with rage and then darting madly, helplessly about, like a cornered animal seeking escape.

He'd seen eyes like that often enough in the mirror, back when Ruth died.

Was *murdered,* damn it, he reminded himself, knocking the drink back and reaching to the mini-fridge for another pair of the miniature brandy bottles. Glossing it over with polite euphemisms was never going to change that fact.

They'd been living in Los Angeles less than three years when it happened, Daniel having finally saved enough from his years on the Cleveland *Plain Dealer* and then the *Chicago Tribune* to take the risk of going full-time free-lance, as he'd always yearned to do. Ruth had been a paralegal—he'd met her during the course of an investigative series on legal malpractice; she'd been enthusiastic about the move, and had prepared for it with extensive night courses in California law. For his part, Daniel had considered the West Coast an ideal base for free-lancing, with its cutting-edge Pacific Rim status and its wealth of emerging trends and technological developments of national or international interest.

They'd been happy there at first, even managed to afford a little house in Sherman Oaks with help from Ruth's modest though adequate trust fund; but then Daniel's work had taken him more and more frequently to distant datelines: Beijing, Tokyo, El Salvador, Panama . . . and the marriage began to suffer from the strain of the unpredictable and sometimes prolonged separations.

Just how much it had begun to suffer, Daniel never really knew until that morning in July when the call had come to his hotel room in Vancouver. He'd been working on a piece about the escalating number of affluent immigrants from Hong Kong, fleeing the Crown Colony before its scheduled 1997 cession to China.

She'd been found in the home of one of the junior partners in the law firm for which she worked, a man named Kyle Shannon. Daniel had met him a few times—at the company Christmas party, in the halls on the rare occasions when Daniel would drop by to see Ruth at work. He'd seemed pleasant enough, unassuming; Daniel had always thought him a bit on the shy side for an attorney.

Ruth's naked body was discovered by a Salvadoran maid, in the master bedroom of Shannon's house in Woodland Hills. She'd been beaten to death with a sharp-edged marble statuette. Kyle Shannon was in the adjoining bathroom, slumped over the edge of the tub, his left wrist slashed to the bone and an open straight razor on the floor beside him. There was no note, no indication at all of what words or events had caused the clandestine affair to mutate into sudden, bloody death.

The news had unleashed a flood of warring emotions in Daniel: anguish over Ruth's violent death, anger at her for betraying him, guilt for having allowed the marriage to deteriorate to that extent, rage and disgust at Kyle Shannon ... and always the unanswerable question: What had happened to spur the man to commit murder-suicide? Had Ruth told him she was ending the affair, that she'd decided to try and repair her wounded marriage? Daniel would never know, and in some ways that was the most tormenting aspect of the whole insane tragedy.

His head was swimming from the three double brandies, from the events of the past few days, from the unwanted return of all the old memories. He needed some food in his stomach, but he was no longer hungry; he wanted to open a window and get some fresh air, but of course this was one of those hermetically sealed modern hotels.

Daniel's eyes focused again on the TV set; now they were showing a dolphin, of all things, playing with a group of children in the calm, shallow water off some beach. He leaned forward to turn up the sound, and caught the reporter's voice in mid-sentence:

". . . almost three weeks now, and it continues to return to this spot on a daily basis. Scientists are unable to explain why this wild creature has suddenly sought out the company of humans, but they note that similar phenomena have occurred in recent years in Australia, England, and various other parts of the world. But the children here who've adopted the friendly dolphin they call "Whizzy" as their favorite playmate don't care why he comes to visit them so regularly; they just hope he'll keep coming back for more fun and games, and the opportunity for some spontaneous affection between two very different species. Jessie Ganzell, CNN News, Fort Myers, Florida."

The camera held on a freeze-frame of a young girl, no more than six or seven, her face alight with rapture as she embraced the wild dolphin. Daniel could not recall when he had last seen such utter joyous transport in a human face.

There was a crisp rap at the door; Daniel's dinner had arrived.

He signed for it, turned off the television, and sat down at the table, engrossed in thought as he picked halfheartedly at the spicy marinated fish with onions and cilantro. Then he pushed the food aside and reached for the phone, to cancel tomorrow's connecting flight to Los Angeles. What the hell, he thought, Fort Myers was only a couple of hours' drive from Miami.

The waters were noticeably cooler now, and with her head above the surface Ch*Tril could see the rugged contours of the land jutting high above the waterline, the dry rocks and vertical slopes rising directly from the white-waves. When they had started out, the land to their right had been lower, browner; groups of land-walkers could be seen dashing about on the flattest and smoothest sections. Sometimes the land-walkers would jump into the waves and awkwardly attempt to swim, but Ch*Tril could see from her far-off vantage point that even the strongest of them could barely maneuver in the water.

On other occasions the land-walkers would come farther out into the sea, moving across the surface atop hard hulls with tall white fins. Tr*Til was intensely curious about these, never having seen them quite so close before; but Ch*Tril made sure their little traveling pod stayed at least a hundred beak-to-flukes from the intruders.

Tr*Til and Nk\Jin showed little interest in the changing nature of the remote land itself, however, while Ch*Tril was fascinated, as always, by its ever-transforming shapes. The land had reached higher and higher upward since they'd started traveling, and had lost its sparse brown look. Now the steep hills were covered with large green growths as high as kelp stalks were deep.

Looking at the land made Ch*Tril think of the fanciful scenes Dj\Tal had imaged to her from time to time, as real as if he had truly beheld the very breadth of that alien and unreachable world, had soared above it with the flying-creatures. How could one with such an imagination have become so taciturn?

Except for that one odd moment just before she'd left, she

thought; well away from the rest of the School, near the kelp beds where they'd mated. He had Linked her something at once highly detailed and yet abstract: neither concepts nor emotions, but rather . . . a *structure,* a pattern of pure thought that resembled an extremely complex image based on numerous interlocking circles.

Ch*Tril had asked him to explain what it was all about, but he'd refused; it was something she might need, he'd told her cryptically, and then had Touched her farewell.

No time to wonder about it now, though; there was a great deal of distance yet to cross, and much to do. And where in sea was Tr*Til?

]Cessation of Motion[, Ch*Tril imaged to Nk\Jin, and she stopped and did a turning-scan. No sign of Tr*Til. She turned slowly in place once more, this time extending the range of the scan, and spotted her: heading straight for the white-waves and the rocks.

Ch*Tril sent Nk\Jin a quick no-follow image, and made at top speed for the perilous spot her friend was approaching. Tr*Til was riding the waves toward the largest of the rocks; it was at least eight beak-to-flukes across, and protruded more than half that height above the white-waves that constantly smashed against it.

Ch*Tril found the energy for an even greater burst of speed, and whistled a loud alert, but Tr*Til showed no sign of hearing. The white-waves lifted her higher with each new surge, steadily closer to the jagged perimeter of the rock.

Suddenly Tr*Til dove, and slowed, holding her own against the currents that were creating the mighty froth above. Ch*Tril did the same, following her companion into an area of relative calm on one side of the rock. There she saw Tr*Til ease ahead at a stalking pace, scanning something on the surface.

Ch*Tril scanned it, too: a small floating creature, about a quarter of her own size. It looked like a land-creature, with its fur and four limbs; but it seemed quite at home in the water, rolling contentedly about, using its broad flat tail for balance. As it rolled, Ch*Tril could scan that it clutched a shell-creature against its front, and in the other forelimb it held a small rock with which it was trying to break open the shell.

Tr*Til spurted upward, catching the otter unawares from beneath, and easily lifted it with her snout. She tossed it a beak-to-fluke across the water and it flailed wildly in the air, dropping its shell-creature before it fell back into the sea with a splash.

Despite her upset at Tr*Til's reckless excursion, Ch*Tril couldn't help but enjoy the humor of the trick, and she chittered funny-funny sounds to herself. She did an inner scan of the fur-thing to make sure it wasn't hurt, then dove to retrieve the sinking shell it had dropped.

Rising back to the surface, she tossed the shell-creature just out of reach of its indignant former owner, which immediately swam to reclaim its prize. When the fur-thing almost had it within its grasp, Tr*Til darted in to flick the shell away again with a twist of her flukes.

They continued this game for ten or twelve more tosses, then let the otter have its intended meal back. It clutched the shell tightly in its forelimbs and swam away quickly to a sort of inlet in the rock face that was too small for Ch*Tril or Tr*Til to enter. There it selected another small rock for a tool and resumed its efforts to crack open the shell, all the while keeping one wary eye on the strange and bothersome newcomers.

Tr*Til imaged a series of the most comical moments in the fur-thing's struggles, and she and Ch*Tril both made funny-funny sounds; but then Ch*Tril regained her composure and imaged a horrific, bloody scene of Tr*Til riding the white-waves straight into the monstrous rock and being torn apart on its sharp edges.

Tr*Til was chastened. She arched sideways in the position of remorse, and imaged what the fur-thing had scanned like from a distance, how intriguingly it had rolled and wriggled about.

As she was making her apologetic explanation, the otter suddenly dashed up from behind and gave her a firm swat on the snout with its wide flat tail. Tr*Til squawked and jerked back in surprise, and the little creature hurried back to its pool of sanctuary amid the rocks.

The funny-funny sounds Ch*Tril made in response to this went on for quite some time, and eventually Tr*Til joined in. A good trick was a good trick, no matter who—or, in this case, what—had pulled it off.

Their return to where Nk\Jin was waiting was far easier than the swim to the rock had been. They swam deep, far below the turbulence of the white-waves, where the incoming currents gave them only token resistance. When Ch*Tril had scanned that the sea above was relatively calm again, they hurried together to the surface and soon spotted Nk\Jin.

He was not pleased. As the two females excitedly took turns imaging the frightening approach to the rock, the odd little fur-thing and the games that had gone on with it, Nk\Jin made no response. Only when they had begun to repeat themselves did he harshly image back a view of himself shivering and swimming in circles. He'd had to keep moving to stay warm, but where was he to go? This was strange territory, and so while the females were off adventuring he'd been able to do nothing but swim around and around for what had seemed forever.

His irritation was understandable. To be placed into a circum-stance of enforced boredom was an insult of the deepest order, an affront ranking with denial of food-sharing privileges.

She gave Nk\Jin a Touch, and imaged to Tr*Til that she should follow suit. The two of them began to caress him with alternating gentle strokes and rubs, much as they and the other females had comforted Ek*Tiq during her time of bringing-forth . . . but this time, the Touches were distinctly sexual.

Nk\Jin made himself erect as Ch*Tril and her friend continued to glide past him, their soft undersides brushing ever so lightly, teasingly, against his own. As they swam, they imaged to him scenes of the most vigorous intercourse, of willing female undersides presented by the score.

Tr*Til at last granted him the release of entry, as Ch*Tril kept up her caresses and her images; then Nk\Jin slid from one into the other, and back again, sending ecstatic images of his own, until it seemed there was a multitude of them copulating there in that isolated sea off the rocks and the high green cliffs.

When their sex was done, they realized that a cool mist had rolled in over them, and the stark land was no longer visible. They dove, and scanned to get their bearings, and were on their way once more.

The drilling ship *Alicia Faye* was anchored just four miles out in the channel, plainly visible from the marina where Jeb caught the PetroGlobe shuttle boat, a clean, sleek forty-foot cabin cruiser that didn't look at all out of place amid the white forest of sailboat masts and the rows of pricey motorized pleasure craft. Jeb supposed the company must use it for cocktail parties and sunset cruises when it wasn't ferrying workers back and forth to the offshore rigs; a handy way to entertain visiting executives or clients ... maybe even, discreetly and privately to be sure, a member of the Coastal Commission now and then, when drilling or tankering permits were up for review.

The seas were choppy, and Jeb stayed put in his seat, beer in hand: the last alcohol he'd see until it was time for his land rotation, if the rules on the drilling ship were the same as those on the big floating or permanent rigs. Life was difficult enough on the offshore installations, and the population—ninety-eight percent male—sufficiently rowdy that adding booze to the mix would have been a superfluous, even dangerous, catalyst; so the rigs were all as dry as a Wahhabist wedding in Jeddah.

Interestingly, though, the two-and-a-half-hour flights back out to the North Sea rigs from Aberdeen had always been strangely quiet, the rough-and-tumble workers in the plush, airline-style seats of the big forty-four-passenger Chinook helicopters as subdued and thoughtful as a platoon of soldiers on their way back from R&R to a distant battlefield. Which, in a sense, is exactly what they were.

At least on the rigs you had that regular break from the regimentation and the enforced sobriety; in the North Sea fields the tours were usually "fourteen-and-fourteen," meaning two weeks at sea and two weeks on land, to spend drinking or whoring or tending to family, as each man chose.

In Saudi the oppressive, rigidly moralistic atmosphere lasted week after week, month after month, and it affected not only the workers but their wives and families, if they had them. And if they stayed.

God, the commotion Lindy had raised when she'd learned she wasn't allowed to drive a car anywhere outside the American compound in Dharan: "That's the only goddamned thing that kept me sane in Scotland," she'd protested, and Jeb had had the sense not to question the possible hyperbole of that statement. Who knew, maybe she even meant it; when he was home on his two-week leaves, they seldom stayed at the immaculate though sterile flat in the dull granite city of Aberdeen, opting instead for endless drives through the birch-strewn hills and amethyst moors of Royal Deeside, or along the coldly beautiful, deserted beaches of the northeast coast. Lindy would drive as often as he, and would always take the wheel of the old Range Rover when they'd been following the peat smoke of the whiskey trail, he sampling twice her ration of Glen-this and Glen-that single malts at the region's ubiquitous, and peculiarly odiferous, distilleries.

Not *allowed* to *drive*?? Lindy, not unreasonably, had taken the proscription as a personal insult, a direct and malicious slap in the face aimed specifically at her by the collective male descendants of Ibn Saud.

Jeb tossed back the last of his Tecate and crumpled the can. The boat's engines were throbbing in reverse now, as they edged alongside the *Alicia Faye*. Typical, Jeb thought; half the rigs in the North Sea were named for the wives or girlfriends of the original wildcatters and oil-company execs who'd persevered when no one else had thought it possible to build and operate a single well, let alone a series of entire fields, out there on those impossible, turbulent seas. *Mabel, Josephine, Beryl, Joanne* ... who had all those women really been, and had their oil-obsessed men actually believed that applying the women's names to those massive, incongruously unfeminine platforms would compensate for the months of separation, the familial plans deferred or dashed?

"Sir? Gangway's ready when you are. Not sure how much longer we can hold it, in this chop."

Jeb looked up at the young ferry pilot, nodded, and made his way with his duffel bag to the swaying canvas walkway that temporarily connected the two craft. It shook and swung like a rope bridge across a canyon in one of those old *Indiana Jones* movies that Jeb had enjoyed in college; and at the other end of the gangway, waiting, was a smiling face that took him back to those same college days as surely as if the wobbly little canvas bridge had been a time machine.

"Son of a bitch!" Bryant Emerson exclaimed. "They told me it'd be you coming out, but I don't think I really believed it till right this minute."

"Good to see you, Bryant," Jeb said, shaking the man's hand and clasping his upper arm with the other hand. "Long damn time."

"Jee-sus, tell me about it! Last time I saw you was, what, '88, '89?"

"That night at Antone's," Jeb recalled. "Bobby 'Blue' Bland, remember?"

"Shit, that's right, I was with that freaky little brunette, what was her name, and ... hey, but what the hell are we doing standing around out here? Come on inside and let's get you settled."

Emerson took Jeb's bag and led the way through the corridors of the ship, a medium-sized vessel maybe half the length of an average cruise liner. The warren of corridors led past several dozen doors, many of them standing open to reveal empty cabins.

"This damn thing's twice as big as we need, with the new laser equipment," Emerson noted. "Guess the next generation of drilling boats'll be a hell of a lot smaller, but for now, this is what we've got."

"Beats being overcrowded," Jeb said.

"Oh, hell, yeah; I spent a tour on one of the old platforms off Yucatán. Jesus, it was like a matchbox. With roaches."

Jeb grunted his understanding, and followed Emerson into a spacious galley area, the brightly painted walls and sculpted tables illuminated by rows of recessed track lighting. There were maybe half a dozen men scattered around the room, reading, eating, or sipping coffee.

"If you'd rather go straight to your cabin, just say so," Emerson said. "Otherwise, I thought we could grab a bite and catch up on old times."

Might as well be sooner than later, Jeb thought with resignation. "Sure, sure," he said with what he hoped was not obviously false heartiness. "Been looking forward to it."

There was a cafeteria setup at the far side of the room, with no one in line and a single crewman behind the counter to handle everything from salads to hot dishes to beverages. Emerson loaded his tray with a meat-loaf platter, three-bean salad and a slice of lemon cake; Jeb, his stomach still unused to the pitch and roll of the anchored ship, took only a hotpot of chicken broth, two packets of Saltines, and an iced tea.

"So," Emerson said when they'd sat at an empty table and taken the dishes off their trays, "how's Lindy?"

Right to it, Jeb thought, no delays. What the fuck. "She's gone, Bryant."

Emerson stopped still, salt shaker held in midair above his salad. "*Gone?* My God, you don't mean—"

Jeb shook his head irritably. "No, no, she's not dead. She's just . . . gone. Left. Back home in Dallas, last I heard."

Bryant let out a breath of relief, and set down the salt shaker, but the look on his face was still one of surprise and concern. "I just never figured . . . Jesus Christ, man, what the hell happened?"

What had happened, really, that he could say and be understood? The world had happened. The goddamned job had happened, just as Jeb had wanted, and it had sent them to hell, together and apart. But he couldn't say that, could he?

"I don't know, Bryant, it just ... it all got to be too much for her, you know?"

That had been part of her appeal at the beginning, Jeb remembered, that unique combination of strength and delicacy. She could whack a 240-yard drive or maneuver a Jeep down a boulder-strewn creek bed with the best of them, but a foul smell or a gruesome sight would cause the Texas tomboy in her to instantly revert to a sort of pre-feminist southern girlishness, eyes scrunched shut and nose wrinkled in repulsion. Even the butchers' shops in Aberdeen had disgusted her, with their whole plucked geese and gutted hogs hanging from the ceiling; her banker's-daughter childhood in Dallas had clearly been a world removed from the relatively hard-scrabble life Jeb had known when he was growing up. Why, his grandmother in Denton used to—

His own stomach churned as the random memory of the chickens in his grandmother's yard suddenly gave way to that indelible scene outside the mosque in Riyadh, the smell of it, the crowd cheering and chanting, surging forward as he and Lindy tried to push their way through against the tide, caught at the forefront of the encircling mob. . . .

"Oh, man, I'm so sorry to hear that."

Jeb licked his lips; it felt like there was sand in his mouth, sand or maybe dried blood. He took a big gulp of the iced tea: bitter, he'd forgotten to sweeten it first.

"It goes with the job, I guess."

Emerson shook his head sympathetically. "I've still never gotten married, but five other guys I know, three engineers and two geologists, same story. Mexico, Nigeria ... hey, weren't you there a few years ago, yourself?"

Jeb nodded. "Port Harcourt."

"God, talk about your basic hellholes . . . if Lindy was going to crumple, I'm surprised she didn't do it there."

"Damn near did."

"Ah, Jeb, Jeb . . . I used to envy the two of you so."

Emerson had introduced them actually, in a casual and round-about way, back at U.T. Austin: Some girl he'd been briefly dating had been invited to a party some other girls were throwing, and she'd asked Bryant to bring along an extra guy or two. The extra guy had been Jeb; the party had been at a condo in the Orange Tree complex, three sophomore girls sharing a two-bedroom place that one of their daddies—Lindy's, as it turned out—had bought. She got the place rent-free for four years, plus the monthly shares her roommates paid; her father got a tax write-off and a nice little income property that he could rent to U.T. students for decades to come after Lindy graduated.

After that, the three of them—Jeb, Lindy, and Bryant—had hung out together constantly, the fourth wheel of the group changing as Bryant's tastes in, or luck with, women changed. Pizza and beer at Milto's or Mike & Sal's, studying at the Castaneda Library, the Oklahoma game every year; and the music—God what a place for music that town had been, probably still was: country sounds at the Broken Spoke, big names like Waylon or Willie or Jerry Jeff at the Austin Opera House, R&B at Antone's . . .

"We had us some times, didn't we?" Jeb said.

"Oh, yeah. Hell, yeah."

Jeb broke a Saltine into half a dozen pieces and dropped them into his soup bowl. They floated there, sodden and colorless, held suspended by surface tension as they soaked up the thin broth.

"How soon can I get to work, Bryant?"

5

Sheila stood in the waist-deep water, her toes dug into the soft sandy bottom to keep her balance. The reel-to-reel digital recorder was heavy, and she was grateful for at least the little buoyancy it acquired in its watertight case. The dolphin had shown immediate interest in the equipment, scanning it from all angles, and had continued to cooperate with all of Sheila's tests.

She gave the yellow foam-rubber cube in her hand a toss; she'd introduced it to him today, following their previous games with a pyramid-shaped object and two balls of different sizes. The dolphin caught the cube in his mouth and threw it back to her, and Sheila put it back into the opaque vinyl pouch that was slung over her shoulder on the opposite side from the recorder. The dolphin waited a moment, then swam impatiently to her and nudged the pouch. She could see by the VU meter on the face of the recorder that he'd given off an ultrasonic burst just before his snout had touched the pouch; it wasn't likely to be a scanning beam, since he'd learned on the first day that his sonar couldn't penetrate the vinyl. The tape was rolling, and Sheila hoped that what he'd transmitted was a signal that might include the image of the cube.

She pulled the toy from the pouch and tossed it across the placid green water again. The dolphin raced after it, and when it fell this time he whacked it with his tail like a tennis ball, sending it flying straight up into the air. Twice more he slapped the bouncy cube aloft, and on its third descent he gave it a mighty swat toward the beach where the children stood watching.

Sheila smiled tolerantly. "O.K., big fella," she said under her breath. "You want to go play with the other kids, you go right ahead. School's out for now."

She'd established a pact of sorts with the children over the last four days: The dolphin was their exclusive companion and playmate for at least an hour after he arrived each day, and then they could quietly observe as she made her recordings and observations. When she was done they could resume their games, and ask her as many questions as they liked about cetaceans.

Now she waved the children on into the water, and they ran out to greet the dolphin again with a great show of communal splashing. One little girl picked up the floating yellow cube and threw it, but the dolphin swam to her with a piece of seaweed in his mouth instead. He knew the distinction between work and play.

Sheila retrieved the foam rubber cube and waded back up to the beach, the plastic-encased tape recorder growing heavier with each step. She sank to her knees at the water's edge, set the burden down and sat to watch the children playing with the dolphin.

"So I guess that's it, huh?"

"Pardon?" Sheila squinted up into the sun to see who'd spoken. It was a tall, lanky man in shorts and sneakers; she couldn't really see his face because of the sun behind him.

"I said, that must be the famous dolphin, right? The wild one that comes in to play with humans?"

"That's him, all right. Whizzy, they call him."

"Mmmh." The man scrunched down into the sand beside her, and she could see that he had an interestingly angular face; a man's face, unlike the tanned but doughy California-boy look she was so accustomed to seeing.

"Is that one of your kids down there with him?" he asked.

"No." She started to elaborate, to tell him she didn't have any children, or . . . but it wasn't any of his business, why should she tell him that?

"You on vacation?" he asked.

She shook her head. "Work. How about you?"

"Same here." He smiled, spread his hands to indicate the beach, the water, the brilliant sky. "Tough jobs we've got, huh?"

Sheila laughed along with him. "I'm Sheila Roberts," she said.

"Daniel Colter." They shook hands, and he held on to hers for just a beat longer than she'd expected. She was suddenly aware of the relative brevity of the white bathing suit that she normally thought of merely as her working clothes.

"So, what's with the fancy tape machine?" he asked, trying to recover from the slightly awkward moment.

"It's for underwater stereo recording," she told him, tugging at where the bathing suit had ridden up in back. "I'm taping the dolphin."

"For one of these New Age CDs? Songs of the whales, that kind of thing?"

"No, no. It's all strictly ultrasonic, inaudible. I'm carrying out a research program at U.C. Santa Barbara, and . . ."

She gave him the condensed layman's version: short on cetacean physiology and algorithmic theory, long on colorful analogies to 3-D television. He seemed duly impressed by the complexity of the experiments, but that familiar look of skepticism on his face was unmistakable.

"You really think they can do that? Send each other pictures through the water?"

"Yes," she said simply. "I do."

"I don't know . . ."

"That's exactly the point," she said. "You don't *know*, and neither do I. That's why I'm testing the theory."

"It would be a hell of a discovery if you were right, I'll grant you that. Hell of a story."

"You're a reporter?"

He shrugged. "Not like the Woodward-Bernstein kind, no. I'm a free-lance writer, working on a piece about dolphins right now. So what you say intrigues me, even if I don't necessarily buy it. Not just yet, anyway."

"At least you have an open mind. That's more than I can say for some people." She looked at him quizzically. "What kind of story are you doing about dolphins? 'Our Friends in the Sea,' that kind of thing?"

"No, not exactly. More an ecology-related approach."

"Like the tuna-boat issue, you mean?"

He turned his face away, squinted toward the lowering sun. "Yeah. Like that."

Sheila noticed his sudden change of expression, and took it for lack of interest. "You know, most people think it's all fine now," she told him, "because of the Starkist deal. But they're wrong, it's still going on. And do you have any idea what they actually *do* on those boats, what happens to the dolphins?"

"Yeah." He shifted his weight in the sand. "Hey, so have you got some good recordings from this dolphin here? Or do you really know yet?"

"It's hard to tell," she said curtly, a bit miffed at his refusal to discuss the tuna-boat controversy. If he was writing an ecology-oriented article about dolphins, you'd think he'd want to learn more about that.

"So when will you know?"

"I need access to the mainframe back at the university." She sighed. "Or maybe I just need to come up with a whole new approach."

They stared out at the water in silence, watching the children at play with their alien but highly sociable visitor.

"Have you met one yet?" Sheila suddenly asked.

"I'm sorry?"

"A dolphin. Have you actually met one as an individual, or have you just been researching the species in general?"

"Well . . . more the latter, I suppose. But I don't see what difference—"

"Come on," Sheila said, standing up and brushing the sand off her elbows and her bottom. "I'll introduce you."

Daniel took off his sneakers and put his watch and wallet in one of them, then followed her down the beach toward the water. Her legs were in great shape, he couldn't help but notice; must swim every day. Probably that's why she kept her hair so short, too, but it suited her. She must be, what, thirty, thirty-two? Looked younger, though, except around her eyes. Very intelligent eyes.

He waded into the bathtub-warm water behind her, and together they made their way to a spot about thirty feet from where the children were playing with the dolphin.

"Squat down," Sheila told him, lowering herself until the tiny wavelets lapped around her chin. Daniel frowned curiously, but followed her lead; the water felt good anyway.

Almost immediately, he felt an odd vibration in his chest and abdomen, a not-unpleasant thrumming sensation that seemed to pass right through him.

"What the hell—?"

Sheila grinned. "He's scanning you," she said. "Feels funny, doesn't it?"

"I wasn't expecting that."

"He's just curious, that's all; taking a look at you from a distance."

The tingling stopped, and the dolphin swam toward them, its fin slicing the placid surface of the Sound.

. . . *Something gray,* Daniel suddenly thought, *something gray in the water* . . . but neither the rest of the thought, nor the source of it, would come.

"Can you keep your eyes open underwater?" Sheila asked.

"Yeah, I suppose; I mean, I could when I was a kid."

"Try it," she suggested. "Meet him on his own turf, so to speak."

He took a deep breath and ducked his head beneath the clear, green water. Despite the surrounding liquid warmth, he felt a shiver run up his back as the dolphin darted straight toward him, stopping with its snout no more than a foot away from his face.

Its eyes ... they were bright and knowing, full of eager curiosity and a strangely moving serenity. These were not the eyes of a dog or a monkey; instead, they conveyed the unmistakable impression of full sentience, of an intelligence equaling or surpassing Daniel's own. They differed from mere animal eyes in the same way that Sheila's eyes had revealed her as unique, apart, before she'd even spoken.

Daniel lifted his head from the water for a breath, and the dolphin did the same, regarding him still with the same calm interest.

"Jesus," Daniel said, "it's ... it's like looking into a *person's* eyes."

Sheila nodded, smiling. "I'm convinced he is a person, every bit as much as you or me. Just made differently, that's all."

"Can I touch him?"

She shrugged. "That's up to him, not me. Just don't make any sudden moves toward him, and don't touch the area around his blowhole. And take that ring off first, his skin's very sensitive."

Under the dolphin's watchful eye, Daniel removed the Sigma Delta Chi ring he'd worn since college and stashed it in the buttoned pocket of his now-soggy shorts. He reached out slowly, deliberately, and stroked the rubbery smooth skin. The dolphin chittered once and rubbed his head against Daniel's hand like a kitten being petted.

"Here," Sheila said, pulling the foam-rubber cube from the pouch around her waist and handing it to Daniel. "He likes to play with this."

"What do I do with it, toss it to him?"

She smiled again. "You guys make up your own game. He's very creative."

Daniel ducked his head under the water again and waved the cube back and forth in front of his face; the dolphin watched for a moment, then gently took the toy from Daniel's hand with his teeth, reared his head back up above the surface and threw it some fifty feet away.

Daniel felt a rush of amazement. He was actually playing with this wild creature, bigger than he was, in its own environment! He swam quickly to retrieve the cube, brought it back, and waggled it in front of his face again. The dolphin took it in his mouth again, and once more tossed it a dozen yards across the water.

Swimming toward the floating yellow cube again, Daniel suddenly realized what was happening: The dolphin was teaching *him* to play fetch.

Daniel started to laugh as he swam, so hard he almost swallowed a mouthful of seawater, so hard that—well, he couldn't really remember when he'd last laughed that thoroughly or spontaneously. Not for a long, long time.

And that, he suddenly knew, had been the dolphin's gift to him.

Ch*Tril and her companions swam in tight formation, almost touching, the better to share warmth in the deepening cold. The land they could see was wilder now, more starkly defined, with fewer traces of land-walkers visible either there or on the frigid, tossing seas.

The inner tugging of Ch*Tril's direction-sensors was growing stronger by the moment. A spot of intense magnetic energy was located here, as she knew from past journeys; it lay near the place where the sea floor fell away into the great depths, where they would need to turn away from their course paralleling land and head outward to find the Sources.

This energy-spot, and others like it, had confused many travelers. It was easy to mistake these lesser magnetic nodes for the Primary Node, which lay somewhere unreachable in the distant frozen land but could guide the careful from warm seas to cool and back again. An error such as that could easily be fatal; Ch*Tril knew of a number of her kind, and even some of the Sources, who had swum directly onto the land as a result of that sort of miscalculation. Most had died there, unable to return to the sea.

Ch*Tril was familiar with this route, though, and as the invisible tugging at her brain reached its peak she led the others in a tight turn leftward, toward the limitless reaches of the cold sea. Scanning ahead and downward, she located the dropoff.

She signaled the others to follow on her flanks, then filled her lungs with air and dove to the sea floor, some twenty beak-to-flukes below the surface. A multitude of bottom-dwelling creatures inhabited these chilly waters; Tr*Til nudged one fat, red-orange crawling thing with her snout, and was rewarded with a quick warning snap from one of its two sharp pincers, while Nk\Jin cautiously watched a long, black, sinuous creature that slithered along the sand.

Then all at once the sea floor disappeared. Ch*Tril was expecting it, but still the moment nearly stopped her heart. What had been a benign, lively bottom of sand and plants and funny crawling things, where a dim light still shone, became in an instant a black nothingness where even the longest-range scans revealed only void, without apparent end.

They swam together quietly above the great watery pit, chastened into silence by the sheer immensity of it. Nk\Jin was the first to need a breath; he imaged this, and the three of them rose to the surface, staying fin-to-fin as they ascended.

They broke through to the choppy waves above, and Ch*Tril spotted a pod of six Danger-Cousins ahead, coming in their direction. She steered her two companions in a detour to the right, and the big black-and-white orcas sliced past without incident. Probably going after land-prey, Ch*Tril thought; she had seen Danger-Cousins take the whiskered awrk-awrk things that lived on big rocks in these regions, had seen them lift their massive heads from the water and simply pluck off awrk-awrks the size of herself with their teeth.

It was best to stay away from the Danger-Cousins, she knew, to keep out of their paths and give them right-of-way if they crossed yours. An uneasy truce prevailed between her kind and theirs, but violent encounters still took place from time to time.

The ancient enmity had its roots in different interpretations of how the seas had come to be, and of how life had been brought forth to occupy them. The Danger-Cousins believed the vast blue emptiness high above was another, far-off sea, and the many tiny lights in the darktime blackness were the spiritual glow of great Cousins who dwelt in that sea. This world, they believed, had been nothing but uninhabitable dry land until the Cousins above had chosen to share their water, drop by drop, in the form of thunderous tempests which had also brought, in jagged strokes, the lights of life.

First had come the light of the Sources, the story went, followed by those of the Danger-Cousins, of Ch*Tril's kind, of the fishes . . . and finally, so that all this wondrous life could be admired and envied from afar, they had sent the light of the land-walkers.

Ch*Tril's kind had never held with such tales of Cousins on high, doling out life as a random gift. They believed the seas and the land had always coexisted, and that one day a huge burst of hot red liquid had come spewing from the bowels of the earth; as the burning spray had risen into the air above the mountain that its birth had given birth to, it looked down and thought:

—I shall be neither sea nor land. I shall be life.

And as the millions of molten droplets fell, some into the oceans and some upon the land, they each became one of the myriad different forms of life, separately yet perfectly suited for the various spots at which they had come to rest.

Ch*Tril thought both these stories were nonsense. She knew from her historical research that there had indeed been many incidents of fiery liquid spewing into the air; but when the liquid landed, at least when it landed in the sea, it became plain black rocks, not life. And as for the Danger-Cousins' myth, well, above the water there was lack of water, which was air; above the air, then, should be merely lack of air, not a second ocean. Of course, that didn't explain all the various lights up there, large and small, bright and dim; but Ch*Tril was still working on that one.

A school of bright blue fish swam past, just the right size for eating. Tr*Til and Nk\Jin noticed them immediately, too, but hesitated a moment until Ch*Tril had imaged her permission to go after the fish. That pleased her; perhaps her little band had begun to learn discipline after all.

Momentarily braving the cold in favor of the prospects of a much-needed meal, the three of them swam apart, each taking up a well-practiced herding position: Nk\Jin ahead and to Ch*Tril's right, Tr*Til in a somewhat closer position ahead and to the left. As they approached the school of fish, the two in the lead spread their pattern, swimming to keep pace with the school and staying on either side of it.

Ch*Tril, bringing up the rear, rushed the school from behind. At first the fish tried to escape by darting away straight ahead, as fast as they could; but their speed was no match for that of their pursuer, so in desperation the school abruptly split into two halves, one feinting right, the other left . . . directly into the waiting mouths of Tr*Til and Nk\Jin.

The three held back a bit after that first pass, allowing the remainder of the school to regroup; then Ch*Tril moved into what had been Nk\Jin's position, and Tr*Til took up the chase. The stupid fish, having no memory, responded in exactly the same way as before. Ch*Tril and her friends feasted.

It was on the third pass, just as Nk\Jin was about to rush the fish from the rear, that Tr*Til suddenly sent out a danger signal. Five times she sent it, the last two garbled in incoherent panic, before Ch*Tril was able to scan her whereabouts and discover the source of her fear.

White hard-water, a huge sheet of it, floating in the area where Tr*Til had been swimming. Tr*Til was underneath the ice, frantically scanning for a way out.

]Follow-CLOSE[, Ch*Tril imaged to Nk\Jin, and she made a dash for the frozen island. Just before they reached it she led Nk\Jin to the surface for a deep, deep intake of air; then they dove, he directly at her side and emulating her every move.

It was darker beneath the expanse of hard-water, with confusing spots of brightness where the cold crystal latticework caught the light from above and diffused it. Ch*Tril could scan Tr*Til ahead, just a few beak-to-flukes away, but Tr*Til was no longer able to scan or image. She was in a state of hysteria, thrashing wildly about and beating her head against the underside of the ice, struggling futilely to get to the surface for a breath.

Ch*Tril imaged Nk\Jin to move in tight on the other side of Tr*Til, and together they began to push her back to where they'd entered this glacial trap. Tr*Til continued to twist madly with fear, slapping her rescuers with her flukes; a mist of blood was rising from her snout, where she'd tried to smash her way through to the surface.

Suddenly they were out, and the three of them broke the surface together. All were urgently in need of air, but Tr*Til was gasping too much of it, too fast. Ch*Tril gently pushed her back below the water so her blowhole would close; otherwise she'd soon be sick with dizziness. Her injuries were minor, Ch*Tril scanned with relief, but that emotion quickly gave way to anger.

In any three-point herding, it was the responsibility of the one in the lead to scan for obstacles or hazards ahead. Tr*Til hadn't been paying any attention to where she—where all three of them— were going, and her negligence had put them all into a potentially fatal situation.

Still, Ch*Tril knew that she herself shared the blame; she was leader of this journey, had traveled these waters before and knew of the dangers of floating hard-water. She should have warned the others more clearly, should have been constantly scanning their route on her own.

Embarrassed at the realization of her own carelessness, Ch*Tril now did a mid-range and a long-range scan of the ocean ahead. Quite a ways off, there seemed to be . . . another big sheet of hard-water? Two more?

No. The gigantic things she scanned were moving, were propelling themselves through the cold waters with majestic grace, now breaching the surface with their impossible bulk: a hundred, three hundred times the size of Ch*Tril.

She signaled her companions to halt, and raised her head above the choppy waves. In the distance was an arcing spout, and the dark shape of a stately, massive head; then those tremendous flukes lifted regally above the sea—*its* sea.

The first part of her journey was complete: She had found the Sources.

Now the Melding could begin.

The last few days had been lucky ones for Batera. He'd put the nasty incident with the Greenpeace types out of his mind, and had managed to find replacements for them in Mensabe: a couple of Panamanians, hard workers with years of experience on the boats. Their last skipper had tossed them off for drinking too much, but by the time Batera found them they'd been desperate for work and neither of them had touched a bottle since they'd come on board.

Then there'd been today's set, a beauty if Batera had ever seen one. They'd brailed fifty tons of yellowfin aboard, not a skipjack in the load and hardly any sharks. Each of the two forward wells was three-quarters full now, a thousand or more of the big tuna heaped in brine while the ammonia pipes hummed to keep them frozen.

Giant goldfish, Batera thought with a chuckle, that's what they were: 100- or 200-pound fish as good as gold, and if they kept on piling up like they had today, the *Sea Master* would be headed back to San Diego in record time.

The heavy tropical sun was dropping ever faster toward the horizon now, a great red globe that cast a burnished glow over the men stacking the net. Batera watched the scene contentedly. The two Panamanians, the ones who were supposed to be drunks, had taken the most demanding job: stacking the corkline. They worked diligently and skillfully, constantly twisting the line to keep the corks in their proper places as the men laid them in an eight-foot strip along the starboard side of the netpile.

The cook's bell gave off one short ring: cocktail time. Batera stepped into the deckhouse and walked past the cabins to the galley. Carlos Donato, his chief engineer, was the only one there as yet; he was sitting under the faded reproduction of *The Last Supper*, nibbling crackers smeared with pâté and sipping vodka on the rocks.

Antonio nodded to Vinicius, the cook, and made himself a Chivas and soda. He looked over the appetizer tray that had been set out on the wide counter separating the eating area from the kitchen, and selected a couple of pickles rolled in thin ham. He dipped them in a little pot of mustard and went over to sit across from Carlos.

"How's she running?" he asked.

"Smooth, Toninho, nice and smooth. Only problem I got is a filler tube clog in number-six well. Gonna have to drain her to clear it out."

"Tomorrow?"

"I'd like to. How's it look?"

He meant the weather, Batera knew. Emptying any one of the room-sized storage wells of its brine meant draining the opposite well at the same time, to maintain the boat's stability. The process required precise timing, and wasn't something you'd want to do in heavy seas.

"Last report I got was good."

"I'll check again in the morning."

"Yah," Batera said.

"Good set today."

"The Panamanians. They brought us luck."

"Could be."

They chatted about the set, about the seas, and had another drink each. Neither of them mentioned the men with the camera, the sickening sight of the one who'd fallen being crushed by the boat's sharp prow. All the luck they'd just started having might be reversed by talking about that kind of thing while they were still at sea.

The aroma of roasting meat permeated the galley, and soon Vinicius rang the double chimes of the dinner bell. Most of the seats were now occupied by men having drinks as they came off duty, and with the dinner call the rest were quickly taken. Meals were important on these long trips; the skippers of the different boats vied with each other to see who could hire the finest cook, who could stock the most elaborate foodstuffs.

Tonight, Carlos chose butterflied shrimp with salsa, and Batera went for the rare prime rib and a baked potato. He ate in silence, listening to the hubbub of a happy crew laughing and reliving the near-perfect set. It was a welcome relief from the palpable anger and depression that had hung over the boat since the ugly incident with the Greenpeacers.

Once the dinner plates were cleared, one table was turned over to the ongoing nickel-ante poker game, and the rest of the men went out for a smoke by the netpile or back to their cabins to listen to music. Batera stopped by the bridge, where he monitored the latest weather reports and watched the dark rolling sea for a few minutes. Then he left Manoel at the wheel and headed for his own cabin.

He poured himself a nightcap from the well-stocked bar, settled down in his leather recliner and rummaged through the box of videotapes he'd brought along for the trip. There were several episodes of *60 Minutes* and *Nightline* that he'd set the VCR timer for at home during his last trip; a couple of old John Ford westerns; a miniseries about Army Air Corps pilots in World War II; and several recent cop-thriller movies that the guy at the video store ran off for him in the back of the store, for a reasonable under-the-table fee.

None of it really appealed to him right now, and he didn't feel like reading, either. He swirled the Scotch in his glass and stared around the comfortably appointed but confining cabin. Times like this, nights usually, he sometimes hated being at sea. Nowhere to go, nothing to occupy his mind.

His eyes fell on the Greenpeacers' duffel bag and backpack, crammed between his closet and the bulkhead. He'd stuck them there to keep the crew from picking through them, but now his own curiosity was aroused.

Batera pulled the duffel bag out and opened it. The camera was on top of the clothes and other belongings; he had one almost exactly like it himself back home; he'd bought it for his and Maria's last trip to Portugal. He didn't use it much, mainly just when Jorge—George—brought his wife and little boy from Phoenix to visit in the off-season.

Jesus, he thought, holding the compact unit in his palm; a man had died just so he could bring this thing on board the boat. Where was the sense in it? How could anybody think a bunch of porpoise were worth a human life?

He turned the camcorder on; the battery was still charged. He rewound the tape and dug through the duffel bag in search of the cables that would connect the camera to a TV set as a playback unit. They were at the very bottom, in a plastic bag otherwise stuffed with dirty socks and underwear.

Batera attached the cables to the camcorder, then pulled his television set out from its cabinet so he could plug the other ends of the wires into the video and audio input sockets. He pushed the TV back into place, turned it on and hit the Play button on the camcorder.

The first thing he saw was a shot of his boat, this boat, from a distance, from somewhere off Harbor Drive in San Diego within sight of the docks. The picture zoomed in on the bow, and the bold blue letters SEA MASTER filled the screen. Batera was livid. He'd given those idiots a *job,* and this was how they'd repaid him; they'd been planning to nail him personally, turn him and his boat into some kind of symbol of whatever it was they thought was wrong with the whole goddamned tuna industry.

Now the scene had shifted, and the image was tilted, unsteady: the speedboats, heading out to round up the porpoise. There was a fast, blurry pan, and a zoom-in on the encircling net, on the porpoise trying to get out, the porpoise drowning. Batera had seen all this ten thousand times before, but he'd never seen it so . . . close.

The net drew closed, was lifted from the water. The shaking camera focused on one porpoise that was mashed up against the heavy strands of the net, its head half in and half out; there were deep bloody cuts in its skin where the net pressed against it, and you could see one of its eyes darting around, mad with terror.

Batera held his breath, wanted to turn off the TV set but couldn't.

The net had dumped its load on the deck now, and the porpoise were all flopping about. One of them had the big fin on its back ripped off, and it was spurting blood. The camera zoomed in again on its eyes, its goddamned eyes. This was obscene, you never looked at their eyes like that when you were working a set, you always ... you always looked away.

Those eyes, they were so like—something, a memory or a dream of a memory. Batera shook his head to try to clear it, but the connection wouldn't come. Eyes. What the hell did they remind him of? No matter how hard he tried, he couldn't quite recall.

Now there was Carlos's dog, he was running around in all the blood on the deck, he was worrying one of the porpoise, snapping at it. A crewman, Roderigo it looked like, pointed and laughed.

Manoel was walking toward the camera; his bulky frame filled the picture, and the tape ended.

Batera watched the static for a while, then he switched off the TV and poured himself another drink. He turned off all the lights in the cabin but one, and he sat in his leather chair and he drank his Scotch and he thought.

Ch*Tril approached the huge gray Source with the utmost respect, mindful not merely of its exalted mental state, but also of its massive and unimaginably powerful bulk. She observed its every movement, each random flex of its gigantic musculature, with highly focused interest; the slightest inadvertent or unexpected twitch of those enormous flukes could crush the life from her in an instant.

The danger was real, Ch*Tril knew, because the Sources were largely heedless of their immediate environment. Instead, they were almost always occupied with the infinite workings of the great Source-Mind that linked them all from one sea to the next, across the watery expanses of the entire globe. The Sources had long ago ceased to exist as individuals in most ways; their feeding and mating and migrating were done on a semi-automatic level, as far beneath the concerns or even the awareness of that vast shared mind as were the moment-to-moment details of the circulation of their blood.

Tr*Til and Nk\Jin hovered some distance away, well within scanning range but safe from accidental injury by the Sources. Ch*Tril scanned to check on them, and saw with relief that they were swimming in a tight keep-warm formation, never straying more than a beak-to-fluke or two from the spot where she had left them. Even the flighty Tr*Til had been sobered by the nearly disastrous incident of being trapped beneath the sheet of white hard-water.

Ch*Tril turned her attention back to the Source she had selected, a female with two young ones in tow, each of them already several times as large as Ch*Tril herself. Intellectually, she knew that it made no difference which of the adult Sources she chose for the Melding; they were all equally a part of the ocean-spanning Source-Mind. Still, Ch*Tril had her own methods of operating, and over time she had come to feel that certain nonrational factors seemed to facilitate the Melding, for her at least.

The Source was coming up for a breath now, water streaming in torrents from its colossal head as it lifted above the surface. Ch*Tril moved back a ways, alert to the currents created by the enormous creature's movements. It spouted, the misty spume rising ten beak-to-flukes above the surface and then curving to fall back in a fine spray near where Ch*Tril had temporarily retreated.

Its voluminous breath completed, the Source dove, though not so deep that Ch*Tril would have trouble following. She wouldn't need to be in direct physical contact with the immense female, anyway, just close enough so that her own relatively weak Link-Talent could enable her to Meld with the Source-Mind, as represented through this single Source.

Her mother's father had been the first to recognize in her the ability that he had also possessed. Tx\Vir, his signature had been, a name revered still among her kind as one of the finest Master Imagers of the old tales. He had nurtured her Link-Talent from the start, had taught her and encouraged her and ultimately had sponsored her for full membership in the ranks of the Melders.

Ch*Tril's use of the Talent had taken a different turning from his own, but his pride in her had remained undiminished to the time of his death. Tx\Vir's gift had been in the finding and reproduction of fantastic-tales, those groupings of images that represented imagined scenes and events. The creation of these stories was an almost lost art now, but multitudes of such ancient tales were stored in the deepest reaches of the Source-Mind, and Tx\Vir had been one of the most adroit at seeking them out and re-imaging them in his own special fashion.

(Ch*Tril often thought that Dj\Tal held that rare ability to create wholly new fantastic tales, as witness the strange images of land-scenes he had begun to share with her when they first met in the lagoon of the Sources; but he refused to make public use of his apparent gift, and had cautioned her to make no outside mention of such things.)

Ch*Tril's skills and interests had proved somewhat more prosaic, more utilitarian than those of Tx\Vir. Her Link-Talent seemed always to lead her to Meldings that traced the actual doings, the catastrophes and the triumphs of her kind over the course of many thousands of cold-to-cold cycles.

It had been she, in fact, who had uncovered and revealed the realities behind the myth of the Ending of the Lk\Jal-Vn*Kir School. Prior to her discoveries, it was assumed that the bizarre accounts of a fiery disaster from the sky had been fantastic-tales of the sort her mother's father could image so well; but her findings had been so precise as to the long-ago date and location of the event that a scanning expedition had been dispatched to the region. They had found, scattered across the seabed, the broken remains of a large scarred rock that had apparently entered the water from above, at an amazing rate of speed. Any life within a wide radius of its impact would have been extinguished instantaneously. Ch*Tril's work had shown the old myth to be true, after all.

Now she had been entrusted with an equally daunting, and even more intriguing, task. Qr*Jil, the Old One of her School, had ordered her to research the earliest stored records of contact between their kind and the land-walkers that were sometimes glimpsed along the shore, or atop their odd floating hulls.

The prospect of this search excited Ch*Tril, for she had long felt a great curiosity about those peculiar nonswimming creatures with their flailing limbs and their strange conveyances and devices. She had never dared approach any of them, although that was permitted within certain rigid restrictions; her pod-sister Ch*Stri had once swum several times around one of their hulls that had come to rest on the surface, and had even played some rudimentary games with three of the land-walkers who had been splashing awkwardly about in the water. Contact beyond that level, though, even discussion of such contact, was a taboo so firm that Ch*Tril and her friends had seldom even thought to question the reason for it.

Oh, there had been some secret imaging when she was a young one, fanciful scenes that never appeared in the well-repeated tales of Tx\Vir and the other Master Imagers: sequences that pretended to show members of her kind who had once had regular contact with the land-walkers, who had even shared unspecified areas of learning with the semi-furry creatures. Ch*Tril supposed all young ones probably passed such absurd depictions back and forth before they were old enough to know better. The land-walkers couldn't image, could they? And if any of them had the Link-Talent, surely that would have been common knowledge by now.

No, the only reason for the taboo on extended contact with them must be that the land-walkers could be either friendly or dangerous by turn, and since those poor creatures were unable to communicate, there was never any way to know which response to expect. The safe course was simply to stay away from them, as with the Danger-Cousins, and Ch*Tril couldn't imagine any adult being foolhardy

enough to disobey that stricture on an ongoing basis. Not even
Tr*Til!

So why, then, had Qr*Jil suddenly decided that information on
the history of such unwise contact was needed? The question was
not properly Ch*Tril's to ask, but it was difficult to restrain herself
from wondering.

She maneuvered herself into the Melding position that she fa-
vored, just above and to the right of the Source's massive head. The
two young ones were out of sight behind her in this arrangement,
but she knew she had nothing to fear from them despite their own
large size; they would exactly mimic every motion of their mother,
so Ch*Tril need monitor the movements only of the one adult
Source.

She proceeded to shut down most of the conscious areas of her
mind and give them over to the Link-Talent, excepting only mini-
mal scanning and the swim-breathe functions. The sensation was not
one of an outward-reaching toward the Source, but of an inwardly
directed ... *wave,* it seemed to be, a liquid surge of something
familiar yet still strange within her, moving swiftly toward the
central spot where there would be

>Acceptance<

pure and unadorned, within her yet outside her, contained and
containing. Unlike her occasional private Links with Dj\Tal, the
Melding carried with it no undertones of affection or communication
or anything whatsoever except that simple, bare

>Acceptance<

dispassionately informing her that she had gained access to the
limitless reaches of the Source-Mind.

No matter how many times she Melded, Ch*Tril would never
cease to be quietly astonished, not merely by the infinite complexity
of the Source-Mind, but also by its extreme orderliness. It seemed
as if the whole of that unfathomable vastness was overlaid with a
clearly defined structure of some sort, a guide—not seen or scanned,

but somehow *there*—to any area that she might wish to reach. She had often pondered whether the Source-Mind was in fact so perfectly categorized, or if that was no more than a helpful illusion to enable her own small mind to maneuver meaningfully within it. Most probably, the Source-Mind existed within itself on a plane surpassing all her petty notions of design or classification.

She selected an area that defined itself as "land," and as her mind effortlessly entered that region she sensed the unfolding of thousands more categories, each related to the concept of "land." She took her mind into the subset that called itself "land-walkers," and from there to "contact," and at last into the one referring to her own kind.

The landscape of choices had narrowed now to a single, long continuum that Ch*Tril knew represented "time." She focused on a segment some distance back from the moving end-point that was the present, made one final selection from a great virtual sphere which delineated all the regions of all the seas, and—

As explicitly as if she were there, or as if a Master Imager were sending it to her, a scene appeared: a small School of her kind, perhaps a hundred strong, swimming through a calm, clear sea. Seventy or eighty beak-to-flukes away was a stretch of land, the low sort but with high peaks in the distance behind the waterline, and lush, green growing things in tremendous abundance. Not far ahead, a large group of good-eating-fish was being corralled by the School, but none of its members were splitting off to flank the other side. Instead, they were herding the fish toward the land, toward . . . hulls, with land-walkers atop them, coming closer and closer.

Just as it seemed a collision was imminent, the land-walkers tossed out a number of flexible web-things, each of which was like hundreds of strands of seaweed strung together to form patterns of squares. The School with which Ch*Tril seemed to be swimming veered away, and the land-walkers pulled the web-things, now full of fish, onto their hulls. The two groups had been cooperating, Ch*Tril realized; her own kind had purposely driven those fish straight toward the hulls, so the land-walkers could capture them.

She watched the School repeat the maneuver several times, pausing between each herding to feed on the leftover fish that had been trapped between their own numbers and the hulls. The strategy, it seemed, was mutually beneficial.

When Ch*Tril had tired of watching the shared herding, she withdrew her mind from the scene and chose another segment of the time-line at random. It might take a while, but she wanted to get a general feeling for her search, establish a flow or pattern of some sort.

The next scene was of a violent sea, no land in sight; harsh sheets of falling water drops beat down on the sensitive skins of a pair of her kind, swimming alone away from their School. Each breath brought them to a surface that was turbulent with white-topped swells, rising and breaking with great force. The male of the pair turned to look behind him; Ch*Tril could see another of the land-walkers' hulls back there, tossing wildly on the huge waves.

The male of the pair dove and swam back toward the hull, surfacing at its side and then turning to leap forward again, once, twice, a third time. The land-walkers atop it were covered with shiny yellow things, and they were gesticulating with their forelimbs, aiming them at the male; they had seen him, they were somehow making the hull turn to follow him.

Ch*Tril tracked the scene for some time, watching the male and female take their turns at leading the land-walkers on a steady course through the worsening seas; then at last the wind and the waters began to die down, and the pair was entering a tranquil bay with the white-finned hull coming safely along behind them.

She pulled her attention away from that sequence and chose one from a more recent point along the continuum. This time only one of her kind was in the scene, again swimming out of sight of land, but in peaceful seas. There was a small hull ahead, at rest on the surface, and two land-walkers with no coverings were trying to move around in the water, their limbs churning with a pitiable lack of grace. No, Ch*Tril saw, there were three of them, and one was only half the size of the other two.

The male of her kind swam nearer the hull, right up to the side of it; Ch*Tril could see the odd little protruding features on the front and sides of the young land-walker's head, could see its eyes growing wider, could—

>Non-Acceptance<

The scene cut off abruptly, going to total blankness. Ch*Tril was perplexed; she had never before had such a thing happen during a Melding. She moved to pick up the scene anew where it had broken off, but—

>Non-Acceptance<

It was refusing her. The Source-Mind was denying her access. She tried once more, to no avail. Ch*Tril didn't know whether to be angry or simply amazed; the Source-Mind, that unending and eternally open fount of knowledge and history and myth, was hiding something from her.

Ch*Tril gave up, selected another point, and allowed herself to enter its own flawlessly preserved reality.

She and three others were in a shallow, warm sea; there were land-walkers coming toward them, moving from the nearby shore through the green water on their lower limbs. Their sun-darkened skins were bare, but Ch*Tril could see others of their kind on the rocky land, watching, and those were wrapped in long, loose robes of translucent white.

The ones in the water were still coming this way, she could see their close-set eyes and the long, black strands that flowed in waves from the tops of their heads. All of them were females, she scanned; one was holding its forelimbs out and moving its flat little mouth, she could hear—

>Non-Acceptance<

The image ended, giving way to silent blackness, just as had happened the last time.

Bleak frustration began to overtake Ch*Tril. She had never before been unable to complete a Melding; how would she possibly explain her failure to the Old One, and to Dj\Tal?

Dj\Tal. A hint of a memory hovered at the edge of her partially disenabled consciousness; careful not to break the Melding, she reactivated that one small portion. It was the strange thought-pattern Dj\Tal had Linked to her before she'd left, the intricate arrangement of interlocking circles. He'd told her she might need it.…

She Linked the pattern to the Source-Mind, and—

The land-walkers were back, balancing themselves upright on their lower limbs directly in front of her. The one in the lead was making low-pitched sounds with its mouth, and looking straight at her, close enough that the spindly appendages at the ends of its forelimbs were almost touching her. The noises it made were unintelligible, and yet she could somehow understand it, was conscious of greetings and polite reminiscences of earlier meetings being passed back and forth between her and the ungainly, brown-skinned creature.

It was Linking to her!

Or rather, Ch*Tril corrected herself, it was Linking to the female of her kind whose long-ago reality she temporarily inhabited, through the auspices of the Source-Mind.

The land-walker was discussing fantastic, barely comprehensible things with her, and she—or her "host"—was responding in kind. Surreal concepts, having to do with land-walker activities, and modes of thought, and physical structures … like that large structure she could see on the nearby rocks that jutted out into the sea, its top perfectly rounded, the whole of it surrounded by smooth, white columns.

Ch*Tril struggled to understand the rapid communication taking place between the land-walker female and the one of her own kind. They were obviously familiar with each other, had Linked many times before; Ch*Tril could piece together only a portion of what they were sending back and forth, images and ideas here and there that fell into some kind of rough context.

There was something important about that structure she could see on the land; it had to do directly with this encounter and others before it. There were rituals involved, and mutual learning ... a sense of beneficence, of growth, hung over every aspect of this Linking.

Some of the concepts related to the sounds the land-walker was making, Ch*Tril realized; it seemed to be reinforcing its Link-Talent by mouthing certain of its thoughts aloud. It wasn't imaging, the growls it issued forth were far too primitive for that; but each separate utterance apparently carried a specific meaning. They were symbols, of a sort, and Ch*Tril listened attentively to them, trying to figure out how they correlated with the segments of the Link:

"Awr-uh-kuhl" she heard, and "Ah-pahl-oh," and "Del-Fi" ... that last one seemed to be connected with the growls the land-walker used when referring to Ch*Tril's kind, but it was also rife with mythic, even religious, connotations. Ch*Tril could sense that the sounds were also somehow related to simple, but incomprehensible, visual symbols in the land-walker's mind: μαντεῖον, Ἀπόλλων, Δελ Φός ...

The thoughts that the female of Ch*Tril's kind was Linking in return were even more confusing, and they went by at a pace Ch*Tril found difficult to follow. She caught random snatches of the surging flow, things about social organization and ruling bodies and moral concepts, all of it conveyed with the utmost seriousness of purpose.

And then it struck her. The female wasn't merely conversing with the land-walker; she was acting as a conduit for the Source-Mind. These were Directives, vaguely similar to the governing precepts that had so long guided the lives and the social order of Ch*Tril's own kind, yet adapted to the needs of land-based, object-manipulating creatures.

Here in this meticulously recorded moment, a vision of a time thousands of cold-to-colds ago, the Source-Mind was instructing the land-walkers ... was molding them even, for its own reasons and to its own unfathomable ends.

6

The wind was up, and a thick line of dark clouds scudded across the horizon, headed out to sea it looked like. As long as the wind didn't change.

Antonio Batera held the wheel steady, maneuvering the *Sea Master* into the swells, riding the watery hillocks as they came and went, came and went. A fine spray fanned across the forward window of the bridge as the boat bottomed out in each trough, and it trickled down off the glass as the craft rose upon each crest.

The radio crackled: "Hey, Toninho, you on this side?"

Batera grabbed the mike for the VHF in his left hand and keyed it to transmit.

"Yah, I got you, 'Nando."

Fernando Guimares was skipper of the *Diego Queen,* one of the eight other tuna seiners that were either owned or managed by the same exporter Antonio had signed up with a few years back. The nine boats belonged to their own "code group," which meant they'd share information about weather and fishing conditions, up to a point.

"—up here, so I don' know."

"Say, you broke up on me there, 'Nando, come back."

"I said we got some pretty good whitecaps here, maybe workable, maybe not."

"Anything to work?" Batera asked.

"7564 last few miles, 8795 this area. How 'bout you?"

The information might or might not be reliable. It was bad form to mislead your fellow code-group members, and the company would get on your case for it if they found out, but they were still more or less in competition with each other for the best and earliest catches. 7564, Batera knew, meant "nothing sighted," and 8795 meant "lots more of nothing."

"What course you keeping?" Batera asked.

Fernando read him off the latitude and longitude numbers; they put the *Diego Queen* about twelve miles northwest of the *Sea Master,* moving on a roughly parallel westward course.

"—for you?" the voice from the radio sputtered.

"Come back, 'Nando, come back."

"I say, what kinda seas you got?"

"Right heavy swells, no good to work and 7564."

"Hope you come on out of that, Toninho. Talk at you later."

Batera put the microphone back on its hook and took the wheel with both hands again, guiding the boat through the tossing waters with an easy, practiced touch.

"What's the word on up ahead?" came a voice from behind him.

Batera didn't bother to turn around; he knew the mate's voice as well as he knew the sound of his boat's engines. "Could get rougher. Could clear up. Same as always, down here."

"You want I should take it for a while? You maybe go for some *café?*"

Batera maneuvered the big boat downward into another oncoming blue valley, and watched as the view through the window became rippled and distorted with the fuming sea, then cleared again as they scaled the other side.

"Yah, maybe for a bit. Thanks."

Manoel moved ably into place, taking his position at the wheel in a smooth, almost delicate transition that belied the man's hulking size. He steered the boat expertly into the next wave trough as Batera made his way back toward the galley.

Even from the hallway, it was evident that Vinicius had just put a new pot on, and none of your commercial stuff, either; Batera liked his coffee brewed from fresh-ground beans that the cook selected personally in the *mercados* of Panama or Colombia, where they sometimes put in for repairs or supplies.

"*Olá,* Skipper! I figured you about due for a refill. Here, gimme that mug, I get you a fresh one."

Batera handed over the mug he'd been drinking from since early morning. Vinicius set it aside to be washed later, when the seas had calmed down, and took a duplicate from the cabinet above the big oven.

"What you think, Skipper, you think our luck turned?"

Batera gave a noncommittal grunt.

"I mean, after that big set the other day," the cook went on, carefully pouring the steaming coffee from the pot into the non-spill mug, "maybe we not due any more for a while. You think?"

The skipper shrugged. "I don't know, Vinicius. Things always go different, you know? Never can tell. How about a drop of honey in there, O.K.?"

"You got a cold?" Vinicius asked solicitously. "Sore throat?"

"Nah, I'm well. Just want it sweet this time."

The cook added a dollop of wild-clover honey to the coffee and reclosed the sip-through lid. "You want a sweet roll? Coffee cake, Danish?"

"This'll do me," Batera said, taking the mug. "What's for dinner tonight?"

"Rack of lamb, or *frango com piri piri.*"

Batera smiled, for the first time that day. His mouth had already begun to water in anticipation of the Portuguese-style grilled chicken marinated in a sauce of olive oil, garlic, and hot *piri piri* peppers. "I won't be late," he told Vinicius, and headed back for the bridge.

Manoel obviously had the boat well under control, so Batera hung back and sipped his coffee. He put on his glasses to compare the compass readings with their position on the chart, then reviewed the latest changes in the numbers for the code group. When he'd finished the coffee he looked up to see that the swells had begun to subside.

"Lookin' better, Skipper," Manoel said.

"Yah, a bit."

"We could cut south southwest a ways, and—"

The mate's suggestion was interrupted by a shout from the man in the crow's nest:

"Porpoise to starboard, two o'clock! Three mile, maybe three and a half!"

Manoel and Batera both turned to look out the side window to their right, but from the height of the bridge they could see nothing but the rolling sea.

"You want to take over, Skipper?"

"Not yet. Just hold your course."

The boat cut on through the water, its rises and falls less dramatic now than they had been only minutes before. A prismatic shaft of sunlight was breaking through the tumbled clouds off to the north.

"Porpoise at three o'clock!" came the call from the crow's nest. "Two mile!"

Antonio looked out the side window again, and there they were: a thousand or more of them, leaping in pairs and groups as they sped on a course that would soon converge with that of the *Sea Master*.

The door to the bridge flew open, and Paulinho, the head of the speedboat crew, burst in. "Ho, Skipper, *muitos toninhas!*" he exclaimed with a huge grin. "So many yellowfin gonna be under that bunch, we be home next week, hey?"

Batera stared out at the massive school, its wide path edging ever closer to the direction the boat was headed.

Paulinho couldn't stay still; he was rocking eagerly back and forth from one foot to the other. "I get the boats ready, O.K.? An' tell the net crew to hit the winch, *sim?*"

The skipper looked at his crewman, and said nothing. He turned his face back to the window, where individual dolphins could now be plainly distinguished among the larger school.

"Hard aport, Manoel," he said.

The mate turned his head and frowned, the wrinkles expanding across his broad forehead. "You say *port*, Skipper?"

"That's what I said."

Paulinho opened his mouth to say something, then seemed to think better of it. He stood there in silence, rocking on his heels, waiting to see what was happening and why.

"All we got to do is stay the course," Manoel said. "Don't even have to turn; the porpoise they gonna meet us."

Batera looked down at his charts. "I don't like the weather," he muttered.

"Weather's not so bad now," Manoel insisted. "Not so bad at all; we made sets in way worse seas than this."

"I told you to take her hard aport," Batera said with a sharp edge to his voice.

"Skipper, we do that we gonna miss out on a—"

"Can you do what I tell you to do? Or do I have to take the fuckin' wheel myself?"

Manoel shot him a look, then turned his thick-jowled face back toward the front of the boat and the steadily lessening swells. "I got the fuckin' wheel. Skipper."

"Then take her hard aport."

The mate angrily spun the wheel to the left, and the heavy boat came about in that direction, cutting sideways across the oncoming current and moving away from the converging school of dolphins.

The radio came to life again, Fernando's voice coming through a blur of static. "Hey, Toninho, you still back there?"

Batera keyed the microphone. "Yah, 'Nando. I'm takin' us south-west, see if it clears up any faster down that way."

"I got you on that. Lemme know, will ya?"

"Will do."

"How's everything your way otherwise?"

"8795," Batera told him, "8795 all the way."

Paulinho, the speedboat driver, backed silently out of the doorway, frowning with disbelief. First the skipper had turned away from what would have been a damn good set, and now he'd lied to one of the other code-group skippers about it. It was almost like he didn't want *anybody* to make that set.

When the crewman was gone, Manoel turned to Batera, his eyes full of fury. "You shouldn't oughta done that," he said. "Shoulda give another man a chance at least."

Batera returned the mate's gaze, his face without expression. "You just drive the boat for a while, Manoel. You leave the decisions up to me."

Behind them, well beyond the *Sea Master*'s spreading wake, the dolphin school moved on, unharmed, unhindered.

Tk\Lin scanned the land-walkers waiting for him near the waterline of the small-quiet-sea. Most of those splashing about in the shallow water were again the young ones, he noted as he sped toward them. Some made touchingly awkward attempts to swim along the surface, managing at least to keep their front-mounted blowholes generally free of the water. They propelled themselves in slow, ungainly circles with their four spindly appendages, the water around them frothing with their efforts. Others made no pretense of trying to move naturally through the water; they remained upright, moving laboriously through the shallows, supported on the sea floor by the stubby, flat proto-flukes at the ends of their lower limbs.

When he was a hundred beak-to-flukes from the expectant gathering, Tk\Lin leaped twice to announce his arrival, then slowed his approach so as not to frighten the smaller of the young ones. The long adult female, the one with the smooth-strange things that made false images, was here again, too, he scanned, as was the even longer adult male who had joined her the last time.

Both of them were Receptives. Both! When he'd been given this assignment, Tk\Lin had estimated the chances were perhaps one-in-forty that his recurring presence here might attract one of the rare land-walker Receptives. Instead, his visits had drawn a pair of them. He'd immediately relayed this news, and now the original plan for individual Preparatory Contact was in abeyance while the Old One of Tk\Lin's School pondered the import of this unexpected circumstance.

Was it mere coincidence that the two who'd come were of opposite sexes, Tk\Lin wondered, or might they be planning to mate for his edification? That would be extremely interesting; he had never seen land-walkers mating, and marveled that they never seemed to do so. The existence of so many young ones, though, obviously meant the adults must couple at least occasionally. They were fairly well-constructed for it, with the males' penises permanently extruded; but Tk\Lin had seldom seen a male make himself erect, and it seemed that all those flailing limbs would make a graceful mating difficult at best.

Perhaps it was their custom to mate only on the land, though that made little sense when the rippling, erotic buoyancy of the shallow sea was so readily available to them. Then, too, there was the matter of the way in which they all, males and females alike, encased their genitals in tight wraps of various multihued but unnatural materials. What could be the purpose of that? The practice only further inhibited mating, and impeded the wonderfully sensuous caress of water against those most sensitive areas. There could be no pleasure in such constriction. The females even wrapped their mammaries, making it impossible for the young ones to nurse!

With some disappointment, Tk\Lin put the hope of a land-walker mating display from his mind. He gave the long female a brief Touch, then turned his attention to the young ones. They swarmed around him, reaching out to touch him with the squirmy little growths that sprouted from the ends of their upper appendages. He allowed the contact, even enjoyed it when they stroked him gently; but he remained alert, because each of those wriggling growths was tipped with something hard and sharp, like miniature crawler-claws. He'd received a few painful scrapes on his delicate skin during the first few of these encounters, but the young ones seemed more careful now, and usually only touched him with the soft pads beneath their claws.

One young female, smaller than the others, was standing hesitantly aside from the boisterous group that had rushed to meet and touch him. Tk\Lin scanned her internally and saw that her heart was racing, the muscles around her stomach were tight. An adult male was urging her forward in the water, but she held back, clearly afraid.

Tk\Lin peeled away from the crowd of fearless young ones around him and made his way slowly, ever so slowly, toward the trembling little female. He stopped two beak-to-flukes from her and raised his head above the surface, swaying it to and fro in a gentle rhythm timed to mimic the normal land-walker heartbeat. The young one watched, entranced, but still she clung to the lower limbs of the long male behind her.

Two of the bigger young ones came splashing toward Tk\Lin, eager for more active play, but he warned them away with a slight *thwap!* of his flukes against the water. They retreated, and Tk\Lin turned his attention once more to the frightened little female. Keeping his distance from her, he rolled methodically from one side to the other, showing her his dorsal, his pectoral fins, his soft white belly. She watched in silence, her eyes round.

One of the many-colored spherical things filled with air that the young ones often tossed to Tk\Lin was floating nearby. He nudged it with his beak, and it rolled across the placid surface to the young female. She reflexively let go of the adult's limbs and caught it between her own upper appendages. She stared at the toy for a moment, then at Tk\Lin, and gave the weightless sphere a push back in his direction. He chittered his approval and bounced it back toward her, a little harder this time.

The young one's face contorted, her mouth curling upward at the sides in the land-walker gesture that Tk\Lin had learned to recognize as indicative of amusement or contentment. She slapped the toy back again, through the air above the surface; her aim was off, but Tk\Lin easily darted to meet it and toss it back to her. The young one squealed and tossed the brightly colored sphere again and again, ignoring the adult behind her. Her muscles were relaxed now, Tk\Lin scanned, her heartbeat steady and normal. Soon she had joined the others in a wide circle around him, taking her part in a vigorous game of toss-catch-toss, with Tk\Lin lobbing the air-toy to a different young one each turn.

After a time the young land-walkers began to tire, and Tk\Lin saw that the long adult female and her male companion were still patiently waiting a bit farther out in the water. He ended the game by giving the sphere a powerful slap of his flukes, sending it soaring all the way to shore, and then he swam to join the long ones.

The female stroked his side as he came to her in the shallow water; the male held back, but Tk\Lin could scan no signs of fear in his abdomen. The land-walkers' mouths worked, and they made sounds at each other and at him. He supposed they must be primitive greetings of a sort, but the frequency of the sounds these beings made was so low that they could scarcely contain much useful information. Certainly the land-walkers were incapable of imaging, although the female had been making serious efforts in that direction with the help of the smooth-strange objects she always carried. Such attempts were unique, and had further complicated the plans for this encounter.

Even now, the female was touching and turning the little round and square parts of her black smooth-strange objects. She lowered one of them into the water; it hissed for a moment, and then it imaged. A fuzzy, somewhat indistinct image, to be sure, as if from very far away; but it was definitely recognizable as an image.

Tk\Lin had been astounded the first time she had done this; he had immediately imaged a response, but she had seemed oblivious to its meaning, and the black object had come back with an irrelevant image in return. He had recently taken to responding in the simplest terms possible: echoed images of his own scans of her and the various objects she sometimes showed him. Maybe she'd be able to make sense of those. She was obviously in control of the smooth-strange imaging thing, and could make it work at will; but if she didn't understand the content of the communications, why was she doing this at all? More to the point, *how?*

The images that emanated from the black object were real, yet not real; false, yet genuine. An incomprehensible paradox. They seemed to be coming from one of his own kind, but there was something odd about them, even aside from the fact that they were blurry. Some of the scenes were quite strange: rough white-water seas breaking on large, jagged rocks, for instance, rocks on which dwelt bizarre whiskered creatures that emitted *awrk-awrk* sounds; and land that did not slope gradually from the sea into a low, flat expanse of brown or green, but rose precipitously from the water to great heights above.

Likewise, a number of the symbols that came from the smooth black thing were different from those with which Tk\Lin was familiar. He could grasp the sense of them, from the overall context, but they were not symbols or gestures that he or any of his School— indeed, any School that he had ever encountered—would use. A head-down arch to convey apology, for example; everyone he'd ever known used the half-roll-to-side to indicate that.

Tk\Lin knew a little, of course, about the others of their kind in other seas . . . how the adjoining land, the creatures, the customs were all subtly or dramatically different. It was frequently his task to relay communications that he assumed had originated or would end in far distant seas, but such differences in symbology and experi- ence would usually be smoothed out or translated by the end of the relay.

How, then, could this *land-walker,* of all things, be bringing him direct messages (albeit trivial, even nonsensical) from those mythic reaches? This was most assuredly not part of the plan. The female meant no harm, he was sure; quite the opposite, if anything. But her actions were an anomaly, something the Old One of his School had not prepared him for. This was not how the Preparatory Contact was supposed to take place, not at all.

Regretfully, Tk\Lin wheeled away from the land-walker pair

and headed back out to sea, after giving each of the two a brief Touch. He must confer again with the Old One, who he hoped had by now decided how—indeed, whether—they should proceed with Contact.

The drilling had started well, as silent and as smooth as Jeb remembered from his one previous experience with the new laser equipment. Quieter even; in Saudi, all the paraphernalia of the apparatus—cables, switching devices, focusing coils, refrigeration units—had been aboveground, operated hands-on by his tower-of-Babel mixed-nationality crew (American, Spanish, Pakistani, German . . . anything but Saudis, who tended to consider actual work, of any sort, beneath them). Here, all the heavy stuff was underwater, much of it 250 feet down on the sea floor itself, and the control mechanisms were soundless electronic remotes.

The place where Jeb was to oversee the drilling looked like a miniature version of NASA's JPL operations center, from which the world had received those astounding close-up views of Saturn's rings, of Jupiter and its volcanic moons, back in the '80s. Someone at PetroGlobe with a taste for science fiction had dubbed it the "command module," and the 15 × 20-foot room was actually a one-piece prefab unit of molded fiberglass, freshly painted computer-beige and hoisted intact onto an open area of the ship's aft deck.

Inside the windowless, UFO-shaped compartment (yet another SF touch; Jeb had begun to suspect that some tech designer's sense of humor was at work here), there were seating positions for four people, including one centrally placed swivel chair from which Jeb could observe the various screens and readouts at each of the other three workstations. The contoured white desk in front of his seat was also fitted with a full set of override controls, allowing him to take over any function of the operation in an instant if necessary; indeed, if he were a glutton for work overload, or merely insane, he could run the entire process himself from that one station.

The laser drill itself was contained in its own submersible component, entirely separate from the ship and the command module aside from a tow line. All commands to the unmanned drilling unit and its accompanying robot mini-sub were issued by radio, again just as with the JPL center and its Pioneer or Voyager spacecraft; except that here, the mechanized probes exploring an alien world were only a few hundred feet away, rather than tens of millions of miles.

As exciting as the laser drilling equipment was—the technology behind it still new and relatively untried—Jeb found himself equally fascinated by the mini-sub. The drill was extraordinarily fast, and quiet, but the task it performed was still essentially the same as that of the old, mundane mechanical drills: boring a hole in the earth, straight down to—it was hoped—a pocket full of petroleum. Once the shaft had been started, there was little to do but monitor its progress, and less to see other than the effluvia spewed up by the drilling device.

The nose-mounted cameras of the mini-sub, by contrast, provided dramatic visual relief from the monotony of the drill, an ever-changing view of the turbulent events beneath the nearby waves. On the color monitors before him, Jeb could see the laser-molten rock as it oozed from the bore hole, the orange-hot liquid earth bringing the seawater to an instant, violent boil.

At the surface, some quarter of a thousand feet above, this tumultuous meeting gave birth to great billowing clouds of steam rising hundreds of feet higher still. The image was awe-inspiring from the decks of the *Alicia Faye,* a few hundred yards west of the actual drilling site, and was undoubtedly quite a sight even from the slopes and beaches of the town, four miles away.

PetroGlobe's P.R. department had gone into high gear to explain away this highly visible phenomenon, as Jeb had seen on the local newscasts: The steam was supposedly a byproduct of a new process the company was testing to harness the potential of geothermal energy, as simulated by an underwater laser. God forbid the environmentalists should find out that the laser was instead being used as a more efficient way to tap into the offshore petroleum reserves;

there were already protests against what the public believed to be merely a resumption of ordinary exploratory drilling.

There was nothing environmentally incorrect about the majestic white plumes of steam themselves, of course; depending on the heat of the day, they would either dissipate to nothingness or coalesce and blossom into true clouds, gathering still more moisture as they rode the currents of the wind until their wet and heavy burden became too much for them, until at some distant point—over Idaho, perhaps, or Nebraska—the troubled molecules of water that had begun their journey in a burst of submerged and superheated ferocity would fall to earth and begin the long, arduous cycles of trickle and flow that would ultimately lead them back to the seas from which they'd come.

On the sea floor, however, the molten rock from the depths of the burnhole remained, leaden and thick, freezing in place like the syrupy whorls of some monstrous hot-fudge sundae. This is where the mini-subs truly came into play, not as mere passive observers/recorders of the undersea spectacle, but as active participants in it, a means by which to reignite and prolong the colorful display.

Which was not to say the devices were being put to frivolous use, Jeb hastily reminded himself, not in the least; the fact that their intended purpose here happened to result in an eminently watchable ongoing show more impressive than the best Hollywood special effects was no more than a fortuitous accident, an odd little fringe benefit that helped distract him from the essential boredom of so much of the rest of the job.

The laser drill was clean, quiet, safe, and easy to operate; those were both its benefits and its drawbacks. For good or for ill, Jeb had spent his professional life growing accustomed to the eardrum-shattering whine of steel drill bits, the hoarse shouts of workers against the incessant metallic pounding of tons of filthy, potentially deadly machinery. Even the offshore rigs had been dirty, deafening places outside their air-conditioned, soundproofed living quarters and control rooms. Jeb had learned to love that noise, learned to depend on it and to gauge the state of an operation by the various nuances of its attendant cacophony; here there was only silence, the low hum of the module's ventilation system accompanied by nothing louder than the soft clicks of keyboards and solenoids, the ebb and flow of quiet, orderly conversation.

"Left thirty degrees, up fifteen," Jeb said, and watched the scene on the monitors change at his command. There was no pretense at nautical language here, no mention of "aft" or "starboard" or the like; despite the fact that they were on board a ship, despite the quintessentially aquatic spectacle being relayed from the mini-sub, the crew considered the sea itself all but irrelevant to the task at hand. Indeed, the two-hundred-some feet of water beneath them could be thought of as no more than an annoyance, a minor impediment to the business of getting to the sandy bottom of it and burning a hole there that would descend far deeper into the earth's crust than the puny relative depth of that troublesome film of water on which the ship floated.

The image on the screens shifted gradually from the bubbling column of superheated water, fresh from its encounter with the uprising molten rock, to a great mound of that liquid rock itself, cooling and hardening as it piled upon itself, layer after layer.

Was that how he had coped with the varied pressures of his peripatetic career? Jeb wondered. Hardening himself in stages, taking on difficulty after difficulty and turning the very problems themselves into a sort of carapace against the ones yet to come ... while Lindy shrank and withered beneath the strain of it all, hating their life together/apart, resenting it and him all the way until the horror of that dusty, reeking square in Riyadh. . . .

Jesus, he thought, blinking away the memory, *enough*. It happened, it drove her away from him, there was no changing any of that. So why the fuck did every random thought, every image, still somehow bring him back to it, as if it had happened this morning, not six months ago?

"Steady in place," he ordered. "Twenty-degree sweep."

On the monitor, twin beams of deep, fiery orange shot from the nose of the robot sub and began to remelt the cooling mass of rock, spreading it across the sea floor like candle wax, dissipating it, and in the process creating another boiling column of bubbles rushing upward to become steam, maybe even clouds.

Left alone, the layers of molten rock would pile higher and higher still toward the surface, an artificial geological feature that could have unpredictable effects on the undersea ecology of the region. If they let the stuff pile up high enough, it could eventually even become a hazard to shipping. Hell, Jeb thought, smiling, if they drilled for a year or two and never melted away the debris, they could build themselves a goddamned island!

Sheila smiled with amused understanding as Daniel recounted yet again his story of the dolphin teaching him to play fetch. Several of the other patrons of the antebellum-style restaurant back on the mainland cast odd glances in their direction as he mimicked the dolphin's actions, but Sheila ignored them and Daniel either didn't notice or didn't care.

His attractively angular face had undergone something of a transformation since that initial session with the dolphin. When Sheila had first met him on the beach, there'd been something guarded, almost hollow, about those deep-set eyes of his; now they shone with an undisguised boyish enthusiasm. She rather liked the change, she decided.

"Amazing," Daniel concluded, "just absolutely amazing. Do they still make you feel that way? After all the time you've worked with them?"

"Sometimes," she admitted. "They're such fabulous creatures, such *individuals,* it'd be hard ever to take them for granted." She broke off a piece of a sweet corn muffin and began to spread it with pepper jelly.

"How did you ever get involved with all this, anyway?" he asked. "Did you grow up around the ocean?"

Sheila laughed. "Hardly. New Mexico, just outside Santa Fe." The dry, unending emptiness, broken only by the Sangre de Cristo mountains ... like a vast prison, it had seemed to her as a child.

His face showed interest, and she could see he was waiting for her to go on. "My father worked at Los Alamos," she told him. "I got my interest in science from him, but I hated what he did. He took me up there a couple of times, to the nonclassified areas, and I was terrified of the place. They even had a little museum with all these pictures of atomic bombs, and my dad was in a couple of the pictures. It made me sick.

"Anyway, my mom was from Boston—Winthrop, actually, right out in the Harbor—and every time we went on vacation she'd insist we go someplace where she could see the ocean, smell the salt air. So that part I got from her."

"And your interest in dolphins? When did that start?"

—Dark in the water, moving this way fast ...

"Hey, are you O.K.?" Daniel asked with sudden concern, and Sheila realized her bare shoulders were shivering despite the warmth of the Florida night.

"Yes, I'm all right. Just one of those weird ... you know, déjà vu, or whatever. Like when a piece of a dream suddenly pops into your head for no reason."

"A bad dream? Nightmare?"

"It's not important." Sheila had shut the vaguely unsettling errant thought away, and didn't want to risk reviving it. "You were asking ... well, I majored in biology at UCLA, and the guy I was living with brought home a couple of John Lilly's books one day. I started reading those, and ..." she shrugged. "Here I am."

Daniel gave her a wry smile. "And the guy?"

"Long gone. Story of my life; none of the men I've known since then have been able to put up for long with my 'obsession,' as they've been known to call it." The thought of Richard Tarnoff, of the way he'd sabotaged her grant, caused her stomach to turn suddenly sour.

She pushed away her half-eaten meal. "Why don't we have some brandy?" she suggested, averting any further questions.

He signaled for the waiter and ordered them each a Rémy-Martin. "Now it's your turn," Sheila said. "What, exactly, is a Daniel Colter?"

Daniel fished a cigarette from the pack in his shirt pocket, tapped it on the edge of the table, and lit it, holding it so the smoke wouldn't drift toward her. "Raised in North Carolina. English major in college. Worked on a couple of newspapers in the Midwest, then moved to L.A. and went free-lance about six years ago."

Sheila waited expectantly, but he didn't say anything more. "That was concise," she finally said, disappointed. The excitement in his eyes when he'd talked about his encounter with the dolphin had seemed to vanish entirely when she'd inquired about his past. "Tell me more about this story you're working on now," she suggested diplomatically. "I'd be curious to know what you've learned so far."

He took a deep drag of the cigarette. "I've met some people, seen some things."

"What kinds of things?"

Daniel looked away across the garden of the restaurant, toward the little pond surrounded by towering palms and spreading jacarandas. "You wouldn't want to know."

Sheila's temper flared; the man's studied emotional distance had become tiresome, annoying. "Look, I don't know what's bothering you," she said angrily, "but whatever your problem is, you don't have a monopoly on personal troubles. You might just remember that the next time someone's trying to be socially pleasant with you."

He looked surprised at the heat of her retort. "I'm sorry, I didn't mean to—"

"This is my last chance," she said, and she could feel unwanted tears welling up in her eyes. "My grant's been canceled. Do you understand what that means? You sit there doing your 'cynical journalist' pose, and my career, my whole life, are falling out from under me."

"Jesus, I'm sorry to hear that. I had no idea."

Sheila blinked the tears back, suddenly contrite. There'd been no reason for her to jump all over him like that; none of this was his fault.

The fireflies had come out, were winking prettily among the bougainvillea and the oleander. One of them started circling the table, attracted by the glowing end of Daniel's cigarette. He extinguished the butt and the blinking firefly went away.

"You're right," he said apologetically. "I do tend to retreat into my shell. I don't mean to, it's just that . . ."

And he began to tell her, tell her all of it: the slaughter of the dolphins, Creighton falling to his death . . . and then the sick, sad story of his wife, of her betrayal and her murder, and of how the two were inextricably woven into one unfathomable whole in Daniel's mind.

Sometime during the telling, Sheila put her hand over his, and long after the litany of fear and pain and distrust was over, their hands remained entwined, their eyes locked in quiet understanding.

The enormous sheets of white hard-water were far behind them now, and the three travelers no longer needed to huddle close for warmth, or to keep up such exhausting, incessant movement. They could swim at their own pace for the remainder of the return journey, could maintain their own individual spaces except for periodic Touches and sex.

Ch*Tril was grateful for the opportunity to spend some time to herself. She had much to think about.

The secrets she had learned from her Melding with the Source-Mind had left her stunned; even now, her mind still reeled with the enormity of what she had uncovered.

Her own kind and land-walkers—partners once, long ago, in free and open contact with one another. *Linking* to each other, even; two of the oldest, and strongest, taboos broken simultaneously.

And what had been the role of the Source-Mind in all that? She was certain she was right in her perception that it had instigated the contact, had been directing it; but why? Had the Source-Mind truly hoped to shape the development of the land-walkers' primitive society, and if so, to what purpose?

More to the point, why had the contact ceased? Ch*Tril had tried to follow up on that extraordinary scene of the ritualistic meeting between the female land-walkers and the ones of Ch*Tril's kind, but she had again been denied access, and even the key-pattern that Dj\Tal had given her would not open those stored memories.

There were a thousand things she was impatient to ask her mate when they returned to the School; and this time, she vowed, she would not allow him to evade her questions.

She scanned ahead to where Nk\Jin and Tr*Til were swimming and leaping. Tr*Til's wounds from the time she had spent trapped beneath the hard-water were healing well, she saw; she hoped that experience had taught her friend the importance of discipline and caution.

This portion of the route home had always been Ch*Tril's favorite, and now it intrigued her even more, because here there was more evidence of the land-walkers' strange way of life than in any other place she had ever seen. To the right was a group of rocky islands with no sign of land-walker habitation or influence; but to the left was a magical place like something out of the bizarre fantasy images Dj\Tal would sometimes send to her.

The entrance to the place was marked by a tremendous span stretched high above the water, from one outcropping of land to another, a distance of perhaps two thousand beak-to-flukes. The great span was the deep-orange color of a starfish, and it was supported by two straight, tall towers that rose from the sea itself and went through the span and high above it.

What lay beyond the span was even more incredible: dozens more huge towers, one of which came to a sharp point at the top, were packed together on the undulating land; and below the towers ran a long gray ribbon on which large, shiny objects moved at high speed, one after the other. Inside these objects one could sometimes see the heads of land-walkers.

In the water around them were many of the tall-finned hulls on which the land-walkers rode, and other hulls without fins. Some of these were extremely fast, and a few were even larger than one of the Sources. They moved incessantly beneath the massive span, coming and going between the sea and the forest of towers. The swifter ones trailed boiling wakes behind them; Ch*Tril knew from occasional experiments that these could provide an exhilarating ride if approached from the proper angle, but she didn't want to encourage—

The Death-Creature came from her right, its gaping maw already open to devour her. She saw the ridges of its shell-sharp teeth and she dove without thinking, without even taking a breath.

Deep below the surface, her brain crying out for oxygen, she wheeled abruptly to the left and turned to scan behind her: The shark was still coming, unhindered by any need for air. Three times her length and girth, pale as bone, mindless and relentless in its pursuit of meat.

Had the thing already taken Tr*Til and Nk\Jin? No time to scan for them, she could only flee, and she needed air, needed it *now*.

She suddenly doubled back, hoping to take the brute off guard, but its feeble brain was incapable of registering expectation or surprise; all it knew was feeding, constant and inexorable. Ch*Tril sped past it toward the surface, almost brushing the thing's massive jaws as it turned to follow her.

Breaking the surface, Ch*Tril gasped deeply, filling her lungs in an instant, then darted away at peak speed toward the islands silhouetted against the horizon. Almost immediately, the sea darkened and there was a foul taste to the water, a taste that in itself was enough to terrify her.

She was swimming through a cloud of blood.

Ignore it, she told herself, don't think about what it might mean. Swim!

There were rocks not too far ahead, she scanned, and shallows; if she could get there, the Death-Creature might not be able to follow.

All at once it was upon her, its hideous mouth looming no more than six or eight beak-to-flukes away to the left, and closing fast. The sustained burst of speed had exhausted Ch*Tril, had left her with no reserves, no hope of escape. She allowed herself a brief, sad thought of Dj\Tal, and of her son Dv\Kil.

At that moment a streak of gray shot from behind her, straight toward the head of the Death-Creature. It collided with the beast, striking it directly in one of its dull, dead eyes. The big white head jerked upward, rearing above the surface, its mouth still wide and a stream of clear, viscous fluid oozing from the demolished eye.

Tr*Til imaged a quick depiction of diving, and Ch*Tril dove, her lungs still full with what she had thought to be her final breath. Above her, she scanned Tr*Til darting beneath the belly of the thrashing creature, then ramming its remaining eye.

Evading the blinded giant's convulsions, its randomly snapping mouth and flailing tail, Tr*Til dove to join Ch*Tril near the sea floor, with Nk\Jin close on her flukes. Tr*Til imaged a sequence of the Death-Creature biting one of the large awrk-awrks in half; that had been the source of the blood-cloud through which Ch*Tril had swum.

Together, the three of them scanned as first one, then four, then a dozen much smaller Death-Creatures began encircling the monster, nipping at its fins and its belly as they instinctively recognized its helplessness. The great feeder had itself become food, and the sea was black with its vital fluids, was thick with the chunks of flesh and gristle and organs ripped from its dying hulk.

Ch*Tril imaged her profound gratitude to Tr*Til, adding a symbol of high respect; her friend had proved her mettle on this journey, after all.

Taking advantage of the Death-Creatures' preoccupation with devouring the big one that Tr*Til had killed, the little pod of travelers slipped away into the blood-darkened sea and resumed their progress southward; and Ch*Tril's thoughts were soon consumed once more with the multitude of questions she would have for Dj\Tal when this journey was complete.

The great subterranean chamber was filled to bursting with the super-heated molten earth that had welled upward as the oceanic plate had slid and shuddered its ponderous way northward . . . but still the rock walls held, still the dense layers of granite resisted the heat, the pressure, from so far below.

Earth containing earth, one more small battle fought to a draw in the ancient and ongoing war of the planet against itself, its painful and unceasing evolution. A stasis had been achieved, a delicate symmetry between the immovable barrier of the thick, hard crust and the irresistible force of the rising magma, expelled by the expansive power of the planet's furnace core.

Far above, a beam of light burned downward through the upper layers of the crust. Star-hot, unbending and unchallenged, the light burned its steady way toward the newly, and precariously, stable environment of the buried chamber.

7

Sheila sat up abruptly, still half caught in the dream; the same dream, the one she'd been having almost every night for the past two weeks.

She slipped quietly out of bed, careful not to wake the sleeping figure beside her, and pulled on a light cotton robe. The window was open, and the full moon's light inked her shadow sharply across the floor. She drew the flowered curtains closed so the brightness wouldn't disturb Daniel, and then she let herself outside.

The motel consisted of a secluded cluster of efficiency units over-looking a quiet, blue river that meandered westward toward Sanibel Island and the Gulf. The property was more Old South than New Florida, with sprawling oak trees draped in Spanish moss and a tangled carpet of crepe myrtle growing all the way down to the river.

A length of rope was strung across the entrance to the motel's little fishing pier, presumably to keep tipsy late-night revelers from wandering off it into the river. Sheila crawled under the barrier and padded barefoot to the end of the dock, stepping carefully to avoid any splinters or rusty nailheads.

The moon had tinted the languid river silver, and as she sat down at the edge of the pier Sheila saw a fish jump, breaking the flat surface into a spreading series of concentric circles, each carrying with it its own distinct shimmer.

Her recurring dream involved water, too; a great deal of water, and she was immersed in it ... but in the dream she was a child, not an adult. That was one of the odd things about it: Most of her childhood-reminiscence dreams were set among the arid sands and hills surrounding Santa Fe, or along the chilly shores of her grandparents' house on Cape Cod; but in this one the water was bathtub-warm, she could taste the salt on her lips, and from the distance something indefinable was moving toward her, fast. . . .

Sheila shivered and drew the thin robe tighter around her, despite the warmth of the night. So much had happened in so short a time, and being plagued by this eerie dream wasn't making it any easier to sort out all the conflicting emotions she suddenly had to deal with.

Conflicting emotions. Jesus, who the hell was she to complain about that, compared with what Daniel had told her about his wife's death? After four days, her mind still recoiled every time she thought about it. How on earth had he lived through that, let alone retained his sanity?

The dolphin made him laugh though, made him smile; and so, now, did she. They'd both come to Florida looking for something else, and although she might not have had the same success in saving her grant as Daniel had in expanding the story he was writing, at least they'd discovered each other.

And what, exactly, did that mean?

"Mind some company?"

"Oh! God, you startled me. What woke you up? I tried to be as quiet as I could."

"No, no, it wasn't you." Daniel took a seat on the pier, his legs dangling above the water beside hers. The night was warm, and he was wearing a pair of jeans with no shirt. "More the absence of you, if anything. I've gotten used to you being there, these past few nights."

She smiled and fluffed her short dark hair with her fingers. "What time is it, anyway? I didn't look at my watch when I got up."

Daniel shrugged. "Neither did I. I'd guess three, three-thirty. You had trouble sleeping?"

"Just this weird dream that keeps coming back."

He frowned with interest. "You know, I've been bothered by something like that myself, it's really—"

"Nothing to worry about, I know." God, Sheila thought, how could she have been so stupid as to bring that up? His own dreams must be a torment of horror beyond her capacity, or desire, to imagine. "Aren't you chilly?" she asked, eager to change the subject.

Daniel was barefoot, too, as well as shirtless. "No, it's nice out here. Warm."

He took her hand and they stared out at the river together. A palm frond floated by on a slow and random course, the only visible sign that the smooth blue water was moving at all.

"Do you think the dolphin will stay around here long?" Daniel asked.

"There's no telling. This kind of thing has happened before, a dozen or more times over the last forty years; mostly in the past decade. Some of them would spend a few weeks socializing with humans, then disappear; others kept returning for years."

"Why do they do it?"

Sheila laughed and reached out to caress his bare shoulder. "That's the first thing I'd like to ask him, if I ever get the chance."

Daniel grinned sheepishly, pulled a crumpled cigarette pack from his jeans pocket and lit one. "Sorry. I just can't help wondering, ever since . . ."

"Since you got to know him."

"Yeah. Yeah, I guess that's the only way to put it, isn't it?"

She nodded. "So maybe that's his motivation, too. Just to get to know a few of us. Sheer curiosity."

"What about his own kind, though? How come he deserted his school?"

"Maybe he didn't. They could be hanging around just offshore;

these are pretty rich feeding grounds. He might be going back to join them every night. And their sonar has a range of four or five miles, so he could even be keeping in touch with them while he's visiting us."

Daniel pondered this. "You really do think they can send each other pictures? Clear, recognizable images?"

"If that's not what they're doing, then they're talking in sentences about as long as *War and Peace.*"

He finished his cigarette, started to flick it into the river and then caught her scowl. He crushed it out on the dock and returned the butt to the half-empty pack in his pocket. She nodded her approval and leaned over to kiss him.

"Ready to get back to sleep?" Sheila asked.

He kissed her back, longer this time. "No," he said, cupping her breast through the thin material of her robe.

She looked back up to the cabins; no lights were burning. Daniel's hand had found its way inside the robe, and she felt her nipple stiffen as he ran his fingers lightly back and forth across it.

"What if somebody—"

His lips had moved to her neck, and now her ear. "There isn't anybody. We're the only ones awake."

He opened her robe, and she felt a warm breeze across her naked breasts just before he took the other nipple into his mouth. His hands were on her back, her belly, moving downward. She parted her legs slightly, and the lower half of the robe fell away from her thighs. His probing fingers found the cushioned moistness there.

"Oh. Daniel, let's go back to the room...."

His only answer was to pull the flimsy robe back from her shoulders, and down her arms. There were no sounds other than their quickened breathing, and the occasional soft splash of fish leaping in the river below.

Sheila lay back on the discarded robe, her naked skin alive with warmth now, and watched in the dim moonlight as he stood and pulled his jeans down over his slim hips.

"What about splinters?" she asked, with a throaty laugh.

Daniel grinned and put his bunched-up jeans under her head
and shoulders. He knelt between her legs, lifted her buttocks up
onto his thighs, and entered her.

She gave way to the rhythm, to the smells of the night, to the
subtle sounds of the river mingled with the delicious noises of flesh
against flesh.

She came, and he spurted within her moments later. Still joined,
he gently massaged her belly and her breasts as she spread her arms
out in the welcoming night air and began to laugh. He looked at
her face and gave her a quizzical smile.

"It just struck me," she said with lazily contented humor, "dolphins *always* fuck outdoors."

Antonio Batera picked at his *parrillada* of sweetbreads, Argentine-
style, and stared across the galley at the faded print of *The Last
Supper*. How much of an appetite did those guys have that night,
he wondered idly. Did Jesus polish off his roast lamb or whatever?
Did Judas order dessert?

Across the table, Manoel was finishing his third stuffed crab, on
top of a double portion of *ceviche*. Batera pushed his plate away,
drained the glass of wine in front of him and refilled it from one
of the two bottles of '89 Spanish *rioja* on the table.

"You change your mind, Skipper? Maybe want the crab instead?"
Vinicius, the cook, hovered anxiously at his side.

" 's O.K. Not too hungry tonight, that's all. Was good *parrillada,*
though."

Vinicius hesitated over the half-empty plate. "Maybe you want
the rest for a late snack, huh? I can heat it up, anytime you say."

"Yah, maybe so. Keep it in the fridge, O.K.?"

The cook took the plate away, headed back toward the kitchen.
On the way he flicked a light switch; the dull red glow of dusk
had begun to cast a gloom over the crowded galley, and now Batera
blinked in the sudden fluorescent brightness. He took another long
sip of wine, started to set the glass down and then sipped again.

The chief engineer, Carlos, finished wolfing down his own *parrillada* and replenished his salad from the big wooden bowl in the center of the table. He sat at Batera's left, but he kept his eyes on his food. There'd been no conversation at the table other than grunts and "pass the mustard, willya" since they'd sat down to eat.

"Storm to the south, eighteen, twenty miles," Manoel said, making a stab at it.

"Unh," Batera said. Carlos ground some pepper on his after-dinner salad and started eating it.

The normal din of the galley at mealtimes was tonight no more than a low hum of mutters and whispers. Somehow the relative quiet made the overhead lights seem brighter, more intrusive; Batera wished Vinicius would turn them off again, just let the tropical day fade away naturally and the darkness roll into the room, covering it all like a deep blue blanket.

He glanced up, saw that Manoel was staring at him. The mate held the eye contact for several seconds, then looked away.

Batera pushed his chair back and slowly stood, steadying his wineglass as he did. He picked up a soup spoon and struck it against his bread plate five times, six, seven.

"Everybody listen up," he said loudly. "I'm gonna say this once."

The newly sober Panamanian deckhands frowned at each other, leaned toward their seatmates for a whispered translation. Everyone else went silent, put down their forks and looked expectantly at the skipper.

"We got a new policy, starting now," Batera said. "New rule." He cleared his throat, took a gulp of wine. "No more porpoise kills. I mean, none. Not *one*."

The room buzzed, and Batera banged the spoon on the plate again, harder.

"I don't mean we can't set on porpoise," he told the crew. "We still set on 'em, we still find the tuna. But none of 'em die no more, none of 'em get hurt. We don't use the seal bombs, we don't herd 'em with the speedboats. We just wrap the net around the porpoise best we can, and nobody pulls it closed or winches it on deck till every last one of 'em is out over the side. Anybody lets a porpoise get pulled up in the net, that man forfeits his share of the catch."

"Hey, but, Skip—"

"I didn't say there was gonna be any questions, did I?" Batera shouted. "I just said there was a new policy, and I was gonna say it once. And I did." He finished his wine and walked out of the galley toward his cabin, a wall of silence behind him.

Manoel was close on his heels. By the time he knocked on the skipper's door, Batera was already pouring himself a Chivas and water.

"Fix you one?" he asked as Manoel came into the cabin.

"No. I'm not here to drink."

Batera shrugged, added an extra dollop of Scotch to his already almost-brimming glass. "So, you drop by to watch a movie maybe? Or talk some more about that storm to the south?"

"You know damn well, Toninho. We fish together what, eleven years? Twelve? I don' question you, I don' talk back. You the skipper, you gotta be right. Simple as that. For twelve good years."

Batera gave a mirthless smile and stirred his drink. "Until now."

"Fuckin' right until now! You know what you asking those men to do?"

"To not kill any more porpoise."

"How we gonna make our load we don' kill a few goddamn porpoise? It goes with the job!"

Batera shook his head. "Not anymore. Not on the *Sea Master*."

"You just decide that, hey, all alone? Fuckin' company still owns seventy percent of this boat; what you think they gonna say we come up with our wells half empty?"

"We'll fill 'em."

"How long's that gonna take, we be pussyfootin' around looking out for them son-bitch porpoise so they don' get hurt none? You tell me, how long? We end up maybe six months out here!"

Batera sat in his leather recliner, drink in hand. "Whatever it takes. I said what I had to say."

"These men got families, they got car payments, mortgage . . ."

"So they'll have to work harder for it. We all will."

"Where the fuck you come off, Toninho, all of a sudden you acting like these Greenpeace assholes. They get to you or somethin'? What happen?"

The skipper turned away, stared out at the black ocean. Venus was rising, the evening star. "See the men do like I told 'em, Manoel."

The big man balled his fists in frustration. "They gonna be trouble, Skipper. I'm tellin' you now, they gonna be big trouble over this. Sooner more than later."

Dj\Tal was engaged in a spirited debate over fish-herding techniques with his friend and colleague Vl\Kal when the news came through that Ch*Tril and her traveling companions had been scanned by the School's perimeter scouts.

]Time-Later[, he imaged to Vl\Kal, and hurried to greet his mate. He felt buoyant with relief, as he always did when Ch*Tril returned safely from a Journey; no matter how capable or experienced she might be, the dangers for a small traveling pod were many.

The returning trio was just entering the center of the School when he got there. Almost everyone had taken a pause from tasks or games to welcome or simply observe the travelers, who were now the focus of hundreds of curious scans. Dj\Tal did his own quick scan, glad to see that Ch*Tril was unhurt; but he could tell that Tr*Til had been wounded, and that disturbed him. Ch*Tril spotted him amid the crowd, and after a series of grateful Touches they swam away together toward the periphery of the School.

She imaged him the highlights of the Journey's events, and Dj\Tal could tell that she was downplaying the incidents with the hard-water and the Death-Creature, which served only to heighten his concern. The hazards must have been substantial, and she was lucky to have survived them; but she seemed impatient to get the recounting of the stories over with, as if something of much greater importance occupied her mind.

She switched from imaging to the Link-Talent to describe the Melding, and the memory-scenes of those long-ago contacts between their kind and the land-walkers filled Dj\Tal's brain, as fully realized as if they were happening now and Dj\Tal was a participant. He absorbed the ancient scenes in silence, waiting for her to finish.

Ch*Tril conveyed the great frustration she had felt when the Source-Mind blocked her access with a wall of Non-Acceptance that even Dj\Tal's key-pattern could not penetrate, and she concluded with a strong interrogatory image, a request for answers and explanation that was more demand than plea.

>Agreement<

Dj\Tal Linked to her;

>It Is Time You Were Enlightened<

She waited expectantly, but still Dj\Tal hesitated. How would she take this? he wondered. She had spent her life as a Historian, exploring the vast archives of the Source-Mind as familiarly as the lesser members of the School roamed their well-charted feeding territories, and uncovering a wealth of previously lost or untapped information about the history of their kind.

Among her finds had been the moving saga of the Dispersed School, which had made the error of imposing insufficient unifying discipline on its members. They had been swimming in a noncohesive gathering one darktime in an unnamed sea, one of the very warm ones, when a vicious storm had struck. By the time the torrent had subsided, the School no longer existed: Its thousands of members had been hopelessly separated, pod from pod, mothers from young ones, mates from mates, beyond their ability to find one another and regroup. Those who had not drowned in the awful fury of the storm had been doomed to spend the rest of their lives in a futile search for their friends and loved ones. A fortunate few had been able to join unfamiliar Schools, while the others had been relegated to eking out dangerous, solitary existences with none to give them aid or comfort.

Ch*Tril had pieced together the bleak story of the Dispersed School over the course of nearly a dozen Meldings. Now it was taught to every young one, both as a tragic drama and as an object lesson demonstrating what might happen if customary School discipline were to go unheeded.

Her life was devoted to the seeking, and the teaching, of truth; what would her reaction be when he told her that the greatest Truth of all had been kept secret from her, and by *him*?

Ch*Tril imaged a symbol of impatience, and echoed his earlier promise of enlightenment. He had no choice but to plunge ahead.

Dj\Tal began simply, with a Link re-creating that same shallow sea at the place of Del-Fi; but this time there was no ritualistic gathering, no harmonious encounter between the land-walkers and the representatives of his and Ch*Tril's kind. This time the rocky shore was a scene of brutal chaos, of land-walkers killing one another with abandon. The females in their flowing white garments were being butchered, their mutilated bodies thrown into the sea; the water was fouled with their blood, and the temple that had been their home was being ransacked, demolished.

Ch*Tril recoiled in horror, as Dj\Tal had known she would, but he pressed on, expanding and elaborating the ancient story.

The densely packed, fast-flowing Links she had witnessed between their kind and the land-walkers had indeed originated with the Source-Mind, he informed her. They were similar to the almost-mythic First Teachings with which the Source-Mind had, millions of cold-to-colds ago, inculcated his and Ch*Tril's own early ancestors. Philosophy, culture, School organization ... the seeds of all these Directives had been implanted by the Source-Mind in Time-Before-Memory, and had been nurtured ever since through the tradition of the Melding.

Just as the Source-Mind had discovered and utilized the existence of the Link-Talent in a select few among Dj\Tal's and Ch*Tril's kind, so had it much later recognized the same potential among a small minority of the land-walkers. The Links Ch*Tril had found evidence of had been part of the First Teachings for the land-walkers; but, as she had seen, the Teachings had been viciously interrupted by barbaric, non-Linking factions of the species.

Since that time, the lives of the land-walkers had been dominated by one form after another of violence and cruelty. The ability to Link had come to be viewed with grave suspicion or disbelief among their kind; those who had learned to use the Talent hid or suppressed it, and in later generations, most of the ones who inherited the skill were no longer even aware of their latent power.

The Source-Mind had decreed that the land-walkers were to be left strictly to themselves. Over time, the origins of this Directive had been forgotten, and it had become so ingrained that it was eventually considered to be an inherent taboo among Ch*Tril's kind. Only a small group in each School was permitted to retain and selectively pass on the true history of these events; this was the Circle of which Dj\Tal had long been a member.

The Source-Mind had hoped that the land-walkers would eventually outgrow their violent tendencies, or at least keep their depredations confined to the land. Such hopes had been in vain.

Even when the land-walkers had begun to venture out onto the seas to hunt down and kill the Sources, a few hundred cold-to-colds ago, no action had been taken. The Source-Mind concerned itself little with the individual existences of its components, and it had been thought best to simply ignore the scattered attacks by the land-walkers with their primitive hulls and sharp sticks.

The merit of that aloofness had since been reconsidered. In the last hundred or so cold-to-colds, the land-walkers had achieved great expertise in the fabrication of killing devices, both those intended for use against their own kind and the ones designed for the slaughter of the Sources. As the number of individual Sources had continued to decline, it had become clear that the existence of the Source-Mind itself was threatened: There was now a danger that the quantity of

Sources might fall below the critical level at which the Source-Mind was able to coalesce.

The hunting of the Sources was not the only problem; indeed, that brutal business had in recent years been largely halted, for reasons not yet fully understood. But as the land-walkers had expanded their skills at object-fabrication, they had not only plundered their own dry regions but had increasingly fouled the seas with the detritus of their frenzied activities; and the spreading contamination was now a threat of crisis proportions.

The Source-Mind had therefore Directed that contact with the land-walkers be tentatively and gradually reestablished. Perhaps it was too late for the First Teachings to do the creatures any good, but an attempt must be made.

Dj\Tal's own father had taken part in some of the initial steps, more than thirty cold-to-colds ago. One or more Circle members would approach a land-walker young one and scan it to see if it possessed the Link-Talent; if so, a preparatory Link would be sent to the creature's half-formed young mind, along with a key-pattern that would block its memory of the Link until reactivated.

Thus had the fulfillment of the New Directives begun; and though some, including Qr*Jil, the Old One, had opposed the plan and tried to slow its progress, its ultimate realization was now imminent.

Ch*Tril herself, Dj\Tal told her, would—

The sea around them suddenly turned red, and a large shape etched in stark black and white came racing toward them, its razor-toothed mouth agape.

Dj\Tal pushed Ch*Tril roughly out of the way of the oncoming orca, and its big flukes stunned him with a heavy blow. Ch*Tril darted upward to distract their attacker, and when Dj\Tal had regained his orientation he swiftly followed in the direction she had gone.

He scanned through the murky red water, but Ch*Tril was nowhere to be found. Directly overhead, the Danger-Cousin was breaching, rising clear above the water. Dj\Tal twisted to one side and dove out of the way, but the shock waves from the Danger-Cousin's impact on the surface rocked him painfully.

He tried to scan, and couldn't. His eyes were still all right, but the water was so dark and disturbed that he could see no farther than a beak-to-fluke in any direction.

The tip of a huge black dorsal passed alongside him, almost brushing his right pectoral fin. The heavy body was out of sight below; but how could it have gotten beneath him so fast, it had just breached, hadn't had time to dive yet—

An expanse of bright pink moved above him, descending: the first Danger-Cousin's white belly, discolored in his view through the bloody water.

Dj\Tal rammed the soft belly with his beak, then somersaulted in place and swam away between the two big sets of converging flukes. He could no longer see the Danger-Cousin he'd hit, had no way of knowing how bad an injury he might have inflicted.

He zigzagged through the water blindly, unable to scan, searching for an unclouded area where his eyes might be of some use; but there was a thick haze of blood wherever he swam.

Another shape moved toward him through the reddish fog, and he prepared to strike again with his snout, but then he saw that it was one of his own kind. Dj\Tal felt the thrumming in his thorax that meant the other was scanning or imaging, but his receptors were still numbed by the violent buffeting he'd received when the first Danger-Cousin had breached so close to him.

Deaf, mute, and nearly blind, Dj\Tal communicated the situation to the newcomer as best he could by use of postures and motion-mimicry. The other was a male he didn't even know by signature, but Dj\Tal's improvised sign-language seemed to get the message across. His School-brother responded shakily in kind, acting out a near-duplicate of the sudden onslaught; the Danger-Cousins had struck simultaneously on at least two flanks of the School.

Dj\Tal struggled to image details of Ch*Tril's disappearance, but could emit only the faintest of signals. The unfamiliar School-brother strained to understand, and Dj\Tal could see that he was picking up at least a portion of an image here and there. If he could only get the gist of it, then he and Dj\Tal might be able to—

There was a flash of black and white, and the stranger Dj\Tal had been trying to image to was left writhing in agony, his flukes gone entirely and an inconceivable amount of blood gushing from his sundered hindquarters.

Dj\Tal automatically tried to scan the dark waters from which the Danger-Cousin had lunged, and into which it had now invisibly withdrawn. He caught a brief impression of its broad, notched flukes, then nothing; his scanning powers were beginning to return, but with excruciating slowness.

No matter; he must find Ch*Tril, and do what he could to help defend the rest of the School, despite his temporary handicap.

He swam back toward what he hoped was the center of the School, scanning ahead weakly and intermittently. He passed a dozen of his own kind, mutilated, dead or dying, before he found what he had most feared.

The Danger-Cousins, at least ten of them, were herding hundreds of the survivors together just as Dj\Tal's kind herded fish. They seemed to be concentrating particularly on females and young ones, though Dj\Tal could not scan Ch*Tril anywhere in the terrified crowd. One young male tried to break through the encircling ranks of the orcas, and was hit in the head, hard, with a blow from a pair of those deadly flukes. The injured male went limp, his eyes closed, and he floated slowly toward the surface without moving.

Dj\Tal retreated several beak-to-flukes from the hostages and their captors, and swam in a careful course around the edges of the area in which the females and their young were imprisoned. He scanned more dead and wounded, then came upon a zone of all-out battle.

One Danger-Cousin had suffered numerous bites on its large, rounded pectoral fins; little chunks of the fins hung suspended in the turbid water, trailing strings of muscle and fat. The commotion, and the omnipresent meat and blood, had already attracted a small swarm of sharks; thankfully, none of them were big enough to pose an additional threat.

The injured orca thrashed violently about, his powerful jaws snapping at all who came near. A phalanx of Dj\Tal's School-brothers maneuvered around the invader, nipping now at his tender dorsal.

Another Danger-Cousin, a female, had come to the aid of the wounded one, but she was in trouble, too: Twenty or more of Dj\Tal's kind had formed a column across her back, their combined strength holding her down so she could not surface for air.

Dj\Tal swam on, his scanning powers almost back to normal. Just ahead he noticed a throng of several dozen of his kind in what appeared to be an emergency strategy session. Ch*Tril, he was relieved to see, was among them.

He made his way hastily through the assembly, scanning signs of fear and rage at every turn. Kr\Val, one of his fellow Circle members, was imaging to the crowd, exhorting that the majority of the School should take flight and abandon those trapped by the pod of Danger-Cousins.

]Negation[, Dj\Tal interrupted, imaging as forcefully as he could.]Necessity/Protection/School-Entire[.

]Threat/Excessive[, Kr\Val retorted.]Invincibility/Danger-Cousins[.

Dj\Tal sent out several graphic images of the wounded and helpless Danger-Cousins he had passed on his way here.]Possibility/Triumph[, he concluded;]Assistance/Weak-Ones[.

He caught a brief scan of Ch*Tril in the midst of the mob; she was imaging him encouragement.

]Agreement/Tactics[, someone else imaged, and was echoed by another, and another.

Within a hundred heartbeats, the retaliatory charge was under way. As the now-cohesive crowd came near the place where the hostages were being held, it broke off by prearrangement into five separate flanks. Dj\Tal led one, Ch*Tril another.

Each of the groups bore down from above or behind, focusing on two Danger-Cousins at a time; the squadrons' members dove in two by two, starting with those on the leading edge. Their targets were the orcas' tightly sealed blowholes.

Dj\Tal and his randomly chosen partner were among the first to strike. He could feel the rubbery consistency of the watertight blowhole as he hit it with his snout, and then the weighty black-and-white enemy flung the two of them away with a toss of his head.

They moved to rejoin their group at the rear, and Dj\Tal scanned another pair immediately on the attack. This time the Danger-Cousin wasn't in position for such an easy and effective head-toss, and the blowhole parted slightly under the force of the two-pronged assault, letting in a small quantity of seawater.

The Danger-Cousin quickly expelled the water, and a column of rising bubbles came out after it. Even as he exhaled, he was set upon by two more of Dj\Tal's squadron, one of whom got his beak into the half-open blowhole and ripped a three-teeth-long tear in the sensitive tissue with a jerk of his head.

The flow of bubbles was constant now, and mixed with blood. The Danger-Cousin crushed the next diving pair with a swing of his flukes, but the two after that made it through and widened the bloody split in his blowhole; the bubbles ceased.

The drowning Danger-Cousin fought to make his way to the surface, but half the attacking squadron followed him as he rose, battering his soft white underside and tearing the damaged blowhole to mere shreds of flesh. The other half of the group, including Dj\Tal, broke off into quarters to join the assault on the remaining nine marauders.

One was already dead, Dj\Tal saw, but its corpse was surrounded by the broken and mutilated bodies of half a dozen of Dj\Tal's own kind. He had no time to scan for Ch*Tril among the victims; he was positioned for the second wave of an attack on a Danger-Cousin whose dorsal was by now almost severed.

With three of the invaders dead or disabled, a potential escape route for the captured females and young ones had opened. A rescue party hastened through the raiders' depleted ranks, and began leading the frightened captives to safety.

Dj\Tal hit the new target blowhole with all the strength he could muster, and felt a sickening pulpiness as it gave way under the battering of his and the others' rigid snouts.

The battle had turned. Scanning, Dj\Tal saw that the blood-dimmed sea was filled more with the aftermath of conflict than with actual fighting. The surviving orcas, those who were able, were fleeing.

Dj\Tal and the rest took up the chase; he scanned Ch*Tril among the pursuers, and was gladdened. Then he saw one of the Danger-Cousins veer abruptly to the left, and he swerved to follow.

The starkly colored creature moved with astonishing speed for its size, and Dj\Tal was a thousand beak-to-flukes away from the School before he realized that none of the others had noticed the fugitive's change of course. He was on his own.

The massive Danger-Cousin stopped, and turned to face him.

Dj\Tal came to a halt, paralyzed by the hopelessness of his situation, less than ten beak-to-flukes from the Danger-Cousin's fearsome head. It regarded him with its glistening dark eyes, and he stared back, mesmerized.

Resigned to impending death, Dj\Tal was utterly unprepared for what happened next: The menacing creature *Linked* to him. Then it wheeled about and sped away, disappearing into the measureless sea as suddenly and surprisingly as it and its ravaging accomplices had arrived.

Shaken to his core, Dj\Tal swam slowly back toward the School.

The tasks ahead would not be pleasant ones. The damage to the School must be assessed, deaths and injuries tallied, farewell rituals performed for murdered friends and colleagues. An explanation must be sought for why the School was taken so unawares by the attack, and how such unpreparedness might be rectified in the future.

Most difficult of all, however, would be the report Dj\Tal must now deliver to the Circle, describing the Link he had received from the Danger-Cousin. Its message had been alarmingly simple, though couched in layers of meaning that would be thoroughly analyzed and discussed. Many painful Choices would be necessary in the wake of what the Danger-Cousin had communicated:

>War<

it had Linked to him;

>Herewith Commences War<

8

They'd taken Daniel's rented Taurus today, since it had more trunk room for Sheila's equipment than the Escort she'd been driving. Sheila waved familiarly at the woman in the tollbooth at the causeway entrance, and the woman smiled back, pleased that "her" dolphin continued to attract so much attention.

The makeshift parking lot near the sand dunes was empty. Daniel looked at the digital clock on the dashboard. "We must be early," he said.

"Sometimes he is, too," Sheila noted. "Maybe we can grab a little time with him before all the families show up."

They stripped to their swimsuits and unloaded the equipment from the trunk, Daniel carrying the lion's share of the heavy recorders and oscilloscopes and underwater speakers. The sun was hot as they trudged across the dunes, along the path where the tall sea grass had been pushed aside and trampled flat. He was looking forward to getting into the water whether the dolphin had arrived yet or not.

Sheila walked ahead of him as they came over the top of the last dune and started down toward the beach, and he watched the sway of her perfect little bottom, the grace of those swimmer's legs, with pleasure. What an extraordinary few days these had been, he marveled; the unexpected rush of emotions he'd experienced, first in his encounter with the dolphin and then in the rapid blossoming of his affections for this bright, charming woman, were very nearly overwhelming—but in a wholly positive way. He'd been devoid of feeling for so long, this sudden explosion of joy was like being released from prison, like getting stoned ... everything he saw or touched or smelled seemed to take on new meaning, new life. Even the—

"Oh, my God!" Sheila cried out, breaking his reverie.

"What—" he looked down at the gently lapping water and saw what she had seen, the image rooting him to where he stood even as Sheila ran headlong toward the shore, dropping her recording equipment in the sand.

Footsteps sounded behind him, bare feet scrunching through the fine sand. Daniel turned to see a man and a woman leading two excited children, the boy about eight and the little girl no more than five.

"Get your kids away from here," Daniel said in a harsh whisper, putting his hands firmly on the man's arms.

The man jerked away from him, his face reddening with quick anger. "Hey, what the hell, buddy?" he protested. "This is a public beach; we've been coming down here the last three days. You think you own the place or—"

He peered over Daniel's shoulder, blanched, and reached down to stop the scurrying children. "Come on, guys," he said to them, "we're gonna go over to the Gulf side today and collect some shells, how about that?"

"No, Daddy, no!" the little boy insisted. "We wanta play with Whizzy!"

The man's wife looked puzzled. "Honey, if they want to see the dolphin again I don't see why—" Her husband stopped her with a look.

"Special treat," he told the children. "You can ride the go-carts. And Chrissie, I'll help you drive; won't that be fun?"

The girl pouted. "I don't want to, I want to play the beach-ball game with—"

"Let's go," the man ordered, "before the big kids get all the go-carts." He nudged the children back toward the parking lot, ignoring their whines.

"Hey, mister!" Daniel called out after him. "Give a call to nine-one-one, will you?"

The man nodded once and led his family across the dunes, away from the beach.

Daniel hurried to join Sheila at the water's edge, his heels digging into the sand with every loping step.

The dolphin was floating on its side in the shallow water, rocked by the barely perceptible waves of the Sound. The water all around it was a cloudy pink, and a thin line of red flowed from its head, just above the blowhole.

Sheila was kneeling in the water beside the dolphin, her arms wrapped around it and her face streaked with tears. As Daniel approached, the agonized creature's eyes sought his, and he wanted to look away, but couldn't. He remembered the lonely, searching eyes of the dolphin he'd videotaped on the deck of the tuna boat, and was suddenly sick with hurt, with rage.

What had happened here today was hideously obvious; Daniel had seen humans in the same condition too many times, in far too many places. The thin trickle of blood from the dying dolphin's head was coming from a gunshot wound.

The sharp-eyed young crewman on early watch in the crow's-nest had spotted the porpoise at first light, and they'd made the set just after dawn. Now it was midafternoon, and the men were still working the net in the water, carefully and laboriously freeing every porpoise caught in its huge circumference.

Nobody'd had time for either breakfast or lunch. Vinicius, the cook, was quietly indignant; he'd laid out a lavish Mexican-themed spread for lunch after it had become clear that breakfast wasn't going to happen, and now all his painstakingly prepared chimichangas and guacamole and black beans with salsa were drying out in the midday heat.

"How long before we can start brailing?" Batera called to Manoel down on the deck.

The big man looked up toward the bridge, squinting against the burning afternoon sun. "Up to you, Skipper," he shouted back. "All up to you."

"How many porpoise left in the net?"

"Too fuckin' many," the mate said, and turned his back and walked toward the bow. The men on deck should long since have stacked the netpile, but instead they milled around the empty space, scrubbing at oil stains and doing whatever else they could to stay busy and stave off their hunger. They wouldn't eat as long as their *companheiros* in the boats were forced to go without; tomorrow, or next week, any of them might be the ones out in the boats struggling all day to let the porpoise loose. No point just taking turns pissing each other off.

Manoel stood with his hammy fists on his hips, watching the men go about their make-work chores. Off the starboard side, he could see four other crewmen in the water, splashing about in the enclosure formed by the net as they worked to lead the porpoise out over the cork-strung top of it. Every so often a porpoise that had been steered out of the net to safety would reverse itself and leap back in, forcing the men to lead or cajole or push it out all over again.

The skiff that had trailed the net out in its half-mile circle bobbed at idle on the listless waves. Its driver was helpless to proceed with his own job until every last one of the porpoise had been removed from the net without so much as a bruise or a scratch, just the way the skipper had ordered it.

Nine hours of work, Manoel thought disgustedly, and not one goddamn tuna hauled on board. The cold, briny wells that by now should have been packed to capacity with the big fish were less than two-thirds full. Shit, at this rate they'd be out here another month.

Paulo, a crewman who'd been needlessly polishing the steel cleats on the gunwales for the past hour, came up to Manoel and offered him a cigarette. They smoked together in silence for a minute or so, watching the swimmers in the net wrestle to set the porpoise free.

"Hey, Senhor Ricosta?" Paulo finally said in a tentative tone.

"Yeah, what?"

"A couple of the guys and me, we was wondering . . ."

"Sim, sim?"

"What we done wrong?"

Manoel frowned, perplexed. *"Que queres dizer?"*

"Must be we fucked up some way or other, the skipper treatin' us like this. *Mas eu não sei como.*"

"Nobody fucked up," Manoel said between his teeth.

"Então, que esta o problema? We had a good trip goin', some great sets, and now—"

"Skipper run this boat the way he wants. You got that?"

"Bom, sim, but to me an' the guys it look like—"

Manoel tossed his cigarette into the torpid ocean. "I don' give a shit what anything look like to you, boy, understan'? You just do like you told, earn your share an' keep you mouth shut."

The crewman waved his hand in a placating gesture. "All it was, we was just thinkin'—"

"Show me your *cabeça,* boy," Manoel snapped. "Point at it for me."

The deckhand cocked his head in confusion and slowly pointed his right index finger at his temple.

"Now lemme see your arms. Hold 'em out for me."

Paulo complied, sticking his ropy, tanned bare arms out in front of him.

"Now which you think we payin' you for? Your arms or you head?"

"Arms, I guess," the crewman said after a brief hesitation.

"Yeah, well, you guess right. An' that's the last thinkin' you gonna be called on to do this trip. You hear what I'm tellin' you, or I gotta say it one more time?"

Paulo returned Manoel's level stare without blinking. "I hear you, all right."

"That's good, that's real good. You just go back and tell your *amigos* what I tol' you, O.K.?"

They held each other's gaze for several moments before the deckhand looked away. *"Sim, certo,"* he muttered, and walked back the way he'd come.

Manoel stared after him, saw him squat down and start talking quietly with two of the other crewmen. Their hands flew as they spoke, and one of the men suddenly threw a wrench overboard. Manoel decided to let it pass.

He looked around at the other side of the deck and saw a couple of men arguing. One of them reached out toward the other, and the second one took a step back, almost stumbling over a length of rope where the net should have been piled. It was the two Panamanians, Rico and Xavier.

Manoel walked to within earshot of them, and listened:

"Dame eso!" Rico demanded.

"No es tu botella."

"Dámelo ahora!"

"No hay más para ti," Xavier said with disdain.

"Hijo de perro, dámelo!"

"Qué dices?! Chinga tu madre!"

The knife was out and in Xavier's hand before Manoel could move. It cut through the still, hot air, slicing open the other Panamanian's loose shirt. Suddenly they both had blades out, and were circling each other in an unsteady street-fighting crouch.

"Gimme the fuckin' knives, right now!" Manoel shouted. *"Dámelos!"*

The Panamanians ignored him, and Xavier suddenly swung out at Rico's head with an almost-empty whiskey bottle, feinting forward with the knife in his other hand as he did so. The slight but wiry deckhand saw the bottle coming at the last instant and raised his knife in time to inflict a deep slash on Xavier's wrist, but the heavy bottle had acquired a momentum of its own. It smashed into Rico's right ear with a meaty thud, then shattered, sending splinters of glass flying across the oily deck.

Xavier switched the knife to his left hand, oblivious of the blood spurting from his other wrist. He lunged at the shorter man, who had dropped to his knees, and Manoel caught him from behind, heavy arms around the Panamanian's thin chest.

"Drop it, motherfucker! Drop it!"

Manoel lifted him in the air, shook the bleeding man violently until the knife fell to the deck. The other one, Rico, had collapsed on his side, his legs jerking convulsively, the right side of his head a mess of bloody, matted hair and hanging strips of flesh that had been his ear.

"*Ajuda!*" Manoel yelled to the men who'd been watching the fight. "*Ataduras, sem demora!*"

Somebody scrambled belowdecks and fetched Carlos, who came running with the first-aid kit. He looked from one wounded man to the other, made a quick decision and started applying a tourniquet to Xavier's arm while Manoel still held the struggling man in an unbreakable grip. There was a potent stink of alcohol on the Panamanian's breath, and Manoel turned his head away as the chief engineer bandaged the damaged arm.

Carlos pulled the tourniquet tight and turned his attention to Rico. The spasms hadn't ceased, and the man's eyes had rolled up so that only the whites were visible.

The engineer shook his head. "We've gotta get these men to a hospital, right away."

"We twelve hours from Costa Rica," Manoel said. He looked across the calm sea, saw a line of whitecaps whipped by a rising wind toward the eastern horizon. "Maybe more."

"Get hold of the Coast Guard, then. They'll send a helicopter."

"You really think . . .?"

"Skipper doesn't give 'em a call, he's gonna have one dead crewman in five, six hours, and another one with gangrene setting in."

Manoel lowered the now-sedated but still drunken Xavier to the deck and released him. The other deckhands had stopped tending to their superfluous tasks and were watching the aftermath of the excitement.

The mate walked back along the deck with a show of unruffled dignity, and mounted the companionway to the bridge. Batera was inside, at the wheel, watching the scene on the main deck through the thick glass windows.

"Some trouble, huh?" he asked, staring straight ahead.

"You could say. Got two men damn near kill each other, I call that trouble."

Batera nodded distractedly. "They need to be taken ashore?"

"Carlos say they need a fuckin' Coast Guard chopper, right now."

The skipper picked up the mike of the VHF radio, keyed it, and calmly called in the request for emergency assistance. The Coast Guard operator asked for verification and coordinates, then promised a jet-copter within the hour.

"I don't like to say ..." Manoel began when the call was done.

" 'I told you so'?" Batera said. "Good American expression, but everybody always claims they don't want to say it. When you know damn well they do."

"Yeah, well ... this ain't no damn good, Toninho. Them Panamanians, they ain't had a drop of booze since they signed on. What you think turn 'em around like that all of a sudden, huh? We two men down now, rest of the crew ready to swim home, an' the wells still not full."

"So what you suggesting, Manoel? You tell me."

The big man clenched and unclenched his fists, wiped at the perspiration on his dark brow. "I say 'less you change your mind about this porpoise shit, we cut our losses an' head back with what we got. Maybe we find a new crew, some fellas need the work bad enough."

Batera pursed his lips and gave a curt nod. "Soon as they pick those men up, we can get under way. Tell the skiff driver to undo the net, men on deck can start piling it."

Manoel stood where he was, his heavy-lidded eyes on the skipper.

"You waitin' for something?" Batera asked. "Call on down to the skiff."

Manoel grunted, turned away, and left him there, alone at the wheel, watching the sky for the helicopter.

There was something strange up ahead, Dv\Kil scanned, something unlike any creature or object he had ever scanned before.

He moved closer to the unknown entity, scanning it all the while to make certain that nothing it might do would take him completely by surprise. The whole School was in a state of high alert since the unexpected attack by the Danger-Cousins; Dv\Kil's own position here as a perimeter scout was a direct result of that startling, if ultimately failed, assault on the School. This was the first truly significant task he had ever been assigned, and he would have been bursting with pride at having been entrusted with such responsibility, had not the circumstances leading to the assignment been so fraught with tragedy and terror.

Even now, his concentration on the task at hand was ever in danger of interruption by his concern for the safety of his new mate, Lr*Xin; he must constantly remind himself that by guarding the borders of the School itself, he was doing the most he could to protect Lr*Xin. Indeed, this task put him in a position of helping to oversee the safety of all the members of the School, including even his parents, Ch*Tril and Dj\Tal; he couldn't allow anything to distract him from such a weighty mission.

Dv\Kil suddenly worried that his curiosity about this strange object might be just the sort of distraction he had been warned against. He was here to look out for marauding orcas, not to investigate whatever random oddities might catch his notice. Still, anything unusual this close to the edges of the School seemed to him to merit some degree of scrutiny; if the regular perimeter scouts had been

181

paying closer attention earlier to everything even vaguely out of the ordinary, the School might have had more warning of the Danger-Cousins' raid, and at least some of those who had been killed or injured might have survived unhurt.

He was almost close enough now to have the mystery object in visual range. It was obvious even from a distance that the thing wasn't alive, despite the fact that it moved through the water with apparent purpose, if not intelligence: His scans had shown it to be rock-hard, its interior impervious to his scanning sense; no heart could pump within that cold, metallic shell, no stomach could hunger there for nourishment. It was clearly an artifact of the land-walkers, and seemed to stay within a certain distance of one of their large metal hulls, floating on the surface. How strange, then, that the submerged object's shape should be so similar in many ways to the streamlined bodies of his own kind, so smooth and symmetrical, as if designed to exist and maneuver here beneath the surface like a creature of the sea.

The water was becoming warmer now, Dv\Kil noticed, and murky. No, not murky really, not infused with sand or particles of organic matter, but *disturbed,* a white opacity of millions of minute bubbles, as if this spot had just been the scene of a great struggle of some sort; but Dv\Kil knew from his regular scans as he had approached the area that no such battle had taken place here, and the land-walker artifact was moving much too slowly to whip up such an irritated froth.

Dv\Kil moved in closer; the sudden warmth of the surrounding water was no longer comfortable, but unpleasantly hot, and growing hotter still, the nearer he came to the area around which the self-propelled metallic device was moving.

Then he saw it, sharp and distinct even through the hazy barrier of bubbles: a thin, brilliantly glowing beam, red as coral, *burning* its way into the sea floor, turning the sand and the rock beneath into a glowing, rising liquid.

That must be the source of the disturbance in the water, Dv\Kil knew instinctively, even though he'd never witnessed such a phe-nomenon himself; the heat from that remarkably powerful beam of light, and from the searing-hot molten rock and sand, must be creating that thick curtain of bubbles.

All at once the glowing beam disappeared, and the big squarish device from which it had been emanating with a low hum went quiet. Even as it died, an identical beam suddenly sprang from the snout of the small moving projectile that had been hovering and circling around the spot where the sea floor burned, where the rock gushed up like a thicker, heavier, and far hotter form of water, then cooled and solidified once more in a growing mound.

The beam from the moving object, the thing that acted like a living creature but was not, focused on the mound of newly solid rock and made it liquid yet again, burned it and melted it until the freshly created hillock was flattened, its component materials spread out over a wide area around the spot where the first beam had burned its way into the earth beneath the sea.

Dv\Kil watched this inexplicable activity in fascinated silence. Clearly, the devices and their burning beams belonged to the land-walkers on the hull above; but could the land-walkers be responsible at a distance for the behavior of these bizarre objects, or were the artifacts somehow acting on their own? Both possibilities seemed equally unlikely, but one or the other must be true.

The sleek mobile object with the burning snout had made its way to the edges of the debris field now, still moving as if it were aware of its surroundings, as if it could actually see or echolocate. Dv\Kil looked back at the center, at the hole from which the quantity of molten earth had been exuded. A few tiny droplets of glowing, liquid rock were still seeping from the hole, were solidify-ing into porous black pebbles as they oozed forth, sizzling, into the cool water.

But the beam that had made the hole was no longer burning into the sea floor, Dv\Kil thought with puzzlement; what, then, could be melting the rock?

It came to him in an instant, the memory of a myth all young ones knew, and of the more realistic, if no less terrible and dramatic, factual version that his mother had told him.

Dv\Kil spun and sped away, heading back toward the School as fast as he could swim. This took precedence even over his orders to patrol the perimeter and watch out for Danger-Cousins, he realized; this was news of the most stunning import, and the School must be informed at once.

They took the Super Shuttle from LAX to Union Station, where Daniel had left his ten-year-old Toyota when he'd taken the train to San Diego with Mitch Creighton. Had it really been only two weeks ago? He found that hard to believe, with all that had happened since.

Sheila had taken the Santa Barbara Airporter van down when she'd left for Florida, so now they could drive up together. The cases of equipment she carried filled the trunk and most of the backseat of his little car, and she had to ride with her feet propped on her flight bag.

Daniel headed up Sepulveda and took the San Diego Freeway to the westbound Ventura. It was early afternoon, well before rush hour, but the roads were choked with traffic, as always. The time of day, the recently added extra lanes, the city's constant pleas for carpooling ... none of this mattered anymore. Los Angeles had truly become Car Hell, even for those people who had found the freeways readily negotiable in the '60s and '70s.

He turned the radio on; it was set to his usual station, KLSX "classic rock," but Creedence's "Bad Moon Rising" didn't seem like the most appropriate background music right now. He punched a button and switched over to the New Age station, which was playing an Andreas Wollenweider album with ocean sound effects in the background.

"Do you mind?" Sheila said quietly.

"Hmmh?"

"I'd rather listen to something else, if it's O.K. with you."

Daniel turned and saw that her eyes were brimming again, as they had done several times on the plane.

"Sorry," he said with chagrin, and flipped over to the AM dial. Michael Jackson, the talk-show host, was interviewing some self-styled "expert" who had the audacity to claim that he had some reasonable idea for how the Russians might be able to bring themselves out of their ongoing economic quagmire.

"This all right?" he asked.

"Sure. Fine."

They passed through Encino and Tarzana and Woodland Hills, and the traffic started to diminish by the time they entered the dry, brown hills between Calabasas and Agoura. The radio signal was beginning to fade, too, so Daniel fiddled around with the dial until he found another talk station out of Ventura. This time Bruce Williams was advising callers from around the country on mortgages, taxes, and landlord-tenant disputes.

There were two more spurts of semi-urban traffic as they drove through Oxnard and Ventura, and then the number of cars around them dropped off once more just as the highway made a sweeping curve to reveal a vista of sky, ocean, and a sparsely populated beach jutting up against the desert hills. On the radio, a confused woman from Milwaukee was being told that she should hire an attorney to help her settle a disagreement with a neighbor over property lines. Sheila shut it off.

"This wasn't the first time, you know," she said.

"Are you talking about ... ?"

"Yes."

"Do you mean other dolphins coming up to where humans were, or ... ?"

"I mean both."

"Jesus," Daniel whispered, appalled. "When did this happen? Where?"

"New Zealand in the '50s, Spain in the early '70s . . . there've been cases all over the world, going back centuries. First time we know of was in a Roman town in Tunisia, second century A.D. It's always the same story: A dolphin approaches people near a beach, particularly children, plays with them regularly for a few weeks or months . . . then somebody kills him. Usually in the dead of night, and nobody ever gets caught."

"Why the hell would anybody do such a thing?"

She shrugged, her eyes fixed on the road ahead. " 'Sport,' I suppose. All that crap about 'dominion over the creatures of the land and sea.' "

Daniel rolled his window down and stuck a cigarette between his teeth, crushing the filter. "What about laws? Aren't dolphins at least protected from that kind of stupidity?"

"Some places. But then, so are humans, supposedly."

"I just don't understand—"

"Neither do I. And those are only the most publicized cases, the ones where the media get to 'personalize' an individual dolphin. The mass slaughters get less attention."

"Yeah, I know, the tuna boats. But I'm trying to—"

"I'm not talking about the tuna boats. Have you ever heard of Iki Island, for instance?"

He shook his head. "I don't think so. The South Pacific?"

"Japan. The fishermen on the island resent the fact that dolphins eat the same kind of fish they do, so they hunt them down and slaughter them."

"Do they use nets?"

"No. Just knives."

Daniel didn't quite understand. "Why don't the dolphins just swim away?" he asked. "They're faster than most boats, and they can dive."

Sheila sighed and bit her lower lip. "The first thing each boat does is capture a young dolphin, a baby if possible. Then they wound it—they don't kill it, they just wound it, so it bleeds—and they tie its flukes to the back of the boat. The young one's mother answers its distress call, and her mate answers hers, and so on . . . and the fishermen methodically stab to death every dolphin that tries to help."

Daniel stubbed out his cigarette in the overflowing ashtray. Neither of them spoke again until they'd reached Santa Barbara, and Sheila gave him directions to where she lived.

Water, as much water as all the sand in New Mexico, maybe more . . . warm on her body in the little two-piece suit, her first, didn't really need the top part yet but Mommy said . . . Mommy yelling now, far off behind her, and Daddy too, Daddy screaming LOUD, can't tell what he's saying but here comes something toward her in the water, coming fast, she looks and it's getting closer, she sees a fin, sharp and gray, cutting through the sparkly blue water, coming right at her. . . .

Sheila opened her eyes and found that her hands were clutching the sheet. She let go of it, absentmindedly smoothed the wrinkles out, and reached for the glass that she always kept on the nightstand next to the bed. Sipping the lukewarm water, she noticed that the other side of the bed was rumpled but empty; Daniel must have woken up early.

She got up and wandered into the kitchen, naked. Cold orange juice in the fridge, better than the stale overnight water. She pressed the icy, beaded pitcher against the back of her neck, then between her breasts, savoring the coolness that spread through her sweat-soaked body. A dip in the pool with Ringo and Georgia and Paulette, that's what she needed. They'd be ready for breakfast now, anyway.

She put the orange juice back in the "people's" refrigerator and opened the other one, where she kept the raw, whole fish. Will and Janette, the grad student couple who looked after the dolphins in her absence, had stocked it with a fresh supply.

She padded out to the lab area with a bucket of fish. Daniel was already there, wearing swim trunks, sitting by the edge of the pool with his feet dangling in the deep end.

"Morning!" he shouted when he saw her coming. "I like the outfit," he added with a smile.

"Strictly utilitarian, Mr. Colter," she said. "It's what all the best-dressed scientists aren't wearing this year."

"Don't you feel a little ... self-conscious, though?"

She sat down next to him and set the bucket beside her. "Around the dolphins, you mean?" It was her turn to smile. "Makes no difference to them. They're all naked to begin with, and they can scan through that bathing suit of yours as well as you can look through a sheet of Saran Wrap."

He looked as if he were about to blush, an incongruity on his rangy, slightly weary face. "Guess I never thought about it quite that way. Do they really notice the difference ...?"

"Between male and female humans? Absolutely. Paulette's an aggressive little flirt with just about any man who comes around, and I think Ringo still believes I'll mate with him eventually. He's the jealous type, too, so watch out for him; he might give you a little swat with his flukes if he sees you getting too close to me."

"Warning heeded," Daniel said, his gaze passing along the slim curve of her hips to her flat, brown belly and her taut little breasts. "Though you do make it difficult."

"Have you been in to meet them yet?" she asked. When they'd come in the day before, the dolphins had been out at sea, and they hadn't returned until late that night.

"I thought I'd better wait for you," he said. "From what you tell me about the male, sounds like that was a good idea."

"Oh, don't worry about him, he won't hurt you; the worst he'll do is maybe put you through a bit of a dominance routine to make sure you know your place."

"Hey, the water's all his. No argument there."

Sheila took a fish from the bucket and waved it above her head. "So, how're they doing? They been up to check you out, or show off a little?"

"No, they haven't paid me much attention."

She frowned. "That's odd; usually they want to see what a

stranger's like right away." She tossed the fish toward the far side of the pool, where the dolphins were swimming in tight, rapid circles. They ignored the fish, and it sank to the bottom, untouched.

"Jesus, that is weird, they ought to be starving by now." She stood up and carried the bucket to the other end of the pool, Daniel following behind her.

"Ringo! Georgia! Breakfast!" She pulled another fish out and held it by the tail, just above the surface. One of the dolphins surfaced for a breath and gave her and the fish a cursory glance, then dove and resumed its frantic swimming.

"Paulette!" Sheila called. "Come on, Miss Finicky, here's some fresh mackerel!"

The dolphins paid her no mind, and continued their brisk, aimless circuit at one corner of the pool. The water hummed with the vibrations of their ultrasonic emissions.

"Looks like they're just not very hungry," Daniel said.

Sheila shook her head. "There's something wrong. The way they're swimming, so preoccupied . . ."

"You think maybe they're sick?"

"I'll have to check them over, but I doubt it. When they're sick they usually get listless, not agitated like this." She put the bucket of fish down and walked to a metal cabinet against the wall.

"Why don't you fix us some breakfast?" she said, taking a bulbous thermometer and a wide, flat stethoscope from the cabinet. "If I need a hand, I'll let you know."

He kissed her and then looked toward the pool with mock apprehension. "Ringo'll get you for that one," Sheila whispered, and pushed him toward the kitchen.

As he chopped the ingredients for their omelets, he watched her through the windows overlooking the pool: chasing after the dolphins, stroking them, soothing them . . . lithe and naked as a dolphin herself, her wet-slick black hair the only indication that she was a creature of the land rather than of the sea.

He'd spent more time thinking about the ocean on this project than he had in years, he reflected; decades. Hell, he'd even started dreaming about it. One dream in particular had kept recurring over the last couple of weeks, a frustrating one that never came to any conclusion: himself as a kid, moving over the surface of the water at high speed like he was in a boat, only he couldn't really see the boat, all he could see was the water rushing past, and . . . something coming toward him through the water, coming fast.

He tossed the diced onions and garlic into a pan to sauté, and started cutting strips of Swiss cheese into the bowl with the eggs. He tried to concentrate on what he was doing, but that dream kept nagging at him, like there was something important about it that just kept eluding him, something momentous; if only he could figure out how it was supposed to end.

Sheila came back into the kitchen, her hair still dripping, wearing a short blue terry-cloth robe. "I can't find anything wrong with them physically," she said, shaking her head. "Temperatures are normal, pulses are steady. . . . I just can't figure it out."

"Maybe it's their mating season," Daniel said, pouring the eggs and cheese into the pan.

"You do have a lot to learn. Dolphins mate all the time, as often as they can."

"Like some people I know," Daniel said, smiling, but her expression remained somber.

"What am I going to do if they're still like this when my grant runs out?" she asked with real concern. "There's no aquarium or research facility in the world that'll take them if they look like they're ill, or mentally unbalanced. And the way they're acting, I don't know if they could survive for long in the wild."

Her face took on a pensive look as Daniel flipped the omelet and turned the heat down a bit. "Maybe it was something that happened when they were out there in the ocean," she speculated. "They could have run across some wild dolphins, but . . . why on earth should that have upset them so?"

9

"Are you sure you wouldn't ..."

Another jet came screaming overhead, and the red-haired receptionist busied herself with her nails, not even attempting to speak over the piercing roar. Her nail polish was kelly green, which looked a bit punkish but went well with her hair and eyes.

"... like a cup of coffee, Mr. Batera?" she finished smoothly as the plane landed and the noise was reduced to a mere background whine.

"Thank you, no," Batera said. "Had too much on the boat this morning already."

The young woman gave him an empty smile and reached for a blinking phone. "Sea Banquet Exports," she answered, and Batera tuned her voice out.

He looked around the reception area as he waited, thinking as he always did when he came here that the mustard-colored carpets and the pictures of French châteaus on the walls didn't really jibe with the location: Kettner Boulevard, right smack between the freeway and the railroad tracks, and not more than two blocks from the end of runway 27 at Lindbergh Field. He didn't hardly expect them to spring for some penthouse digs around Horton Plaza, but still ...

"Mr. Batera?" the girl said. "Mr. Schofield will see you now." He could feel her green eyes on him as he walked past her desk, and he momentarily wished he'd taken the time to go home and change clothes, have a shower. Fuck it, though—these people sell fish; let them at least have a whiff of their own product every now and then.

He rapped twice at Gerard Schofield's door and went inside. "Gerry," he said, taking a seat in front of the uncluttered oak desk.

Schofield looked at him a moment, then nodded. "So, Antonio," he said. "Lot of trouble these last few trips, huh?" He picked up a pencil from the immaculate desk and twiddled it between the thumb and first two fingers of his right hand. "Hell of a lot of trouble," he added, answering his own question.

Batera said nothing. Through the window behind Schofield's desk he could see a USAir 727 coming in for its final approach. It looked like the plane was on a direct collision course with the building.

Schofield turned to the computer on his desk and tapped at the keyboard, calling up a colorful Quattro spreadsheet. He stared thoughtfully at the screen until the jet had landed, then looked back at Batera.

"The accidents on the last couple of trips, those could happen on anybody's boat. And I suppose most anybody could've gotten fooled by those Greenpeace types you let on board. Hell, we won't even talk about the goddamn knife fight this last trip, or the bill from the Coast Guard for the MedEvac service. So fishermen drink, they fight. What else is new, right?"

"If I'd thought they were gonna start hitting the bottle again—"

Schofield held up his hands, palms out. "I said we wouldn't even talk about it, Antonio. Comes with the territory."

"Yah, Gerry, well ..."

"This right here, though," the man behind the desk said, jerking his thumb in the direction of the computer, "this right here is a different matter. This we have to talk about."

Batera looked at the screen, a meaningless jumble of numbers in red and blue and yellow rectangles. His son Jorge—he knew all about computers. Bet he could show Gerry plenty, by God.

"Five hundred tons, Antonio. Not eight, not seven, not even six hundred and fifty; *five* hundred fucking tons!"

Batera shifted his gaze back out the window over Schofield's shoulder, hoping to see another big, loud jet on its way in. The sky was empty.

"And what was the problem?" Schofield went on. "Hurricane, maybe? Boat's engines broke down? No, unh-unh. The problem was that *you* all of a sudden decided you had to look out after the health and welfare of every goddamn porpoise in the ocean."

"It's my boat, Gerry."

"No, it's *our* boat, and our asses. Sea Banquet bought seventy percent of that boat, and of your catch, after Starkist knuckled under. You knew then you'd go broke saving porpoises; what's so different now?"

"I sold you majority interest so long as I could stay on as skipper," Batera said. "I don't care how big a piece you own, I *run* that boat. Look at the contract."

"You look at the fucking contract, Antonio! There's a guaranteed minimum average tonnage specified in there, and if you keep going at this rate you're not gonna be running shit. We'll put a new skipper on, buy you out, whatever it takes. Got that?"

Batera took a deep breath and let it out slowly. "I run my boat how I see fit."

"Without a deck crew? All but two of them walked the minute you docked, is what I hear. Those guys want to work tuna boats, not goddamn Sea World."

"I'll find a crew."

Schofield glared at him, hard, but whatever he'd been about to say was cut off by a DC-9 coming down the glide path, threading its way between the downtown skyscrapers. If they didn't move the airport there was gonna be another bad crash here before long, Batera thought, maybe even worse than that PSA midair back in '78.

"Have you been listening to me at all?" Schofield asked when the high-pitched din subsided.

"I heard enough, Gerry." He stood up to go.

"You make the damn quota next trip. I mean it."

"Yah. Don't get your ass in a sling."

"Hey!" Schofield shouted at his back. "And keep the other boats in the code group informed, by God. You spot a big enough school of porpoise, you let them know. Don't go lying about it anymore."

Batera shut the door behind him and went back down the corridor, past the desk where the girl with the green nail polish sat typing a letter on her own computer terminal. She didn't say anything as Batera walked by. Given his mood, it was just as well.

Schofield was right, he knew; the word would spread fast around the docks, around the fishermen's bars: Stay away from Batera's boat. A jinx boat, they'd call it, and he could imagine what they'd have to say about him behind his back, about his orders to keep the porpoise kill to zero.

Maybe he would end up losing the boat, he thought as he stepped out into the incongruously sun-drenched industrial slum that surrounded the Sea Banquet offices. His whole goddamn life's work, thrown away on some stupid whim.

But it was more than just a whim—somehow he knew that; even though he couldn't say exactly how it was, or what it was, that he knew.

He settled himself into the plush leather seat of his big boat of a car and headed toward the house in Point Loma, struggling all the while to pin down that strange something that seemed to hover just beyond the edge of his awareness ... trying to *remember*, goddamnit, and whatever the hell it was that kept eluding him, he was sure it was plenty important.

Jeb Sloane lifted himself, headfirst and face skyward, out the exit hatch of the drilling command module and onto the deck of the *Alicia Faye*. There was plenty of room for the designers of the module to have just put a door in the goddamned thing, but, true to form, they'd made it so that anyone entering or leaving would have to do so in the style of the astronauts who'd ridden the old Gemini and Apollo capsules.

Bryant Emerson was waiting outside the hatch. "How's it look down there?" he asked, as if Jeb had just physically returned from the bottom of the sea, rather than emerging from an overly high-tech room where he'd been watching events down below on a television monitor.

"Still going well; we're down to one-point-six K," Jeb answered, meaning the laser drill had penetrated to a depth of 1,600 meters, or about 5,300 feet, beneath the sandy level of the sea floor.

"God, can you believe it?" Bryant said, shaking his head. "A mile down, in just four days."

Jeb nodded, equally impressed. "Wish we'd had this equipment in Nigeria; I could've cut that posting down to a couple of months."

"Buy you a beer?" Emerson asked.

Jeb looked at him, surprised.

"Things're a little looser here than they are on the rigs," Emerson explained. "Least they are in *my* cabin. What do you say?"

"Absolutely. Cold one sounds great."

Jeb followed him along the gangway and into Emerson's cabin, where his old school buddy opened a mini-fridge and withdrew two bottles of Rolling Rock.

"To old times," Emerson said when he'd popped the caps off the bottles and handed one to Jeb.

"Let's make it to new ones."

"To *good* times, then, whenever and wherever."

Few and far between, Jeb thought as he raised the cold green bottle and drank. There was a long, awkward gap in the conversation, then both men spoke at once.

"I don't mean to—"

"I wish there was—"

They paused again, then Emerson gestured with his hand out, palm up, meaning "You go ahead."

"Ah, shit, Bryant," Jeb muttered, shaking his head. "I'm sorry to be such a pain, but I—it just all went straight to hell, you know? And it wasn't all that long ago, so I guess I haven't really come to terms with it yet."

Emerson took a long pull on his beer, then wiped his mouth with his sleeve. "You want to talk about it?" he asked, uncomfortably.

"Fuck, no," Jeb said, and meant it. What he'd already said qualified as an exhaustive admission and discussion in his book. "If I decide to go all talky-feely, I won't bug you with it, I'll take my act to Oprah."

"Cause if you really—"

"I said no," Jeb told him, and realized with mild chagrin that there was more of an edge to his voice than he had intended. It was discomfiting to still be this upset about it; part of him instinctively felt that he should have perceived the end of his marriage as no more than a brief, and minor, inconvenience—or at least that he should present that impression of nonchalance in the face of personal disaster to the outside world.

It was more than just the breakup with Lindy, though; it was what had caused it, the specific incident that had, in a moment, severed the bond between them. And it was the fact that Lindy had *blamed* him for it, blamed him and his work, as if Jeb had planned the whole revolting spectacle, as if his entire career had been somehow purposefully leading up to that one awful scene . . . as if he had been any less dumbfounded and appalled than she.

They'd been in Riyadh for the day, on a shopping expedition, though there was little to be bought there that couldn't be found in greater variety, and at better prices, in one of the company stores back in Dharan's sprawling American enclave.

Much of Riyadh was deceptively modern in appearance, blocks of cleanly designed white office towers that could as easily have been in New York or Atlanta or Hong Kong, and streams of Mercedes or BMW sedans racing past shops with small metallic plaques discreetly identifying them as the local outlets of Gucci, Cartier, Armani, and the like.

He and Lindy had been in the old town that day, though, the warrens of the city's southern part, where the walls of the plain, low buildings sloped inward at the top, somehow rendering them even more austere and uninviting. No one lounged in the streets, no children played; this was the stronghold of the Wahhabists, strictest and most humorless of the country's Muslim sects.

The Gold Souk was in this area, as was the *Suq al Harim,* or Women's Market, and Jeb and Lindy had spent the morning browsing through them both. She'd bought a filigreed silver bracelet and a small piece of Bedouin pottery, and they'd made their way out of the Souk just before noon, both of them hungry and Jeb longing hopelessly for a beer to counteract the dry, stultifying heat.

The *mutawiyyin* had been everywhere in the market that day, babbling their incomprehensible calls to prayer or whatever. Jeb and Lindy had ignored the religious vigilantes as best they could, paying them heed only when one of the men had whacked Lindy sharply across the shins with a stick. Her "sin" had been to bend down to inspect a carpet, allowing her long dress to ride up an inch or two above her ankle.

"Up yours, you sorry little goat-fucker," Lindy had hissed at the man, and Jeb had urgently squeezed her elbow to quiet her. The scowling fanatic had appeared not to understand, and had moved on through the crowd, his ferrety eyes ever alert for other violators of his religion's myriad proscriptions. The very word *Islam,* Jeb recalled with distaste, was Arabic for "submission."

They'd made their way out of the market, past the increasing numbers of ululating *mutawiyyin,* and only when they were about to emerge into Dira Square did it occur to Jeb that the remarkably large crowd, including an unusual number of the patrolling religious vigilantes, might portend something out of the ordinary.

Dira Square was Riyadh's version of the Piazza San Marco in Venice, or Moscow's Red Square, though considerably smaller and less interesting, architecturally, than either. It was bordered not only by the two bustling Souks, but also by the *Oasr al Adl,* or Palace of Justice; the *Oasr al Hukm,* where the king traditionally met with tribal sheikhs; and the Great Mosque, erected on the site where Emir Turki ibn Abdullah, great-grandfather of the legendary ruler Ibn Saud, had been assassinated in 1834.

By the time Jeb and Lindy entered the square, they were no longer really moving on their own, but were being pushed forward by a tide of sweaty, shouting humanity, almost all of whom were men. The crowd pulsed and flowed as one organism, its focus clearly and intently directed at a small tableau of people on the north side of the square, in front of the mosque.

The little gathering had immediately struck Jeb as somehow theatrical, even operatic: There was a staged quality in the men's stances, in their movements; a certain forced dignity of purpose that set them apart from the milling, unruly crowd of onlookers.

Then Jeb noticed that the small assembly in front of the mosque was larger than he had thought, by one person. There was a young woman in the center of the group of formally robed men; she, too, was clad in immaculate white, but hadn't been noticeable at first because she was at such a lower height than the men, considerably lower even than would be expected due to the ordinary height difference between most men and most women.

The young woman was buried up to her chest in a four-foot pit that had apparently been dug in the asphalt of the square, and then refilled with heavy dark earth as she had stood in the hole. Her shoulders were thrust back in such a way as to suggest that her hands were tied behind her back, below the freshly tamped earth. Her eyes were blindfolded with a white silk ribbon, and her cheeks were wet with thin lines of perspiration—or tears—that trickled from beneath the tightly knotted ribbon.

"Oh, Jesus," Lindy had said with something akin to a whimper, "they're not going to—"

"Let's get out of here," Jeb had said, recognizing what was about to happen, but the way back out of the square was a solid mass of people now, impenetrable, fervid with zeal and righteous expectancy.

Jeb took Lindy by the arm and tried to open a path for them through the crowd, to at least get them away from the forefront of the mob, but their way was forcibly blocked by two of the berobed, stick-wielding *mutawiyyin*. One of them was the man from the marketplace, the one who had struck Lindy earlier.

"You watch, American whore," the holy man spat out, in clear though accented English. "You watch and you learn!"

A pile of rocks, ranging in size from walnuts to baseballs, had been heaped together not far from where the young woman was half buried. The eldest of the presiding officials selected one mid-sized rock, and threw it at the woman's head. His pitch was impassioned, but feeble; the rock glanced off the woman's forehead, causing her to cry out more in alarm than in pain.

The first stone cast, a dozen of the nearest onlookers then scrambled to collect their own missiles. They threw them with calculated purpose: A heavy blow to the temple with one of the largest rocks would have killed the woman instantly, but the hurlers seemed more interested in prolonging her agony, inflicting maximum torment while deferring the coup de grâce.

The minutes of torture stretched on like hours in the dusty heat. The young woman's nose was broken again and again, her lips shredded as one stone after another smashed against her screaming mouth, breaking her teeth. Her ears were torn from her head, her black hair matted with clotting blood. A roar of approval went up from the crowd as one lucky toss of a lemon-sized rock caught the socket of one blindfolded eye, crushing it with a sickening, pulpy sound that was clearly audible where Jeb and Lindy stood, weak-kneed and sickened.

It had taken the rock throwers a full fifteen minutes to murder the young woman, and the crowd had buzzed with angry disappointment when at last she was pronounced dead. Jeb had never learned what her supposed crime had been; most likely a matter of falling in love, and of acting on her desires rather than suppressing them.

KEN GRIMWOOD

Lindy had left the country—and Jeb—on the next available flight out. He had spoken to her only by telephone since, to arrange the details of the divorce.

As if that episode of horror had been *his* doing, the insanities of Wahabbist fanaticism his own creation. As if he, Jeb Sloane, had personally and maliciously arranged that three quarters of the world's petroleum deposits be placed beneath the most barbaric and benighted of its nations.

"You got another beer in there?" he asked Emerson, and took the proffered icy bottle, and spent the remainder of the day drinking with his friend and talking of inconsequential things, things unencumbered by memories or meaning.

Daniel took the first State Street exit he saw, and soon discovered he was still two or three miles from downtown, where his appointment was. He didn't know the area very well; he'd been up here only a couple of times before, and he'd stayed at the beach then.

Santa Barbara was, he thought, the most strikingly attractive small city in the country, and the town planners had obviously had that goal aggressively in mind when they'd rebuilt it after a major earthquake in the twenties. They'd had a beautiful setting to work with, the town cradled between the Santa Ynez Mountains and a sheltered, southward-facing stretch of Pacific beaches; and they'd made the most of what they'd been given.

The city now had a distinctively Mediterranean look, and not by accident. Strict zoning laws and construction codes had mandated that no new buildings be higher than three or four stories, and that almost every public or commercial structure adhere to the basic theme of white stucco walls and Spanish red-tiled roofs. More subtly, there were no billboards to block the mountain and ocean views; their absence added considerably to the town's appeal, though it took a while to realize they weren't there.

He turned left on Micheltorena, then south on Anacapa, past a palm-shaded park that reminded him of the Plaza San Martín in Buenos Aires. The nearby County Courthouse, a masterpiece of Spanish-Moorish arches and towers framed by tropical gardens, was the town's centerpiece. Its image of lush and carefree beauty was marred only by the knowledge that there were people in there on trial for their freedom, even their lives; and by the presence of a dozen or so orderly protesters carrying signs that read NO MORE OIL and STOP THE DRILLING.

Daniel pulled into the parking lot for the Santa Barbara *Herald* building, gave the guard his name, and got a visitor's I.D. badge.

Inside, the newsroom was like any other: big U-shaped city desk, frazzled reporters and harried editors shouting at one another, and almost as many computer terminals on the desks as there were coffee cups. Much as he'd enjoyed free-lancing, he could never enter a working newsroom without a familiar twinge of nostalgia and a vague half-regret at having gone solo.

Sam Jenkins was in the catbird seat at the city desk, and he was currently engaged in a heated debate with a young black woman. Daniel hung on the sidelines until the woman abruptly walked away, still in a huff, and Jenkins waved him over.

"You old son-of-a-bitch!" Sam exclaimed with a grin, squeezing his hand with a painful grip. "God, it's been—what, four years? Five?"

"More like six," Daniel said.

"Jesus fucking Christ, I couldn't believe it when you called. Saw that piece of yours on Boris Yeltsin in *Rolling Stone;* first-rate stuff, I always knew you had it in you."

"So what's the view from the other side of the desk?" Daniel asked. He and Jenkins had been in the reporters' trenches together at the *Chicago Tribune*, and had spent many a bourbon-soaked evening in one or another of the city's dives commiserating on the stupidity of editors in general and in particular.

"Hell, I was born for it!" Jenkins roared. "Finally figured out I was too goddamn mean for anything else. Plus, I got sick of the wind-chill factor, and this was the only job open out here. Never would've dreamed the only way to paradise was to become a city editor, would we?"

His hearty demeanor suddenly changed, the wry smile left his face. "Hey, listen, I was—it was a shock to hear about Ruth. A terrible, terrible thing. I'm so sorry."

Hearing her name spoken aloud still made Daniel's stomach clench, even now, but he managed a shrug. "Been a long time," he said.

"Are you—"

"Remarried? No, haven't even thought about it yet. Seeing somebody now, though, very interesting lady. She's a scientist, does research on dolphins here at UCSB."

Jenkins smiled again, clearly grateful to have been steered away from the murky topic of Ruth's death. "So that's what brings you up our way."

"Partly," Daniel said. "There's also a story I'm doing background on—her work kind of ties into it. That's why I asked you the favor."

"No problem. Come on, I'll show you where you can work." Sam stood up and led him through the newsroom to a cramped, glass-walled cubicle near the sports desk. Inside was a large, stand-alone computer terminal and a bookshelf full of manuals and reference materials.

"You ever used NEXIS before?"

Daniel shook his head. "Never could afford an account, free-lancing."

"Best thing is to plan your search before you get it fired up. Lot cheaper that way, and less chance of the front office giving me any static."

"Understood."

"Now, you want info about dolphins, right?" He thumbed through a thick user's guide and handed it to Daniel. The page Sam had opened to showed a long list of scientific journals under the subhead "Biology": the *Journal of Cetacean Studies,* 1977–present, *Natural History Abstracts,* 1973–present, *Cetacea,* 1983–present . . .

"I don't need anything this far back," Daniel said. "Just from the last few days."

"Like wire stories, you mean?"

"Yeah, that should do it."

"O.K.," Sam said, scribbling notes on a memo pad. "We'll start with ALL WIRES; that covers AP and UPI national and all fifty of their state wires, plus Reuters and the New York, L.A. and Chicago city wires."

"How about newspapers?"

Sam made another note. "ALL PAPERS," he said. "That's the *Trib, New York Times, L.A. Times, Washington Post,* plus a dozen or so more from Miami, Seattle, Denver, like that."

"Jesus," Daniel said. "Does this just give you summaries, or what?"

"Nope. Complete articles, every word of everything they print. It's a monster of a data base, cost you a goddamn fortune to search if you're not careful."

"O.K., then. What I'm looking for is any reports of dolphins acting . . . weird, or agitated. Anything out of the ordinary."

Sam nodded, thought a moment and wrote something at the bottom of the memo pad. "Grab a chair from out there," he said. "I'll get us on the system."

When Daniel returned, Jenkins was telling the computer exactly what he wanted:

```
SEARCH:   ALL WIRES
          ALL PAPERS
DEFINE:   dolphin AND behav OR acti AND odd OR unusual
          OR strange
LIMITS:   AFTER 10-11 CURRENT YEAR
```

"What's 'behav' and 'acti'?" Daniel asked, puzzled.

"It'll look for any words with those strings of letters," Sam explained. "Behavior, behaving, behaved, actions, activity, acting ... 'course, if there's a story about a strange guy named Mobehaven who built a statue of a dolphin in his garden of cacti, it'll give us that one, too. But this ought to keep it pretty well confined to what you're looking for."

He hit a key and the screen told them SEARCH IN PROGRESS. In less than a minute the message had changed to SEARCH COMPLETE: 32 STORIES FOUND.

"That's not so bad," Sam said. "Might as well print 'em all." He struck a key labeled PRINT, and the built-in laser device began churning out pages. "Some of these interns, you let 'em in here they'll search for everything with the word 'the.' One of my reporters was on deadline for a White House story back during the Gulf War, goddamn intern came up with nine thousand entries. He told it to search for 'bush,' and didn't add 'AND george OR president'; we not only got every article about roses and garden hedges for the past year, but all the stock-market wheat futures, too ... bushel after bushel."

The printer stopped its whirring and Sam signed himself off, then shut down the terminal. "If you want to look those over now, just take any empty desk," he said. "I've gotta go take a hatchet to some poor guy's copy."

Daniel thanked him and found a place to sit where he could stretch out his legs. He desperately wanted a cigarette, but there was a large NO SMOKING sign next to the bank of clocks above the city desk. Jesus, what were newsrooms coming to? The haze-free air and the silent computers made the place feel more like an insurance company's office than one of the loud, smoky, free-for-all newsrooms that had once been the norm.

He flipped through the stories Sam had printed for him, skimming their headlines:

DOLPHINS: OUR STRANGE AND WONDERFUL COUSINS OF THE SEA
LOCAL ODDFELLOW SOCIETY ADOPTS DOLPHIN
ODD DOLPHIN BEHAVIOR PUZZLES SCIENTISTS

That last one was more like it. He tossed the first two stories into an already overflowing wastebasket and started reading the one that had caught his eye:

MIAMI (UPI) Scientists at the Devore Marine Mammal Institute here say they're not sure what to make of an unexpected change in the behavior of six Atlantic bottlenose dolphins whose mating patterns they've been studying for the past three years. The normally cooperative creatures, whose intelligence has been estimated to be on a scale approaching if not equaling that of humans, began acting in an unusual manner last Thursday. Dr. Louis Friedman, director of the Institute, says the dolphins are healthy, but have been refusing to eat and have appeared to be highly agitated. Attempts to calm the animals have been to no avail, and they continue to swim in random circles in their tank, rejecting all human contact. Dr. Friedman adds that . . .

Daniel set the single-page printout aside and went back to the small stack before him. There were several versions of the next article, all essentially identical to the original AP wire story:

KILLER WHALE ATTACKS TRAINER

ORLANDO (AP) Officials at Sea World have declined to speculate on the reason behind a near-fatal attack here Tuesday by a killer whale against its longtime trainer. The ordinarily tame sea mammal, named Blackie, suddenly lunged at its trainer, 23-year-old Barbara Sherwood, and bit a large chunk of flesh from the woman's thigh. Ms. Sherwood is in serious but stable condition at a local hospital, and says she had done nothing unusual or threatening to provoke the attack, which occurred during a rehearsal for one of the oceanic theme park's popular shows. Sources say that immediately following the attack on Ms. Sherwood, the 28-foot, five-ton creature turned on a group of smaller common dolphins that were swimming in the same tank and the animals engaged in heated fighting until they could be separated. The killer whale has reportedly been quiet since the incident, while the dolphins have become increasingly agitated and withdrawn.

Killer whales, also known as orcas, are ferocious predators in the wild, but have rarely if ever been known to attack humans. Orcas and dolphins are related species under the order *Cetacea*, which also includes . . .

What the hell was that all about? Daniel wondered. At least the dolphins in Orlando had good reason to be upset, but could the incident be related to Sheila's problem, and the case in Miami? He took a paper clip from a cracked coffee cup on the desk and put the Sea World stories together, then turned to the next printout.

—*Cincinnati Enquirer:*

DONNIE AND DAPHNE
WON'T COME OUT TO PLAY

Boys and girls at the Cincinnati Ocean Zoo have been disappointed this week because two of their favorite stars, Donnie and Daphne Dolphin, haven't been acting their usual friendly selves. The normally "flipper-ti-gibbet" pair won't even eat their daily 20 pounds of raw fish each, like good dolphins should; and instead of performing their spectacular repertoire of tricks like jumping through hoops and playing volleyball, all they want to do is swim around in circles . . . going nowhere! The dolphins' trainers say their unusual standoffishness might just be a touch of the "Ocean blues," and they hope that by next week . . .

There were seventeen more stories, detailing eleven different instances of peculiar dolphin behavior from around the country, and one case each in France, Germany, and Australia. As far as Daniel could see, nobody had yet come up with a good explanation for what was going on.

More important, nobody seemed to even know there *was* anything going on; he could find no indication that anyone other than himself had pieced the widely scattered reports together and recognized them as a generalized phenomenon.

"So, you find what you were looking for?"

Daniel started; he'd lost track of where he was, and hadn't seen Sam Jenkins come up behind him. "Nah, guess my hunch was wrong," he said, folding the pages and sticking them in his jacket pocket. "Thanks for the computer time anyway, though."

"Hey, no problem, anytime. Gimme a call if you're in town a few more days, we'll grab a beer. Thursday, maybe?"

"Sounds good," Daniel said, and made his way out of the busy newsroom. Once he'd left the building's parking lot, he gunned his protesting old Toyota and raced down Anacapa Street, searching for the nearest pay phone. He knew he had an exclusive here; but what the hell it meant was another question altogether.

Ch*Tril's stomach was tight with apprehension as she swam toward the center of the School. A state of high alert had been in effect ever since the unexpected orca attack, and no one knew when or whether another onslaught might take place; but her present anxiety was more immediate, more personal.

The Circle had been in emergency session on an almost constant basis, and she had seen little of Dj\Tal in the past few days. Now she had been summoned to appear before the Circle herself, for what reasons she could not guess. Had the Old One somehow learned that Dj\Tal had told her everything, or almost everything? She only hoped his own position was not in jeopardy because of what he'd revealed to her.

Qr*Jil, the Old One, was holding forth as Ch*Tril quietly approached the gathering and hovered on the sidelines. Qr*Jil was more than twice Ch*Tril's age, and in her prime she had Melded with the Source-Mind a hundred times or more. A crescent-shaped segment of the Old One's dorsal fin was missing, the result of a

long-ago encounter with an angry Danger-Cousin, and her flanks
were streaked with the scars of many other brushes with disaster.
The risks she'd taken had been worth it, though, for Qr*Jil's numerous Meldings had produced a great trove of historical information.

The saga of the Great Water Hardening, for instance: For hundreds of generations, until Qr*Jil had unlocked the full story from
within the deepest recesses of the Source-Mind, such tales had been
dismissed as at best a wild exaggeration, at worst a ludicrous myth
with no basis in fact. Now everyone knew of the age when the
sheets of ice like the one that had almost claimed Tr*Til's life had
expanded into all but the warmest seas. Millions of their kind had
died, and the survivors had been forced into a shrinking band of
relative warmth in which they had been effectively imprisoned until
the encroaching hard-water had at last begun to recede to its present
boundaries.

How, Ch*Tril wondered, could one who had dared so much in
the search for knowledge be opposed to the New Directives Dj\Tal
had described? Ch*Tril could think of nothing more fascinating,
more thrilling, than to finally break the old taboos prohibiting full
contact with the land-walkers. There would be so much to learn,
to teach, to share. . . .

Someone was Imaging something about Dj\Tal, and she turned
her attention back to the Circle meeting. A lengthy discussion was
under way about how best to respond to the Danger-Cousins' unpro-
voked attack, and judging from the vehemence of the general imaging, the debate was nearing a climax.

]Retaliation/Imperative[, insisted Jr*Zin, whose mate had been
killed in the attack. Her desire for revenge was understandable,
and Dj\Tal leavened his response to her with sympathy, but he
reminded her and the rest of the Circle that such an action would
be contrary to the First Teachings of the Source-Mind.

Surely the attack by the orcas had not been mere random mali-
ciousness, he argued; what was truly imperative was that they learn
the cause behind it, so that a basis might be found for negotiation
to end the sudden hostilities.

208

His suggestion was not a popular one, Ch*Tril noted with dismay. Jr*Zin was not the only Circle member who had suffered personal loss in the recent battle, and the anger ran as high here as in the rest of the School.

Qr*Jil, the Old One, had been regarding the proceedings in silence, as if from a regal distance; now she cast a cloudy, omniscient old eye on Dj\Tal, and Linked her decision to the assembly at large:

>Dj\Tal Proposes the Concept<

>Dj\Tal Shall Initiate the Negotiation<

He had no choice but to accept, Ch*Tril knew. His pride would not permit him to refuse, despite the obvious danger. Ch*Tril's only hope was that the rest of the Circle might Choose to override Qr*Jil's decision, but none came forward with an objection. The Old One's solution seemed to strike everyone as a satisfactory compromise. If Dj\Tal were killed in the attempt to reason with the Danger-Cousins, a full-scale retaliation would be even more justified; if he succeeded, peace might indeed be reestablished.

>The Choice Is Affirmed<

Qr*Jil Linked to the assemblage after several seconds of silence. Ch*Tril wanted to go to her mate's side, to give him a Touch and offer him her sympathy and support, but she didn't dare initiate a private contact with him now. All she could do was look at him, and he back at her, each knowing what the other must be feeling now.

>Welcome to Our Circle Historian Ch*Tril<

Qr*Jil Linked next, and all at once Ch*Tril found herself the object of a dozen simultaneous Links, a mental suffusion of warmth and acceptance reminiscent of a Source-Mind Melding. Dj\Tal's revelation of the Circle's secrets had been by design, she suddenly realized; she herself had been Chosen to be a member of the group.

>Proposal of Assignment for Historian Ch*Tril<

Dj\Tal Linked formally;

>Initiation of Next Phase in New Directives<

Ch*Tril looked at her mate with surprise; they'd never discussed this—he'd never even hinted at such a thing. Could he have had this in mind all along? Was this what he'd been planning when he'd first given her the key-pattern that had allowed her access to some of the Source-Mind's secrets?

The Old One rocked slowly from side to side, her eyes half closed, apparently mulling over the idea. Ch*Tril tried to will her heart to slow its sudden pounding, aware that any member of the Circle could easily scan how excited she was. This would be the greatest opportunity of her life, the chance to play a major role in the history of her kind rather than merely studying and analyzing that history.

Qr*Jil's blurry, unreadable eyes opened at last, her ruminations done.

>The Time Is Not Now<

she Linked with finality, and the blunt decision was buttressed by a dozen accompanying images, most of them violent, only a few of which Ch*Tril understood. The current conflict with the Danger-Cousins, that was obvious enough, but there were also references to members of their kind dead and bleeding in shallow waters, injured in some incomprehensible way by land-walkers. The Old One's Link implied that at least one of these events was quite recent, though the image was clearly of a foreign sea and shore; this must have been relayed information that only the Circle was privy to, and it gave Ch*Tril pause.

Dj\Tal caught her eye, and his look was full of reassurance. That quick glance was enough to calm her; he would never knowingly send her into a situation of real danger.

>It Is Crucial That the Time Be Now<

he Linked to the Old One and to the Circle at large, and his own Link carried with it a host of supporting images that outlined his plan: The contact would take place at sea, he explained, not near the shore. No potentially hostile land-walkers would be involved, only the chosen Receptives.

Ch*Tril remained silent while the debate raged; it was understood that, were she to join in, she would argue in favor of the mission, but the Choice was not hers to make.

The passions on both sides of the question ran high: Qr*Jil was adamant in her insistence that the establishment of contact with the land-walkers be delayed until the conflict with the Danger-Cousins was resolved, but Ch*Tril knew this to be mere subterfuge on the Old One's part; Dj\Tal had told her that Qr*Jil had done everything she could to block the implementation of the New Directives from the beginning. Perhaps the Old One had simply focused for too long on the past, and was unable to accept the imperatives of the future.

Dj\Tal had no such qualms; his own father had been among those to establish the Preparatory Links with selected land-walker young ones, and the promise of the New Directives had been Dj\Tal's dream for all his life. He had infected Ch*Tril with that vision, too, even without her knowledge; for she realized now that those strange, seductive images he had shared with her from the time of their first mating were not fantasies, but were genuine images of the land-walkers' way of life, gleaned by Dj\Tal's father in the course of those Preparatory Links and passed on through his son to her.

Now she, too, had at least vicariously participated in such contact with the land-walkers, during her most recent Melding with the Source-Mind; and if Dj\Tal could persuade the others to ignore Qr*Jil's objections, she might soon be doing so for real.

Ch*Tril wanted a breath, wanted to dissipate her rising tension with some rapid movement, but the debate was coming to a close and she didn't dare risk rising to the surface for fear of missing the moment of Choice. This would be the most important Choice that had ever directly concerned her; it might even be the most significant ever made, for her kind as a whole. *This,* she thought with a sudden thrill, was history.

There was a sudden commotion off to one side, a flurry of activity among Qr*Jil's protector/companions, who waited silently nearby whenever the Circle met. Dv\Kil—it was Ch*Tril's son, Dv\Kil, swimming toward the gathered Circle at top speed.

Ch*Tril felt a rush of fear; was Dv\Kil all right? Were the Danger-Cousins attacking the School again?

Dv\Kil came to a sudden halt directly in front of Qr*Jil, casting only the quickest of acknowledging glances at Ch*Tril, and began to Image to the Old One. Ch*Tril moved discreetly behind Qr*Jil, so that she could more clearly perceive the Images that Dv\Kil was directing to the Circle's leader.

What he communicated was as mysterious as it was disturbing: Lifelike metallic objects that swam without swimming, burning beams of light that emanated from them and from another, larger object . . . and, most worrisome of all, red-hot liquid rock oozing from the sea floor even when the land-walker's peculiar beams ceased their burning.

Ch*Tril knew all too well what that portended; and the prospect of something that incomprehensibly violent was more terrifying than any number of marauding, warring Danger-Cousins. Despite the mythic connection of such an incident to the creation of life, Ch*Tril knew from her research that it would, in reality, bring only destruction and death.

The Choice now was a foregone conclusion: The Circle would override Qr*Jil's veto, even if the Old One was blind enough to persist in her objections. The land-walkers *must* be contacted now, Ch*Tril thought: They must be warned; they must be stopped.

10

"Pobres! Depois todos êstes anos, seremos pobres!"

"English, English . . . talk English, will you?"

"Why for? We must to go back in Portugal, you go on this way. *Não mais America, por causa de teu estupidez!"*

Batera rubbed his eyes with the back of his hand, sick of the way this day was going. Bad enough that most of the crew had quit on him when they'd docked this morning, worse that Gerry Schofield had jumped down his throat about the short tonnage . . . and this was what he'd walked into when he'd come home looking for some peace.

"Leave it be, Maria, O.K.? We not gonna be poor, we not movin' back to Portugal. So don't worry."

"What you care about these damn *toninhas,* anyway? The men don't got enough to do on the boat already, they got to save one kinda fish to catch another?"

Funny, Batera thought, he'd never paid much attention to how close the Portuguese word for "porpoise" was to the familiar form of his own name. *Toninho e as Toninhas,* it sounded like some kind of title, a song maybe. Children's song.

"You know what ever'body sayin'?" Maria asked, her voice thin with mixed hurt and contempt. "The wives, the men ... they all sayin' you go soft *em la cabeça*. They say you get fooled by damn Greenpeacers, go over their side. What can I say, I hear that kinda talk?"

Batera pushed his recliner back, tried to relax. "You tell 'em my business ain't their business, that's all."

His wife tossed aside the knitting she'd been working on when he'd walked through the door; socks, it looked like, blue and green wool socks.

"Bom, verdadeiro bom," she said sarcastically. "Easy for you to say, you don' have to hear them talk ever' day, see how they look at me. I got to hear it, though, all the *mexerico* about how you can't handle your crew no more."

He stared at the wall, trying to lose himself in the smooth, creamy texture of the new paint they'd had put on last year ... but one of Maria's Jesus portraits kept looking back at him, a stern-faced one done on cheap black velvet; she'd bought it on one of their Sunday drives across the border last time he'd been in port for a while. Whose side would Jesus be on in this mess? Batera wondered; would he think the porpoises were worth all this grief, or would he say a man's work and his family came first?

"At the *supermercado,* even, I hear it, do you know? Last Friday, while I stand in line at Lucky, *a esposa de Fernando Guimares,* she say to me ..."

Jesus, Jesus, Jesus. She just wouldn't let it alone. Batera closed his eyes, but it didn't help. If anything it only emphasized the sound of her voice droning on and on about how stupid he was, how much he'd embarrassed her. He could tell her a thing or two about embarrassment! But, hell, even her damned fado records would be better than this. He got to his feet and halfway considered actually putting one on the stereo, turning it up loud enough to drown her out. Instead, he grabbed his cap and jacket and headed for the door, as she had driven him to do so many times before.

"*Porquê sais?* I want you explain to me why—"

"I have to go out, Maria." He closed the door behind him before he could hear any more.

He found Manoel at Nunu's, sitting in one of the dark leather booths with the engineer and the mate of another tuna boat that had docked at the G Street Mole this morning, just after the *Sea Master*. Batera slid in to join them, and the men's previously animated conversation went into an awkward lapse.

The crappy music, barely a step up from Muzak, played on in the background: Barry Manilow, Neil Diamond, somebody like that; not rock, not standards, but some lukewarm mush in between. The waitress came by, and Batera ordered a sausage-and-pepper sandwich and a Dos Equis.

"So, Toninho, you guys home early." The engineer's tone and expression were neutral, but after today it was hard for Batera not to read them as taunting.

"Yah, few days. Lookin' for a fresh crew don't mind hard work."

Silence, except for the whiny singer on the radio.

"Fuckin' Panamanians," Manoel said. "Can't keep 'em off the sauce."

The other men nodded solemnly, as if a sage universal truth had been proclaimed.

Batera's sandwich came, hot out of the microwave. His table companions talked of storms and engines and Costa Rican whorehouses while he ate.

The place was filling up with the cocktail crowd; about half of them were in the business, or their husbands or brothers or sons were. Fernando Guimares, skipper of the *Diego Queen,* came in and took a seat at the bar. He was still blinking from the bright sunshine outside, and when his eyes had adjusted to the dimness he spotted Batera and gave a grinning half-wave, half-salute.

"Hey, Manoel," Batera said, nudging the mate with his elbow. "What say we get outta here, maybe hit the union hall?"

Manoel glanced around, saw Guimares at the bar. "Sounds good," he said, putting a twenty on the table for the drinks and food. "You guys be in town long?" he asked the men from the other boat.

"Couple days," the engineer said. "Waitin' for a new compressor."

"See ya here or the Lamplighter, then."

"Yeah. Good luck on the crew."

Batera nodded curtly, still unsure whether the sarcasm he couldn't help hearing was intended.

He'd parked his Chrysler in the lot behind the bar; Manoel's Trans-Am was across the street, in front of a used book store. Batera eased out slowly, singing along with Mel Tormé. He put the big car on cruise control when he hit the Cabrillo Freeway; Manoel passed him, doing 80 or 85, and was soon out of sight.

When Batera pulled into the parking lot of the union hall down near the docks, the stocky mate was leaning against his car, smoking a cigarette. Out in the bay, a battleship slid past, escorted by a dozen smaller vessels. On the superstructure of the battleship shone the bright red star of the Russian Navy. Batera shook his head; times changing everywhere, for everybody.

The union hall was painted a drab institutional green, inside and out. Tacked on to the cork bulletin board near the information desk was a mixed array of pension plan booklets, sample insurance forms, and ads for companies that promised to clear up bad credit. Toward the back of the room was a table with a coffee machine, Styrofoam cups, and a box of stale-looking doughnuts. Ten or twelve men, all with skins dark from a combination of genes and constant exposure to the sun, had pulled some of the patched vinyl chairs into a circle around the table.

"Inglês?" Manoel asked the group. A couple of the men shrugged and looked away; the others nodded or raised their hands.

"I'm fillin' out a crew," Batera told them. "But I don't want nobody's gonna lounge around, not pull his share. Anybody interested?"

Most of the hands went up again; then one of the men who hadn't responded spoke up. "Ain't you Batera?" he asked. "Off the Sea Master?"

"That's my name, an' that's my boat. You want work, or you wanta hang around here?"

"I heard stories . . ." the man said, leaving his comment hanging.

"Women tell stories," Manoel said. "Men work."

"You that porpoise-lovin' skipper, *não?*" another of the men asked, squinting at Batera. "Bad-luck boat, too, I been told."

"Nothin' wrong with my boat," Batera said gruffly. "Had some bad-luck crew, rather drink or fight than work. You that kind?"

The man's thick arms tensed, stretching the cut-off sleeves of his white T-shirt. "Nobody ever complain about my work. But I catch tuna, I don't train no fuckin' porpoise."

"You want to go after tuna?" Batera challenged. "Then what you sittin' here for?"

"Boats all full," the man admitted, dropping his gaze to the floor.

"Not mine," Batera told them all. "I got twelve crew slots, and anybody that's man enough can have one."

"What about that porpoise stuff we hear?" someone in the back wanted to know. "That true, or not?"

Batera crossed his arms and looked the man straight in the eye. "I got a rule of my own," he said. "My boat don't kill porpoise. You understand that goin' in, we won't have no problem."

"I don't know . . ."

"Yah, it means more work. Means more money, too."

Manoel glanced at him and frowned questioningly.

"How's that?" asked the one who'd first brought up the rumors.

"I'll split my own share. Most skippers, you know, they take maybe five times a crewman's share of the profit from the catch every trip. On my boat, all that extra's goin' to the crew."

Manoel was looking at him with amazement, and seemed about to say something. Batera hushed him with a glance.

By the time they left the union hall, three crewmen had signed on for the *Sea Master*'s next trip, and the names of a cousin and a brother-in-law had been put forth as seasoned hands who might also be willing to join in for the unprecedented share arrangement Batera was offering. Now it was on to the Lamplighter and back to Nunu's to repeat the same spiel, and he figured he'd probably have to return to the union hall two or three more times until he had a full crew.

That meant the better part of a week, most likely, before he could head out to sea again. More days of listening to Maria gripe and groan; more nights of that weird, confusing dream, where he was a young boy and there was something racing through the water toward him, like it knew exactly who he was . . . like it had plans for him.

There was something terribly wrong with the sea.

Dj\Tal had been swimming for half a light-time, with Vl\Kal as his companion—the pod-brother had insisted on coming along, even though Dj\Tal had planned this as a solo mission—when suddenly they had found themselves surrounded by a slimy film that floated on the surface of the water for hundreds of beak-to-flukes in every direction. In places it was dark, almost black, and in other areas it gleamed reflectively like the brightly colored sky-arches that often appeared after a storm.

The slick was some sort of detritus from the giant floating hulls of the land-walkers, he knew; but why did they so often foul the seas with such noxious stuff? Every time he and Vl\Kal were forced to surface for a breath it stung their eyes and burned their blowholes, and the greasy film stuck unpleasantly to their skin. They stayed as deep as possible for as long as they could between each breath, and wriggled as they swam to clean the pernicious substance off them. There were many dead fish floating on the surface, and dead flying-creatures, too.

This was reason enough to make it imperative that contact with the land-walkers proceed with due haste, Dj\Tal thought. The threat presented by the burning sea floor that Dv\Kil had discovered was serious indeed, but in the end it was a danger only to this small portion of this one sea; the hazards represented by the patch of vile effluvium, however, were an ongoing menace to all life in all the seas.

It seemed an eternity before they were free of the contaminated region, and for some time after there was a foul taste in their mouths and their eyes still smarted. Vl\Kal imaged a depiction of gagging with disgust, and Dj\Tal echoed it as the two of them pressed on, leaving the filthy slick behind.

Dj\Tal desperately needed a rest, and he was sure Vl\Kal felt the same. Neither of them had gotten a moment's half-sleep since the attack on the school, two full light-and-dark cycles ago. There was no time for any sort of respite now, though, and no telling when there would be; he had to find the Danger-Cousins soon, had to do whatever he could to negotiate some sort of peace.

There were moving shapes ahead, he scanned, large ones; but as they came within better range he saw that it was merely a group of hard-backed sea/land creatures paddling laboriously through the water.

]Memory/Funny-Funny[, Dj\Tal imaged to Vl\Kal. When they'd been young ones, the pod-brothers had come across one of these lumbering creatures and had spent most of a dark-time playing with it, watching it jerk its odd little head and walking-appendages in and out of the hard, round covering that concealed its body. The things did not seem truly suited for either the land or the sea. Vl\Kal imaged back his own nostalgic pleasure over the memory, and the hard-backed creatures warily watched them pass.

Empty sea again, except for scattered fish; the two travelers fed haphazardly as they swam, whenever a likely-looking fish came within their immediate reach, but there was no time to pause for a herding maneuver.

The orcas came upon them from behind, without warning. Dj\Tal cursed himself for lack of vigilance: If he'd had even a little rest before leaving the School, he would've remembered to do a turning scan every hundred or so beak-to-flukes, and wouldn't have allowed himself to be taken by surprise.

There were three of the massive black-and-white beasts, and Dj\Tal had no doubt that many more lay in wait beyond view. A quick long-range scan verified his suspicions: At least twenty other Danger-Cousins hovered less than fifty beak-to-flukes away. If called upon, they could instantly supply heavy reinforcement for the three who'd made the initial approach.

]Desire/Dialogue[, Dj\Tal imaged to the nearest of the three;]Intent/Negation/Violence[.

]Immediate ... Recurrence ... Alter ... [, the Danger-Cousin imaged, or something like that. This was hopeless, Dj\Tal realized; there was too much to be discussed, too many crucial fine points that must be conveyed with absolute precision. He'd forgotten how far apart the imaging idioms of the two species were.

>Mind-to-Mind Communication Is Preferable<

he Linked, hopefully.

The Danger-Cousin simply stared at him. Was the look one of arrogance, or simply lack of comprehension?

>Is Self-You a Possessor of the Link-Talent<

he asked, and waited for a response. The Danger-Cousin maintained his enigmatic silence, but then Dj\Tal scanned another large male coming forward from within the nearby School.

Dj\Tal thought it might be the same one that had Linked to him before, just after the attack, but he couldn't be sure. The earlier encounter had happened so unexpectedly, and had been so brief; besides, he had little experience in direct dealings with Danger-Cousins, and they all looked roughly alike to him. This one was heavily scarred, almost as much so as Qr*Jil; Dj\Tal seemed to recall that the one he'd met had borne similar marks of age, but there was no way to be certain whether they were one and the same.

>No Need Exists for Further Communication<

the orca Linked without preface;

>War Is in Process<

The Links were resonant with meaning, with wide-ranging undertones, all of them overtly hostile. Dj\Tal stared back at the
hulking, arrogant Danger-Cousin; if he read its posture correctly,
it was about to leave with no further discussion.

>It Is Imperative That We Negotiate<

he implored.

>Present Your Reasons<

the battle-scarred orca demanded with a Link full of enmity and
suspicion.

>The Mutual Survival of Our Two Kinds<

Dj\Tal offered in an even manner,

>And Achievement of the New Directives<

The Danger-Cousin looked at him with contemptuous eyes.

>We Repudiate the New Directives<

it stated simply, with condescending overtones reminiscent of those
Qr*Jil so often used.

>Mortal Danger Is Imminent<

Dj\Tal implored, including in his Link a graphic image of the
burning sea floor, and the ultimate consequences that image portended. The Danger-Cousin merely jerked its great head in a
scoffing motion.

>Land-Walkers Exemplify Greater Threat<

it asserted;

>We Are Sufficient unto Ourselves<

>The New Directives Will Be Disavowed<

Dj\Tal fought to restrain his anger. First Qr*Jil, now the Danger-Cousins . . . how could they not see the desperate necessity of what was planned, and beyond that, the beauty, the *rightness* of it?

>The Source-Mind Requires That We Comply<

Dj\Tal reminded him, as he had reminded the Old One.
The Danger-Cousin tossed its flukes dismissively.

>The Source-Mind Is in Error<

it Linked with vehemence;

>We Refuse the Directives<

This was unthinkable. Dj\Tal's kind no longer literally deified the Source-Mind, as had once been the case, but the fact of its ultimate authority was beyond dispute. Explicit Directives from it were few, but when issued they were to be heeded without question. To defy them was—

>War Shall Continue<

>The Directives Will Not Be Fulfilled<

the Danger-Cousin Linked with finality. Then the seas churned and it was gone, along with all the others.

Dj\Tal made no move to follow them; it was clear that no further negotiation would be permitted. At least he and Vl\Kal had survived the encounter, no doubt only in order that they might convey the orcas' unremittingly antagonistic message to the Circle and to the rest of their School.

Qr*Jil would secretly welcome this turn of events, he knew, would use it to bolster her own argument against the New Directives. Now she could insist, with sound cause, that peace would be achieved only through capitulation to the Danger-Cousins' demands.

The only ray of hope, as Dj\Tal saw it, was that Ch*Tril had already left to initiate preliminary contact with the first land-walker Receptives. If her mission was successful, maybe . . .

This was not the time for idealistic speculation, though. The School was in more peril now than ever, and Dj\Tal's place was there with them, with his son and his pod-brothers and his friends who stood ready to defend the School against all odds.

He signaled wearily to Vl\Kal, and the two of them began the long and melancholy journey home.

The story was on page 3 of the *Los Angeles Times:*

UNUSUAL DOLPHIN BEHAVIOR
PUZZLES SCIENTISTS WORLDWIDE

the headline read, with Daniel's byline immediately below.

"My God," Sheila said, turning to where the story was continued on the back pages of the paper. "It's been happening everywhere; Australia, Italy . . ."

"Still no solid explanation, though," Daniel noted. "Not from anybody I talked to. They're pretty much split between its being either some kind of new disease or solar flares screwing up the dolphins' navigational abilities."

Sheila shook her head emphatically. "There's no way a virus could have spread from Australia to here to Europe in a matter of days," she said. "And if it were solar flares, they'd have been beaching themselves, by the hundreds at least."

"So what else could it be?"

She folded the paper and turned on the poolside computer console. "Maybe they're doing it on purpose," she said, and was relieved to see that he didn't laugh.

"Whatever it is, I want to find out," Daniel said, sitting down at the edge of the pool and letting his bare feet dangle in the water. The dolphins continued their interminable, seemingly compulsive circling. "I think there's more than a page-three story in this, somehow."

"Hmmh," Sheila grunted in assent, calling up the latest version of her attempt at an image-translation program. It contained more than eleven thousand lines of code, none of which resembled English, and none of which seemed to have brought her any closer to success.

She selected one of the digital audiotapes and set it up to play back in a forty-five-second loop consisting of six distinct bursts of ultrasonic output. According to her index, the dolphin in Fort Myers had emitted these signals right after she'd shown him a set of plastic geometric shapes: circle, square, and triangle, in that order. If she was ever going to decipher any images from the tapes, these should be among the simplest to translate.

She stared at the monitor where her algorithms were displayed, meticulously examining the endless rows of numbers, and began to tweak one here, another there, reverse a pair somewhere else. With each minute alteration or addition she ran the audiotape through the revised program; each time the result was visual gibberish, or static.

Sheila sat back from the screen and rubbed her eyes, exhausted from the tedious repetition, the—wait a minute, she suddenly thought: *repetition*. What if it wasn't enough for the tapes of the ultrasonic signals to be passed *through* the translation program; what if each component of the signal were to be noted there, redigitized, and sent on to the monitor anew? That might more closely mimic the process that the receiving dolphin's brain went through. Maybe the problem wasn't in the translation at all, but in the reception.

Her fingers tapped furiously on the computer keyboard, inserting the new instructions into the program. When she was done she saved copies of both the old and new versions to backup disks, then started the tape loop again.

A circle appeared on the screen, wavery and indistinct, but unmistakably a circle. Sheila inhaled sharply through her open mouth, and held the breath. She reached forward to adjust the monitor; the image cleared, then moved offscreen and was immediately replaced by a picture of a square, an open square whose sides were made of thin round tubing. In the lower right-hand corner there was ... a human hand, holding the square.

"Daniel!" she shouted. "Come look at this!"

"Got a problem with the computer?" he asked.

"Get over here!"

By the time Daniel joined her at the console, the ghostly hand on the monitor was holding a triangle, about eight inches on each side.

"Jesus Christ," he whispered hoarsely. "Is that ..."

"Yes, it is. Images. From the dolphin."

"Oh, my God, Sheila, my God; you did it. You really fucking did it!" He put his hands on her shoulders, squeezed them hard. Sheila's own hands were shaking so much she could barely keep them on the keyboard.

The dolphin, the one who had befriended the children of Sanibel Island, had been dutifully repeating the images of the geometric shapes she had shown it, like a human repeating words and phrases in a foreign language ... or, more accurately, like a human speaking his or her *own* language, slowly and distinctly, to someone who could not understand.

"Jesus, look at this part!" Daniel exclaimed.

A second sequence of images had begun, this time clearly depicting a sand dollar lying flat on the ocean floor, then a smooth, four-sided rock, and finally the undulating delta form of a manta ray's fin. Then the loop started again with the plastic shapes in Sheila's hand.

"Analogies," Sheila said quietly. "He was making visual analogies to what I'd shown him: a circle, a square, a triangle."

Daniel was talking again now, excited, congratulating her ... but all she could think of was the dolphin who had made these images, who had sent them to her ... and had then been slaughtered by the humans it had trusted, only hours after this tape was made.

Sheila had succeeded at last; and it was, she realized, one of the saddest moments of her life.

This was the pits, Kimberley thought; the absolute, what's-the-point-of-living-anymore pits.

If only she hadn't skipped third grade, she'd still have almost all of her senior year in high school to go. Not that she cared that much about school, particularly not the trig class she'd had to repeat with that geeky Mr. Halverson, but at least she'd be with her *friends,* at least there'd be some *boys* around, for Christ's sake.

Yeah, sure, she could've gone to college, to Tacoma Community, anyway; but that was like a pretend college practically, and she'd still have been living at home. Most everybody else in her class, the ones that hadn't flunked trig or physics or whatever, had all gone away to school, even if it was just to U. of Washington or Seattle U.

She'd figured she could get a job and an apartment for a year or two until she applied again—after all, she *was* a high school graduate—and her friend Jennifer had wanted somebody to share a place in Portland where she'd got this great job at Nordstrom's ... but you think her dad was buying that? Hunh-unh, not till she turned eighteen in April, anyway.

Instead he'd had this great idea—right, spare me, she thought—that he should take six months off from his practice and sail this precious boat of his down the West Coast, all the way to Mexico. With the whole family, for Christ's sake.

So here Kimberley was, stuck out in the middle of the ocean, or anyway far enough out so that most of the time you couldn't even see any land, with her mom and her dad and her eleven-year-old brother, Jason. Sean was the lucky one; he was twenty-three and in his first year at UCLA med school. They'd stopped off to see him a couple of days ago. He had this great little apartment in Westwood, and a girlfriend that Kimberley figured was really living there, too, though they'd pretended not for Mom and Dad.

But Kimberley? Well, what could you say, here she was. Sitting in the cramped little kitchen that Dad always wanted her to call a "galley," like they were all in the goddamn navy or something, sitting alone in the kitchen and listening to an old Nirvana bootleg on her Walkman. Not even any MTV, for Christ's sake.

One thing, at least—she had a great tan now, for all the good it was doing her. Except her parents wouldn't let her wear that red thong bikini Curt Collier had given her for a "joke" graduation present—yeah, he wished—so every time they stopped someplace long enough where she could get off to a beach by herself and wear it, she had these wuss white marks on her butt. Even when the guys were looking, she couldn't help but wonder if they were really laughing at her.

"Kim! Come on up here, you've got to see this!"

She heard her mother's voice in the hissing silence between cuts on the tape, and moved the headphones away from her ears. "I'm busy, Mom!" she shouted back.

"No, seriously, Kim, you don't want to miss this! Come on, hurry!"

"What is it?"

"Just get up here!"

Kimberley knew that tone of her mother's, so she sighed and turned the tape off. It was probably some other boat. Her parents were always pointing out boats that were bigger or slower or smaller or faster or whatever, who gave a crap? If she didn't go see what they were so excited about now, though, she'd be washing dishes for a week, so she tossed the Walkman on one of the cushioned benches that doubled for storage compartments and pulled herself up the little ladder to the deck.

"What *is* it, Mom?" she said petulantly. "I was listening to a really good—"

"Look," her father said. "Just look over there, to the west!"

Kimberley didn't know which way west was and didn't care, but she turned to look in the direction he was pointing, and squinted against the lowering sun.

"I don't see any—" she said, and then she did. Fins, big black fins, a dozen or more of them, and here and there a large black head with a white lower jaw and a round white spot on either side like huge eyes. They were coming straight toward the boat.

"Oh, my God, Daddy, it's sharks! Big ones!"

Her father laughed and tousled her hair the way he had when she was a child. "They're not sharks, honey, they're orcas; killer whales, so-called like in *Free Willy,* remember? Aren't they gorgeous?"

Kimberley relaxed a bit, feeling foolish; her little brother was looking at her with that superior expression he had, like what did she know, she was just a girl even if she was six years older. Sure, she knew all about killer whales; they did tricks and stuff, they let people ride them.

"They are kind of interesting," she admitted, hating to let her parents know there was anything about the trip that had actually impressed her.

"Orcas are toothed whales," said Jason, the know-it-all. "And they don't just eat fish, they also eat birds and porpoises and sea lions. Sometimes even littler whales."

"Oh, honey, we don't need to know about all that," their mother chastised. "Just look at them; it's so amazing to see them up close like this."

They *were* getting awfully close, Kimberley noted, and they didn't seem to be slowing down any. It was pretty neat, though, like being in the front row at Sea World, only better.

"I guess they'll veer off pretty soon, go around the boat," her dad said, shading his eyes with his hand as he watched them approach, each one trailing a wake as wide as a good-sized speedboat might kick up.

No sooner had he said it than the orcas disappeared, diving beneath the surface of the water as if on cue.

"Well, that was quite a show, wasn't it?" her father said. "Keep an eye out to port now, and let's see if we can spot them when they come back up over there." He turned to look that way, but Kimberley and Jason were still peering off to the right, what he always called starboard.

"Hey, Dad?" Jason said. "They're still coming this way, and they're not very deep."

Kimberley saw the black shapes, too, big as trucks, racing toward the side of the boat no more than five feet under—

There was a tremendous thud, and the boat suddenly lifted from the water, tilting crazily to one side as it was borne upward. Kimberley wrapped her arms around the mast at the front of the boat without even thinking, and she could feel her legs flying out in the air behind her. Then the boat came down with a jarring crash, water splashing everywhere, and finally righted itself.

"Jason! Jason!" her mother screamed, clutching at the raised metal railing that ran all the way around the boat. Kimberley looked and saw that her little brother was half in and half out of the boat, stuck at his waist in the space between the railing and the edge of the deck.

Her father scrambled across the soaking wet deck to help her mother free the boy. Her father's glasses were smashed, and he was bleeding badly from his forehead where his face had hit something when the boat had gone up out of the water.

"Here, Annie, I've got his shoulders, you pull from the chest!" her father commanded, twisting his head to rub the blood from his eyes with his sleeve. Her brother was crying; one of his arms was twisted all funny. Kimberley could feel tears welling up in her eyes, too.

She looked off the other side of the boat, didn't know what she could do to help and couldn't stand seeing her family all hurt and desperate like that; sure, they were a pain in the butt sometimes but when it came right down to it she really—

"Dad!" she screamed. "They've turned around! They're coming back!"

11

Like a desperate, trapped creature, the magma sought release from its imprisonment. Exerting its pressure and its searing heat in all directions outward from the core of the chamber, the molten earth found here a fissure, there a cleft: none large enough to permit the passage of more than a few droplets at a time, none weak enough to allow the full, explosive rush of the expanding magma to burst forth through the sea floor above.

From the quiet, cool regions of that distant sea floor, the burning light continued to tunnel its way downward through the barrier crust . . . opening a smoothly cylindrical corridor directly toward the powerful, insensate beast that struggled against the confines of its subterranean keep.

Qr*Jil was furious, as Dj\Tal had expected; worse, she was smug in her anger.

>It Is As I Have Long Maintained<

she Linked imperiously, the message rife with implications of Dj\Tal's wrongheadedness;

>The New Directives Bring Only Turmoil<

There was no use arguing, Dj\Tal knew. The failure of his attempted negotiations with the Danger-Cousins was a crisis of the first order. The best that could be hoped for now was that the School might be able to stave off the predations of the warring orcas long enough for Ch*Tril to locate the land-walker Receptives with whom she was to establish preliminary contact.

>Defense Plans Must Be Made<

Dj*Tal Linked to the Circle at large, and his pod-brother Vl\Kal immediately launched into a review and analysis of the strategies the School had employed in response to the Danger-Cousins' attack.

The Circle was engaged in an open debate on the merits of Vl\Kal's theories when Dj\Tal's son, Dv\Kil, approached, swimming hard and fast.

]Apology/Interruption[, he imaged, and went on hurriedly to describe what he had just scanned while on perimeter duty: a pod of Danger-Cousins, not headed directly toward the School but moving with ominous and disciplined purpose.

Qr*Jil ordered him to pursue and observe the orcas, and Dv\Kil turned to go. For Dj\Tal, the decision was instantaneous, knowing that his son was ill-prepared for a confrontation with the powerful creatures should they turn on him:

>I Will Accompany My Son<

he informed the Circle, and was quickly joined by Vl\Kal, then four more.

Dv\Kil led the group to the area where he'd scanned the pod of Danger-Cousins, and Dj\Tal soon spotted them. They showed no signs of doubling back to attack, but swam as if they had a specific destination in mind. Dj\Tal switched to long-range scanning to see if the orcas' School was ahead, and saw no signs of it; only a white fin-topped hull of the land-walkers in the distance.

The Danger-Cousins were fast approaching the hull, he scanned; they would have to swerve soon. Even as the thought crossed his mind, the big black-and-white creatures dove, maintaining their tight formation as they did. They were going under the hull instead of around it.

Dj\Tal and the others moved to follow them, then stopped dead still, shocked by what they saw before them: The Danger-Cousins had reared up beneath the fragile hull, heaving it roughly, purposefully, upward on their broad backs. Dj\Tal quickly overcame his astonishment and shot to the surface, where he saw the hull lifted clear of the water, tipping precariously to one side. The land-walkers on its flat top were clearly visible, struggling to hold on; one of them had been slammed against a hard object, and its head was bleeding profusely.

The hull fell back into the water and floated unsteadily. Dj\Tal dove again, and scanned that the Danger-Cousins were not continuing on their earlier course; they had reversed direction, and were homing in on the battered hull once again.

]FOLLOW[, Dj\Tal imaged to Vl\Kal and the others, and took off toward the land-walkers' hull as rapidly as he could swim. Side by side, he and Dv\Kil sped on a collision course toward the leader of the oncoming formation of Danger-Cousins.

The orca didn't seem to have noticed Dj\Tal's group until now, and he instinctively veered to avoid hitting the unexpected intruders. The rest of his pod stayed with him, brushing just in front of the white hull and almost swamping it in their combined wake.

Dj\Tal surfaced again and looked back at the hull. The land-walkers were hustling desperately about, attaching puffy orange things to their torsos. The biggest of them, the one with the blood all over its head, was using its forelimbs to do something to the tall white fin that rose above the hull.

Dj\Tal ducked his head back beneath the water, and scanned a pair of large, notched flukes ascending straight toward him. He did a twist-and-roll, narrowly avoiding the blow as the Danger-Cousin's flukes slapped heavily on the surface at the spot where he had been.

Then the sea was quiet, the orcas nowhere to be scanned. They must be regrouping at the surface on the other side of the hull, Dj\Tal thought. Would they emerge from beneath it, or—

Right and left, swooping in a pincer configuration, they came at him from around each pointed end of the hull. Dj\Tal dove, and the Danger-Cousins followed suit, right on his flukes.

When he was twenty beak-to-flukes down, he sensed that the two closest to him had abruptly fallen back. He whirled to scan the situation: One of the pursuers was writhing in pain not far above, and Dj\Tal scanned that its spleen had been crushed. Another was in furious pursuit of Vl\Kal, and the rest of the pod was locked in combat with Dj\Tal's other comrades.

Dj\Tal rushed upward to join the battle, and as he did a dying-image pierced his sense. He passed the broken, floating body as he rose: Jr*Zin, one of the few in the Circle who had supported his initial attempts to negotiate with the Danger-Cousins.

Dv\Kil was trapped between two of them, Dj\Tal saw as he neared the fighting; they were circling him, preparing for the kill.

Dj\Tal sped straight through the center of the enclosing ring, drawing one of the deadly pair after him as he went. He was tiring already, he needed to fill his lungs; the bulky marauders had a much larger capacity for air, could outswim him and outlast him.

He made a sudden tight reverse arc past the pursuing orca's side, forcing it to pivot along with him. If he could compel it to keep on changing direction he might be able to turn its unwieldy size to his advantage, might—

The Danger-Cousin was scanning something, he realized, and the deep vibrations he could feel in the water indicated it was a long-range scan. Dj\Tal scanned in the same direction: There was another pod of orcas, thirty or forty strong, headed swiftly toward them. Death, black-finned and certain.

He could give up the struggle now, could grant his aching muscles and lungs a final respite before submitting to those dreadful jaws. Why not? The fight was over—he and Dv\Kil and Vl\Kal and the other few hadn't the slightest chance against the horde of Danger-Cousins rushing to finish what their brethren had begun....

No. He couldn't allow himself to simply give up like that, despite the inevitability of the outcome. The hostilities between his kind and the Danger-Cousins would not cease upon his death; there would be many conflicts ahead for the survivors, and it was important that the orcas know his kind would resist to the very end.

The sea around him filled with the grim, black shapes of Danger-Cousins; if Dj\Tal moved fast enough, he could inflict some painful wounds before they took him.

There was a sudden, terrible thrashing nearby, and a cloud of blood billowed in the water.

The Danger-Cousins, the newly arrived ones, were attacking their own.

Dj\Tal scanned the scene again in confusion: There was no mistake, the larger pod was fighting the original seven that had tried to smash the land-walkers' hull. The one he'd been contending with was already dead, its head gouged open to reveal its bare skull, and now the newcomers were moving in on the area where Dv\Kil and the others still battled for their lives.

Dj\Tal hurriedly followed, and the Danger-Cousins all around him ignored his presence in their midst. He saw two of them ram the one nearest Dv\Kil, crushing its abdomen between them. Dv\Kil wheeled about, startled, ready for an expanded fray that miraculously did not ensue.

The bigger pod swept on remorselessly, hunting down the remaining five of the first group. One of them fought back with savage strength, even though its flukes were mangled beyond use; another was held down by three of its kindred, and struggled desperately until it drowned.

Dj\Tal surfaced for a breath, saw the seas red. The hull carrying the land-walkers was cutting across the water now, rapidly distancing itself from the carnage.

Suddenly he was aware that a Link was being directed at him, and not from Vl\Kal or any of the others in his party, but from one of the orcas:

>It Is Imperative That We Consult<

the message came. Dj\Tal tried to focus on the source of the Link, but the scene was still too chaotic; there was no way to tell which of the many Danger-Cousins had issued the call.

>I Concur<

he Linked back, in the general direction of the blood-dimmed region where the orcas swarmed; then one of them moved out of the pack to hover before him.

>We Are Grateful for Your Assistance<

Dj\Tal Linked. The Danger-Cousin rolled its huge head back and forth in acknowledgment and replied:

>There Is Disagreement Among Our Kind<

Dj\Tal felt a thrill of hope; if the ones who had attacked the School and the land-walkers' hull were merely a rebellious minority, there might be no War, after all, and the New Directives could be fulfilled without delay, the awful danger of the burning rock perhaps averted.

>Inquiry: Proportion Desiring War<

he asked.

>Two of Every Three<

the Danger-Cousin answered, and Dj\Tal's rush of optimism faded. This War was far from over; if anything, it would be even fiercer and more prolonged, and its outcome every bit as much in doubt as before.

Dj\Tal and the Danger-Cousin continued Linking well into the darktime, sharing their ideas and plans and aspirations; but even as their unexpected camaraderie deepened, Dj\Tal found himself increasingly skeptical that any of the long-held visions toward which he had worked for so long would ever come to fruition ... or, worse, that the potential cataclysm of the burning rock could be contained much longer.

There was no moon that night, and the bloodied seas soon turned to black.

The *Sea Master* pulled away from the pier and moved slowly northward into the long, looping passageway to the sea. Antonio Batera stood on the bridge, letting Manoel handle the wheel.

They chugged past the old square-rigged merchant ship *Star of India,* its iron hull burnished as smoothly and brightly as when the elegant vessel had begun plying the Pacific trade routes in the 1860s. Just beyond her now-permanent berth were the docks of the main portion of the tuna fleet. There were only a couple of boats docked there, both fitted out for line fishing; the dozens upon dozens of purse seiners that had once crowded the piers were mostly gone now, junked one by one after 1990, when the major U.S. canneries had bowed to all the pressure and stopped buying any tuna that wasn't caught by hook and line. Only a few seiners, like the *Sea Master,* were left in San Diego, their markets limited to exporters and pet-food companies and other less particular customers.

What's old is new, Batera thought; he'd grown up learning bait-boat fishing from his father, could well remember what it was like to stand on one of those racks outside the boat's rails while another crewman tossed chum into the water to attract the tuna. If you wanted to work the boats in those days, strength counted even more than it did now; there were no hydraulics, no powerblocks, just a bamboo pole and a line and your own muscles to jerk the hooked tuna over your shoulder and onto the deck. For the bigger fish you sometimes needed two or three poles on the same line, and to this day the size of a tuna was gauged in terms of one-pole, two-pole, or three-pole.

Batera had been in his twenties when the seine-net boats began to take over the industry. "Factory boats," his father had called them derisively, but he and his son had had no choice but to learn the new ways. It was that, or starve.

Now his father was dead, and Batera owned a seiner of his own; thirty percent of one, anyway. If he had his choice, he'd happily unload this goddamned factory boat and go back to fishing with bait, long and hard though those days had been … but who really had a choice, when there were bills to be paid, food to be put on the table? The *Sea Master* was worth maybe half what it had originally cost, and the modern long-line boats were priced way out of reach.

He watched Harbor Island slip past, and as they made the portside turn toward Shelter Island and Point Loma he could almost see his house on the hill above the Navy Training Center. Maria was probably up there now, listening to her fados, still angry with him over the decisions he'd recently made.

Hell, maybe she was right, her and Gerry Schofield and Manoel and the crewmen and everybody. What the fuck did he care about porpoise, anyway? He'd been finding tuna by setting on porpoise for thirty years and it never bothered him before. It'd make life easier all around if he just dropped this crazy notion and went back to doing things the way he had for so many years.

Except he couldn't, goddamnit. He couldn't, and he didn't know why. It was almost like something was telling him what to do, giving him instructions inside his own head, and it confused him as much as trying to remember that … whatever it was he kept trying to remember.

Now he had a fucking headache, on top of everything else. He left Manoel on the bridge and went to his cabin to pour a drink and close his eyes for a while. Maybe that would help him remember, or forget; right now he didn't much care which.

Ringo was gone. He'd been gone for two days, while the others had stayed behind in the pool, endlessly circling, refusing food or contact.

Daniel knew that Sheila was both hurt and distressed by the dolphin's departure, but she never talked about it; it was almost as if any discussion of his absence would be tantamount to an acknowledgment that Ringo might never be coming back.

Rather than give in to grief or concern, she'd thrown herself into her work with renewed vigor, running her earlier tapes of Ringo through the imaging translation program, and Daniel watched the unfolding images with a fascination equal to her own. There were hundreds of the tapes, accumulated over her six years of research: hour after hour of previously incomprehensible signals that were now crystal clear, like letters from a departed friend. Now she was cataloging them and editing together a selection of the most vivid scenes, the reel with which she would announce her achievement to her skeptical colleagues.

"What's this one?" he asked as she threaded yet another tape into the digital reel-to-reel machine.

"You'll see," Sheila told him with a wry smile, and started the tape rolling.

Daniel stared in amazement at the image that appeared on the monitor, and then he started to laugh. It was an imaginative scene of Ringo himself, starring in a highly creative and utterly explicit sexual threesome with the two female dolphins, Georgia and Paulette.

"He transmitted this one just a couple of weeks ago," Sheila said. "It was at the start of one of our sessions, and I'd just shown him a videotape of dolphins having sex."

"So he made his own little porn film to show to you."

"Apparently so."

Now the scene on the monitor changed, and they were looking at a depiction of the open sea from a leaping dolphin's viewpoint: the swift rise through the water, a glittering dance of sunlight on the surface above, then *through* the surface and upward still, soaring . . .

They'd seen a lot of these kinds of scenes on the tapes. Daniel never mentioned it, but he knew Sheila must see them as he did: They were a celebration of life ... of freedom. Sad as she must be to see him go, maybe he was finally back where he belonged.

Suddenly there was an image of Sheila on the screen, slicing through the water alongside Ringo, faster than any human could realistically swim, her body twisting with an acrobatic and balletic grace to match his own, and then—the fantasy image of Sheila was *leaping,* rising impossibly above the waves as if she were flying, as if she were a dolphin at play. There was no mistaking the intent of the ecstatic, breathtaking image: It was a gift, from Ringo to her; a statement of camaraderie, of friendship, of love.

Sheila got up from the computer console, her eyes brimming with tears. "I'm going to go check on Georgia and Paulette," she said, and headed toward the pool.

The tape was still running, and Daniel watched it quietly. The next scene was another one of Sheila, head-to-head with Ringo in the pool, and—

"Help! Daniel, help me!"

He jumped up from his seat, turned around and saw Sheila standing in the pool, waist-deep, her arms streaked with blood.

"Get a syringe and an ampoule of Terramycin from that green cabinet!" she shouted. Only then did Daniel notice that Ringo was in the pool beside her. He was the one who was bleeding; his dorsal fin was torn nearly in half at the base, from the front backward.

Daniel grabbed the hypodermic and the antibiotic and waded into the pool to hand them to Sheila. The other dolphins had stopped circling and were hovering at the deep end of the pool; the water hummed as they scanned their wounded companion ... and no doubt imaged him their sympathy and support, Daniel realized.

"I'm gonna need a bottle of alcohol, too," Sheila said as she took the syringe from him. "And some gauze, and a suture kit. They're on the top shelf of that same cabinet. There's some lidocaine on the middle shelf, bring that, too."

He climbed out of the pool without a word, collected the items she'd asked for, and headed back into the water, holding the things above his head to keep them dry. His jeans and his shoes were soaked, but he didn't pause to take them off.

"Hold him up," Sheila ordered. "This is bleeding too bad; we don't have time to get him out of the pool in a sling. Just keep as much of his back above water as you can."

Daniel slipped his hands beneath the dolphin's soft belly and lifted. The heavy creature was almost weightless in the warm, buoyant liquid.

Sheila cleaned away most of the blood, injected the local anesthetic, and then started stitching the wound with quick, deft strokes. Neither she nor Daniel spoke as she worked, and the other dolphins continued to watch with intent interest.

"I think that's got it," she said at last. "How're your arms doing?"

"O.K.," said Daniel, though his muscles were beginning to cramp from their rigid immobility.

"Hold him just a couple of minutes more, if you can," Sheila said as she moved toward the side of the pool. "I'll set up a sling so we can keep those stitches dry until they take."

Daniel shifted his wrists a bit, flexed his aching shoulders. As he moved, Ringo twisted his head to one side and rubbed his beak up and down along Daniel's right arm, then looked up at him with a beatific gaze that seemed to bore straight through Daniel's eyes.

He felt a chill run the length of his back, looking into those calm eyes; it was as if the dolphin knew his arms were hurting, knew ... all about him, somehow.

Odder still, Daniel had an overpowering sensation that the wounded creature was trying to reassure *him,* instead of the other way around.

". . . the Fort Myers encounter. As you can see, the translated images illustrate a successful attempt by an undomesticated male adult *Tursiops truncatus* to create and transmit, by means of ultrasonic wave patterns, a visual facsimile of the test objects in the precise order that they were shown to him. This series is immediately followed by ..."

The conference room was packed; Sheila's presentation had even been delayed for half an hour to allow the temporary installation of two more video monitors, so everyone could see the tapes. The news of her breakthrough had spread swiftly among the faculty, and the crowd here today included not only the entire staff of the Marine Biology Department, but representatives of the Linguistics, Anthropology, Psychology, Philosophy, and Environmental Studies departments as well. Not to mention a few curious historians and literarians and who knew what else; Sheila had never even met half the people in her audience.

The tape she'd put together switched now to the latest samples she'd taken from the recuperating Ringo: scenes of the open sea, of a large school of wild dolphins ... hundreds of them, maybe thousands, and almost all were exhibiting the same sort of now-familiar agitated behavior that had been observed of late in so many captive dolphins. The picture was wavery, strange, yet somehow unnervingly distinct. Periodically, one dolphin or another would appear in skeletal form, then revert to being fully fleshed; then the viewpoint might abruptly change from far to near, exactly as a motion picture might jump from a long establishing shot to a close-up, with no intervening zoom.

"You're seeing the world as a dolphin does," Sheila explained, "through its sonarlike sense rather than its eyes. The amount of available light is irrelevant; and, depending on the scanning frequency it uses, soft bodily tissues can seem as transparent as water.

"The actual meaning of these images is as yet unclear," Sheila went on. "They may be memories of the dolphin's youth, before his capture; they may be entirely imaginary; or they may represent a contemporary encounter, one that took place during the dolphin's recent two-day absence from my facility here at the university."

She paused, took a long breath, watched the ghostly images build toward what she knew was coming. "This next sequence," she intoned, "and the fact that the dolphin who transmitted it is currently recovering from serious and unexplained injuries, leads me to believe that the events depicted here are real, and of quite recent vintage."

On the screen, a pair of killer whales moved into the school of dolphins, then another, then a dozen more, their starkly patterned bulk suddenly dominating the scene.

There was a sharp collective intake of breath among the watching academics, a scattering of low moans and exclamations as they realized what they were seeing.

The orcas were attacking the dolphins en masse, crushing some with blows from their heavy flukes, severing other dolphins' dorsal fins or hindquarters with their large, conical teeth. Blood gushed everywhere, but the spreading cloud, no more opaque in these dolphin-scanned images than the dying flesh from which it flowed, did nothing to obscure the hideous carnage.

The image on the screen rushed forward with sudden, dizzying speed, as if filmed by a camera bolted to the warhead of a torpedo, and then slammed into the tank-sized flank of one of the killer whales. As it pulled back, a bleeding wound could be seen in the orca's side, and the creature spun angrily, its gaping mouth snapping at the "camera." Sheila recoiled involuntarily, as she had each time she'd watched this portion of the tape; this, surely, was the moment at which Ringo had been so terribly wounded.

A darting, disorienting series of evasive maneuvers followed, then rapid flight into the open sea, away from the killing place ... and the tape ended.

The audience of normally voluble faculty members sat in stunned silence as Sheila turned off the monitors and ejected the cassette from the VCR.

"This, of course, is only the beginning," Sheila said. "I have four years' worth of accumulated tapes, thousands of hours of dolphin images that will take me years more to translate." She looked directly at Richard Tarnoff, who was perspiring lightly in his dark wool suit, and he looked uncomfortably away as her gaze caught his.

"Assuming, of course," Sheila added with a thin smile, "that my grant is renewed."

The awed hush in the conference room was finally broken, first by applause and then by a clamor of remarks and congratulations and questions. Richard shook her hand briefly, then muttered something about being late for a seminar and left the room.

It was almost two hours before Sheila herself managed to get away, and when she did she could still feel her face flushed with a satisfaction that, until a few days ago, she had almost given up hoping for. The response to her presentation had been more than merely gratifying: It was a vindication of everything she'd believed in, a triumphant refutation of the derision and ridicule to which she had been subjected for the past six years.

She took the long route walking back to her on-campus home and laboratory, basking privately in the glow of her success, and what it meant: The continuation of her research was assured now, and Ringo and Georgia and Paulette could stay here safely with her for as long as they chose; all their lives, if they wished. There was so much left to do, and all the time and backing in the world to accomplish it.

"Daniel!" she called as she entered the house, shutting the front door behind her. "You wouldn't believe how well it went!"

There was no reply; he must be out by the pool, she thought, looking after Ringo. Then she heard the drone of the television set from the little den-cum-TV room just off the kitchen.

She found Daniel sitting in front of the set, transfixed. He was watching a report by Charles Jaco, with the familiar CNN LIVE logo prominent in the lower right-hand corner of the screen.

". . . exclusive live interview with Dr. Philip Talbot of Tacoma, Washington," Jaco was saying, "whose family's sailboat was attacked by killer whales off the coast of southern California near San Clemente Island last Friday, and was discovered adrift only this morning. Dr. Talbot, was there any indication of what might have provoked the attack?"

The man being interviewed was in a hospital bed, his scalp and forehead swathed in bandages. "Nothing at all," he said. "There were half a dozen of them, coming at us real fast, and we were just watching them, you know ... my wife, Annie, she called our daughter up on deck to take a look, and then they all dived at the same time, going under the boat ... then they just, I don't know, reared up or something; they lifted the boat clear out of the water. That's when I hit my head on the ice chest, and my boy, Jason, he's eleven, he almost went over the side."

Sheila sat down on the love seat beside Daniel, watching the report with immediate and intense concentration. Daniel reached for her hand, wordlessly intertwined his fingers with hers.

"Well, I thought it was just an accident, you know," Talbot went on, "thought maybe they'd misjudged the depth or something ... but then my daughter, Kim, saw them coming back, straight toward the boat like they were going to ram it, and she yelled out to warn us."

"Is that when the second group of killer whales appeared?" Jaco asked.

"No, that was a few minutes later. The first thing, these dolphins showed up, and it looked like they started to fight the ones that had attacked us. I think a couple of the dolphins were killed; there was a lot of blood in the water by now."

Sheila's fingers tensed, and Daniel squeezed her hand firmly, reassuringly.

"This went on for a little while," the bandaged man on the screen continued. "We were scrambling around pulling on our life-jackets and I was trying to straighten out the mainsail—it was wrapped around the mast, all ripped to hell—so we could get out of there."

"And that's when—"

"Right, that's when the other bunch showed up, more killer whales, dozens of them." The man's eyes filled with tears. "I thought that was it ... you know, I didn't think we had a chance. My family ..."

Jaco paused, nodding, letting the man regain his composure as the camera focused in close on his tormented face.

"... but, so anyway, these new ones didn't pay us any mind at all, they started fighting with the first bunch just like the dolphins had, they were literally tearing them apart ... and by then I had the sail fixed about as well as I could, it was already coming apart, but we got away from there as fast as we could."

"Thank you, Dr. Talbot. Back to you in Atlanta, Bernie."

Bernard Shaw was frowning, and on the wall behind him was a projection of a map of the world, with bright red dots scattered here and there. Each of the dots had been placed in an area representing one of the world's oceans: Sheila counted four dots in the Pacific, three in the Atlantic, two each in the Mediterranean and the South China Sea, one in the Indian Ocean.

"Thank you, Charles," Shaw said, his voice grave. "To repeat, we are now receiving reports of numerous such incidents from around the world. The unexplained attacks have resulted in a total of at least sixty-three fatalities, including fifteen children who perished in a boat that was being used for a school outing off Porto Alegre, Uruguay.

"As bizarre as the attacks themselves may be, scientists are even more baffled by the fact that almost every incident has led to the sort of scene we've just heard Dr. Talbot describe: dolphins and killer whales joining in pitched battle with the attacking killer whales. Untold numbers of the two marine mammal species have themselves died in the astonishing clashes.

"In the CNN newsroom with us now is Dr. Robert Harrigan of the UCLA Department of Marine Biology, who says these incredible events are—"

"Turn it off," Sheila said. "I know Bob, and he won't have anything useful to add."

Daniel clicked the remote and the TV set went blank. "I tried to call you," he said. "This started breaking about three hours ago. They told me you'd already started your presentation, and you'd said no interruptions."

"God," she said. "Ringo must have been trying to warn us, with those images ..."

"I still don't get it," Daniel said, shaking his head. "I thought orcas were supposed to be lovable and harmless."

"This isn't some kids' movie, Daniel; this isn't about 'a boy and his orca.' They're very intelligent, and they can be quite gentle and affectionate ... but orcas can also sometimes be violent, and they have been known to kill dolphins before."

"Aren't they related species, though?"

"So are Serbs and Croats." Sheila stood up and walked toward the kitchen that overlooked the pool area. "I'm going to check on Ringo," she said.

The phone rang as she was leaving the room. "Want me to get it?" Daniel asked.

"Just tell them I'm busy, I'll get back to them when I can," she called over her shoulder.

It wasn't for her, though; it was Sam Jenkins, from the Santa Barbara *Herald*. "Do you have any idea how hard you are to track down?" he said when Daniel answered.

"You managed."

"Yeah, finally. So, 'wrong hunch' you had last week, huh? Thanks a heap, buddy."

"What did you expect, I'd just give it away?"

"Hey, you could've at least let me know the night before that article of yours was gonna break."

"Don't bullshit me, Sam. Nobody else made a big deal out of it, not until yesterday, anyway."

"We'd have been ready, though."

"Maybe," Daniel said. He could hear it coming, and he knew he'd be doing the same thing if he were in Sam's place.

"This lady you're staying with, she's a dolphin expert, right?"

"She doesn't give interviews."

"No, no, no; we're all set on that score, we've got half the marine mammal people from here to Melbourne already lined up."

"So what do you want, then?"

"Look," Sam said, in that cagey tone Daniel remembered from years back. "You knew something was coming down on this before anybody else did, right? So I figure you've got to be privy to some stuff none of these experts are willing to say on the record. Maybe it's something crazy, maybe it's speculation, I don't care. Just, if you hear anything special, doesn't matter how off-the-wall it is, think of me first. Will you do that?"

"Sam, I don't know anything more about this than you do. Neither does Sheila, all right?"

"I'm just saying."

"And I'm telling you, there's nothing else."

"We'll make it worth your while, you know that."

Daniel sighed. "I'll keep it in mind, O.K.? That's the best I can do for right now."

"Fair enough, buddy. For old times' sake, right?"

"We'll see."

Daniel hung up the phone and went out to join Sheila by the pool. He lit a cigarette and watched Ringo hanging impassively in his makeshift sling, half-submerged, as the other dolphins swam their ceaseless circles, but more listlessly now, as if their agitation had given way to depression, even despair.

"We've got to find out what's going on," Sheila finally said.

"How?" Daniel asked, frowning.

Sheila stared out past the pool, past the connecting lagoon, toward the ocean beyond. "Isn't it obvious? We have to ... well, as you might put it, we have to go where the action is."

12

Daniel stood on the aft deck of the rented boat, his eyes searching the water in every direction for large black fins. Sheila, steering, had assured him that killer whales were seldom spotted here in the Santa Barbara Channel; but there was no way to predict how much their patterns of movement might have altered along with their frightening behavioral changes of the last few days.

The boat, a thirty-three-foot Dutch-made model, felt fairly substantial, with its twin diesel inboard engines and steel displacement hull; Sheila had chosen it over other, cheaper fiberglass models for just that reason. Even so, Daniel wondered how well the craft might hold up under a full-scale assault by half a dozen or so two-ton orcas.

He was surprised, and not pleasantly so, by his own nervousness: he, who had weathered missile attacks in Tel Aviv, roving bands of *Road Warrior*–style "technicals" in Mogadishu, and more revolutions than he could count, was suddenly scared to go boating on a sunny day off the coast of Southern California.

The last time he'd felt anything like this was in the Philippines in '91, during the eruption of Mount Pinatubo. Maybe there was a connection there, he thought; somehow, the violence of man, even random terrorist-inspired violence, was more comprehensible—more *expected*—than the freakish chaos of nature gone berserk.

"What's that island up ahead?" Daniel shouted over the wind and the engine noise.

"San Miguel," Sheila yelled back, and eased off on the throttle a bit.

"What's out there?"

"It's a national park," she told him. "Totally undeveloped, though. Strictly for day hikes."

Daniel lifted his binoculars and peered at the deserted island. Something caught his eye: One end of the island seemed almost to be alive, a writhing mass of indistinguishable brown shapes.

"There's something crawling all over that point over there," he said uneasily.

"Sea lions," Sheila explained. "San Miguel has one of the largest sea lion rookeries in the world."

"A breeding ground?"

"Right."

Daniel suddenly recalled an item from his recent research. "Don't killer whales eat—"

Sheila looked at him and nodded. "Yes. Yes, they do."

Great, he thought. Fucking great. No orcas in the channel, she says, but Sheila was taking them straight toward the world's biggest source of killer-whale chow. He started to say something, thought better of it, then redoubled his scanning of the seas around them.

"You sure this is the right idea?" Daniel asked, his eyes flicking from the island to the horizon and back again.

"It's the best one I could come up with," Sheila said, steering the boat in a slow zigzag pattern. "If we can record some images from dolphins who haven't been affected by human contact, who've been totally involved in whatever's happening out here, maybe we can learn something."

It was a vague answer, but Sheila had a look of certitude about her, of conviction. And the funny thing was, Daniel thought, apprehensive though he might be over the possibility of encountering hostile orcas, there was something about being out here that felt indefinably *right,* as if he were fulfilling some deep inner compulsion that he couldn't begin to put into words. It was almost like something was commanding him to be out here, or calling to him with an unheard voice that could not be denied.

"Look over there," Sheila said excitedly, "to the left of that buoy."

Daniel trained his binoculars on the orange channel marker and panned slowly to the left. "I don't see anything."

"Wait a second, just keep looking . . . there! Do you see them?"

He moved the binoculars back and forth, searching the waves, and then he focused on a glistening blur of light gray. A fin; a pair of fins, swimming together straight toward the boat.

"They're coming this way," he said, and shivered as a quick chill ran from the back of his neck to the base of his spine.

Sheila killed the engines, and the silence was abrupt, diminishing; it was like entering a cathedral, and Daniel suddenly felt as if he should be whispering.

"Give me a hand with the anchor," Sheila said in a low voice, and Daniel knew the feeling wasn't his alone. The waves lapped softly against the boat's steel hull, and the approaching fins drew closer by the second.

Together, he and Sheila heaved the anchor over the side of the boat, and the two-hundred-foot length of rope and chain stretched taut as the heavy anchor implanted itself in the unseen seabed below. The boat bobbed, toylike, in the gently rolling waves, and Sheila busied herself with her recording equipment while Daniel watched the pair of dolphins slow down and start circling the boat at a distance of fifteen or twenty feet.

"I wonder why these two are out here by themselves," he mused aloud. "Shouldn't they be with their school?"

"It must be nearby," Sheila said, unreeling a spool of waterproofed audio cable. "Maybe on the other side of the island."

One of the dolphins had stopped swimming, and had raised its head out of the water; its bright eyes regarded Daniel with a look of frank curiosity. Feeling vaguely foolish, Daniel waved at the dolphin, and it moved its head rapidly from side to side, following the movements of his arm.

"We should have brought along some fish," Daniel said.

Sheila had finished unreeling the cable, and now she was attaching one end of it to the computer equipment in the wheelhouse, the other end to the bulky, plastic-encased tape recorder she'd had with her in Fort Myers. "They probably wouldn't eat any if we had," she told Daniel. "Dolphins have to be trained to accept dead fish."

The other dolphin had lifted its head out of the water, too, and they both turned their attention to Sheila as she lowered the tape recorder off the stern of the boat and into the water. One of them dove briefly, and Daniel could see it just under the surface, inspecting the strange new object from all angles.

"Keep an eye on the monitor," Sheila said, stripping off her jeans and sweatshirt to reveal a blue one-piece bathing suit. "Any signals I pick up on the hydrophone will be translated there, in real time. The first ones you'll see will be coming from me, though; I'm going to play them a tape."

"To introduce yourself," Daniel said, grinning.

Sheila grinned back. "That's the polite thing to do, wouldn't you say?" She pulled the snorkel mask over her eyes and nose, and started down the short bathing ladder at the back of the boat.

Daniel watched the dolphins as Sheila entered the water; neither of them seemed frightened by her presence, and one of them, the larger of the two, moved even closer toward her.

"I'm starting the tape now," Sheila said, and ducked her head beneath the surface.

Daniel stepped into the little wheelhouse, which had already been crowded with radio and navigational gear and was now filled to overflowing with the addition of Sheila's computer and video equipment. He left the door open so he could hear her if she called to him, and he turned on the video monitor.

The blank screen gave way to a series of the now-familiar images that Sheila had captured from Ringo and the other dolphins. Daniel noted that for this tape, she'd chosen mainly scenes that included herself at play with one or more of the dolphins, or feeding or caressing them.

Daniel shook his head in wonder, knowing that even as he was watching these translated images, the wild dolphins near the boat were "seeing" the same pictures, picking them up organically from the speakers of the underwater tape recorder. Jesus, what must they be thinking right now? A human being, a stranger in every sense, communicating with them in their own visual language, sending them images of herself in contact with other members of their species.

This was an incredible moment, Daniel realized, even an historic one. Absorb it all, he told himself; you're going to be writing about this soon, and the world will read your words.

He stuck his head back outside and peered over the stern of the boat. Sheila was still just below the surface of the water, manipulating the recorder, and the two dolphins were quietly focused on it with what looked like rapt attention. He glanced back into the wheelhouse at the monitor; the prerecorded tape, and the images, came to an end.

Sheila lifted her head again and looked up at him, her eyes magnified by the clear plastic of the snorkeling mask. "I'm switching over to the hydrophone now," she told him. "Watch the monitor, let me know if they send anything."

Daniel turned back to the wheelhouse and switched on the VCR next to the monitor; if they got anything, it would be captured twice, with the original on Sheila's digital audio master tape and the translation here on videocassette, for immediate reviewing if necessary. He saw nothing but static for several moments; then he heard the computer's hard disk drive begin to whir as it received an ultrasonic signal to process, and shortly after that the screen came to life again.

The first images were blurry, indistinct: a school of dolphins, maybe, but it was hard to tell. The pictures soon began to clear up, though, as the automatic error-detection and enhancement routines

Sheila had added to the latest version of her translation program identified and corrected the fuzzy portions of the signal.

It was a dolphin school, all right, a very large one; and then the image changed, turned into one of those now-familiar point-of-view scenes of a dolphin rushing through the water.

"Anything coming through yet?" Sheila called from outside.

"Yeah," Daniel yelled back, "we're getting images. Dolphin school, dolphin swimming."

The picture on the screen showed the water growing shallower now, sunlight streaming down from the surface, the sandy seabed rising at a gentle slope, a shoreline just ahead . . . then there were—*feet,* human feet and legs standing in the water.

Daniel stared in amazement as the image scrolled upward, above the surface of the water; there was a child standing there, a little girl in a floral-print bathing suit, looking openmouthed toward the "camera," then smiling, reaching out with her tiny hand.

The dolphin, the real one just outside right now in the water with Sheila, was telling them that it—or maybe some other dolphin it had known, might have received these images from—had been in contact with a human being before, with some small girl somewhere, and that the contact had been friendly.

"Sheila!" Daniel shouted, not even knowing if she could hear him or not. "This is fucking amazing! It's showing us pictures of a person, a little girl!"

There was no answer; she must be underwater again, watching the dolphins or fiddling with the recorder, not even knowing yet what a spectacular success she'd already scored. Christ, was this tape going to give her a thrill!

Daniel looked back at the screen; the little girl was still there, beaming with joy at what must have been a wildly unexpected encounter for her, whoever she was; and then Daniel noticed something else in the picture, something in the background, in the sky above the girl's dark-haired head. What the fuck, was that a *rocket* contrail?

The image changed again, and as it did so Daniel's heart began to race, he felt suddenly light-headed and had to reach out and grab onto something, anything, to steady himself.

The little girl on the monitor screen was gone, and in her place was another child, a boy about eight years old; he was in the back of a boat, a weekend pleasure craft, his hand trailing idly in the water and his eyes wide with astonished, entranced surprise.

The boy was Daniel.

Finding the land-walkers hadn't been difficult: A hundred or more of Ch*Tril's kind, all of them, like her, possessed of the Link-Talent, had been enlisted from a dozen different Schools to form the relay network. It stretched for many thousands of beak-to-flukes, giving Ch*Tril ready access to the latest information from the Source-Mind. The relay wasn't as efficient, or as intense, as a direct Melding—it would be hopelessly inadequate for a full-fledged search of the Source-Mind's measureless store of memories—but for a simple task like this one, the long-distance relay was quite sufficient.

Ch*Tril had long known that the Source-Mind, in its unfathomable wisdom, was somehow constantly aware of the existence and precise location of every individual among her kind who had the Link-Talent. She herself had often tapped into this cache of information during a Melding, to check on Dj\Tal's or a friend's well-being or to verify the whereabouts of her School when she was preparing to return home from a journey.

It had never occurred to her, though, that the Source-Mind might also be keeping track of certain land-walkers—or, indeed, that any of the land-walkers might themselves have at least a latent form of the Link-Talent.

Now here they were, merely a half-day's swim from the School, the first two of the land-walker Receptives she had been sent to find; in the same place, *together*. Were they mates? she wondered.

And if their memories of the long-ago initial preparatory contact each had experienced were truly suppressed as she'd been told they would be, what had brought them here together?

]Destination/Loud-Hull[, she imaged to Tr*Til, and the two of them set off in the direction of the floating hull that was rumbling its way through the water near the island just ahead. The island itself, or one end of it, was covered with whiskered awrk-awrks, hundreds of them, thousands. As she swam, Ch*Tril scanned warily in all directions, well aware what a tempting feeding area this would be for Danger-Cousins; she detected none in the vicinity, but cautioned Tr*Til in no uncertain terms against any spontaneous exploration of the rocky shallows at the island's edge.

The loud noise from the floating hull suddenly ceased, and it stopped moving. Ch*Tril surfaced for a breath, and saw the two land-walkers on the hull lift a heavy object and throw it into the ocean. The object was attached to something like a long strand of seaweed, but *very* long, maybe twenty or thirty beak-to-flukes, and thick.

Ch*Tril dove again and watched the object sink to the bottom, where the weight of it forced its pointed end into the sand. The long strand it was attached to was no longer loose, but straight and tight, all the way up to the land-walkers' floating hull.

It was holding the hull in place, Ch*Tril realized; keeping the hull from drifting away with the current. How ingenious!

She rose back to the surface, where Tr*Til had almost reached the hull now.]Circle[, Ch*Tril imaged to her, and the two of them went into a looping circuit three or four beak-to-flukes away from the stationary hull.

One of the land-walkers—probably the female, Ch*Tril surmised, since it was smaller than the other one—was busily at work with some sort of objects on the hull. Ch*Tril stopped circling and raised her head above the water to watch, and then the land-walker began lowering one of the objects into the water.

It was smaller than the heavy object that had secured the hull in place, Ch*Tril scanned, more regularly shaped and with an intricate internal structure. She was inspecting it more closely when she noticed that the land-walker was climbing into the water, too.

Ch*Tril moved to within a beak-to-fluke of the creature, and scanned it: definitely the female, and wearing some sort of partially transparent covering over her face. A breathing apparatus, apparently; these land-walkers were impressively inventive.

The land-walker touched the object that she'd lowered into the water, and—it began imaging! Distinct, coherent images, only slightly distorted, showing the land-walker herself playing games with one of Ch*Tril's kind, a male.

This wasn't what Ch*Tril had expected at all; the land-walker was actually trying to communicate with *her,* instead of the other way around as had been planned. And it was *imaging,* or rather it was somehow making that odd square object do so.

The series of impossible images continued for several moments, then abruptly stopped. The land-walker lifted her head above the surface, made some sounds toward the one who was still atop the hull, then came back down and looked quietly at Ch*Tril.

She was waiting, Ch*Tril realized; waiting for a response. If that square black thing she had with her could create images, it must be able to perceive them, too, and somehow translate them into recognizable form for the land-walkers.

This was supposed to have been a preliminary *Linking* session, though, initiated by Ch*Tril; no one had considered the possibility that the land-walker might inaugurate the contact, and with actual images.

Well, maybe they'd be more comfortable communicating in images, at least at first. But what to send them? What sort of scenes would be most familiar to the land-walkers, would be most apt to put them at ease and prepare them for the Link?

Then it suddenly occurred to her, and the answer seemed obvious. Both of these land-walkers had been contacted before, when they were young ones, though they weren't supposed to remember the event; Ch*Tril had, through the relay, studied the Source-Mind's stored records of those meetings, and could easily re-create the scenes.

She did so, and the reaction was quick in coming, but it came from the one on the hull, not the female in the water. That puzzled Ch*Tril, and then she was disappointed when the female suddenly went back up onto the hull in response to the other one's excited cries.

They must be discussing the images, Ch*Tril thought, in whatever limited way they were able to communicate between themselves. Allow them a little while to do that, she decided; then it would be time for the real communication to begin.

The manic confusion audible in Daniel's shouts alarmed her the moment she raised her head above the water to clear her mask. "Sheila!" he yelled, his voice higher-pitched and raspier than she'd ever heard it before. "Get up here now, you've gotta see this!"

"What? What is it?"

"Just get up here, for God's sake!"

Sheila ripped off the mask, threw it onto the deck of the boat, and clambered hurriedly up the bathing ladder. "Daniel, what the hell is it?" she demanded.

He grabbed her by the shoulders and propelled her toward the cramped little wheelhouse. "You have to see it yourself," he insisted. "The tape in the VCR, run it back five minutes."

Sheila gave him an exasperated frown, but his sudden fervor was contagious. She rewound the tape in a state of high anticipation, and watched with impatience as the numbers on the time counter swiftly reversed themselves. When the counter read "00:00," she stopped the tape and hit the "Play" button.

And saw herself on the screen. Herself at the age of nine, with—

Mommy yelling from the beach behind her, Daddy screaming too and the big gray thing with the fin coming at her fast coming right up to her face it was looking at her it was ...

Communicating with her. The details of the dream, of the long-buried memory, came rushing into Sheila's mind with dizzying completeness.

July 1969. Her parents had taken her to Florida, to Cape Canaveral, to watch the launch of *Apollo 11,* the first moon-landing mission. The rocket had rumbled aloft like a burning spear hurled in slow motion; Sheila had watched it as she stood in the calm shallows of her beloved ocean ... and the gray shape, the *dolphin,* had suddenly approached her.

Her mother and father, standing on the sand, had seen it moving toward her and had panicked. They must have thought it was a shark, because of the fin. By the time her father had reached her, swimming as fast as he could, it had already left.

But not before it had ... come into her mind.

>Harmony<

it had conveyed to her, as distinctly as if it had spoken to her in English; but with far richer levels of meaning and complexity than any spoken words, more as if it had somehow managed to impart to her, in that brief moment, an entire set of attitudes and values, a purpose and a way of being.

>You Are to Be Prepared<

it had told her, had imbedded the notion, the sense of permanent expectation, directly in the deepest reaches of her mind;

>But Now Forget<

And then it was gone, it was speeding back out to sea where she could see a hundred other dolphins, ten times a hundred, jumping and cavorting in the waters that only minutes before had rippled in the thunder of the ascending Saturn V.

The picture on the television screen changed, and Sheila was abruptly torn from her reverie of long-buried memories.

"Is that ... is that you?" she asked, watching the image of the boy in the boat, his startled and delighted eyes.

258

"Yes," Daniel whispered. And . . .?"

"The little girl was me," she verified. "Cape Canaveral, 1969."

Apollo, Daniel said, nodding. "So—did you . . . remember it all?"

She looked at him, saw the intensity in his gaze, and knew exactly what he meant, knew she wouldn't have to face the impossible task of trying to describe for him the enormity of what she'd just discovered within her own mind. "The message," she said.

Daniel smiled a smile of deep relief. "Then it wasn't just me."

"It was telepathic, wasn't it? I mean, I wasn't just hallucinating; that was direct mind-to-mind communication."

"I never thought I'd be admitting something like this, but that's all it could have been," Daniel said.

"My God . . . this changes everything, this—"

"How could this dolphin here have known about it, though?" Daniel interrupted. "Those incidents happened more than twenty, thirty years ago, thousands of miles from here. In a different ocean, for Christ's sake."

Sheila frowned. "Stories, maybe; passed from one dolphin generation to the next."

"On a global scale? And anyway, how did it know where we were? How did it find us?"

It was difficult enough just trying to absorb the reality of that sudden memory, the stunning import of it. Right now, Sheila was incapable of even considering all the new and unanswerable questions that it raised. "I don't know," she confessed. "I don't have the slightest idea."

She stepped back out on the deck and looked down at the water. The two dolphins were still there. Waiting.

"But there's only one way we're going to find out," Sheila said. "Get into your bathing suit; I think we're late for class."

The meeting had been called for 7:00 P.M. but had started twenty minutes late, the arguments among the crew of the drilling ship

Alicia Faye beginning well before the sailors and roughnecks had even reached the lounge where Bryant Emerson had called them all together.

" 's a fookin' suicide post owt 'ere; I'd sooner be back in bloody Araby," thundered one burly, six-and-a-half-foot tool pusher from Merseyside.

"Aw, get fuckin' real, willya?" retorted a ship's crewman whose face was still smeared with engine-room grease. "What you think fuckin' Shamu's gonna do to a boat this size, huh? Eat it?"

That was essentially the way the battle lines had been drawn: between the drilling crew, who may have spent months or even years of their lives on board offshore platforms, but still regarded the sea as something alien, strange, and hostile; and the crew of the ship itself, who, though technically employed by an oil company, considered themselves mariners first and foremost.

"All right, all right, settle down," commanded Bryant Emerson, his arms extended upward, open hands waggling, like a politician acknowledging a well-rehearsed rally crowd. It was obvious to Jeb, though, that there wasn't going to be much unity in this little gathering; even he wasn't one hundred percent certain on which side of the controversy his own true feelings lay.

"Now, then," Emerson went on when the noise in the lounge had diminished to a low grumble. "I understand that some of you have been worried by the reports we've been seeing on the TV news about—"

" 'Worried' my ass," came a shout from the back of the room. "Me, I'm scared shitless and ain't too proud to say so."

That brought a round of laughter from both camps, and seemed to ease the tension in the room a bit.

"Well, Frank," said Emerson with a smile, "I'll admit, to hear that coming from a man of your fearless reputation is enough to give anybody pause. But it also serves to illustrate just how far out of proportion everybody's been reacting to this ... situation."

"What was you about to say there 'stead of 'situation,' Bryant?" demanded a gruff voice in a thick Oklahoma twang. " 'Crisis,' maybe? Or 'emergency'? How 'bout jes' fuck-all *calamity,* how's 'at?"

"Goddamnit, Henry, just hear me out, will you? Now, I know that most of you men aren't accustomed to working at sea, except on permanent platforms the size of a small city, so I just want to remind you first of all that this is a damned big boat we're on here. It's a goddamn *ship,* is what it is; this thing's two hundred feet long, it's got a solid steel hull that's in perfect condition, and it weighs *seven thousand tons.* There's not a killer whale in the world that could so much as put a dent in it, even if one tried!"

Jeb looked around the room, listened to the tone of the low hum that permeated the lounge. If Bryant kept to that kind of clear, simple logic, Jeb thought, he just might be able to make a dent of his own in the state of general near-panic that had been building since the first CNN reports had electrified the men on the early lunch shift yesterday.

A hundred rumors had swept through the *Alicia Faye* after the news of the worldwide orca attacks on boats: It was said that the drilling ship had a rusted hull that could easily be punctured by a creature so large and so strong . . . that a navy radarman had spotted a huge swarm of killer whales headed straight toward the Santa Barbara Channel, but the government was keeping it secret . . . that PetroGlobe had decided to sacrifice the crew if the ship were attacked . . . that the company's lawyers had determined that employee health and life insurance did not cover attacks by "wild beasts," on land or at sea. Jeb had heard all those, and dozens more, in the past thirty-six hours.

"Let's say that's true," said Frank Hickham, the muscled roughneck who'd earlier proclaimed himself to be "scared shitless." "Let's say one of those killer whales couldn't damage the ship. But from what I hear, the damn things have been ganging up together in these attacks. What if ten of 'em ram the hull at once? Hell, what if a *hundred* of 'em come at us?"

The tone of the murmurs filling the room veered back toward the anxious mood with which the meeting had begun. "Fookin' well told," declared the angry Brit whose complaints had been the first raised.

"Shit, they don't even need to do that," said someone else. "They want to hurt us, all they got to do is sink that shuttle boat when some of us is goin' or comin' from shore time."

A thin film of perspiration was breaking out on Emerson's forehead, Jeb saw, and the project supervisor began to hem and haw, grasping for answers. Jeb didn't envy Bryant the task; both men had raised valid points, according to the hasty research Jeb had managed to do since yesterday. Even before the current problems, orcas had typically traveled in cooperative packs of five to forty individuals, hunting seals, sea lions, dolphins, and even other whales considerably larger than themselves; despite the benign, friendly, Barney-the-dinosaur image with which they had been publicized in recent years, orcas had a hell of a lot more in common with the dinosaurs of *Jurassic Park*. They were known, quite accurately, as "wolves of the sea."

As far as their attacking the shuttle boat, that forty-foot cabin cruiser on which Jeb and everyone else here relied for transportation to and from land, the men's fears were also well justified. An average adult orca was only slightly smaller than that boat, and two or three of them working together could easily destroy it; several of the boats reported sunk or crippled in the recent attacks were as big as, or bigger than, PetroGlobe's handsomely appointed little shuttlecraft. There was no other option available, either; the only area of the *Alicia Faye*'s deck large enough for a helicopter to land on was now taken up by the UFO-shaped command module for the laser drilling operation.

"What we need is some fuckin' guns!" came a shout from the back of the room, followed by a loud, rough chorus of agreement. Emerson had clearly lost whatever hold he might've once had on the crowd that was nominally under his supervision. Jeb could see where this was headed, and he silently prayed that no one in the raucous crowd would make the next connection; but of course it was too obvious a leap not to be made.

"To hell with guns," Frank Hickham yelled, drawing the mob's curious attention. "With the lasers on those mini-subs out there, we can cut a goddamn killer whale in two!"

The water was colder than Daniel had expected, much colder than the warm waters off Sanibel Island where Sheila had persuaded him to swim with the doomed wild dolphin that had been visiting there.

Had that dolphin, too, been seeking them specifically, Sheila and him? The thought was impossible, insane; but no more so than what he was already thinking, and doing, now.

He pulled the face mask over his eyes and nose, and bit down on the rubbery breathing valve of the snorkel tube. Sheila looked at him, nodded, and together they ducked their heads beneath the surface.

Maybe it wasn't just the water temperature, Daniel thought, shivering, as his eyes focused on the form of the waiting dolphin. This wasn't like going into a battle zone or a revolution, where the dangers were all clear-cut and well defined; this was more like the first time he'd dropped acid in college, those uncertain minutes between the irrevocable commitment of swallowing the drug-soaked little square of blotter paper and the onset of ... whatever it was that might await, be it ecstasy or madness or revelation, or some unimaginable combination of all those things and more.

The dolphin turned slowly in the water, looking first at Sheila, then directly at Daniel. Its eyes were clear, bright almost to the point of luminosity, and full of intelligence and mystery in equal measure.

It moved forward a few feet, now no more than an arm's length from Daniel's face, and—

>Welcome<

The greeting filled Daniel's mind with a rush of inner warmth, like a time-lapse image of a flower unfolding in the sunlight. It seemed to spring spontaneously into being inside his mind, though he knew it had not originated there. The message was distinct and unmistakable, but immensely more encompassing than the single English-language word into which Daniel automatically translated it: The salutation somehow managed to convey the entire concept of welcomeness, of companionship pleasurably accepted and offered, along with a sense of shared well-being and contentment and a joyful anticipation of camaraderie to come.

Daniel turned to look at Sheila; she nodded in slow motion, the tendrils of her short dark hair billowing about her head like the petals of a sea anemone. She'd heard it—or sensed it, or received it, or whatever—too.

He closed his eyes and felt a sudden, gentle sort of tugging from the deepest reaches of his brain, something pulling at him, at the essence of him. His stomach lurched at the unfamiliar sensation, but he willed himself not to resist it, to see whatever was happening to him through to the end.

>There Is Pain Within You<

came that inner voice again, and the pain it so eloquently and instantaneously described was indeed his own, was in one broad, swift stroke a comprehensive representation of that labyrinthine tangle of emotions attendant upon his wife's murder, the wounds of her revealed betrayal and the horror of her brutal death, the loss, utter and irrevocable, the *loss* . . .

Dimly, Daniel became aware that a tiny pool of tears had begun to collect at the bottom of his face mask, and that Sheila had reached out to him beneath the chilling water, had taken hold of his hand.

He felt the tugging at his brain again, and it was as if a barrier had come down, a wall of his own construction, and that dreaded morass of conflicting emotions surrounding Ruth's death began to coalesce into a tangible and finite whole, at once less confusing, less troubling than before. He could feel it all receding, somehow, being put away into some shadowy corner of his mind along with the fears and disappointments of his childhood, sorrows he had long since deemed no longer worthy of consideration.

>Acceptance and Forgetting<

the presence in his mind encouraged, and it was so.

There was a long moment of heady buoyancy, of release, his mind floating unaccustomedly free of all the searing emotions that had so long isolated him, had so very nearly consumed him . . .

And then the flood came, a great perceptual tide of thoughts, sights, memories, sensations both physical and emotional. . . . Daniel felt himself swept inexorably along with that inner current, swept into it and absorbed by it, becoming part of it even as it became the whole of him.

Somewhere in the distance, he could still hear the steady, labored sounds of his own breathing, the singsong rise and fall of the air passing from his mouth to the snorkel tube and back again; but the essential He was elsewhere, was a hundred different wheres and whens, and Sheila was there with him, not beside him but within him, and he within her, throughout it all.

Together, they became dolphins, dozens of different dolphins one after another, racing gracefully and smoothly through a sea of millennia and of astonishing visions and events, of meetings with naked or white-robed humans and of mergings with an all-inclusive Mind whose enormity constituted a veritable ocean of its own, an ocean of memory and wisdom and design, of purpose clear yet comprehensible only in the smallest and most tantalizing of fragments.

Together, they rode this coursing sea of time and thought, and knew that they were forever changed.

Ch*Tril swam at a relaxed pace, letting her friend Tr*Til lead the way as they headed toward warmer waters.

The partial Meld with the land-walkers had been exhausting, but it had gone even better than she'd hoped. She'd known they were classified as Receptives, but had expected to encounter at least some difficulty in stimulating their dormant Link-Talents to life; not so.

The hardest part had been for her to concentrate on the task at hand, the passing on of the First Teachings and then the warning about the dangers of the burning rock, when there had been such a wealth of fascinating new detail about the land-walkers themselves to discover. Even the most mundane matters, things the land-walkers took for granted to the extent of ignoring them, had filled Ch*Tril with wonder: what it felt like to have limbs, for example, to manipulate objects with such ease and precision.

And what objects! The land-walkers' minds had contained a profusion of object-oriented memories, many of them mystifying, all of them intriguing. There were objects that created light, objects that stored images and ideas, objects that carried the land-walkers hurtling at high speed across vast stretches of land or sky . . .

And there were objects that inflicted death.

Ch*Tril had been stunned and appalled by the pain she had seen within the male land-walker's mind, and by its origin. How could a sentient being slaughter another that was not its enemy, and then destroy *itself*, in a manner too terrible to contemplate? Worse still, how could such atrocities, such grief and torment, have resulted from something so innocent, so joyous, as the act of mating?

Clearly, the land-walkers were creatures of great complexity, capable of creating and performing the most astounding marvels, yet prone to acts of seemingly random and inexplicable violence.

She would do well to keep this in mind, Ch*Tril knew; for the next land-walker she was due to contact, as the Source-Mind had relayed to her, was far to the south of here, in a large floating hull . . . a very dangerous hull.

A killing hull.

13

They lay side by side on the aft deck of the boat, drained of all strength, breathing together in great labored gasps. Sheila's mind still raced at amphetamine speed, overwhelmed by the task of sorting and evaluating all that it had just absorbed.

Think of the sea, she told herself, trying to slow the headlong, disjointed rush of thoughts. *A warm, calm sea. Still and empty.*

"You were there," she heard Daniel saying between gulps of air. "With me. Inside . . ."

Sheila turned on her side to face him, opened her eyes. He was sitting up now, his head on one knee, both knees clutched against his heaving chest.

"You were there," he said again with emphasis, as if straining to convince himself of the veracity of his own words. "Right? Am I right?"

"Yes," she told him. "I was there."

He raised his head and looked at her, frowning. "So, tell me, then. Put it in your own words."

Sheila pulled herself to a sitting position and leaned her back against the bulkhead of the wheelhouse. "You—you were in a lot of pain," she said, then hesitated, unsure how to proceed. "I don't know if I can . . ."

"Just tell me," Daniel said. "What you saw."

"All of it," she said. "You relived the—the death of your wife. And then you came *through* it, you resolved it; but not by yourself."

"No," he said. "Not by myself. Then what?"

"We . . . merged. All of us, so many—you and me, and there were the dolphins, scores of them, and people standing in the water wearing robes . . . my God, that was Delphi, wasn't it? The temple of the Oracle. Daniel, that was Greece, ancient Greece."

His frown was gone and a look of bemused amusement had taken its place. "You *were* there," he said hoarsely. "I didn't just imagine it."

"And there was something overriding it all," Sheila went on in a rush, the memories coalescing now, her mind beginning to accept them and define them. "Some sort of . . . intelligence, something transcendent. Like a guiding force, that put it all together."

"This is insane," Daniel rasped.

Sheila reached for a blanket and put it across her trembling shoulders. "But it was real," she said. "As real as anything I've ever experienced."

Daniel stood up shakily and clung to the boat's railing, staring out at the ocean. There was no longer any sign of the smooth gray fins; the dolphins were gone, God knew where.

"So," Daniel said; "what do we do now?"

"I don't know," she said, a quaver in her voice. "It was so beautiful, so optimistic, but . . . it was frightening, too, especially that part at the end, with the—"

"The fire," Daniel whispered, nodding. "The fire in the sea. What the hell was that supposed to *mean*?"

"Say, 'Nando, lookin' for you on this side, come back."

Fernando Guimares ignored the sputtering transmission from the VHF radio and kept his gaze on the ocean ahead. He swept his eyes left and right in a slow, distinctive arc as the *Diego Queen* rode the swells; if he stared in one direction too long, he knew, it would all become a meaningless blur.

"You gonna pick up?" his mate asked.

Guimares shrugged. "Wha's the point, huh, Paulo?"

The radio crackled again. "'Nando, *Sea Master* here, you copy?"

Left and right, he scanned the horizon; right and left.

"Company say we always answer the code group," Paulo said uneasily.

"You think the company give a shit about Toninho Batera? This gonna be his last trip out, I bet you anything." Guimares laughed. "As skipper, anyway; maybe he be a deckhand next month, we hire him on an' you can put him to work on the nets. See how he'd like that."

"Come back, *Diego Queen,* come back," the voice on the radio implored. Fernando reached out and turned the volume down, leaving it just loud enough so he could hear if any of the other boats in the group, any of the *real* tuna fishermen, called in.

"You remember last trip," Guimares said, his eyes still scanning the horizon, "day we had those big whitecaps all morning, cleared up around lunchtime?"

Paulo nodded.

"I checked with Batera that day, he was about twelve miles southeast, said it was 8795 all the way, no porpoise. You remember that?"

"Sure. Was slow a long time after that, ten days before we make another decent set."

"That's when it was, all right. Well, this last time we was back in San-Dee, I was down to Nunu's, I run into Manny Rodriguez, you know?"

"Yeah, yeah," Paulo said, "I know Manoel. We go back a long time, before he even sign on with Batera."

"Well, you know what Manny tell me? I mean, after a few rounds of Black Label, this was, you know what he say?"

269

"No, I don' know."

Guimares took his eyes away from the sea for a moment and looked directly at his mate. "He tell me that day, they spot a big school of porpoise. I mean, *big*. An' Batera, he lied about it to the code group."

"Maybe he was way behind, had to make up tonnage. Sometimes we don' share, less there be plenty to go around."

"No, Paulo, you don't get it. Batera, he never even set on the damn porpoise. I mean, he turn his boat around, leave 'em there in the fuckin' water!"

The mate's eyebrows went up in disbelief, but Guimares was scanning the horizon again, left to right. *"Não,"* Paulo said. "I hear he make his crew work double time, get all the porpoise outta the nets, but—"

"He leave 'em in the fuckin' water! Don't even touch 'em, don't let nobody else come in and make a set. Now, I should pick up the radio an' answer him? You tell me, Paulo."

As if on cue, the radio came to life again, no louder than a whisper. "'Nando, you out there? Gimme a position check if you copy, *Diego Queen,* I need a fix so I can reset—"

Guimares snapped the radio off. "Who's up in the nest today?" he asked angrily.

"That new boy," Paulo said.

"Can't he spot shit? There's porpoise out here, I can smell 'em."

"He's not so bad, use to spot for Carlos Abonando before he retire. They porpoise aroun', he'll see 'em."

The reassurance didn't help; Guimares was pissed, and he needed somebody closer than Antonio Batera to take it out on.

"Well, how come everybody's so fuckin' quiet, huh? Breakfast this mornin', I thought somebody died."

"Some of the men, they . . ." Paulo licked his lips nervously; he didn't want to make the skipper any madder than he already was. "They kinda spooked, you might say."

"The fuck does that mean, spooked? They see a ghost on board, what?"

"It's this thing in the news, you know, Skip. All the killer-whale thing."

Guimares slapped his hand on the wheel and laughed, more a bark than a laugh. "They think we gonna get sunk, huh? Some damn fish gonna come up, knock a hole in six inches of steel plate with their heads?"

"The speedboat drivers, they a little worried. Those boats is small, Skip."

"They worried now, you tell 'em wait till—"

He was interrupted by a shout from the crow's nest: "Porpoise at eight o'clock! Three miles!"

The mate smiled with relief, glad to have a positive end to this conversation. "I tol' you he spot 'em, they out there."

Guimares wasn't listening; he was already spinning the wheel hard aport, and staring toward the flecks of gray that dotted the sea to the northwest. Porpoise, hundreds upon hundreds of them, and a wealth of tuna sure to be found beneath them. It would be a fine day after all, and that traitor Batera wouldn't hear a fucking word about it, not from Fernando Guimares.

"Goddamn it, Sam, I'm telling you this would be an exclusive; isn't that what you were begging me for just a week or so ago?"

"Well ... Daniel, you've got to look at it from my viewpoint, you understand?" The editor's voice on the other end of the phone line was detached, distant. "I mean, this is not exactly what I had in mind when—"

"Oh, for Christ's sake, what are you saying? The only stories you want are the ones you already know in advance? This is fucking *news,* Sam. Remember that, news? The stuff that jumps out at you because you never expected it to happen?"

Daniel tapped a pencil angrily against the back of his hand, and listened to the long uneasy silence.

"Look," Jenkins finally said, "I've got a certain responsibility here—"

"Damn right you do!" Daniel exploded. "A responsibility to tell your readers what the hell's happening right in their backyard, the biggest goddamn story since—"

"I know you took it to the *Times* three days ago," Jenkins interrupted. "And *The Washington Post,* and who knows where else. Word gets around, old buddy. I don't have to tell *you* that."

Daniel closed his eyes and cursed under his breath. He knew all too well what Jenkins meant. A few years back, he'd done a feature piece for *Playboy* on how jokes get started, how they spread so fast; he'd investigated the subject as thoroughly as if he were working on an exposé of the nuclear power industry, and even he had been surprised by the answer: The most common origin of widely told jokes in the United States, particularly those of the black humor variety, wasn't late-night talk shows or comedy clubs; it was newsrooms. Somebody comes up with a wicked, topical wisecrack one night around the newsroom at WGN-TV in Chicago, or at the national desk of *The Miami Herald,* and by noon the next day it's being told from coast to coast, thanks to a legion of reporters and editors making their daily nationwide checks of contacts and affiliates and stringers.

And now Daniel himself had become a joke, within that loose but ubiquitous network of his peers.

"Sam, I'm not bullshitting you. You know damn well I'd never fall for a hoax, and I haven't gone off the deep end. I *know* how bizarre all this sounds, but damn it, this is the real thing."

"It's just that it's so—"

It took great effort for Daniel to restrain himself from shouting into the phone. "This is Prize material, goddamnit, the big one! I don't care how hard it is to believe right now, just think how you're gonna feel down the line if you let it get away from you."

He could hear the sound of Jenkins breathing, could see in his mind's eye the worried furrow of his old friend's brow.

"I'm sorry, Daniel. I'm gonna have to take a pass on this one. Nothing personal, O.K.?"

Daniel sighed and tossed the pencil across Sheila's study, hitting a wall of books. "Yeah," he said. "Sure, I understand. But when it does break, don't forget: I tried to give it to you."

He hung up the phone, frustrated and discouraged. Jenkins had been right: Every other editor of any consequence had already turned the story down, for the same, obvious reasons that Sam had cited. The kinder ones had refrained from laughing, at least while Daniel was talking to them.

Hell, he thought, what else did you expect? He'd had a choice: Tell the story straight and risk coming up against exactly the sort of reactions he'd encountered; or lie, withhold what he knew to be accurate and monumentally important information, and get into print a watered-down, self-censored version of what had happened.

Daniel had made the mistake of opting for the truth, and by so doing had managed to seriously damage—if not destroy—his professional credibility.

"You want some coffee?" Sheila asked, poking her head into the room.

"Yeah. With a double shot of Jack Daniel's in it."

"Another turndown?"

He nodded dejectedly. "I don't know where else to go at this point. I've used up all my options."

"Maybe we—" she broke off, interrupted by the sound of the front doorbell. "We'll think of something," she said, turning to go answer the door.

Daniel picked up the pencil that he'd thrown across the room and put it back in a cup on the desk. The rejections he'd met were as understandable as they were frustrating; a month ago, a week ago, he'd have had the same reaction if someone had tried to sell him on so bizarre a story. Surely there must be someone who—

He heard a commotion from the living room, and although he couldn't make out what Sheila was saying, the irritation in her voice was unmistakable.

Daniel was there in a half-dozen long, striding steps. Three strangers, two men and a woman, were in the room with Sheila. The woman was a heavily made-up blonde with a wireless microphone in her hand, and one of the men had a heavy video camera balanced on his right shoulder.

"... nothing to say to you. Nothing," Sheila was saying with a rising tone of annoyance.

"What the hell's going on here?" Daniel demanded.

The woman with the microphone turned to him. "Daniel Colter? Are you Daniel Colter?"

"What is this? Sheila, who are these people?"

"Dina Mallory, *News Behind the News,*" the woman said. "I'd like to ask you a few questions about your experience with—"

"They just shoved their way in," Sheila said, distressed.

"Well, they can shove their way right back out," Daniel said.

The blond woman was undaunted. "Don't you want to tell us your version of the story?" she insisted, shoving the microphone to within a few inches of Daniel's face. "Is it true that you claim—"

He pushed the microphone away with the back of his hand. "This is a private home," he told her gruffly, "and you've been asked to leave."

"Hey!" Sheila suddenly shouted, "you can't go back there!"

Daniel turned and saw that the man with the camera was walking through the kitchen, toward the pool where Ringo and the other dolphins were.

"All right, that's it," Daniel said, and went after the cameraman. He grabbed him by the shoulder and pushed the man roughly back toward the front door. "Get the fuck out of here, right now. All of you."

The Mallory woman lowered her microphone and gave him a smug smile. "I think we already have what we need," she said. "Tony, Steve; let's get back to the van."

Daniel stood outside the door, his arms folded, as the trio packed their equipment into a Dodge van emblazoned with the title NEWS BEHIND THE NEWS in large, rightward-slanted red letters. Below that, in smaller, blue letters, were the words SYNDICATED NATIONWIDE. Only when the van had backed out of Sheila's driveway and headed away out of sight did he return to the house, locking the front door's deadbolt behind him.

"Where did those people *come* from?" Sheila wanted to know. "How did they find out—"

"I told you, word gets around." Daniel's eyes searched the room, and he noticed that the television set was on. The screen glowed a deep, blank blue, with the words VIDEO ONE in the upper left-hand corner. "What were you doing just before they showed up, when I was on the phone back in the study?" he asked.

Sheila frowned curiously. "I was reviewing the image tape we made on the boat that day; why?"

Daniel walked over to the VCR, knelt down and pressed the "Eject" button. Nothing happened.

"The tape's gone," he said.

Batera leaned forward with his elbows on the railing to steady the heavy binoculars as best he could relative to the rolling motion of the boat. Last Christmas his son Jorge had given him a pair of pocket-sized Nikons that were almost as powerful, but he still preferred the feel and heft of his father's old Zeiss glasses.

He'd known Guimares had been close by, damn it; there was the *Diego Queen* now, idling back in preparation for a set. Through the salt-pitted lenses Batera could see the speedboats being lowered, the skiff driver checking the net he'd soon be towing ... and the multitude of gray fins where the porpoise were already trying in vain to scatter to safety.

Batera lowered the binoculars and went back in to the bridge. Nothing but static on the VHF; Guimares was still ignoring him, disdaining him.

Well, he'd more or less expected that to happen, or something like it. Silence or misdirection, that's all he'd get from the code group this trip. Couldn't really fault 'Nando; he was just doing his job the best way he knew.

Man was right, anyway; it wouldn't work for him or any of the others to share a set with Batera. Different priorities now, and with Batera going for a zero porpoise kill, it'd slow them all down. Whatever changes Batera had gone through were personal; they applied to him and him alone. It wasn't his place to tell another man how to run his own boat; but then, shouldn't the reverse hold just as true?

He looked back on the deck, saw the men he'd hired watching the *Diego Queen* and talking among themselves. The netpile they'd stacked the first day out was still dry and neatly folded. There'd be grumbling, he knew, no matter what they'd agreed to when they'd signed on. Bigger share of the profits wouldn't mean so much if it took them twice as long to earn it.

Ah, shit, Batera thought. Maybe he ought to just give it up altogether. Sell his thirty percent of the boat to Sea Banquet—let 'em catch the damn fish any way they wanted. That'd please Schofield, to see him out; but he didn't know how it'd be on him and Maria, being at home together all the time.

Maybe they could sell the place in Point Loma, too, move to Phoenix to be close to their boy. Or even back to Lisbon: Maria could go to the *adegas típicas* to hear her fados, she could watch her soap operas live on Portuguese TV, and Batera could ... what? Sit around the old Alfama district every day with the old men, sipping their *vinhos da casa* and telling their stories, old men like himself, used up, their lives receding into memory as they drank and talked and watched the cats on the faded stone walls licking their paws and watching them back.

He picked up the binoculars again, focused through the streaked windows of the bridge. Guimares's men were working the porpoise now, herding them together with the speedboats like oceangoing cowboys on floating, motorized steeds. The skiff was coming around; soon the men on deck would start the brailing—porpoise and tuna, lumped together indiscriminately in the big net.

"Pretty good set Guimares got workin'."

Batera hadn't seen Manoel come onto the bridge, absorbed as he was in the view through the binoculars. "Yah, looks it," he answered.

"Guess he was out there all the time we callin' him."

"Musta been." Batera's head had started buzzing, probably some kind of headache coming on. No surprise. "You wanta take the wheel awhile?" he asked.

"Sure," the mate said. "Not much else needs doin'."

Batera ignored the sarcasm. "Let's check it out west of here. Maybe we'll get lucky."

Manoel nodded curtly and took hold of the wheel, spinning it to starboard and revving up the engines. The boat heeled about, and Batera leaned left to keep his balance as he made his way to his cabin.

The buzzing in his head was getting worse. He closed the door and reached for a bottle of Scotch, then checked himself. Just aggravate it, no point in that. He rummaged around in a drawer, found some Advil, and washed a couple of them down with water. Putting the bottle back, he noticed a picture of his father at the back of the drawer: about ten years younger than Antonio was now, his hair thick and black, arms ropy with muscles from hauling in tuna on the long lines.

Batera pulled the picture out, along with several others that were stuffed beneath it. There was the old house on Rosecrans, first one his folks had ever bought; he remembered hanging up an old tire from a tree in the backyard there—his mother made him cut it down after his little sister, Teresa, swung too high on it and fell out and broke her elbow. He flipped the pictures; there she was, too, Teresa, and there was one of his mother, an old print dress on and her hair up in a bun. She'd never adapted to America any better than Maria had; the two of them used to yammer together in Portuguese about how difficult it was to learn English, how expensive San Diego was. She'd died when Antonio was forty-five, and his father not long after.

His head wasn't feeling any better; fucking Advil, he should've had the Scotch instead. He sat down in his leather recliner and went through the rest of the old photos.

Shit, there he was himself, what, eight? Ten? Sitting at the stern of that little fifteen-footer his father and his uncle had gone in on together, used to fish for mackerel in the bay when they weren't out on the big boats. Antonio there with his bamboo pole in hand, serious look on his face like he was gonna hook a tuna right off Harbor Island.

Damn that fucking buzz in his head, he couldn't take it anymore, he—

Remembered.

Remembered what it was he'd been trying to think of ever since he'd watched the video those Greenpeace types had made, remembered the image that had been stuck in his head like a splinter in a calloused thumb, buried too deep to see. Now, in one sudden timeless rush, it all came out of its own accord:

... him no bigger than belt-high, him and his father out in the little fishing boat with his tio João, *off Point Loma in the blue water where they could maybe land some bonito, or some snapper ...* pai *driving the boat, João baiting the hooks and Toninho just looking at the water, looking down so maybe he could see some tuna like his* pai *pulled in with the big poles, and here comes something up from the water, coming right at him, looking at him ... eyes like a human, teeth like a shark, but he wasn't scared, and now here it was, head out of the water with that long beak, smiling at him,* thinking *at him, what the hell was that, his head buzzing and the fish with the human eyes in front of him and inside his head at the same time....*

His father had seen it, too, had seen the thing—the porpoise—lift its head up beside the boat and look right at the boy; but his father hadn't heard it thinking. He'd whipped him good that night for telling such a story in front of João, told him not to ever talk about it again. Didn't matter anyway—the next morning Toninho had forgotten all about it, never remembered it had ever happened, until ... now.

His face was covered with sweat, his back, too, shirt sticking to the leather of the big armchair. Batera wiped his dripping face with his sleeve, got up from the chair and poured himself a double Chivas, no ice. He downed it in one gulp but his hands were still shaking, so he poured another.

There was nobody he could talk to about this. Not on the boat, not back home, noplace; they'd never listen to him, no more than his father had that time when he was a boy.

And why should they? They—any of them, Manoel or Gerry Schofield or Maria, it didn't matter who—they'd know what had happened to him just as well as he did.

Batera had seen it before, how the sea could sap men of their reason; he'd seen it, but he'd never imagined that he himself would someday succumb.

Now the time was here, and there was no avoiding it: The sea, Batera's hated and beloved and familiar sea, had, he finally knew, at long last driven him insane.

14

Richard Tarnoff's normally imperturbable face was a study in barely contained fury as he turned down the volume on the conference room's television set. "Well?" he demanded in the sudden silence. The tendons in his neck were rigid with anger in the confines of his tightly buttoned collar and immaculately knotted tie, and a thin film of perspiration shone on his upper lip.

Sheila shook her head in dismay. "This is none of my doing," she maintained, hating the plaintive tone with which the words emerged. She felt violated, victimized; the taped segment of the tabloid "news" show that Tarnoff had shown her was a loathsome mix of distortion, mockery, and insinuation.

Tarnoff scowled; the incredulity in his eyes could not be more apparent. "Is this what it's been about all along, this . . . *research*"—he spat out the word with distaste—"of yours? What's next, will you be showing up on *Geraldo*? Have you arranged a book contract, is that it?"

"Damn it, Richard, you saw what happened! They all but broke into my house! Did it look to you like I was cooperating with them?"

"That was a good act, Sheila, I must admit. Very believable, you and this . . . Colter individual, both of you. Is he the one who put you up to it? Are you splitting the money with him?"

Now it was Sheila's turn to be furious. "There isn't any money involved! I told you, they stole that tape!"

She closed her eyes, still hearing the Mallory woman's sarcastic and hopelessly muddled voice-over narration of those wondrous, highly private images of Sheila's and Daniel's childhood dolphin encounters: ". . . *claims that she can not only read the dolphins' minds, but that she's discovered some sort of secret process to—are you ready for this?—record their thoughts on film. The maverick professor also professes to believe that—*"

"If that's true," Tarnoff asked, "then why haven't you filed criminal charges? Why haven't you brought suit?"

Sheila sighed. "Would it make any difference, now that they've broadcast this . . . this crap?"

Tarnoff looked at her long and hard, then shook his head. "No, I don't think it would. The damage has already been done, and the university has suffered enough embarrassment already."

"To hell with the university!" Sheila exclaimed. "It's *my* reputation that's under attack here. I'm the one who has to bear the brunt of—"

"That's been your problem all along," Tarnoff said primly, "always putting yourself and your absurd theories first. I don't have that kind of luxury; I have to think of the good of the department, and of the university as a whole."

"Meaning?" Sheila asked, but she knew damn well what he meant, knew what he was leading up to.

Tarnoff took in a deep breath, let it out slowly. "As of today," he said, "you and your . . . project are no longer affiliated with this institution."

Sheila nodded grimly. "You've been waiting a long time for the chance to say that, haven't you, Richard?"

Tarnoff busied himself with the papers in his briefcase, refusing to meet her eyes. "I expect you to arrange for the immediate disposal of the dolphins you've been keeping. The proceeds of any sale will, of course, go to the university."

All the years, the effort, the love . . . the *success,* above and beyond anything she had ever dared to imagine. "You really don't understand what you're doing, do you? You're turning your back on one of the most—"

He snapped the briefcase shut and stood to go. "The laboratory and residential facilities you've been occupying have already been reassigned. You have thirty days to move your personal belongings."

"Richard, I—"

He stopped at the door and turned to look at her again, a flash of anger lighting his eyes once more. "And if I hear of you ever again mentioning the university's name in connection with any of this, there'll be hell to pay, I assure you."

Sheila rested her head in her hands as Tarnoff left. The videotape of the tabloid broadcast continued to play, mutely, on the monitor before her. Now they were showing the last part of the image tapes from that day on the boat, the segment that showed the puzzling images of burning rock beneath the water, of glowing beams emanating from fishlike, yet metallic, moving objects.

There was a soft double rap at the conference room door, and the graduate student whose turn it was today to answer the phones for the Department stuck her head in the room.

"Miz Roberts? I'm sorry to bother you, but there's a call for you on line three."

"Who is it?" Sheila asked wearily.

The student glanced down at a pink memo slip on which she had written the message. "It's a man named Sloane," she said. "Jeb Sloane. He says it's urgent."

The young ones, drowning . . .

So like his own kind's young, Dj\Tal thought, for all their differences. Fur-topped heads or smooth, limbs or fins, the physical dissimilarities became irrelevant when one considered the shared fact of *mind*. It was there in the eyes, so full of wonder and joy and curiosity.

Full now of terror, and despair. Widening with dread before that final closure.

He had done everything he could, they all had. The hull had been a small one this time; it had splintered and sunk on first impact when the renegade Danger-Cousins had rammed it. Five land-walkers on the doomed hull, three of them young ones: a female and two small males. Dj\Tal had kept one of the males afloat as long as possible; it had clutched at him desperately with its tiny limbs as the battle raged around them ... but it had slipped from his back too many times in the confusion, its lungs filling at last with the bloody water.

Unlikely that it would have survived, in any event; the attack had been too far from land, with no potential rescuing hulls in sight. Still, Dj\Tal could not forget its eyes, nor its cries of fear as death encroached. So many others had also died in that encounter, Danger-Cousin allies and members of Dj\Tal's School alike; but it was the young land-walker he remembered most.

He had Linked to it, near the end, though he'd had no time to determine whether the little creature had possessed the Talent.

>Warmth/Calmness/Infinitude<

Dj\Tal had sent, with all the power he could muster. He only hoped the young one had perceived some portion of it, that the Link had helped to blot out at least a little of the horror and the pain. Other such Links, in other times, had carried far greater promise; but in this grievous instance, alleviation of suffering had been all Dj\Tal could offer.

The news had been no better upon his return to the School: Three hundred and more had now been lost, one of every ten. At least Dv\Kil and his young mate, in whose womb had now come into shape a young-one-to-be, were not among the dead or injured; not yet, at any rate.

Dj\Tal's gloomy musings were broken by the sight of Vl\Kal,

swimming toward him at full speed. His pod-brother was frightened, Dj\Tal scanned, and that put him instantly on alert.

]Danger-Cousins/Numerous[, Vl\Kal imaged, and rose immediately to the surface for a much-needed breath.

Dj\Tal turned in the direction Vl\Kal had indicated, and did a long-range scan; he saw nothing there other than the perimeter scouts and the edge of a kelp forest, but—

The Link came to him suddenly, from somewhere beyond the School's perimeter:

>Communication Is Desired<

it proclaimed, the pronouncement bolstered by a surprising aura of openness, of trust both given and entreated.

Vl\Kal descended again, his weary lungs replenished, and Dj\Tal told his friend of the unexpected message.

]Opportunity/Peace[, Vl\Kal imaged eagerly, his pulse rapid with elation at the prospect.

]Possibility/Deception[, Dj\Tal reminded him, and was about to ask his pod-brother to warn the others when all at once the orcas were upon them: fifty or more of the great black-and-white beasts, forcing their way through the edges of the terrified School in a massive, irresistible swath. Dj\Tal recognized several of them as survivors of battles recently fought; one in particular, a blunt-headed male, was missing a chunk of left pectoral fin that Dj\Tal himself had bitten from him.

>Dj\Tal<

the lead Danger-Cousin—not the injured one—Linked, and Dj\Tal moved to face it directly.

>I Am Dj\Tal<

he told it, betraying none of the fear he felt.

The orca regarded him impassively.

>Our Second Meeting<

---

it noted, and Dj\Tal scanned the Danger-Cousin carefully. Yes, he realized, it was the same one with whom he had Linked before, the one who had helped him and Vl\Kal and Dv\Kil in the aftermath of that first attack on the land-walkers' hull.

>Your Recollection Is Correct<

Dj\Tal confirmed;

>My Gratitude for the Previous Assistance of Your Pod<

The Danger-Cousin twisted its head in a startlingly sinuous motion for such a large creature. The movement could have signified almost anything, but it was clearly a nonthreatening gesture.

>Considerable Change Since That Encounter<

the orca Linked;

>Diminishment of Dissension Among Our Kind<

Dj\Tal hesitated, afraid to hope for too much, afraid of hearing too little.

>Proportion of Dissension Time-Now<

he asked, and even though he needed a breath he stayed below the surface, waiting for the Danger-Cousin's response.

>Obliteration of Dissension<

it answered;

>Cessation of Hostilities Is Requested<

>Unity in Support of New Directives<

Dj\Tal maintained the dignity appropriate to the moment as the Danger-Cousin described the renegades' defeat and capitulation; but when he rose to take his long-delayed breath he did so with a tremendous leap, reveling in the brilliance of the warm-light high above as he had not done since the orcas' first attack on the School.

VI\Kal had understood nothing of the Linking session, so Dj\Tal described it to him now.]Notification/School[, Dj\Tal concluded, and VI\Kal dashed away excitedly to inform the others that the fighting between the two species, the anguish and the fear, the needless dying, had at long last ended.

Dj\Tal and the orca resumed their animated discussion, now with so much more cause for optimism than when they had met before, in the midst of War between and among their kinds. They would have gone on Linking until the warm-light sank into the distant sea, had Dj\Tal not received a message with the unmistakably imperious overtones of Qr*Jil.

>Your Presence Is Required Time-Now<

the Link came, and after observing the formalities of farewell with the Danger-Cousin, Dj\Tal hurried toward the center of the diminished School, now athrum on all sides with gleeful images of celebration at the news of the long-awaited peace.

The Old One and her entourage were waiting quietly when Dj\Tal reached them. Her attendants hovered close by on each side, ready to give Qr*Jil a lift to the surface at a moment's notice. They seemed reluctant to abandon their positions when she dismissed them, but at her urging they finally withdrew to a discreet distance.

>Dj\Tal Has Achieved What He Desired<

Qr*Jil Linked, after her attendants had retreated.

>At Great Cost<

Dj\Tal replied carefully;

>Too Many of Our Kind Suffered<

>Too Many Died<

The Old One regarded him with her rheumy eyes.

>The Death of One Would Have Been Too Many<

she Linked back. Dj\Tal did a half-roll left and right to acknowl-
edge the truth of her pronouncement, his body bent as well in
sorrow.

>There Is Further Sadness<

Qr*Jil Linked, and paused a moment before going on:

>The Deaths of Land-Walker Young Ones<

Dj\Tal scarcely managed to conceal his surprise. The Old One
had never expressed the slightest affinity or compassion for the land-
walkers; she had seemingly feared and despised them and had
opposed every suggestion of contact with them, even in the face of
the Source-Mind's mandate.

>I Share That Sadness<

Dj\Tal answered, prudently minimizing the overtones that would
reveal too fully his own depth of feeling about the horrors he had
witnessed, his wrenching sense of personal loss at the many land-
walker deaths he had tried and failed to prevent.

>Assistance in Breathing<

the Old One Linked, and at first Dj\Tal thought she was referring
to his abortive effort to save the young land-walker who had died
along with the rest of his pod; but then he scanned her and saw
the weakness in Qr*Jil's aging muscles, the labored pumping of her
heart.

He moved to her immediately, and gave her a gentle boost to
the surface. He held her there as she wheezed heavily several times,
and when she was done he quickly breathed his own fill.

>Gratitude<

she Linked, and hovered a few moments with her eyes shut, her
body limp. Dj\Tal waited patiently, and then the Old One roused
herself with a shiver and Linked to him:

>The New Directives Must Be Realized<

This time Dj\Tal made no attempt to hide his astonishment. He started to Link a reply, but Qr*Jil interrupted him:

>I Am Incapable of This<

she confessed, and Dj\Tal politely wriggled his disagreement, but the Old One would have none of it:

>My Concepts Are Rigid<

she Linked;

>Your Old One Is Too Old<

Once more Dj\Tal attempted to respond, and once more she cut him off:

>The School Requires Leadership<

>You Shall Provide It<

She closed her cloudy eyes again, exhausted by the prolonged Link. Dj\Tal was at a loss for an appropriate reply; instead, he scanned Qr*Jil, saw her lungs nearly empty, and helped her back to the surface for another breath while he considered the magnitude of the responsibility she had just placed upon him.

There was no possibility that he could refuse it; even had The New Directives not been his driving goal, his obsession, for as long as he could remember, the pronouncement of the Old One carried a weight second only to a Directive by the Source-Mind.

She had had her say, and there was nothing more to add. It would be improper of him even to express his honor at having been chosen to succeed her, and to oversee the fulfillment of such a monumental task; Qr*Jil had made her declaration, and the opinions of another—even respectful gratitude—would be deemed irrelevant.

Dj\Tal held the frail Old One at the surface until her attendants relieved him, and by the time he took his leave he had already formulated his first order of business as leader of the School.

There would be much to do, many relays to initiate, and little time to prepare; but none would soon forget the Journey they were all about to undertake.

For the moment, though, all that was secondary to the success of Ch*Tril's current mission. With the opposition defeated on all sides, there would be time enough and more for the forging of bonds, the sharing of knowledge between their kind and the land-walkers; but before that could happen, there was a potential cataclysm to be averted, an event of such violence that it could mean the deaths of tens of thousands, among both species . . . and Ch*Tril was the only one who could prevent it, who could convey the necessary warning in time.

Dj\Tal no more believed the old myths of all-powerful, noncorporeal spirits of the sea than did Ch*Tril; but a part of him now implored those nonexistent spirits for their help and guidance, all the same.

Antonio Batera lay awake in his darkened cabin, listening to what the voices told him.

That's what they always call "crazy," he thought, when people hear voices out of thin air; but these voices were real, anybody could hear them, they came through the air on radio waves . . . so who was to say that those memories of other voices, the nonhuman and inaudible ones, were less real? Stranger things had happened, hadn't they?

No, he had to admit, they hadn't. This was as strange as it got, he thought, these supposed "memories" of his, these images of the porpoise coming up and looking him in the eyes, these recollected inner voices that had suddenly popped into his head from nowhere. No chance in hell those things were real.

He'd known a man, years back, first mate on somebody else's boat, who'd gone this route. Not exactly the same way, of course, that guy—what was his name, Roderigo, Federico?—he'd started complaining that the FBI was tapping his phone, and then it was the CIA, too, beaming microwaves at the windows of his house....

Humberto, that was his name, Humberto Silva. Good worker, he'd been, a fine first mate and an even better poker player. Last time Antonio had seen him, he'd been begging change down by the docks, and wearing a cap lined with tinfoil to keep the X rays from penetrating his thoughts.

Was that his own future now, Antonio wondered, to be penniless and raving on the streets? Was this how it started? He shuddered, lying there beneath his blankets in the pitch black night. *Jesu Cristo,* what would Maria think, and his boys? How would they react? Would they expel him from their lives in shame?

He wouldn't give in easy, by God; he'd fight it. All he had to do was stay calm, keep his mind focused, his thoughts rooted in reality. Maybe he could ward this thing off, put the evil genie back into whatever bottle it had sprung from.

Antonio rolled over and turned up the radio, willing himself to concentrate on something, anything, other than the incipient madness that seemed to be overtaking him.

"... can *never* entirely eliminate the federal deficit, that's the whole point. And so many of you callers seem to be missing that point, so let's just take a minute here to—"

It was a talk station out of, where, Seattle? Radio waves carried forever out here on the water. He could pick up New York, San Francisco, Boston, all kinds of places. He'd been listening to them for years that way; talk radio had been his English-language teacher and his companion on the boats since he was in his teens. Larry King. Antonio used to listen to him long before there was ever a CNN or a Mutual Network; he remembered hearing him interview Jimmy Hoffa, and Bobby Darin, from a houseboat in Miami he used to broadcast....

"... strength of the yen is eventually a *negative* factor for the Japanese economy, once it rises to a point where it tends to limit exports and—"

Jerry Williams, Long John Nebel, Edward P. Morgan, Ira Fistell ... the names of talk-radio hosts over the decades ran through Antonio's mind like some peculiar mantra. It was almost as if by remembering them all, every professional voice in the night that he had ever heard, he could somehow erase the memory of those other, stranger voices.

John Cameron Swayze, he thought, Ray Briem, Joe Pyne ...

"... assumptions of American decline against the global economy are not only premature, I believe they're indicative of a widespread naïveté. Now, let's take another caller—"

Joe Pyne. Antonio had never cared for him, he was too hateful, too much like that fat one these days who thinks he's funny, but in his voice there's so much meanness, so much gleeful cruelty at the expense of the helpless ...

"... just wondering what you think about these dolphin tapes, Jeff? I mean, do you think they're real, or—"

Antonio sat bolt upright in his wide bunk, suddenly alert, his reveries of the past abruptly broken.

"... said before that I refuse to discuss that kind of claptrap on this show. We're here to discuss reality, not—"

"But, Jeff, they say this Sheila Roberts is a respected scientist, one of the top researchers in—"

"Not anymore," the talk show host said derisively, "not since she started with this 'dolphin telepathy' business. She's been summarily dismissed from her position at U-C Santa Barbara, and her own colleagues now say—"

Antonio reached for the nearby light switch, flicked on the cabin lights. He sat there amid the rumpled sheets and blankets, blinking in the harsh illumination, his heart racing with excitement at the words coming from the bedside radio.

"... don't you think it's worth investigating, though, in light of all the killer whale attacks and—"

"Look, caller, it's one thing for a species of wild animal to go berserk; that may have any number of biological or environmental explanations. It's another thing entirely for some publicity-hungry woman to suddenly claim she and her boyfriend have been communicating telepathically with dolphins since they were children, and—"

Antonio threw off the covers and reached for his clothes, never bothering to look and see what time it was.

". . . the last I'll have to say on that subject. Let's go to a caller in Yakima now. You're on live with Jeff Winston, and I hope you have something more intelligent to share with us than—"

He was *not* insane, Antonio Batera thought with joyous relief as he turned off the radio and started getting dressed. Whatever else all this might mean, he was not going crazy, he would not bring that sort of shame upon his wife and family. Not only that, he now knew where to turn for answers to the questions that had plagued him.

"Sheila Roberts," he muttered to himself as he buttoned his shirt, repeating the name the better to remember it. "Santa Barbara. Sheila Roberts, Santa Barbara."

15

Daniel and Sheila arrived at the restaurant twenty minutes before the scheduled meeting, to make sure they'd be seated at an outside table where they could talk without being overheard. Daniel told the hostess they were expecting someone else, and she led them to a table for four in the corner of the balcony that stretched along two sides of the second-story restaurant. The location afforded not only relative privacy, but a spectacular view of the harbor in which the restaurant was situated.

Several hundred boats were moored in the surrounding slips, ranging from kayaks and outboard runabouts to teak-paneled yachts and barnacle-encrusted fishing boats. One of the latter was being unloaded on the dock directly below, and Daniel watched as three men maneuvered a net full of still-dripping, spiny black sea urchins. A hoist lifted the net from the boat to the open bed of a truck that had backed out onto the wooden-planked dock, at which point the men opened the net and let the ugly little creatures spill out by the hundreds. Next stop, sushi bars from Seattle to San Diego.

A half-circle of tan and ocher mountains cupped the town and the harbor, and between the marina and the sea stood a protective breakwater perhaps fifteen feet higher than the sea. A narrow channel between the breakwater and Stearns Wharf provided access for arriving or departing boats, although there was little outgoing traffic today; here, as in just about every other coastal city on earth, pleasure boating had ground to a halt in the aftermath of the well-publicized orca attacks.

In the distance lay the hazy humps of Santa Cruz and Santa Rosa Islands, marking the spot where that impossible, unforgettable encounter with the dolphin had taken place only a week before. Daniel breathed a sigh of frustration; how could he and Sheila possibly hope to convince anyone of what had happened to them, at a time when the rest of the world was living in sudden and unaccustomed fear of at least one species of the once-beloved cetaceans?

"Can I get you something to drink?" a young waitress asked, shifting her weight back and forth from one Adidas-shod foot to the other as if she'd rather be down at the beach playing volleyball.

"Iced tea," Daniel told her.

"Same," Sheila added, and the girl went bounding back inside to the bar, where a CD jukebox loaded with an eclectic selection of oldies had been playing Willie Nelson when they'd walked in, and was currently segueing from Sinatra to Crosby, Stills, Nash, and Young.

"That must be him now," Daniel said, squinting against the crisp sunlight and pointing toward a big, white-with-blue-trim cabin cruiser that was idling into the harbor from somewhere beyond the breakwater. On the prow of the boat was a colorful logo with a stylized planet earth encircled by the name PETROGLOBE.

"He really didn't give you the slightest clue as to what this was all about?" Daniel asked again, for the fifth or sixth time since Sheila had told him about the phone call.

"Not an inkling," she said. "Only that it was important, and that it had to do with my—with our discoveries."

"*Your* discoveries," Daniel said with a smile. "*Our* ... experiences."

"That sounds fair," Sheila allowed, returning the smile.

The cabin cruiser docked at a slip not far away, and five men disembarked. The first four were burly, roughhewn and clad in various combinations of denim, leather, and flannel, despite the warmth of the day. Two of them were heavily bearded, and all looked as though they were arriving for a Hell's Angels convention. The last man off the boat was tall and thin, wearing a seersucker jacket and a blue button-down shirt with no tie. He looked around the marina, getting his bearings, then headed purposefully for the entrance to the restaurant.

When the hostess had led the man over to the table, as the cursory introductions were being made, Daniel felt sure he recognized something familiar in Jeb Sloane's face, something deep and painful behind the man's outward composure; something grievously distasteful but well buried.

Daniel motioned the waitress back over, and Sloane ordered a Corona—no lime, no glass—and oysters on the half shell. Sheila opted for steamed mussels, and Daniel ordered a cup of clam chowder and the beer-boiled shrimp.

"So," Daniel said when the waitress left, "you're in charge of one of those oil platforms out in the channel, is that right?"

"No, no," Jeb said, "I'm just a project engineer, and I'm based on a ship right now, not a platform." He twisted in his seat and pointed out to the ocean. "Just to the left of the steam plume out there," he said, "that's the drilling ship I'm on, the *Alicia Faye*."

"Wait a minute," Sheila put in, "I thought that boat was doing tests for some new kind of geothermal energy process."

Sloane nodded. "That's exactly what the company wants you to think, but it's actually an oil drilling site. *Laser* drilling, that's what's causing the steam."

"Jesus Christ," Daniel said, the reporter in him coming instantly alert. "That's—I mean, Jesus, that's one of the worst fucking—"

"Blatant corporate lies," Sloane finished for him. "Egregious anti-environmental deceptions."

"That's dreadful," Sheila said with a frown. "Utterly, if typically, unconscionable, and it's very brave of you to give the story to Daniel . . . but I don't understand what it has to do with me, or my work."

"You've got it all wrong," Sloane said, shaking his head. "I'm the drilling engineer on the project, and it's not as if I've suddenly had an attack of the scruples; I wouldn't be here right now if it *weren't* for your work. That's what this is all about."

Daniel heard the man's words, but remained preoccupied with the other things he seemed to sense about the engineer. He'd give heavy odds that Sloane was concealing something far more appalling than deceptive business practices, and that it was something personal . . . ugly, and violent, and unforgettable.

"What do you know of my work, anyway?" Sheila asked skeptically.

"I've seen the reports on television, the—"

"That's all bullshit!" Sheila exclaimed. "They twisted everything I—"

"The tapes, though; the tapes were real."

The intonation made it clear that Sloane intended that as a statement, not as a question. Daniel cut short his musings about the man's inner secrets, and looked at him sharply.

"What makes you say that?" he demanded.

Sloane reached into his jacket pocket and pulled out a small stack of photographs. The one on top was an underwater shot, clearly professional work, showing two scuba divers in red-and-black wet suits with the PetroGlobe logo on the shoulders. Between the two men was a miniature submarine, perhaps five feet long, painted— unashamedly and without a hint of intended irony—bright yellow. A thin, brilliant red beam emanated from the nose of the little sub, and the pile of rocks at which the beam was aimed had begun to glow as well.

Sloane shuffled the photo to the back of the stack; the next shot displayed the same scene as the first, except that the mound of rocks had . . . melted, it appeared, and dissipated across a wide area of the sea floor, like a scoop of ice cream dropped on a hot sidewalk.

"That's the thing in the tapes," Sheila exclaimed, "the metallic thing that looked like it was swimming!"

"It's one of our robot mini-subs," Sloane told them. "This is only the third project they've been tested on. They're about as well-protected an industrial secret as the formula for Coca-Cola."

"Then you know we've been telling the truth," Daniel said excitedly. "The dolphins, the messages, every—"

Sloane held up a hand. "I don't know how much of anything to believe," he said carefully. "All I know is, the images on those tapes of yours are real ... and they scare the hell out of me."

"I know a lot of what we've been saying has some potentially disturbing implications," Sheila said. "But if you think of—"

"That's not what I mean," Sloane cut in. "What I'm talking about is one brief section of the tape, where the mini-subs have turned away from the debris pile. You can clearly see that all the lasers, including the drill, are off."

Daniel regarded him quizzically. "So?"

"There's still molten matter seeping up from the drill hole," Sloane said in a harsh whisper. "I think we're drilling toward a magma chamber."

"No," Sheila said, her eyes round and full of fear. "Oh, no, you can't mean—"

"I'm afraid so," Sloane said flatly, looking back out at the serene waters of the sheltered harbor. "I think we're about to set off a volcano."

"Who is it?" Bryant Emerson called at the sound of the knock on his cabin door.

"It's Jeb."

"Just a minute."

Jeb waited as his old friend unlocked the door that had always before stood open for random visitors; it sounded like two separate deadbolts snapping back.

"Sorry about that," Emerson said, opening the door. "The way things are these days ..."

"Yeah, I guess so." The mood on board the drilling ship hadn't eased since that rancorous open meeting in the crew's lounge. The oil workers were every bit as worried about possible orca attacks as they had been when the news first broke; they'd even managed to infect some of the regular ship's crew with their fears, and new rumors of disaster continued to fly.

If they only knew what kind of genuine disaster was in store directly beneath them, Jeb thought, they'd be jumping off the ship's railings and *swimming* ashore.

"Get what you needed in town?" Emerson asked.

For a moment, Jeb wasn't sure what he meant; then he remembered that he'd claimed his excursion into town was a shopping trip for items he'd forgotten to bring along. "Oh, yeah, sure did," he said. "Stocked up on deviled ham and jalapeño potato chips." It was a believable lie, Jeb knew; stuck out on these ships or platforms, men developed offbeat food cravings as weird and as intense as any pregnant woman's.

"So, how many jumped?" Emerson asked glumly.

Two of the four men who'd ridden the shuttle boat into town with Jeb for a supposed in-and-out supply run hadn't been at the dock when the shuttle returned to the ship. "Just a couple," Jeb said.

"Shit," Emerson cursed, "that makes five now. They want to break their contracts, what the fuck am I supposed to do, hold them out here at gunpoint?"

"We were overstaffed as it was," Jeb said, almost apologetically, as if it were his fault the men had made the right decision, albeit for the wrong reason. "But listen, Bryant, we have to talk. Something's come up, something ..."

"Christ, don't tell me something else has gone wrong. What is it now, equipment problems? The mini-subs? It's not the goddamned *laser,* is it?"

"That's not the point," Jeb said, taking a seat at the cabin's small built-in breakfast table. Emerson wasn't offering any beers today; he was in the foulest of moods, which didn't make Jeb's task any easier. "It's bigger than that. Much bigger."

"What the hell are you talking about?" Emerson asked in an ominously quiet voice as he sat down on the bench seat across the table from Jeb.

It took fifteen minutes to explain, and less than fifteen seconds for Emerson to explode in anger when the telling was done.

"You *cannot* be serious," he said, the hairs on his neck visibly bristling. "I refuse to accept that you actually—that you expect me to *believe* this load of bullshit!"

"I only want you to—"

"I mean, *you* don't believe it, do you, Jeb? *Do you?*"

Jeb hesitated, then said carefully, "I believe it's possible. And if there's even one chance in a hundred thousand that this information is correct—"

"Information? Christ, you call this kind of sensationalistic crap *information?*"

"If there is the slightest possibility of it's being valid, we can't afford to take that risk. Look," Jeb said, and dashed off a crude sketch on a paper napkin:

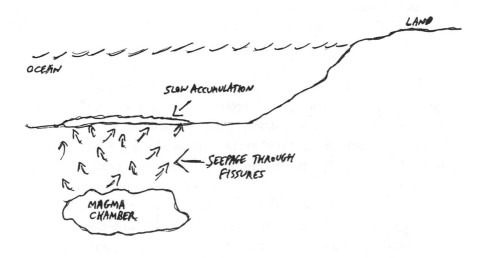

"Now, magma that's released from the sea floor normally cools almost instantly and results in nothing more than a slow buildup of igneous rock at the site. It usually seeps up very gradually, through networks of minute cracks in the earth's crust, and is held in check by the immense pressure of the seawater above and around it. Eventually, if it piles up high enough, it may rise above the surface and form islands. That's how the Hawaiian chain was created, over many millions of years.

"But if we puncture the magma chamber from the outside, with our laser drill, we'd be opening a far larger, more direct passage up through the crust than the magma itself would otherwise find:

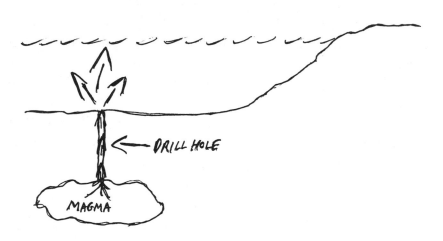

"We might shorten that geologic process by many orders of magnitude, allowing the magma accretion to reach the ocean's surface and beyond in a matter of days ... maybe even hours, or minutes."

Emerson frowned and pulled the napkin across the table toward himself, turning it right side around to study the hastily scrawled diagram.

Jeb began to make a new drawing on another napkin, talking as he did so, taking full advantage of Emerson's sudden silence. "If that happens—if a new volcanic island is created here in the channel, with no time for the pressure in the magma chamber to be dissipated over eons—we could be looking at a monstrously explosive eruption. Santa Barbara could be destroyed, like ... like Pompeii, for God's sake.

"A hundred thousand people, maybe more, buried in a rain of fresh lava. It would be as bad as an atomic bomb, Bryant—it would be a modern Hiroshima, right here in California. Do you want to take potential responsibility for that, no matter what the odds?"

Emerson stared down at the drawing, his face pale. "Jesus, man, I just don't ..."

"If the threat is real, there's one way to stop it ... possibly." He turned the new napkin around and slid it toward Emerson:

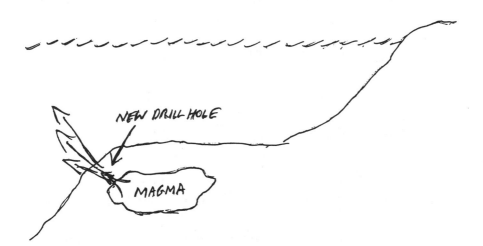

NEW DRILL HOLE

MAGMA

"Right there," Jeb said, pointing at the diagram, "you can see how the sea floor drops off at a forty-five-degree slant, just half a mile from here. Now, if we move the drilling equipment out there, we might be able to open a passage for the magma that would angle the force of the eruption out to sea, *away* from the city."

Emerson studied the sketches for a minute or more, then shook his head resignedly. "It's just too damn far fetched for me, Jeb. I mean, consider the source, for God's sake."

Jeb Sloane's heart sank. For a minute there, he'd thought he'd convinced him. "Fuck the source, and fuck *you* if you drop the ball on this one, Bryant! We're talking a potential catastrophe here, we're talking tens of thousands of lives—yours and mine included, don't forget. You can't afford to ignore something like that!"

"Damn it, Jeb, we've got some of the best geologists in the world advising us on this project; there's nothing but pure shale down there, and we're probably just days away from hitting oil. *Not . . .* magma, for God's sake."

"Look, if you don't want to take responsibility for the decision, let's pass it on to Milt Harris, all right? I can fly down to L.A. tonight, see—"

Emerson's eyes narrowed, and he jabbed an index finger at Jeb's chest. "I don't want to pull rank here, old buddy, but *I'm* the site supervisor on this project, and I expressly forbid you to go running to the president of PetroGlobe with some wild-eyed tale like this. It'd make us both look like idiots—me for not firing your ass the first time you mentioned it." He stood up from the table, crumpling the napkins with their apocalyptic sketches in his fist and tossing them into a wastebasket. "Now, I've got some reports to write," he said with finality, "and if I'm not mistaken, you've still got a drilling job to oversee."

Jeb started to protest again, but knew it would be to no avail; he well recalled that when Bryant Emerson made up his mind, it stayed made up.

No, Jeb thought, backing glumly out of the cabin, now it was time to resort to different—and more drastic—measures.

A pale, cloudless dawn was breaking over the eastern Pacific when Antonio Batera came onto the bridge, two hours earlier than was his custom.

"*Boa-manhã,* Toninho," said a startled Manoel, turning his head from where he stood at the wheel. "First time I know you to skip breakfast in *muitos anos.*"

"Yah, well, I'm not so hungry today. Why don't you go on down the galley yourself, grab some chow? Vinicius got fresh biscuits ready, I could smell 'em when I passed by."

"Ever'thing O.K., Skip?" Manoel asked with a frown. It was unlike the skipper to pass up hot buttered biscuits with honey in the morning.

"Everything's fine. I just feel like taking the wheel for a stretch, that's all. Couldn't sleep."

"Well ... if you say. I could use *uma taça de café,* now you mention it. You sure you don't mind?"

"Like I said, I want to."

Manoel nodded his thanks and handed the wheel over to Antonio. When the mate had gone, closing the door behind him, Antonio reached for the radiotelephone next to the VHF transceiver.

The Miami operator patched him through to information in south-central California, area code 805. There was no Sheila Roberts listed in Santa Barbara, but then he mentioned that the person he was calling had until recently been employed at UCSB, and the local operator suggested trying Isla Vista or Goleta. There was an S. Roberts listed on Lagoon Road in Isla Vista, and Antonio asked the operator to put the call through.

The phone rang seven times before a woman's sleep-fogged voice answered. "Hullo?"

"Sheila Roberts?" Antonio asked. "Is this Sheila Roberts, the scientist? The one that works with porp—with dolphins?"

"Yes, I—Who the hell is this, anyway? Do you know what— Jesus Christ, it's three-thirty in the goddamned morning. What is this?"

Antonio's face flushed guiltily. "I am so sorry, I forgot the time difference." That was a white lie; he knew damn well that California was two hours earlier than this part of the ocean, and under ordinary circumstances he wouldn't have called even his wife at such an hour, let alone a total stranger. "Please forgive me, but this is very important."

"I damn well hope so." Another voice, a man's, spoke a muffled question in the background, and Antonio heard the woman mutter, "I don't know, some nut probably, but he claims it's important."

"Miss Roberts? Please, only a moment of your time. You might— if you can speak with your friend Daniel Colter, you might tell him that it is Antonio Batera, skipper of the *Sea Master*. Tell him that I have come to understand the point that he and his late friend were trying to make ... and much more, besides. It is urgent that we talk, all three of us."

This time the woman must have held her hand over the mouthpiece, because he could hear only the faintest murmurs in the background, but after several moments a man's familiar voice came on the line, sounding both baffled and angry at the same time.

"Batera, from the tuna boat?? Is that you?"

Antonio smiled thinly. "So, Mr. Colter, I see you found your way home from Panama."

"No thanks to you, you son-of-bitch."

"My most sincere apologies for that; however, the circumstances at the time—"

"What the *fuck* do you want now? And how in hell did you ever track me down here, not to mention why?"

"This is not an easy thing to explain," Batera admitted, and proceeded to describe the events of the last few weeks. He began with his viewing of the dolphin-slaughter tape that Colter had made, and ended with his realization that the recurring dream he'd had of a quasi-mystical childhood encounter was neither fantasy nor incipient insanity, but a factual memory only now coming to the surface of his consciousness.

"... when I heard the man on the radio program describe your own experiences, yours and Miss Roberts's, I knew. And now ..." His voice faltered, and he felt an unaccustomed awkwardness. He'd been so caught up in the telling of his tale, so sure in that one purpose, that now it was complete he felt a sudden void. "I don't know what else. I only knew that I had to call you, to tell you what I had remembered. And I've done that."

For several moments, there was no response from the man at the other end of the line. He'd tried to interrupt a few times at the start, but had fallen silent as Antonio's story had progressed. Through the bridge windows, in the pallid light of the borning day, Antonio could see Fernando Guimares's boat, the *Diego Queen*. It was coming about, preparing to encircle and net a good-sized school of dolphins.

"You— Where are you calling from?" Daniel Colter finally asked.

Antonio was disappointed. For all the drama, the sheer unlikelihood, of what he'd told the man, he'd expected something more in the way of a response. He glanced at the navigational chart posted on the bulkhead next to the wheel. "About three hundred miles off Guatemala," he reported.

"You're actually out on the ocean? You're calling from the boat?"

"Yes, that's right. What do you—"

"Mister—Captain Batera, there's so much I want to talk to you about, so much we have to tell you. But we don't have a lot of time right now. How long would it take you to get from where you are to here, to Santa Barbara?"

Antonio frowned bemusedly. "In the *Sea Master*? Three days, maybe four. But—"

"Make it three," Colter said. "We need your help."

Her next land-walker contact was nearby. Ch*Tril knew, but the relay network that had so painstakingly led her here was now more occupied with news of the end of hostilities between their kind and the Danger-Cousins than with the constantly updated position reports that Ch*Tril required.

She was, of course, as relieved to hear the news as anyone; but of necessity, the task with which she had been entrusted must take precedence. Once it had been successfully completed—and that should be soon—Ch*Tril would eagerly return to her School, and would, she hoped find it in a state of jubilant celebration.

Her traveling companion had no intention of waiting that long, she noted wryly, watching as Tr*Til shot upward to execute yet another spectacular leap. Her friend managed two full beak-over-beak flips this time, and Ch*Tril imaged her a polite compliment on the beauty of the leap, though her thoughts were elsewhere. Then she noticed that Tr*Til, who had been swimming in the advance position, was coming back this way as fast as she could swim, and that something had obviously put her in a state of agitation.

Ch*Tril had known there would be risks involved in this segment of the journey; she quickly imaged a query to Tr*Til, asking if her friend had spotted danger in the sea ahead.

]Negative/Negative[, Tr*Til replied, wriggling with excitement.]School/Our Kind[.

Ch*Tril was impatient; the sooner she sould locate the land-walker Receptive and complete her mission, the sooner they could return to their own School, could learn if her contact with the male and female land-walkers had enabled them to avert the potential catastrophe of the fire beneath the sea floor; there was no reason to waste precious time meeting strangers.

It was possible, though, that this School might have received relays of its own, might even have more up-to-date information than Ch*Tril had received. If so, she decided, the brief detour would be well worthwhile. She motioned for Tr*Til to lead on, and followed her friend with mounting hope, even the beginnings of enthusiasm. Surely the land-walkers, with their extraordinary powers to manipulate the physical realm, would by now have contained the explosive threat about which she had warned them; this School might well have heard news of the achievement, might be able to set her fears to rest for good.

As they entered the vicinity of the strange School, Ch*Tril noted that although its perimeter scouts were as numerous as those of her own School, they seemed noticeably less vigilant. Or was it simply that she had grown accustomed to the discipline of a School living on War alert? Of course, that level of watchfulness and regimentation was no longer necessary; the relaxation, the general playfulness that had been the old norms would take some getting used to again.

One of the three scouts within close scanning range finally noticed her and Tr*Til approaching, and swam to meet them. He politely asked the travelers to stay at the periphery of the School, while one of the other guards left to pass along their request for temporary passage to the center.

The scout was young, Ch*Tril observed as they waited; no older than her son Dv\Kil, who had served his own first vigils on the perimeter during the recent War. How much violence had this young male seen, she wondered, how much death?

]Signature/Self-You[, she asked him, as much to initiate a friendly exchange as to garner any specific information.

]Rk\Qal[, the guard imaged hesitantly, as if unsure whether he should be communicating with his temporary charges.

Ch*Tril introduced herself and Tr*Til, then asked the signature of this School's Old One. That request worried the young perimeter scout even more, until Ch*Tril pointed out that she was on a long journey and would be expected to report to the Old One, at which time she would learn his or her Signature anyway.

]Old One/Tl\Xik[, the guard finally imaged, relenting.

]Celebration/Peace[, Tr*Til put in, her image as much a statement or suggestion as a question.

The young guard was unable to disguise his own delight as he answered in the affirmative, with a series of images that bespoke festivities without respite since the War's end.

Ch*Tril could see that her friend was poised to ask him for more details when the scout's cohort returned with authorization for them to enter the School proper.

He led them straight toward the center, and as they passed through the populated regions of the School, Ch*Tril could see for herself that the young guard had, if anything, downplayed the extent of the merriment in which his School had immersed itself. On all sides, at every turn, copulation and play were the only pursuits in evidence. These were rich feeding waters to begin with, and it would require little organized fish-herding to keep the School nourished; at the moment, no one seemed to be involved in any tasks at all save those oriented toward the achievement of pleasure.

Tr*Til was obviously eager to join the general sport, and Ch*Tril could see no reason why she shouldn't, at least for the brief time that Ch*Tril would be consulting with the Old One of the School. She imaged her permission to Tr*Til, along with a reminder not to stray too far, and continued toward the center of the School behind the escort that had been assigned to guide her.

The Old One, Tl\Xik, was as marked with age as was Qr*Jil, the Old One of Ch*Tril's School, and his left eye was permanently covered over with a mass of white scar tissue. He regarded his visitor with the one good eye for some time before he imaged anything, and when he did his greeting was a terse one:

]Link-Talent[, he informed Ch*Tril, in a strong image that indicated he would refuse to communicate in any lesser manner.

>I Possess the Talent<

Ch*Tril affirmed, assuming an air of aloof formality to match his own.

The Old One dismissed his perimeter guard, then turned back toward Ch*Tril:

>Linking Is Much Preferable<

he told her as soon as they were alone;

>Imaging Allows for Insufficient Nuance<

Ch*Tril could easily understand his preference; the Talent he possessed was a powerful one, and even these brief introductory Links had been textured with an enormous richness of detail that hinted at the Old One's vast range of experience and knowledge. Ch*Tril had seldom received such elaborate Links, other than in her most emotionally charged moments with Dj\Tal or when Melding with the Source-Mind.

>Apologies for My Lesser Talent<

she Linked, with genuine humility.

>Apologies Are Unrequired<

the one-eyed old male replied brusquely, but beneath his abruptness Ch*Tril sensed a subtle compliment on the strength of her own Linking ability.

>What Do You Seek from Me and Mine?<

he asked, his one clear eye a study in unreadable calm.

>I Would Learn of Events Far Distant<

>Of Fire in the Sea<

she Linked, interleaving the central message with a subtext to the effect that she and Tr*Til had been traveling for more than six light-to-lights.

>First I Would Know More of Your Journey<

Tl\Xik insisted, all but brushing aside her question.

Ch*Tril pondered how much to tell him, how much he might already know. Outright deception seemed both unnecessary and unwise; his perceptiveness was clearly such that he would recognize a deliberate untruth.

>I Seek to Accomplish a Melding<

she replied simply, with no elaboration.

>Describe the Objective of This Melding<

he demanded, obviously displeased by her elementary attempt at subterfuge.

Ch*Tril made an apologetic gesture and rose to the surface, more as a delaying tactic than from a need to breathe, though she had been mindful first to exhale completely so he could scan her and see that her lungs did indeed need filling.

>My Calling Is That of Historian<

she Linked when she had come back down to face the Old One
again;

>The Melding I Seek Is Scholarly in Nature<

Tl\Xik regarded her carefully with his single working eye, and
it occurred to Ch*Tril that the glint she saw there could indicate
either anger or amusement.

>From Which Direction Do You Journey?<

he asked, and Ch*Tril knew she was caught, knew he would see
through her deception if she tried to lie to him.

>From the North<

she replied.

>Signature of Your School's Old One<

he inquired.

>Our Old One Is Qr*Jil<

Ch*Tril told him.

>Dj\Tal is Affiliated with the School of Qr*Jil<

Tl\Xik Linked, taking her aback. Had this Old One communicated
with Dj\Tal at some point, perhaps even met him?

>Affirmative<

she answered when she had regained her composure;

>Dj\Tal and Myself Are Mated<

The Old One rose to the surface for a leisurely breath of his
own, leaving Ch*Tril to wonder anew just how much he did know.
If he knew Dj\Tal or knew of him, he might even be part of—

>I have Great Admiration for Dj\Tal<

Tl\Xik Linked as he descended once more to the place where
Ch*Tril hovered, waiting for him. Again, the Link conveyed far
more than the simple statement of fact that was at its core; the Old
One's Link was suffused with intimations of a score of thoughts
and emotions that revolved around the basic concept he had expressed. They ranged in degree of complexity from a coarse, almost
primitive appreciation of Dj\Tal's physical courage to a sophisticated respect for her Mate's diplomatic talents ... and there was
something else, some aspect or level of esteem that the Old One
seemed to hold back from declaring as if by a long habit of secre-
tiveness.

>Fire in the Sea<

Ch*Tril reminded him, uncomfortable with the direction this Link
had taken, and how closely it had begun to edge toward matters
both personal and confidential.

The Old One arched his scarred body in acknowledgment, telling
her nothing, and Ch*Tril noticed that his one good eye was growing
dim with the need for half-sleep.

>Knowledge of Fire in the Sea?<

she prodded again, but Tl\Xik made no reply; he merely hung
suspended in place, looking at her with that one sleepy, enigmatic eye.

>Permission to Depart<

Ch*Tril finally Linked, when it had become obvious that her audience with the Old One had come to an end.

>Granted<

he allowed foggily, and she turned to go. As she began to swim
away, Tl\Xik suddenly Linked to her once again:

>Success in Implementing the New Directives<

he bade her, the onset of half-sleep clouding his Link;

>Safe Journey Ch*Tril

>Salutations to Dj\Tal<

Ch*Tril stopped dead still in amazement, and turned back to face him.

>Gratitude<

she replied, and tried to think what else to communicate, but couldn't. She slipped away quietly, leaving the Old One to his rest.

She found Tr*Til near the edge of the School, still accompanied by Rk\Qal, the perimeter guard who had led them to Tl\Xik. Tr*Til was shamelessly flirting with the well-formed male, twisting her body into playful, erotic poses as she swam around him, brushing her belly against his with almost every turn. The guard's interest in Tr*Til's coy maneuvers was blatantly apparent: His penis was fully erect, and he scanned her every move with a degree of attention that certainly surpassed the requirements of his assignment to stand watch over the female visitor.

]Readiness/Departure[, Ch*Tril imaged as she approached the pair.

Tr*Til wriggled petulantly.]Time-Brief Pleasure/Sex[she entreated.

]Negative[, Ch*Tril imaged with a sternness she didn't really feel.]Continuation/Journey Time-Now[.

Tr*Til acquiesced with obvious reluctance, gracing her new near-conquest with a particularly long and sensual Touch before she left his side to rejoin Ch*Tril.

The two of them had swum no more than a hundred beak-to-flukes toward the perimeter of the School, with the disappointed young guard following along to see them off, when Ch*Tril became aware of a strange, irritating vibration emanating from the sea behind them . . . and then, all at once, the waters were fraught with chaos and panic.

It looked as if the entire School was on the move, hurrying away from the center in a state of maddened frenzy. Ch*Tril's heart began to race; had the truce with the Danger-Cousins been only a ruse? Were the orcas attacking again?

But if so, then what was that awful noise, getting louder now and moving around to the right, ahead of the fleeing School?

Ch*Tril's first impulse was to bolt, but she didn't want to make a blind run along with all the others until she knew exactly what they were up against.]Halt/Wait[, she imaged to Tr*Til, and darted up to the surface.

The painfully disturbing din was coming from two—no, three—of the land-walkers' hulls, not the slow, graceful kind with the tall white fins but small ones, mottled red in color. They were encircling the School even faster than she could swim; there was no way past them. In the distance to the left, and coming this way, she could see a much larger hull, and it—

It was the killing hull. The one she had foreseen, had dreaded, since before this journey had begun.

Ch*Tril fought her way back down against the terrified masses of Tl\Xik's School, and found Tr*Til still waiting where she had left her.

]Descent/Immediate[, she imaged.

]Necessity/Breath[, Tr*Til argued.

]Time/Insufficient[;]DESCENT[.

They dove together, and were soon among a large school of fish as big as themselves. Ch*Tril knew from her research that such fish followed beneath Schools of her kind in these warm waters, but she'd seldom been this far south before and had never actually witnessed the phenomenon. She knew, too, that the Schools with which this type of fish swam were in constant danger of—no, she couldn't think about that now, she had to stay calm, had to make sure Tr*Til didn't panic.

]Necessity/Breath[, her friend imaged with urgency.

Ch*Tril scanned her, saw that Tr*Til's lungs were almost totally depleted of air.]Surface/Time-BRIEF[, she told her, and led the way upward.

The School above them was crowded so densely together now that it was a struggle for them to make their way through. When they finally did reach the surface, Ch*Tril saw why: The speedy red hulls, with a lone land-walker in each one, had drawn their circle smaller and smaller, until there was barely room for all the members of the School within its confines.

Worst of all, the enclosure had been secured with a huge, unbroken ring of webbing. Even if Ch*Tril or any of the others found a momentarily unguarded path between the darting hulls, the way out was now sealed.

The big, dark hull had come to a stop right next to the trapped School. There was a tall structure at one end of the hull, and from the top of it dangled a long, heavy strand whose other end was attached to the great ring of webbing. The strand was being pulled steadily upward somehow, and as it rose the circle around the School closed ever tighter.

The crowding was unbearable now; there was no longer enough room at the surface for all the members of the School to breathe. The noise from the hulls had been drowned out by a cacophony of terrified shrieks and squeals.

Ch*Tril looked around for Tr*Til and could no longer see her. She ducked her head below the water to scan, and three others immediately began to jostle each other for the minute amount of breathing space she had left vacant.

Through the crowd, Ch*Tril scanned a glimpse of Tr*Til; her friend was pinned beneath the surface, striving without success to make her way up through the hundreds of others, all equally desperate for air.

Ch*Tril pushed her way roughly toward Tr*Til, shoving through the chaotic mob as best she could. She was buffeted again and again as everyone around her thrashed in a furious fight for life; she could feel bruises already forming from her head to her flukes, but she ignored the pain and concentrated only on moving forward.

Tr*Til was just ahead of her now, her eyes wide with fright; if Ch*Tril could just get underneath her, she might have enough strength left to boost Tr*Til up and free of the crush, at least long enough to—

The crowd suddenly surged to the right, carrying Ch*Tril with it. She fought to make her way back against the tide, but it was no use, the pressure was too great, the ever-shrinking circle too jammed with bodies, many of them dead, and the ones still living were all shrieking together with one awful, cacophonous voice.

Ch*Tril was at the edge of the circle now, near the webbing; the push of the crowd was unbearable; it was all she could do to strain for a moment at the surface, for a chance to breathe. . . .

A look met hers as she struggled upward, one clear, agonized eye beside a white-shrouded, dead one: it was Tl\Xik, the Old .One, pressed hopelessly against the webbing. The strands had cut a hundred wounds in his ancient flesh, and the bright new blood washed over the many scars of his old battles.

Ch*Tril felt herself carried helplessly past him by the living, dying tide, and then she, too, was being squeezed against the webbing, could feel the thick strands of it cutting into her pectoral fin, her beak, her sides. She twisted her head with an enormous effort, and there beside her was Tr*Til, floating limply on one side, her blowhole open to the water.

Suddenly the two of them were pushed abruptly upward, carried momentarily to the surface by the fear-crazed, dying mob. Ch*Tril gasped a quick deep breath, prodded Tr*Til with her snout to rouse her, and took a look around.

The webbing that encircled the School was pulling ever tighter, crushing and suffocating those in its grip. The whole enclosure was beginning to rise above the water now, pulled by a long, thick strand that connected the webbing with the large hull above.

Ch*Tril fought back rising panic and made a rapid inspection of her surroundings: There was an open panel in the webbing not more than three beak-to-flukes away from her, only partially blocked by the lifeless forms of those who had died trying to reach it.

]LEAP/NOW[, she imaged to Tr*Til, and with all her remaining strength she thrust herself toward the opening, without thinking, without hoping. . . .

And they were out, both of them.

The shrieks and wails and high-pitched screams suddenly began anew, and Ch*Tril realized at once how silent it had finally grown inside that webbing, as more and more of those caught there had died. Out here were the survivors, the ones who had escaped the webbing or who had somehow missed being trapped in it to begin with; and they were making their anguish, their grief at the fate of their friends and loved ones, loudly known.

Ch*Tril's entire body was bruised from the horrifying, deadly crush inside that crowded webbing, but her mind would not admit consideration of her own pain, nor any sense of relief that she and her pod-sister Tr*Til had escaped. She could feel nothing but a dreadful, leaden anguish at all the needless deaths they had just witnessed, all the hurt and loss.

The two of them dove deep, distancing themselves as best they could from the sights and sounds of the carnage above. How could she possibly fulfill the remainder of her mission now? she thought. The land-walker Receptive she had been sent to contact was the master of a killing hull exactly like the one from which she had just escaped, the hull that had murdered the knowing and sympathetic Old One, Tl\Xik, along with so many others . . . all of them without blame, none of them deserving of such a horrid, pointless death.

Ch*Tril came to a stop just above the sandy bottom and hovered there, keening softly to herself. In her recent Meldings she had heard the land-walkers make such sounds when they were deeply saddened, a sort of lamentation without rational content; such was her state of mind at this moment.

Tr*Til brushed her bruised and bleeding flanks with a comforting Touch, and imaged her a gentle scene of calm seas and playful young ones.

]Gratitude[, Ch*Tril imaged back. [Time-Future[.

A Link from the relay came through then with jarring abruptness. The members of that staggeringly lengthy chain had no way of knowing what Ch*Tril had just gone through, but she bristled at the intrusion nonetheless.

>The One You Seek Has Begun a Journey<

came the Link, its origins hundreds of thousands of beak-to-flukes away in the recesses of the Source-Mind that remained somehow ever aware of the existence and location of any being, land-walkers included, who possessed the Link-Talent.

>In Which Direction Does He Journey?<

Ch*Tril inquired.

>Northward<

was the answer,

>At Great Speed<

Ch*Tril pondered that information; why should the land-walker have so suddenly departed from this area, just when . . . and then it struck her. He must have spontaneously broken through to the suppressed memories of his own long-ago preparatory Contact, the time when he, as a young one, was approached and Linked to, preparing him unconsciously for the ultimate Contact which Ch*Tril was now about to initiate.

To suddenly have such a memory, and to be at the same time a master of a killing hull . . . his own pain must be extraordinary, Ch*Tril realized, his guilt an unexpected and enormous burden.

She remembered her final Link with Tl\Xik, the Old One of the doomed School; how little time had passed since that brief meeting, and how much in terms of events and consequences. His last Link to her, his last to anyone before his violent death, had been to wish her success in implementing the New Directives, the program of full Contact with the land-walkers. He clearly knew of the plan in detail—knew Dj\Tal, even—and his dying wish had been for its accomplishment.

Ch*Tril owed him that; she even owed the land-walker, she realized, the one on the killing hull who had renounced and disavowed the awful deeds of his lifetime: To him, she owed forgiveness and acceptance. He would need both of those, and need them desperately.

She turned about, scanning to get her bearings, and then she and Tr*Til began the long Journey back in the direction from which they had come.

Ten thousand molten rivulets snaked their way outward and upward through as many tiny fissures, flowing ever away from the mighty pressure of the white-hot mass confined within the chamber.

High above, the earth's crust grew progressively denser and more impenetrable, the available fissures fewer and even more minute . . . but higher still, another shaft of heat and light bored its way steadily downward toward the chamber, leaving in its wake a smooth, straight opening wider and more accommodating than all those microscopic crevices combined.

Entombed within its hidden prison, the superheated magma churned fretfully, eager for release.

16

Jeb Sloane paced the deck of the *Alicia Faye,* his eyes searching the featureless black horizon with equal measures of impatience and dread.

He didn't like this plan, not a goddamned bit; but he hadn't been able to come up with any kind of workable alternative, and neither had Daniel Colter or Sheila Roberts.

Jeb had been back onshore twice again in the last three days to confer with them in secret; his old friend Bryant Emerson hadn't been too pleased about these back-to-back "supply runs," particularly after their little standoff. Jeb was sure that Emerson had called Milton Harris, the company president, after each of Jeb's shore excursions, just to make sure Jeb wasn't going over his head with what Emerson had decided were "wild illusions" about the possible existence of a magma chamber in the area where they were drilling.

The crew was down to a skeleton staff now, as men continued to desert their jobs out of fear of possible orca attacks. That tide might reverse itself soon, since the news on that front seemed to indicate an inexplicable end to such incidents, or at least a lull in the reporting of them. In the meantime, Jeb had managed to use the reduction in manpower, and his own "emergency" trips ashore, as an excuse to slow down the drilling as much as he dared without actually putting a halt to it.

Knowing—or at least suspecting—what he did, it terrified him to drill so much as another foot toward what could be a massive pocket of magma; but the plan, the one and only goddamned plan, required that he stay on the job and arouse as few suspicions as possible, until—

"Taking a little night air, huh?" Emerson said, suddenly at Jeb's side.

"Oh—yeah, just a walk around the deck. Helps me relax."

By the light of the half-moon, Jeb could see Emerson raise a skeptical eyebrow. "I wouldn't think you'd have much to relax from, judging by the amount of work you've been doing the last few days."

"We should be back to speed tomorrow or the next day," Jeb said, hoping the lie came out believably. "All these guys quitting on us has put a helluva crimp in the schedule, you know that."

"Yeah. Yeah, I know. I didn't mean to—ah, Christ, Jeb, it's just that this project started out so well, and now all this bizarre shit—well, it doesn't do either one of us any good, you hear me?"

Jeb looked out at the dark sea again; there was a boat in the distance, apparently headed in their direction. From farther out at sea, from the south, not from the nearby harbor. "I know what you mean," he told Bryant, swallowing the shame he felt, knowing the depth of the betrayal he was about to commit against his old friend.

"I figured you'd come to your senses," Emerson said with a smile. "Well, I'm gonna pack it in. We've all got a long day tomorrow, playing catch-up."

"You bet. Good night, Bryant."

"Good night."

The oncoming boat was closer now; Jeb could see that it was pretty large, about the same size as the two hundred-foot *Alicia Faye*. He took the powerful little flashlight from his pocket, pointed it toward the advancing vessel, and clicked a sequence of one long flash and one short one, another long and short, a pause, then three short flashes. Morse for "JS," his own initials; that was what they'd settled on.

The response was swift in coming: A bright light on the other boat winked back a dot, a dash, brief pause, then a dash and three dots. "AB," the initials of the man whose arrival Jeb had been awaiting.

Jeb walked back toward the stern of the *Alicia Faye* and turned his flashlight on with a steady beam directed downward along the side of the ship, where the emergency ladder was in place. The boat doused its running lights, and Jeb could no longer see it, though he soon heard the low thrum of its engines and then could discern its outline against the dim moonlight.

Jeb looked around to make sure no one had observed his signals, or the approach of the boat; he was relieved to see that he was alone on the deck. Thank God so many of the men had left the drilling ship; no more than a dozen remained on board, and it appeared that most, if not all, of those were now asleep in their cabins.

The other boat came to a halt about twenty yards away, and its as-yet-unseen crew lowered a thirty-five-foot motorized skiff into the water from its stern. After a minute or so, the runabout moved directly alongside the *Alicia Faye,* and Jeb could see that there were at least ten men crowded aboard it.

The first one up the ladder was a wiry, deeply tanned man, older than Jeb had expected—fifty-five, fifty-seven, thereabouts.

"Sloane?" the man asked.

"That's right. Are you Batera?"

The man nodded, and turned to give a hand to the next man up. "We don't have much time to waste standing here," he said, with barely a trace of an accent. That, too, surprised Jeb; Colter had said the man was Portuguese, and somehow he'd expected—

"Where's the man in charge?" Batera wanted to know. "Him first."

This was the part of the plan that Jeb disliked the most. "Look, are you sure we can't just take the module, and not—"

"It's decided," Batera said. "Show me the man."

Six of the dark, muscular men from the boat were aboard now, and the rest were scrambling up the ladder. Jesus, Jeb thought, maybe this was a mistake after all, maybe—

"What the *fuck*?" The voice came from an open doorway, one that led into the crew's cabins. "Sloane, who the hell are these people? What are they doing—"

One of the newcomers delivered a swift jab to the crewman's gut, and he doubled over in pain as the wind went out of him with a heavy grunt. Two more of the intruders pinned the man's arms behind him, and one of them barked at him to keep his mouth shut.

"Let's go," Batera hissed to Jeb. *"Now."*

Bryant Emerson was ready for bed, stripped to his Jockey shorts, when he opened his cabin door in response to Jeb's insistent knock. His eyes went wide with shock when he saw the darkly clad strangers standing there, one of them holding a shotgun at the ready.

"What the—"

"Bryant, I'm sorry," Jeb said contritely. "There was just no other way, and the stakes—"

"*Fuck* you, Sloane. What is this all about?"

"The laser drilling equipment. We're taking it."

"You are crazy, aren't you? Much as I tried to cover for you, you were crazy all along. I should've—and who the fuck are these assholes, anyway?"

"That's no matter," Batera said. "But you and your crew are gonna have to transfer over to our boat for the time being, just so nobody calls the Coast Guard."

"You can't be serious," Emerson said, still talking to Jeb. "This is kidnapping, for Christ's sake, it's *piracy,* attempted murd—"

"Nobody's looking to hurt anyone here, Bryant. We're trying to *save* your lives, and thousands more besides."

There were the sounds of a fistfight from a nearby cabin, seeming to belie Sloane's words.

"This'll mean prison for you, Jeb. You know that, don't you?"

"It doesn't matter. In a few days, we'll know who was right . . . one way or the other."

The men from the tuna boat took Emerson and his crew to the skiff, and ferried them the short distance between the two larger vessels. When the drilling ship's crew had been safely locked away, the *Sea Master* edged even closer to the *Alicia Faye,* so close that for a while Jeb feared they might actually collide.

Another man had come on board now, beefier and more menacing in appearance than any of the others. There was some sort of bitter disagreement between him and Batera, but in the snatches of conversation that Jeb overheard, the big man couldn't hide his essential respect for the captain, no matter what.

"... *é criminoso, Tonhino; é vergonhoso!*"

"Gotta be done, Manoel. Many people gonna die, we don't do this."

"*Jesu Cristo,* these ideas of yours, I just don't know . . . and to pay the men triple wages, outta you own pocket, what you thinkin'?"

"You think they do this for me, I don't pay like that?"

"*É muito errado, Tonhino,* a big fuckin' mistake."

Despite the two men's bickering, the crew of their boat worked swiftly and steadily in the faint moonlight, and had soon enveloped the entire UFO-shaped drilling command module in a huge net that they'd deployed from a tall winch at the stern of the tuna seiner. When it was secured, Batera gave an order and Jeb watched as the entire module was lifted from the deck of the *Alicia Faye* and transferred, swinging like some enormous Gouda cheese in the bottom of a mesh shopping bag, to an open space on the *Sea Master*'s deck.

They'd really done it, Jeb thought in amazement. They'd actually stolen the entire drilling rig, with no one the wiser except for the temporary hostages locked in the cabins of the tuna boat.

Now came the most difficult—and the most treacherous—part. Now it was time to let loose the volcano.

"I just wish we could know for sure," Sheila said, pacing back and forth at the edge of the pool. Ringo swam alongside her as she walked, his eyes worried and intent, watching her.

"They can't risk using the radiotelephone anymore," Daniel reminded her. "Besides, hearing nothing is as good as a confirmation; if they'd failed, it'd be all over the news by now."

"And we'd all be in jail," Sheila couldn't resist pointing out.

"Well, yeah, that was a chance all of us agreed on."

"I still think we ought to have tried *telling* somebody, getting a warning out. . . ."

"Sloane did try, and he was the only one of us with any credibility left. You know damn well that nobody would have listened to you or me, not at this point."

She sat down, dangling her feet in the water, and stroked Ringo's head as he rested his snout on her lap. "I just think people deserve a warning, whether they believe it or not."

He sat down beside her, put his arm around her shoulders. Ringo cocked his head and gave Daniel a cautionary look, not unfriendly but ever protective of Sheila.

"I know how you feel," he said sympathetically, "but it wouldn't have done any good. At best it might've caused a panic; at worst it would've tipped the authorities off to what Sloane's trying to do. We might have ended up *causing* a disaster instead of preventing one."

"We still don't even know if this is going to work," she said, her eyes beginning to fill with tears. Ringo chittered at her, confused and concerned.

"No, but it's the best chance we have." Daniel hoped his voice carried more optimistic enthusiasm than he felt. Sloane's plan, even if it was proceeding as projected, offered only the thinnest chance of success; and Daniel knew all too well what to expect if their efforts fell through. He'd been in the Philippines in '91, when Mount Pinatubo erupted; he'd seen the showers of hot ash and fist-sized burning rocks that destroyed Clark Air Base, and it took little imagination to envision a similar rain of death and devastation coming down on the picture-perfect little city of Santa Barbara.

Worse still, what if it went off with an explosive blast like Mount St. Helens, rather than the sustained, relatively gradual eruption of Pinatubo? What if this turned out to be another Mount Pelée, the Caribbean volcano that had wiped out the town of Saint Pierre on the island of Martinique? St. Helens had killed sixty people, Pinatubo had claimed almost six hundred lives ... while on Martinique, the morning of May 8, 1902, *thirty thousand* men, women, and children had died in a matter of minutes as a rolling, superheated cloud of ash and gas had descended upon them at a hundred miles an hour, setting the city and its inhabitants ablaze. There had been only two survivors, one of them a convicted felon who owed his life to the fact that he had been imprisoned in a windowless cell when the death-cloud struck.

"There's nothing more we can do here," Daniel said with abrupt finality. "It's time to leave."

"What about Ringo, and—"

"Let them go. They'll soon learn what's happening and find their own way to safety." Again, he said this with more confidence than he felt. Maybe the force of the eruption wouldn't bury the city in ash, but drown it in a tidal wave, fifty or a hundred feet higher than the breakwater, slamming in at five hundred miles an hour and snapping the masts of every boat in the harbor as the cold waters engulfed the town so picturesquely, so innocently, nestled beside the ill-named Pacific.

Some say the world will end in fire, /Some say in ice....

"But my equipment," Sheila protested, "all my—"

"Start packing it up," Daniel said in a tone that made it clear he would brook no argument. "We're getting the hell out of here."

"And this handle thing here, what's that for?" Batera wanted to know.

"That's called a joystick," Jeb explained. "We use it to guide the mini-subs." He pulled back on the joystick, and pointed at one of the television monitors in the command module. The image went from a shot of the new drill point to a slow pan upward past empty sea, and finally a live picture of the *Sea Master*'s keel, as seen from a hundred feet below.

"Over on the left side of this console," Jeb went on, "is the firing switch for the lasers on the mini-subs. We would *not* want to hit that right now," he added, nodding toward the TV display showing the underside of the boat they were on.

The control module was now firmly tied down to the aft deck of the *Sea Master,* between the speedboats and the netting. The laser drill was in place on the sea bottom where the continental shelf angled off; for two full days, the device had been burning its way into the earth's crust, toward where the magma chamber was believed to be.

"These are the controls for the drill itself," Jeb said, indicating a bank of knobs and switches. One of the dials, marked in increments from zero to five, was turning on its own in a counterclockwise direction; it had almost reached the zero mark. Jeb reached out and gave it a twist, setting it back to five. "This operates the drill's main power unit," he told Batera. "It's on a timer, one that can't be overridden."

"What for?"

" 'Deadman's switch,' " Jeb said.

"Deadman ...?"

"Like some locomotives—they require the engineer to constantly and actively keep them running, otherwise the power shuts down and the train comes to a slow halt. That's to avoid a runaway train in case the engineer falls asleep or has a heart attack or whatever.

He's got to be there, awake and keeping the power engaged, every second.

"This timer device is kind of similar; somebody's got to be here to manually reset it every five minutes, otherwise the drill turns itself off. It's a safety precaution."

Batera nodded, then frowned. "But doesn't that mean we'll have to stay here until—"

"No, no; the magma should give us ample warning before it blows, and we probably don't need to drill all the way into the chamber. Just getting the burnhole close to it ought to weaken the crust sufficiently, and still give us time to get safely away."

" 'Probably'?" Antonio said, cutting through Sloane's verbiage to the most relevant word.

"*Very* probably; almost certainly."

Antonio never quite trusted people who talked like that, who always qualified whatever they said and left themselves an out if they turned out to be wrong. Still, Sloane had seemed to know what he was doing so far, and Colter and Sheila Roberts had believed him; who was Antonio to question the word of a scientist, someone who studied these things?

"How do you keep the drill locked in one position?" Antonio asked, changing the subject and easing the momentary tension. They were here to do what had to be done, after all; nobody ever said this was going to be a stroll in the park.

He sat back in the uncomfortable molded-plastic chair and looked around the circular room, the "control module," they called it. Like something out of one of those space shows on TV, the kind his boy Jorge used to like to watch.

It was still hard for him to grasp the whole dizzying chain of events that had brought him to this strange place, had led him to do these bizarre things. The *crimes* he had committed, *Mãe de Deus*, piracy and theft, kidnapping even . . . he shuddered to think of those men locked away in two of the crew cabins, innocent men, imprisoned here on his boat for no reason, for—

Not true, Batera reminded himself for the hundredth time. All of this was being done for the very best of reasons, to save who knew how many thousands of lives. He had to keep that in mind, had to remember that no matter how this might appear to an outsider, it was an act of kindness, of compassion.

But, *Jesu Cristo,* what would Maria say when she found out? If she'd thought he was crazy to insist on a zero porpoise kill, what would she think of *this*? And maybe she'd be right, maybe he had gone too far, maybe he'd stupidly set himself up for a prison term and driven Maria into the poverty she feared so much, destroyed all their chances for . . .

No! He couldn't allow himself to think like that; he had to concentrate on the moment, had to keep on doing what was *necessary.* Just because he couldn't understand it all didn't mean that it was wrong, or that he should not have agreed to help. If it were only Daniel Colter who had told him of these miraculous and frightening things, well, that would be different . . . but Sheila Roberts and Jeb Sloane,—these people were highly educated, they had to know what they were talking about. And what they said made sense; it fit right in with that fantastic memory from Antonio's own childhood. It *explained* things.

With an effort of the will, he set his doubts aside and focused on what Sloane was saying about the drilling equipment. Antonio found the impromptu lecture oddly relaxing, reassuring. It didn't even matter that all the science involved, the lasers and all that, was beyond his comprehension; it was the mechanics of the system, the nuts and bolts of how to operate it, that held his interest.

At Sloane's urging, Batera took hold of the knob they called a joystick, and practiced maneuvering the robot mini-sub, as fascinated as a child to see the changing point-of-view images from the camera mounted in the submarine's nose. It made him feel like he was swimming deep underwater, like he was a fish . . . like he was a porpoise.

* * *

They had been swimming steadily for more time than Ch*Tril cared to compute, and she had never known such exhaustion. The constant effort had helped to keep their minds from dwelling over-much on the many deaths they had witnessed, but Ch*Tril wasn't sure how much longer even she could keep up this grueling pace, let alone her friend Tr*Til. At this point she was taking it moment by moment, concentrating on the crucial tasks ahead in order to forget the pain she felt in every muscle.

She felt Tr*Til's flank brush her with an encouraging Touch—but when she pivoted to return the gesture, she saw instead Ek*Tiq, the pod-sister whose bringing-forth she had attended . . . how long ago? Not more than a single cycle of the orb that lights the darktime, yet it might as well have been a dozen of those cycles, a hundred.

]Welcome[, Ek*Tiq imaged, and gave her pod-sister another reassuring Touch. Her young one circled his mother impatiently, eager to suckle.

Ch*Tril raised her head and scanned the waters above; Dj\Tal was swimming straight toward her, and behind him were her son Dv\Kil and his new mate. The sight was like a fantasy-image, all her dearest and most unattainable hopes made suddenly, wondrously, real.

Ch*Tril brushed her pod-sister Ek*Tiq with a grateful Touch and hurried to meet Dj\Tal, Linking to him as she rose. Within the span of that brief Link she somehow managed to convey all the terror and the grief of what had happened, her anguish at the death of Tl\Xik and so many members of his School, and her own near-loss of faith—not merely in her own abilities, but in the very purpose to which they had been put, the Directives of the Source-Mind itself.

Dj\Tal swam straight to her side and led her away from the assembling crowd, taking pains to stay in physical contact with her at every moment, the closeness of his body quietly suffusing hers with his warmth, his strength, his composure.

He lifted her gently to the surface for a breath.

>The Gathering Is Imminent<

Dj\Tal Linked to her.

>And the Sea-Fire?<

Ch*Tril asked.

>The Land-Walkers Strive to Redirect It<

he replied, his Link ambiguous, not fully readable.

Ch*Tril looked toward the horizon and saw the hull she had Journeyed so far to find, the killing hull commanded by the last of the land-walker Receptives she had been assigned to Contact. Near it, a cloudlike plume of steam rose impossibly high above the water's surface.

>They May Not Succeed<

she Linked back fearfully.

>Our Place Is with the Land-Walkers Here<

Dj\Tal told her.

>The Source-Mind Decrees Our Fates Conjoin<

A shiver ran the length of Ch*Tril's body as she understood exactly what that might mean.

>The Gathering Begins<

Dj\Tal Linked to her, with an urgent dignity. Ch*Tril did a long-range scan, and saw that he was right: Two more Schools were arriving from the south, another from the east, and a large advance party of Danger-Cousins was moving in as well.

>I Must Complete My Task<

Ch*Tril averred, and swam alongside her mate with a final, loving caress. The seas around them were crowded with strangers now, and among them all there was a tangible sense of expectation, of fear, and hope, and awed uncertainty ... all of that and more, the collective thoughts of countless individuals, all waiting to discover

if the impending transformation would see their world destroyed
... or born anew.

Ch*Tril shot to the surface, filled and emptied her lungs half a
dozen times, and headed toward the distant hull. She had devoted
her life to the tasks of a Historian; now she must play her own
part in a moment by which history itself would forevermore be
redefined.

17

 "This, too?" Daniel asked, holding up a small bronze statuette of a dolphin riding the crest of a wave.

Sheila glanced up from the mass of papers spread around her on the living-room floor in a dozen seemingly random piles. She paused in her sorting, looking at the figurine; the sight of it took her back to a time that now seemed as distant as childhood, as irretrievable as last night's dreams. Richard had given her the little statue soon after they'd become lovers, when her research had been just beginning and the limitless possibilities of life had all seemed within her immediate reach.

"No. Leave it."

Daniel glanced nervously at his watch. "You know, we've really got to—"

"I'm almost finished," Sheila snapped, and then regretted her tone. "I'm sorry, I just ... if I'm ever going to have any hope of picking up my work again somewhere, I need some of these. But I'm almost done."

Goddamn Richard Tarnoff's eyes, she thought, reaching for another stack of file folders; there were so many things that might never be known now, because of him. Would she have gone through the struggles of the last four years at all, Sheila wondered, if she had known what the outcome would be?

"Are those ready to go?" Daniel asked, pointing at a small stack of cardboard boxes.

"Yeah, they're done."

"I'll just take them out to the car, then. You think, what, another ten or fifteen minutes?"

"I'll try to make it ten. Believe me, I don't want to hang around here any longer than you do."

Daniel nodded grimly, picked up the boxes and headed for the door.

It was going to be hard to leave here, Sheila thought, but the hardest part had been closing the underwater doors that linked her pool to the inlet below, thus locking out Ringo and Georgia and Paulette. She'd never be able to forgive herself for doing that, even though she knew it was the only humane alternative: to give them a chance to seek safety on their own, to rejoin their kind.

Still, what must they have thought? Sheila wondered with a sharp stab of guilt and sorrow. That she was simply abandoning them after all this time, that she no longer loved them? Oh, God, she hoped they hadn't thought that. But how much could they have known of what was happening, and were they sad about it all, or afraid, or angry? Even if she'd been able to communicate to them, how could she ever have explained that she would no longer be a constant, loving presence in their lives? No matter the difficulties and the danger involved, that surely would have seemed to them the rankest of betrayals on her part.

She was wiping the tears from her cheek when she heard Daniel shouting.

"Sheila! Ringo's out here, he's swum back up the channel!"

That started the tears flowing in earnest, it was just too god-damned much to bear; he was trying to come home, he couldn't understand why she had shut him out . . . and now she was going to have to leave him like that, knowing that his life was in danger if he stayed where he was, knowing that his own confused and selfless love for her might end up killing him, even as she ran to safety.

"Sheila!"

"All right, all right, I'm coming!" She couldn't avoid facing the dolphin, and her own guilt, just because she was ashamed at her failure to save him, to stay with him. She at least had to do him the honor of bidding him farewell, painful though that would be.

When she stepped outside, Ringo leaped ten feet in the air, splashing her with water as his 450-pound bulk came smashing back down into the water of the channel. Then he gave a long burst of high-pitched chittering and squawking, and tossed his head repeatedly in the direction of the inlet below.

"He's not trying to get back inside," Daniel said. "He wants you to go down to the beach."

"Maybe—maybe he just wants to play."

"Or maybe he understands; maybe he wants to say good-bye."

"I'll just go on down there, and see if he follows," Sheila said, turning her face away so Daniel couldn't see her tears.

"You want me to come with you?"

"If you like," she said, and started down the walkway that curved toward the beach. Daniel followed, and they were alternately paced or led by Ringo, swimming in the man-made channel that paralleled the path. The three of them reached the lagoonlike inlet adjacent to the ocean at the same time.

Ringo's companions, Georgia and Paulette, were already in the lagoon, along with a dozen other dolphins Sheila had never seen before. They all had their heads above the surface, bobbing up and down excitedly as they regarded the two humans with keen interest.

"What the hell—" Daniel said under his breath, and stopped dead still. Sheila had knelt to greet the two female dolphins, but he was staring beyond the lagoon, toward the wide expanse of beach and shoreline beyond and below.

"Oh, my God," Daniel whispered, and put his hand on Sheila's shoulder, softly beckoning her to follow his gaze. "Look," he said simply, in a voice hushed with awe. "Look down there."

* * *

"Skipper?" The voice at his cabin door was loud and insistent, the pounding fists louder still. "Skipper, you got to get up on the bridge! Right now, Manoel say!"

What could the goddamn hurry be? Batera wondered. Wasn't no storm up—he could feel how calm the seas were; why couldn't Manoel just deal with it, whatever it was, and leave him the hell alone?

Then he remembered where they were, remembered the new and improbable task that he—and his crew—had taken on. The crewmen had done it for the promise of money; right now, foggy and half awake, Batera couldn't entirely reconstruct his own rationale for being here.

"Yah, yah, I'm comin'," he said, and extricated himself from the twisted disarray of sheets and blankets.

The sunlight stabbed at his eyes as he stepped onto the bridge. Manoel was there, along with the oil man, Sloane.

"So, what's the trouble?" Batera asked.

"Aquêle-lá," Manoel said, pointing to the north.

There was a plume of steam, three hundred feet high, rising from the ocean. It looked exactly like the hot cloud that still emanated from the spot above the drill hole, a few hundred yards off the bow of the *Sea Master;* but this one was two or three miles closer to shore, to the city spread out at the bottom of the hills.

"It's coming from the original drilling point," Sloane told him. "Right where the *Alicia Faye* is anchored."

"But—if there's no more drilling there, it must—"

"It's the magma," Sloane said tersely. "It's found a way out, and it's starting to seep up into the old drill hole. Not just a few drops at a time, but steadily."

"He say it's gonna explode," said Manoel, with an anxious uncertainty in his voice that Antonio had never heard from the man before.

"Jesu Cristo," Antonio whispered. "What can we do?"

"Not a fucking thing," Sloane said bitterly. "We've done all we could; we just weren't in time."

"No, you must be wrong, there's got to be *something* ..."

"We have to get this boat moving now, get to the other side of one of those islands ..."

"No! You tell me, goddamnit, what can we do to *stop* it?"

"I already told you, we can't! We tried, we failed, now let's get the fuck *going*!"

"What about the drill, what if we run the power on it all the way up in the red?"

"It wouldn't get deep enough in five minutes, not even at max power," Sloane said.

"Why five minutes? Is that how long before the first hole blows?"

"No, I'd guess another twenty minutes, half an hour. But that barely gives us enough time to get to those islands, and the timer on the drill can't be set for more than five; there's no way to override it."

"Unless ..."

Sloane looked at him strangely. "You can't be thinking of—"

Batera turned to Manoel. "Get the speedboats and the skiff in the water, *rápido*! Let those men in the cabins loose, get everybody on the boats, right now."

Sloane was shaking his head slowly, disbelievingly. "Captain Batera, you do know what—"

"I know just what I'm doin'."

Manoel put his beefy hand on Batera's shoulder. "Toninho," he said quietly, "I say a lot of things these last few weeks, things I don't mean. I was mad, you know? But you the best goddamn man I ever work with, I want to tell you."

Batera clapped his own hand atop Manoel's. "You, too, *velho amigo. Adeus.*"

"*Adeus,* Tonhino."

"Jesus Christ, Batera, you don't seriously intend to—"

"Better get in one of the boats now, Mr. Sloane. Just follow Manoel, he'll give you a hand."

"You've got to—"

"I know what I've got to do. It was a pleasure knowing you, Mr. Sloane. Good luck to you."

Antonio secured the wheel, then took the companionway down to the deck, walked toward the neatly folded and stacked netpile, and hoisted himself inside the saucer-shaped drilling command module. The speedboats and the skiff, all of them packed to capacity with the crews of both the *Sea Master* and the *Alicia Faye*, were being lowered into the water as Antonio shut the hatch behind him.

He gave the control panel a quick once-over, reminding himself of the pertinent operating functions that Sloane had taught him over the past couple of days. He activated the robot mini-subs and their video cameras, then fired up the laser drill and turned the power all the way up into the red zone, as far as it would go. He half expected to hear some sort of ominous hum or whine when he did so, and was vaguely disappointed when no such sound broke the silence inside the clean, starkly appointed module.

He was resetting the timer for the third time when something caught his attention on one of the video monitors: a lone porpoise, swimming straight toward the drilling spot and then up, right up to the boat itself. The sleek gray creature paused there, hovering motionless just off the bow of the *Sea Master*, and—

>Forgiveness<

Antonio heard inside his brain, and at the same time he somehow knew where it was coming from, knew *who* it was coming from, and why, and he felt himself soar with delight at the purity of that clear and guileless absolution, that utter, unquestioning pardon.

>Fulfillment<

>Unity<

he heard, or saw, or felt, and the exquisite truth of it warmed him, was his comfort and his salvation.

Maria, he thought, *eu te amo,* and without another thought he activated the laser drill again, just as the mountain of fire interred so deep below him broke free of its chamber and rose up to meet the sea, the sky.

Sheila raised her head and looked where Daniel was pointing, down toward the beach, where the inlet joined the ocean.

As far as she could see, up and down the coast in both directions, the shallow offshore water was filled with dolphins. Thousands of them, *tens* of thousands, and orcas by the hundreds, not migrating or feeding or cavorting, but . . . waiting, patiently. Looking toward the land, and waiting.

She stood up slowly, reaching for Daniel's hand to steady herself. "It's started," she said in a hoarse whisper. "Whatever it is, it's started."

He nodded, watching along with her as the people on the beach saw what was happening and began to spread the word. Everywhere, the separate knots of sunbathers and volleyball players and solitary joggers stopped what they were doing and began to mutely form a sort of congregation, all of them staring at the extraordinary assembly of cetaceans that had convened offshore.

"What should we—" Daniel started to ask, and then a sudden presence within his head rendered the question irrelevant.

>Unity<

he heard, or felt, and he knew at once that neither he nor Sheila was the sole recipient of the complex and comforting subtext that accompanied that deceptively simple thought.

>Fulfillment of the New Directives<

came the message, more an announcement than a greeting, yet both—and more—at the same time.

One by one, then in groups of three or four, the people on the beach below began to walk into the water, many with their arms outstretched, their expressions an amalgamation of disbelief and joy.

"How many do you think are actually receiving it?" Daniel asked, and was at once surprised that he could speak, could reason. That first contact several days ago had been overwhelming, he had felt engulfed and consumed by it; this, by contrast, was more subtle, more like the beginning of some sort of dialogue.

"No way to tell," Sheila answered, her eyes alert and aglow with exhilaration. "One out of ten, maybe?"

"And the rest believe them, now."

Sheila laughed and swept her hands in a wide arc that encompassed the shoreline as far as they could see in both directions. The entire stretch of water along the coast, north and south, was filled with dolphins, and the humans who were swimming to meet them.

"How could they not?" she said. "It's—"

Her words were cut off by a strange, deep rumbling sound that came rolling across the water like a lion's roar.

In unison, she and Daniel looked out to sea, toward the twin steam plumes that marked the drilling sites where Sloane had been. The farther of the two plumes, the one above the newest site, had suddenly more than tripled in size. As they watched, it doubled in volume again, expanding into what looked like a massive storm front and darkening in color from pure white to a menacing dark gray.

"Oh, Jesus, Jesus—"

The cloud began to glow, dimly at first and then a brighter and brighter red, lit from within, from beneath … and then a great hump lifted out of the sea, a smoking, burning mass a hundred yards wide, then two hundred, then a thousand …

"It's erupting! Oh, God, it—"

The newly created island exploded with a godlike fury, propelling red-black clouds of gas and sheets of incandescent magma into the sky at supersonic speed. There was a terrible silence, which itself lent further incredibility to an already impossible sight: a column of ash and smoke and magma and debris the size of Chicago's Sears Building, formed whole in a single instant amid a stillness so complete that the loudest sound was a single seagull cawing overhead.

Then the shock wave hit, a wall of sound and pressure so intense it buffeted Sheila and Daniel like a hurricane-force wind, knocking them off their feet.

"Cover your head!" Daniel screamed, and assumed the air-raid posture so familiar to a generation of children who had grown up under the daily threat of an explosion of this magnitude, though from a very different source. They huddled together protectively for several seconds, and when it became apparent that no debris was falling anywhere around them, Daniel risked a look back at the deadly cloud.

It was moving away from the shore, the brunt of its overwhelming destructive force projected on an angle, carrying it out to sea. Sloane's idea had worked; the city was saved.

Sheila and Daniel stood up to look around them: Cars were stopping in the middle of traffic along Lagoon Road and Del Playa Drive now, their drivers and passengers abandoning the vehicles first to stare at the awesome sight of the eruption's aftermath, then to race across the sand and wade fully clothed into the water. Off to the left, the brief stretch of freeway that connected the campus with U.S. 101 was filling with bumper-to-bumper traffic, all of it headed toward the beach.

Sheila tore her attention away from the scene below, kicked off her sneakers and lowered herself into the warm, still water of the lagoon. Ringo came to her side immediately, buoyantly gliding against her with a half-lift, half-caress; then he pulled back to hover a few feet away with Georgia and Paulette and the wild dolphins who had followed them into the lagoon.

"Daniel . . ." Sheila said, and then closed her eyes and shivered as she felt the deep, synchronous thrumming of a dozen ultrasonic scans all directed at her, at her belly . . .

>Life-to-Be<

declared the vision/voice that seemed to be nestled gently, protectively, inside her mind, that seemed at once to be speaking to her alone and to the world at large, now and for all time, of life both singular and multifarious, past and present coalescing into future.

Daniel joined her in the water, and the humming in her belly slowly stopped, the joyful chorus in her head quieted to an unobtrusive yet ever-attendant background presence. In its place came a many-voiced sound from the crowd below, a tumult of song and words and laughter that was just beginning but that already sounded capable of endlessly sustaining its newborn vitality.

Ringo and his companions suddenly executed a series of showy, playful leaps and raced away into the channel toward the ocean. Sheila took Daniel by the hand and together they swam at their own speed, awkward and tentative, toward the open sea to join the others, human and cetacean, to join them all.

AFTER

"The Gathering was a global event, of course, but most of those who took part in it found the experience so memorable that they've tended to internalize that first contact as a local, even personal phenomenon. Sheila Roberts and I were no exception; but for a meaningful perspective on what happened that day, it's important to look back at it objectively.

"The scene of chaotic elation that we saw along the beach at Santa Barbara was being repeated around the world, wherever sea met land: on shorelines, in harbors, around ships and islands and boats ... the participants numbered in the hundreds of millions, both human and cetacean. From the stories I've heard, and the video footage we all remember so well, the Gathering was particularly dramatic in places like Sydney and Rio de Janeiro, major cities with mile upon mile of beachfront. Who can ever forget—or recall without a smile—that spontaneous *carnaval* at Ipanema, humans and dolphins by the thousands literally *dancing* together in the water to the insistent, joyous rhythm of a multitude of samba drums.

"Sheila's initial estimate that perhaps ten percent of those involved were capable of full mind-to-mind contact proved fairly accurate; later studies put the figure at approximately eight percent (at least in the industrialized, so-called 'First World'; among such supposedly 'primitive' groups as the aborigines of western and southern Australia, and certain native populations of the South Pacific and coastal regions of Central and South America, the proportion of those manifesting the Link-Talent was shown to range as high as seventy-nine percent).

"Among Westerners, the distribution of this suddenly activated telepathic ability followed no particular pattern of age, sex, race, or any other quantifiable variable. People in their eighties or nineties were as likely to have it as were children; a gang member in South Central L.A. might be blessed with the gift, while a philosopher/poet in Greece, a lover of all things metaphysical and cetacean, might not.

"With nine out of ten people unable to directly experience the Linking phenomenon, there was some initial resistance to accept the authenticity of the Gathering, particularly among those dwelling in inland areas. For the first few days, news coverage of the event varied wildly in tone and content, depending on the individual reporters' and editors' Linking ability or lack thereof.

"Ultimately, what made the difference was the very fact that the eight percent of people in possession of the Link-Talent were drawn from such a wide swath of the population. Within a matter of hours, it was clear that this was not something limited to the mentally disturbed or any other fringe element of society.

"The prime minister of Spain, vacationing along the Costa Brava when the great event occurred, was one of the most prominent of the early Linkers. He played a substantial role in conveying the seriousness of the Gathering to the world's leaders, as did the ambassadors to the United Nations from Argentina, Ghana, Israel, and Jamaica, each of whom also proved to be gifted with the Talent."
—Excerpt from *Daniel Colter: Story of a Lifetime* (c) 2019

"Almost immediately, those of us who'd discovered we had the Link-Talent felt a tremendous surge of sympathy for those who did not. Daniel Colter's published descriptions of how his earliest Linking sessions lifted the burden of some extraordinarily painful personal memories make this point quite well, particularly in his discussion of the empathy we both came to feel for our mutual friend Jeb Sloane, a non-Linker whose struggle with his own personal demons proved long and difficult.

"Daniel and I both felt it our duty to share as best we could the lifelong solace and unending enlightenment that were ours as a result of this enormous, unexpected gift. Indeed, a sensibility of generally renewed and strengthened compassion seemed to be an integral part of discovering and developing the Link-Talent, and swiftly led to a worldwide blossoming among humans of the highly evolved altruistic impulse so long observed in dolphins.

"One of the first, and most dramatic, benefits of this was the speed with which most forms of mental illness came to be fully understood and largely eradicated. Even those psychiatric conditions caused primarily by neurochemical imbalances were soon conquered, as researchers with the Link-Talent were able to use it to directly explore neuronal pathways and identify the specific receptors responsible for various disorders."

—Excerpt from *Sheila Roberts Remembers* (c) 2022

"Perhaps the most appropriate metaphor that one could draw for the whole complex range of events that followed the Gathering, at least from the human point of view, could be summed up in a single word: 'healing.'

"This is not to say, however, that the recovery was in every case an immediate or easy one. Our species had, over the course of a few millennia, forgotten much that was essential to a sane and healthy existence, and had imposed on itself instead a deadly bundle of unnecessary ills. Some of these—the near-despoilment of the planet's environment, for example—had their origins in simple ignorance or greed. Others, sad to say, were rooted in the sort of deliberate mass sadism that gave the twentieth century its terrible distinction as the bloodiest in human history.

"Perhaps the most momentous single event directly attributable to the Gathering was the Chinese Revolution, which belatedly completed the grass-roots drive for freedom that had been cut short by the 1989 massacre at Tiananmen Square.

"The Communist Chinese government's reaction to the sudden appearance of millions of telepaths among its citizens was typical of the world's remaining totalitarian regimes, and the ensuing events there were mirrored on a smaller scale in North Korea, Cuba, Vietnam, Burma (then called Myanmar), and other nations in the grip of despotic rule.

"All the standard repressive measures, including beatings and imprisonment, were called into play against the Linkers, especially those who spoke out about what they had learned of the Source-Mind's teachings with regard to ethical models of social structure.

"The first serious street disturbances and mob attacks on police stations began in smaller cities throughout China, including Foshan, Jinhua, and Guilin, shortly after the executions of imprisoned Linkers had commenced. The government acted with a level of intelligence characteristic of the old communist regimes, by attempting to conceal the officially sanctioned murders of several dozen full-blown telepaths—in a country where almost ten percent of the billion-plus other members of the populace had also become telepathic.

"The United Nations entered the crisis when it was discovered that warships of the Chinese Navy had been issued orders to hunt down and kill all whales found in the country's coastal waters. The U.N. General Assembly voted, by an overwhelming margin, to expel the existing government of China—not merely from its veto-empowering seat on the Security Council, but from any level of membership in the world body. Strict sanctions against trade with China were imposed, and rigidly enforced by a coalition of U.N. forces dwarfing that assembled for the 1991 Persian Gulf War.

"Within a matter of days, antigovernment rioting had spread to Shanghai, Guangzhou, and Beijing. Troops called to put down the unrest refused to fire on the crowds, and when one tank regiment, commanded by a Linker named Li Wei-Jin, turned its guns on the Forbidden City headquarters of the country's aging rulers, the rout was on."

    —Excerpt from *Daniel Colter: Story of a Lifetime* (c) 2019

"The response of religious leaders and their congregations to the event now known as the Gathering, and to subsequent revelations concerning cetacean history and society, was a reflection of both the best and worst of human instincts.

"The more liberal religious bodies were fortunate enough to have little difficulty incorporating the manifold implications of cetacean sentience into their belief systems. It is interesting that those religions which best weathered the transition to a post-Gathering world tended to be those generally considered either the most 'primitive'— the shamanistic and animistic cults of aboriginal Africa, the Americas, Asia, and Australasia; or the most 'sophisticated'—the Buddhists and Shintoists of urban, industrialized Asia, the moderate denominations of 'rational' Christianity, and Reform Judaism.

"Those religions which insisted on unyielding control of their members' thoughts and actions—the more strictly interpreted wings of Islam and Catholicism, the fundamentalist Christian sects, Orthodox Judaism—were openly hostile to any notion of change, and their leaders were quick to reject the First-Teachings of the Source-Mind as 'godless,' 'deceptive,' even 'satanic.' The latter term was most frequently invoked as a rejoinder to any mention of the fact that the cetaceans' thirty million years of preserved memories and observations of the world about them provided, among so many other things, a clear and unequivocal visual record of the evolution of many species, including man.

"Even worse, in the eyes of the zealots, was the behavioral example set by the sexual practices of whales and dolphins. Reports of the cetaceans' nonchalantly playful hedonism and promiscuity unleashed torrents of invective and vituperation from Mecca, the Vatican, and Mississippi.

"This so-called 'moral crisis' reached global firestorm proportions after the discovery of the AIDS vaccine, at which time the long-dormant sexual revolution returned in greater force than ever. The wildest excesses of the '60s were nothing in comparison to the bizarre frolics of the numerous 'dolphin cults' that sprang up to publicly, and often hilariously, thumb their noses (and other anatomical regions) at all humorless prudes of whatever persuasion or nationality.

"As the pace of change in the world continued to accelerate, with new discoveries and new levels of knowledge making it possible at last to turn the corner on the overall betterment of the human condition, the old, unbending religions began to fall by the wayside. Poverty and ignorance had always been the primary allies of the fanatics; as those scourges were defeated, the zealots stood at last revealed for the bitter, egomaniacal autocrats they had always been, and the last vestiges of their unearned and oft-abused power were stripped from them forever."

—Excerpt from *Sheila Roberts Remembers* (c) 2022

"Philosophers and theologians may spend lifetimes debating the spiritual and metaphysical aspects of the Source-Mind, and the long-term implications of its decision to make contact with humanity; but on a simpler level, it might also accurately be said that the human race suddenly found that it had been granted access to the equivalent of a sentient and benevolent alien super-computer.

"Of course, when human researchers these days do tap the Source-Mind's vast power in order to solve even the most abstruse questions of physics or mathematics, they are utilizing only the tiniest fraction of its unknowable, inconceivable whole; but the computer analogy is useful as far as it goes, in much the same way that Newtonian concepts remain a valid way of explaining the observed physical behavior of objects in the everyday world, even though the old theories break down when we move to consideration of the micro- or macrocosmic domain.

"The astonishing array of scientific developments that began to occur soon after the Gathering came as a surprise even to those accustomed to the already dizzying pace of technological advances taking place in the final decade of the twentieth century. In addition to providing scientists with a trillionfold or more increase in available computing power, the Source-Mind also contained a fabulous store of already recorded information—*thirty million years' worth,* including the locations of every oceanic source of food and geothermal energy, precise data on continental drift, the status and progression of undersea fault lines . . . so much new knowledge, in so many disparate fields, that we will probably never be able to complete the task of sorting it all out. Yearly, daily, with no end in sight, human scientists continue to transform this wealth of data into the great strides forward that we have begun to make as a civilization and as a species, thanks entirely to the fact that we are lucky enough to share this planet with the cetaceans."

—Excerpt from *Daniel Colter: Story of a Lifetime* (c) 2019

"Even in the wake of the Gathering, and the opening of telepathic communication with dolphins and the immense Source-Mind of the whales, my own work was far from finished or obsolete.

"With only five to ten percent of dolphin and human populations having inherited the Link-Talent, there was now a compelling need for mechanisms to enable discourse between the non-Linking members of both species. The dolphins' biologic Imaging process was clearly the basis upon which to approach this problem, and the Image-translation programs I had already developed were the nucleus of its solution.

"As chairman of the newly established Department of Human-Cetacean Communication at UCSB—a division which has, I am proud to say, led to the University's current position in independent academic surveys as one of the top two or three educational institutions in this country—I was in a unique position to participate in some of the earliest breakthroughs on that front.

"The design and production of Image-processing software and

hardware swiftly became one of the most significant branches of the computer industry, and has led to the growth of the Santa Ynez Valley near Santa Barbara as a serious rival to the older 'Silicon Valley' farther north.

"Necessity did indeed propagate a prodigious brood of inventions in the field, the most important of which was undoubtedly Lawrence S. Yaeger's seminal design of a system for *reverse* Image translation, allowing human messages to be input via joystick/mouse-manipulated programs and then converted to ultrasonic dolphin Images. The Yaeger Imaging System opened the way for true democratization of human-cetacean contact, regardless of the Link-Talent status of any of the participants.

"As of this writing, fully three-dimensional holographic Image translation displays are available only with the use of suitcase-sized equipment, but it's estimated that underwater-safe notebook holo units will replace the current standard of notebook-sized HDTV communication devices within three to five years."

—Excerpt from *Sheila Roberts Remembers* (c) 2022

"Lewis Thomas, that premier essayist on matters biological and philosophical, once proposed his choice for the most appropriate message that humankind could beam toward the stars and whatever listening extraterrestrials might reside there: 'I would vote for Bach,' he wrote, ' . . . [though that] would be bragging.'

"Few had expected that the first meaningful contact with nonhuman intelligence would come right here at home, as it were; but when it did, more than one eager 'land-walker' elected to make his or her contribution to the widening dialogue by playing recorded selections from the works of Bach, or Beethoven, or Mozart, during their first personal encounters with dolphins. It is gratifying to know that many cetaceans do, indeed, enjoy the elegant sonic structures of such music, as they also savor the clean lines of some human architecture and the interplay of visual effects in certain films.

"Similarly, more and more humans have come to appreciate the stylized flow of creative Imagery in dolphin myths and tales. Some of these have been compared in their simplicity to the Noh plays of Japan, while others are unrestrained extravaganzas filled with effects surpassing even the best computer-generated Hollywood magic.

"My own area of greatest interest, however, is the spectacle of human history and prehistory as seen from a cetacean perspective, a tapestry I have examined at length in my three-volume work *A View from the Sea* (for which I gratefully accepted the Pulitzer Prize in 2011).

"In researching those books through countless Linking sessions with dozens of dolphin Historians, no story I encountered moved me more than that of Kalliste—later known as Thera, and eventually enshrined in hazy legend as Atlantis.

"We now know, of course, that Kalliste was quite real, and that it was the site of the first organized Linking between humans and dolphins, some 3,700 years ago. An island in the Aegean Sea, midway between Greece and Turkey and just north of Crete, Kalliste (its name means 'the most beautiful') was the centerpiece of Minoan civilization, a grand and sophisticated metropolis whose citizens enjoyed unparalleled freedom and the most advanced standard of living yet achieved in those days long before the heydays of Greece and Rome.

"Archeological excavations had revealed, even in the years before the Gathering, a preponderance of dolphin motifs in Kallistan pottery and art; and an exhaustive search of previously closed regions of the Source-Mind has now established beyond doubt that the Kallistans were being prepared for full contact with the cetaceans, and that the Gathering was originally scheduled to take place in approximately 1615 B.C.

"At the height of those preparations, in the autumn of 1628 B.C., the central mountain on the island of Kalliste exploded in a volcanic eruption equal to the detonation of more than a hundred hydrogen bombs. Tens of thousands died, human and dolphin—not merely on and around Kalliste, but as far away as Greece and Turkey, where a tsunami the height of an eighty-story building was driven thirty miles inland.

"The vibrant, fifteen-hundred-year-old civilization of the Minoans—a peaceable, intelligent people who had settled much of the eastern Mediterranean and established a thriving trade with Egypt—was essentially destroyed in a single day. The flooded crater that was all that remained of Kalliste, that 'most beautiful place,' was abandoned to the wind and the waves, and renamed Thera—'fear.'

"Many hundreds of years later, the Greek cult of the Oracle at Delphi marked the second tentative attempt by the Source-Mind to reach out to humanity; and that proffered embrace was violently rejected, perhaps because of confused half-truths and legends associating the earlier disaster with cetacean contact.

"To speculate on what might have happened had the Kallistan eruption not occurred is to invite the deepest, the most immutable, of melancholies. The benefits to mankind that have come as a result of contact with the dolphins, and through them with that global consciousness known as the Source-Mind, are incalculable: a recognition of the oneness of all sentient beings, a panoply of new discoveries for the betterment of the planet as a whole, an effective end to war, to cruelty, to hunger. . . .

"Now imagine the world as it might have been had we gained all those advantages three thousand and more years ago—and weep.

"There could be no more fitting monument to those lost lives and lost millennia than the meticulous re-creation of a sunwashed white Kallistan city that stands now on the black-sand slopes of Batera Island in the Santa Barbara Channel. The opportunity for a new world was tragically destroyed by that ancient eruption of Kalliste; what a strange, sad irony that this glorious new world of ours should have had its triumphant birth in concert with another such violent event."

—Excerpt from *Daniel Colter: Story of a Lifetime* (c) 2019

"As close as I had felt to the dolphins involved in my research project before, my relationship with them deepened considerably in the years following the Gathering. I will always regret that none of the three possessed the Link-Talent, but am eternally grateful that Ringo at least lived long enough to see the development of the Yaeger Imaging System, so that I was able to communicate to him in detail just how much our friendship had always meant to me. His death in 2016 stirred in me a grief equaled only by the sadness that I felt at the deaths of my mother and father.

"I have met and come to know so many dolphins now, through my work and in my personal life, that it's difficult for me to remember a time when anyone could have imagined them to be nothing more than clever animals to be 'trained' for human amusement or indiscriminately slaughtered for the sake of a netful of fish. What an embarrassment it is to look back on those times, as distant and as shameful now as scratchy newsreel footage of any of the other horrors of our savage and murderous past.

"I've always felt that my marriage to Daniel Colter truly began not with the seaside ceremony some months after the Gathering, but in that instant when we simultaneously Linked for the first time with the dolphin we later learned was called Ch*Tril. That moment—this lifetime—of harmonious union will forever define for me the essence of what human-cetacean contact has meant for me as an individual, and for our species as a whole."

—Excerpt from *Sheila Roberts Remembers* (c) 2022

"Much as Sheila and I love our daughter, Marina, I must confess to a touch of envy when I think of how she and her generational cohorts have grown up perceiving the world, the sense of unlimited possibilities which to them seems as natural as the supposed 'inevitability' of war and famine once seemed to people my age or older.

"Marina was, almost from birth, as thoroughly and happily 'of the sea' as her name suggests. She learned to swim at eighteen months, and began to exercise her Link-Talent at the age of two; she was fluent in Imaging before she could read, and since early childhood her closest friends have been evenly split between humans and dolphins. She literally never knew there was a difference between the two, except in such mundane matters as body shape and language. At the time of this writing, she is pursuing a doctorate in cetacean myths.

"Sometimes, watching her in the water with her dolphin friends and colleagues, it almost looks as if she's the forerunner of a new species—the next step forward in human evolution, a return to the sea from which we all emerged. It pleases me no end to know that I played some small part in making this extraordinary world of joy and boundless promise a reality for her and her peers."

—Excerpt from *Daniel Colter: Story of a Lifetime* (c) 2019

"As for the future, we can only begin to imagine what further wonders are in store for the generations who will follow ours. There has been much speculation as to whether the Source-Mind might be gradually preparing us—dolphins and humans alike—to somehow join it, to become full partners in that supracorporeal global existence that the whales have created for themselves, maintaining their individual lives even as they transcend them.

"Beyond that, there have been hints in recent Meldings that the Source-Mind may have come in contact with *other* planetary group minds, in other star systems; that, indeed, there may even be a galaxy-wide or larger aggregate consciousness, a limitless, truly god-like greater sentience pervading the universe—and eternally seeking out newly self-aware worlds, like ours, to join it in jubilant immortality."

—Excerpt from *Sheila Roberts Remembers* (c) 2022

* * *

When their tasks are done, they swim for pleasure: Lx*Chil and Marina, romping and racing together in their beloved sea.

The mother of Lx*Chil's father was a Historian; Lx*Chil is, by contrast and yet in perfect complement to that familial tradition, a futurist. Marina studies the old stories of Lx*Chil's kind, and knows them better than all but the best of the Myth-Imagers. They have been friends since before Lx*Chil can remember.

Lx*Chil is the stronger swimmer, of course, but Marina moves in the water faster and more smoothly than any other land-walker Lx*Chil has ever known; and recently when they have Linked with one another, in that shared place where their minds conjoin, they have discovered that they can swim and leap together far beyond the sea, beyond the sky—that they can soar and swoop and dance their playful impromptu ballet in another realm entirely, among the far-flung lights and Minds that illuminate the great black ocean of infinity.

ACKNOWLEDGMENTS

The author would like to thank the following for their assistance in the research and preparation of this novel: Sam La Budde of the Earth Island Institute, for sharing with me his horrific experiences on board a tuna boat in the eastern tropical Pacific; the captain and crew of the San Diego–based tuna boat (all of whom shall here go nameless) that I myself was able to infiltrate, for unknowingly affording me firsthand insight into the willful denial and the gratuitous cruelty that so long permeated the business of purse-seiner tuna fishing; my editor, Liza Dawson, for her most helpful suggestions that initially had me tearing out my hair but which ultimately led to immeasurable improvements in the manuscript; my agent, Marcy Posner of the William Morris Agency, for her unflagging enthusiasm and support; my friend and former agent, Ned Leavitt, for his ongoing interest in this project and for steering me in the right direction on numerous occasions; my friend and partner Courtney Fischer, for enduring the lengthy process of this book's creation with as much patience as could reasonably be expected; Nancy Myers of Divers' Den in Santa Barbara, who died so tragically young, for teaching me to feel comfortable and confident in the deep, dark environs of the cetaceans' natural habitat; Brigitte Borguss, Lloyd Borguss, and Rick Borguss of the Dolphins Plus research center in Key Largo, Florida, for contributing their extensive knowledge to this project and for introducing me to three of the most fascinating and endearing creatures I have ever known; and above all, Nikki, Sarah, and Dreamer: gentle Touches to you each, and may you swim always in calm seas.